THE SWEETEST REVENGE

A DARK REVENGE ROMANCE

MICHAELA SAWYER

Edited by Damara R. Hill

Alpha Reader: M. Cruz

Cover Design: Vanilla Lily

To anyone suffering in silence...

The epic story of tomorrow can't be written if it ends today.
- Unknown

In loving memory of Josh...

TRIGGER WARNINGS

PLEASE READ BEFORE PROCEEDING IF YOU HAVE ANY TRIGGERS...

Welcome to my dark side!! :).

The Sweetest Revenge is a dark bully revenge romance that contains graphic content and is not suitable or enjoyed by all readers. The MMC comes with red flags, a filthy mouth, and questionable behavior.

If you are sensitive to certain themes and scenarios, this may not be the story for you.

Please visit http://www.michaelasawyerauthor.com/trigger-warnings to view a detailed list of tropes, genres, and trigger warnings before proceeding.

Zaiden Knight

"They say karma is the best kind of revenge, but who has that much patience? Ariella Ledger was going to pay, and I was going to enjoy every minute of watching her squirm."

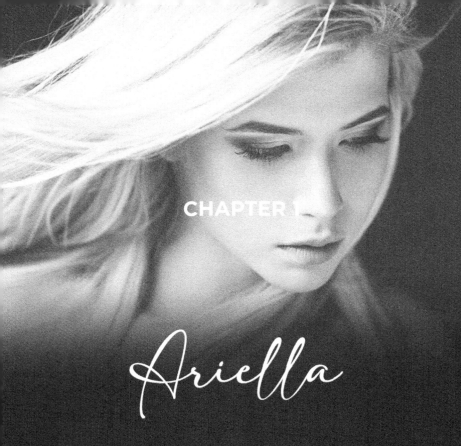

CHAPTER 1

Ariella

Staring up at my new house, I shifted on my feet uncomfortably as I flicked a glance over my shoulder into the black night surrounding me and quickly pushed the doorbell. I'd always been afraid of the dark, of what lurked behind the blackness invisible to the naked eye. It was an irrational fear, but it didn't matter. It was always there, lingering, threatening to consume me.

Footsteps.

Glancing behind me again, I hit the doorbell again. "Come on, Mom," I muttered, humming and bouncing slightly as my nerves began to get the best of me. "What's taking so long?"

Footsteps again.

I spun around, squinting to see through the blackness.

"Who's there?" I couldn't see anything but darkness past the front steps. "Mom?"

Silence.

Blowing out a sigh, I twisted back to the door, wrapping my arms around me. "Get a grip, Ari."

The front door opened. "Ari." My mother stepped back to let me in, and I rushed through the opening. "I was expecting you earlier."

I stopped in the entranceway and turned back toward the night. The door clicked shut, sealing out whatever lurked in the shadows.

I didn't know it then, but what I had to fear was living inside the house, not hiding in the darkness.

I sucked in a deep breath as I turned my gaze, sweeping over the foyer that I never thought I'd be standing in again. It still looked exactly the same: white walls, white and black marble tile flooring, and a tiered glass chandelier hanging low from the ceiling that looked like raindrops descending from the roof.

My chest tightened, and my heart ached as the memories of my best friend Kacie greeting me in this exact spot only two days before her death flooded forward. I wasn't supposed to stand here again, but here I was, standing with the last person I ever thought would answer this door.

"Traffic was terrible," I lied, shoving the memories back as I slid out of my coat.

The truth was I didn't want to come.

I didn't want to live with my mother in her new husband's home. The home where I'd had dozens of sleepovers with Kacie before she died, but I didn't have a choice.

This had never been part of the plan. When my mother

left my father for Kacie's dad, I moved with him hundreds of miles away to a small town after he sold our family home.

I was furious with my mother.

How could she do that to my father?

How could she do that to her best friend, Anne, Kacie's mom?

How could she do that to me?

I planned to live with my dad until I moved into my dorm on the Westbrook University campus, where I had a full dance scholarship, including room and board. However, there was a mix-up, and they gave my bed away. So now I was homeless, and I had no place to go but my mother's new house, which was a few blocks away from campus.

"Well, it's no problem." She smiled, her hair darker and shorter than I remembered. "I'm so glad you're here."

She stepped in to hug me, but I remained stiff. The betrayal was still too fresh.

She pulled back, her smile faltering slightly. "But unfortunately, I have to leave to meet Dennis now."

Dennis. My new stepfather. I bit my tongue to keep from saying what I really thought.

"Come on," she waved for me to follow her, "I'll show you where your room is." I followed her through the all-white pristine living room to the forged iron and mahogany wood staircase. "You'll have the house to yourself tonight. Zaiden had practice, and if he does show up, it's usually only to grab something and leave."

My eyes widened. "Zaiden?" I gripped the banister, my knuckles turning white.

"He goes to Westbrook," Mom said, continuing up the stairs without noticing my reaction.

Zaiden Knight. The same Zaiden who looked me in the eyes at Kacie's funeral and whispered, "You are dead to me." The same Zaiden who was now apparently my step-brother. I hadn't prepared for this because it was never in Zaiden's plans to go to Westbrook.

"I thought he moved away for college."

She shook her head. "No, he changed his mind. Maybe he can show you around campus and introduce you to new friends."

A harsh laugh escaped me before I could stop it. "No thanks." The last thing I needed was for them to try to force Zaiden to have any type of relationship with me. It had been almost a year since I'd seen him, but I didn't know how he would feel about me living here with him. Maybe enough time had passed that he wouldn't still hate me. "I can figure it out."

At the top of the staircase, she swerved left and stopped in front of Kacie's old room. "Suit yourself," she shrugged. "Here's your new room." My gaze followed her hand, and my heart pounded erratically as she reached for Kacie's doorknob, twisted, and pushed the door open.

"Mom." My voice cracked. "No. You can't be serious. This is Kacie's room."

"Ariella." She drew out my name with a sigh.

"Six bedrooms, Mom." I gestured down the hallway. "Six. And you're putting me in this one?"

"Kacie's not here anymore." Her lips pressed into a thin line. "There's no reason for this perfectly good room to go to waste."

My face twisted with horror as my eyes shifted to the room. "Where are all of Kacie's things?"

"Her father disposed of them." My chest tightened, and

it was hard to breathe. "Everything is new for you. It's your room now."

I shook my head, unable to speak. "I—"

"Oh, honey." She placed a hand over her heart. "Kacie would have wanted you to have her room."

My jaw clenched so tight my teeth ached. "Well, she's not fucking here to say that, is she? Would she have wanted you to fuck her dad behind your best friend's back?"

"I know you're angry, and you're saying things you don't mean."

I grunted. I meant everything I said. My mother was always good at being oblivious to reality.

"So, I'm going to let you cool off, and you can apologize later." We both knew I wouldn't apologize, but she spun on her heels and bolted for the stairs.

Watching her disappear down the staircase, a tear streamed down my cheek as the anger boiled over.

I didn't want to be here. My gaze shifted back to Kacie's room. My room. I didn't want to move into it like she never existed.

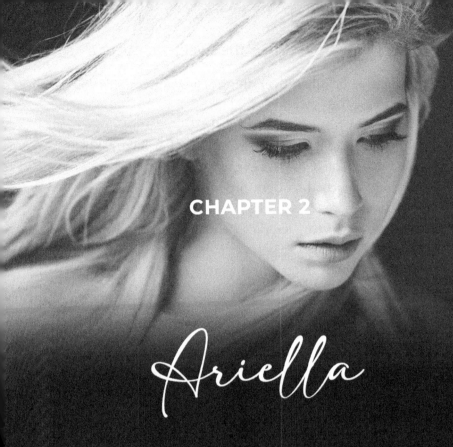

CHAPTER 2

Ariella

Clutching my towel in one hand and my phone in the other, I strolled from the bathroom to my *new* bedroom and stopped. I stood in the doorway, letting my gaze sweep over everything.

A full bed in the corner of the room, dressed in grayish-purple linens. White furniture—a nightstand, two half-empty dressers, and a make-up table—stood stark against the plain white walls and dark hardwood floors. It was the complete opposite of Kacie's vibrant room.

They'd completely erased her.

Blowing out a heavy sigh, I tossed my phone on my bed. I couldn't help but feel like I was being punished for something terrible I'd done in a past life. Having to wake up in her room every day and remember that she was not here with me was a heartbreakingly cruel punishment.

The floorboards creaked behind me. The hairs on the back of my neck stood up before I even heard his voice.

"What the fuck are you doing in here?"

My fingers flexed around my towel as I slowly turned, already knowing who I'd see.

Zaiden.

He filled the doorway with his massive body, wearing black joggers that hugged his thick thighs and a white Westbrook Predators t-shirt that clung to his sculpted chest. His dark tattoos trailed down his tanned and toned arms and up his neck. His grayish-blue eyes swept over the room, and his fists clenched at his sides.

"What the fuck are you doing in Kacie's room?"

The muscle beneath his left eye twitched. I stepped back, my heel catching on the edge of the rug. The words formed in my mind, it's my room now, but my throat constricted, holding them hostage. How could I say those words out loud when I barely believed them myself?

He stepped forward. The floorboards groaned beneath his weight, and the distance between us shrank. I caught the scent of his cologne as he moved closer.

"Where are her things?"

I shook my head because it was all I was capable of doing. They hadn't told him they had discarded her things.

"No, what?" He took one step forward, then another. I could see the muscle in his jaw twitching, the storm gathering in his eyes. I backed away, calculating the distance to the door, knowing I'd never make it. My calf hit the bed frame, and I tumbled backward onto the mattress.

"Zaiden." His name escaped my lips as a whisper, a plea, a prayer.

"Don't," he growled. "Get the fuck out of my sister's room."

"I—"

His fingers curled around my arms, digging into flesh. For a heartbeat, we were frozen, his grip tightening, my pulse racing beneath his touch.

"Get the fuck out of my house."

Time seemed to stretch and distort. The rational part of my brain screamed to stay quiet, to simply leave. Yet something deeper, something reckless, pushed his name up my throat.

"Zaiden—" The word escaped as a broken whisper.

His expression darkened. In one fluid motion, he twisted me from the bed. The world spun—ceiling, wall, door frame blurring together—before he shoved me into the hallway.

His face lowered until we were eye to eye, his breath hot against my cheek. His chest pressed against mine, each inhale pushing me further into the wooden handrail. The spindles creaked behind me.

"If you say my name again, I'll hurl you over this banister."

My heart stuttered. The drop behind me suddenly seemed vast, dizzying. My gaze flicked downward to the first floor, the hardwood far below swimming in my vision. My fingers found the edge of the railing and gripped until my knuckles whitened.

Would he actually do it? The rage in his eyes suggested he might.

I swallowed hard, my voice emerging thin and unsteady. "Please let me explain."

"Explain what, Ariella?" His lip curled into a snarl. "How you got my sister killed? Or how you've moved in like you think you're going to replace her."

I shook my head. "No. I would never—"

"Get the fuck out," he roared, but his grip on me only tightened. Each finger dug deeper into my skin.

"Zaiden—" I whispered, immediately regretting the sound.

His breathing stopped.

"What the fuck did I tell you?" The words came out eerily calm now. Then movement, swift, calculated. He spun me around in one fluid motion that left me breathless. My back pressed against his front, the cold wooden banister digging into my hips, his body a wall behind me. His hand found my wet hair, tangled in it, and then slowly, he pushed me forward until my upper body hung over the rail, nothing but his grip keeping me from falling.

"Please," I pleaded, scrambling to reach back for the railing to catch my fall if he decided to let me go.

He jerked me back by my hair.

I cried out, pain shooting across my scalp.

"Please, what?" His voice was deceptively soft.

The pressure on my hips released. A fleeting moment of relief. He was stopping. He was coming to his senses.

Then—a violent tug. The towel ripped away from my body. Cold air rushed against my exposed skin. My stomach dropped as realization hit: this wasn't over.

I struggled to grab it back, but his hand tightened in my hair, shoving me forward again. He pressed his hip hard against me, pinning me tighter than before so my feet weren't touching the floor anymore and pushing his hard length between my ass cheeks. "I said, please, what?"

"Please, let me go." I cried out. "It's not what you think, I swear."

He ground his thickness firmly into my ass. He

grunted, stepping back, and I hissed as a sharp pain shot through my scalp as he snatched me back by my hair. My hands flew up over my head, gripping his wrist, trying to ease the ache. His free hand slid over my hip from behind and down between my thighs, sliding through my folds. "You're so fucking wet. Does this turn you on?" He pulled his hand free, coated in my arousal, and brought his fingers to my lips. "Open."

What the actual fuck?

I shook my head.

"Open your fucking mouth," he grunted against my ear, tightening the grip on my hair.

"Okay," I whimpered, easing my mouth open as he slid his two thick, wet middle fingers between my lips.

"Suck." I did as I was told and sucked them clean as he moved them in and out, each time going deeper until I gagged. "Does this turn you on, you dirty slut." I assumed it was a rhetorical question, considering he had my mouth full. My small hands wrapped around his wrist as he shoved his fingers deeper.

I hummed a plea for mercy, gagging around him as I desperately tried to pull him out of my throat. "It's bad enough I have to share a house with your whore of a mother." He pulled them from my mouth, and I gasped for air as he released my hair and shoved me forward toward the staircase. "Does it turn you on moving in here and replacing my sister?"

My hands flew up, attempting to cover myself as his heated, dark gaze swept over me. "I don't want to be here any more than you want me here."

"Then get the fuck out." He stepped forward, backing me toward the staircases.

"Fine," I muttered, my gaze fixed on the white towel crumpled on the floor behind him. "Give me my towel, and I'll go."

The corner of his mouth lifted—not a smile, but something darker.

He shook his head. "Not a chance."

The gap between us seemed to shrink without either of us moving.

In the hallway mirror behind him, I caught a glimpse of my face—pale, wide-eyed, exposed. He charged forward like a predator who knew his prey was cornered.

I squeezed my eyes shut, bracing for impact, for the sensation of falling down the stairs. Instead, I was lifted, my stomach dropping as he hoisted me over his shoulder. Each thundering step down the stairs jolted through my body. The cold air hit me first, then the rough wood of the porch against my bare skin as he dropped me outside.

"If you ever come back here, I'll make you regret every decision you've made since the night Kacie died."

He slammed the door, leaving me on the front porch naked, freezing, and furious.

I scrambled to my feet as the wind picked up, raising goosebumps across my exposed skin. I pressed my palms against my eyes until I saw stars, willing the tears back as my entire body vibrated with a mixture of fury and humiliation.

He'd caught me off guard. A mistake I wouldn't repeat.

I looked up at Kacie's old window, which was my window now. I hugged myself tighter, my anger crystallizing into something colder.

Next time, and there would be a next time, I'd be ready.

For now, though, I needed to get back inside before someone saw me standing naked on the front porch. I rushed around the house, stopping at the door to the garage, and tried the knob, releasing a heavy sigh when it twisted open.

Now, I had to wait for him to leave.

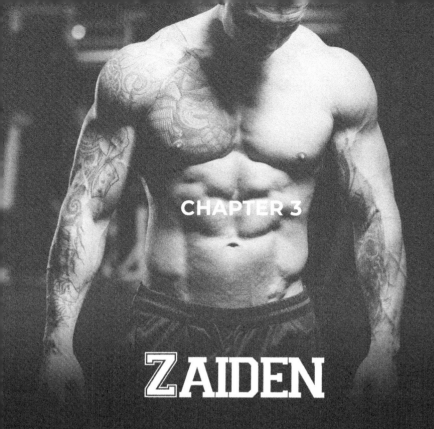

CHAPTER 3

ZAIDEN

My skates bit into the ice. The familiar scrape should have calmed me, but my pulse hammered in my ears, drowning everything else out. Each breath burned in my lungs, a wildfire I couldn't contain, let alone extinguish.

I'd avoided Ariella for the first few weeks of school, hoping distance would dull the edge. It hadn't. My fingers tightened around my stick until my knuckles ached, the same ache I'd felt when I found her in Kacie's room.

The image seared into my retinas, Ariella, water droplets still clinging to her skin, standing in the doorway of Kacie's room like she belonged there.

A year of carefully bottled rage cracked open. A year of restraint shattered in an instant.

It was bad enough that her whore of a mother was

sleeping in my mother's bed, but now Ariella was moving into Kacie's room. It was like they were trying to erase her existence.

Over my dead fucking body.

How could she think it was okay to just slide into Kacie's spot like she never existed?

I'd spent a year plotting and planning my revenge. It was the reason I'd stayed in Westbrook to go to college instead of leaving like I'd planned. I knew this was where she'd be. I hadn't anticipated her moving into my house, seeing her in my sister's room, or how my body still responded to her.

Hate her. I needed to hate her. My body hadn't gotten that memo. It remembered something else entirely.

By the time I left the house, Ariella was gone, but I knew she'd be back. She had nowhere else to go, and I'd made sure of that.

"Get your head in the game, Knight!" Coach slammed his clipboard against the wall, his whistle swinging wildly around his neck.

The rage climbed higher, a dark tide rising. I launched from the ice, my shoulder connecting with Hawk's body with a crack that echoed through the arena. He flew forward. The puck was mine. Blood roared in my ears, drowning out the coach's whistle.

I reared back and swung forward, striking the puck and sending it flying past the goalie.

"That's it." Hawk's words cut through the arena noise. I dug my blades into the ice, spinning hard enough to spray frost. My fingers twitched inside my gloves. Finally. A target.

I needed to hit something hard to release some of this pent-up aggression.

"What the fuck is your problem?" He jerked off his gloves, tossing them to the ice as we skated towards each other.

"You," I smirked. I didn't have a problem with Hawk. He was a good player, and we ran in the same crowd, but today, he was going to take the brunt of my rage because he was here. He bumped my chest with his.

"Woah." Sterling materialized between us, gloves up, voice deceptively calm against the storm building in my chest. His eyes told a different story. Caution. Warning.

"What is up with you today, man?" Sterling shoved my chest, putting some space between Hawk and me. Sterling was my boy, and he'd always had my back. Right now, he was trying to save my ass from getting benched in the first game of the season.

"Hit the showers, Knight." Coach's voice bounced off the plexiglass barriers. "You're done for the day."

The bench door creaked as I yanked it open, the sudden change from biting cold to stale, sweat-heavy air hitting me.

Typically, I would argue, but my mind was preoccupied with a pretty little blonde and making her pay for destroying my family.

I stepped off the ice, pulling my gloves off and tossing them to the bench.

Sterling slid to a stop, ice chips spraying up. Sweat plastered his dark hair to his forehead as he yanked off his helmet, his normally easy-going features hardened into something unrecognizable.

"What the fuck is up with you today?" Steam rose from his dark skin in the cold air, curling around overhead lights.

"When I stopped by the house the other night," I said. "Ariella was standing in Kacie's room in a towel."

His eyes widened. "Ari's fucking hot." Sterling, Ariella, Kacie, and I all grew up together.

"What the fuck, man?" My forearm connected with his shoulder. "She killed my sister."

"Ariella didn't kill Kacie." His shoulders sank. "She died in a car accident."

My jaw flexed, and my nostrils flared. "If it weren't for her, Kacie wouldn't have left that night." The words scraped my throat raw. "And now her whore of a mother broke up my family, and Ariella moved into Kacie's room. She threw all of her stuff away."

"That's fucked up." I nodded, staring forward. "What are you going to do?"

My tongue swept across my bottom lip before my gaze shifted to meet his. "Make her pay."

"I know you're angry, but—" Sterling's eyes tracked mine, searching for something. The rational part of me he'd known since third grade. "Don't do anything stupid."

Translation: Don't do anything, I can't help you cover up later.

"Yeah." I met Sterling's gaze and held it. "Round up the team. Frat house. After practice. I have a plan to run little Miss Innocent out of town."

"Fuck, man." Sterling dragged a hand down his face. A heartbeat of silence. Then another. "Do I—" He stopped, jaw working. "Do I even want to know?"

Something cold settled behind my ribs. My lips curved up as understanding dawned in Sterling's eyes. He stepped back, cocking his head slightly.

"It's her last chance." My lips curled into a sadistic grin.

"After tonight, she'll wish she'd never set foot in this town again."

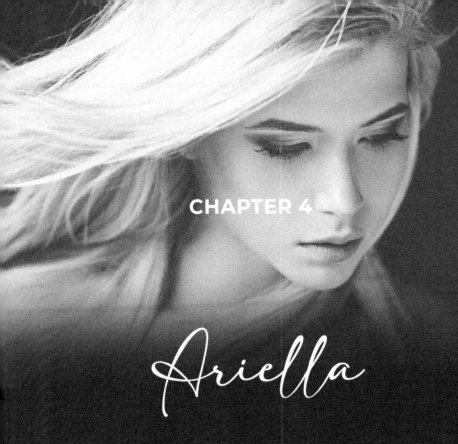

CHAPTER 4

Ariella

Staring at my computer, I smiled with relief. After working on it all evening, I'd finally finished my humanities project. It was only the third week of school. Between classes, practices, my first project of the year, and Zaiden's bullshit, I was already overwhelmed.

I clicked to save the PowerPoint to my OneDrive, and an error message flashed across my screen: No internet connection.

"Shit." The word escaped under my breath as my fingers flew to the WIFI icon.

Disconnected.

I clicked to reconnect, my teeth pressing into my lower lip as the loading circle spun and spun and spun. My knee bounced under the table, each second stretching longer than the last. "Come on, please don't do this right now."

My whisper echoed in the silent room, desperate and small.

Thunder cracked like a whip outside the window. I flinched. The library's ancient WIFI collapsed at the first hint of a storm, reliable only in its unreliability.

I hit the save as button again, saving the file to my desktop, and said a silent prayer that nothing happened between now and the short trip home when I could save it to my drive.

My gaze flashed to the single window in the back of the library. Rain hammered against the glass. I glanced at the time on my MacBook. It was after ten. I scanned over the empty third floor.

During the school year, the library stayed open until eleven, though at this hour, it was typically deserted except for a few high school or college students completing community service hours as librarians. The regular staff departed at five.

Which meant they were hiding somewhere, counting down the time until they could lock the doors and leave.

I closed my laptop at the exact moment a bolt of lightning flashed through the window, followed by an instant boom. The lights went out, and a blanket of darkness covered me.

"Fuck," I muttered as my heart began to race. "Please come back on. Please."

I sat frozen, unable to move, paralyzed by fear.

Every sound in the quiet room was amplified. A floor creaked on my left. Then on my right. The hair on my arms stood up.

"Hello?" The word barely escaped my lips. "Is someone here?"

Nothing.

I cleared my throat, shaking my head. Darkness and fear, a perfect recipe for imaginary monsters.

The legs of my chair screeched against the linoleum floors as my eyes flicked around the dark like something might appear.

Heavy breathing.

My heart jumped, and my hands trembled. "Who's there?"

Nothing.

Something brushed my arm—fingers?—and I flew from my seat, pulse hammering in my throat.

"Who's there?" My voice cracked.

Heavy breathing. Close. Too close.

"This isn't funny." I backed away, hands outstretched in the dark.

Something touched my arm from behind, and I whipped around. Stepping backward, I slammed into something hard.

A scream tore from my throat.

Strong arms wrapped around me, holding me tight against his chest. A mixture of masculine scents surrounded me, making it hard to pinpoint one specific smell.

"Let me go!" I thrashed against his grip, muscles straining.

A palm slapped over my mouth, smothering my scream into a muffled whimper that vibrated uselessly against his skin.

"We don't want you here." His breath scorched my ear, the voice unfamiliar, rough, and distorted.

Then he was gone.

I took off running but didn't make it far.

Tripping, I stumbled forward. Pain shot through my

hands and knees as they slammed against the hard floor. I scrambled to my feet, heart hammering. Where was he? Them? I didn't know how many there were. I shuffled backward, eyes straining, desperate to escape whatever—whoever—waited in front of me.

This felt calculated, planned. The power didn't go out from the storm. Someone turned it off, and if I had to guess, whoever was responsible for locking up for the night was long gone.

The heat of his body reached me before he did, and all the air rushed from my lungs as long fingers wrapped around my throat, shoving me back. My back slammed against something—a bookshelf?—so hard it rattled.

I sucked in a harsh breath, inhaling a scent I'd recognize anywhere.

"Zaiden," I whispered, the name falling from my lips before I could stop it.

My stomach fluttered, a dizzying riot beneath my ribs. My breath came quick and shallow, not just from fear. Heat bloomed across my skin, contradicting the terror squeezing my lungs. I should have been thinking of escape, of survival, but instead, I found myself hyper-aware of every place Zaiden's body nearly touched mine. The wrongness of my reaction only intensified it.

A low growl rumbled deep in his throat as he dragged his nose up the side of my face. "I love the smell of fear." His fingers flexed the tips pressing into my pulse point as his free hand landed on my hip. "Are you scared of me, Ariella?"

He squeezed, momentarily cutting off my air supply and leaving me unable to say, 'fuck no.' That wasn't exactly true, though.

"I'm in complete control." His lips brushed mine, the

touch feather-light despite his words. "I could fuck you against the bookcase, and no one would ever know. I could squeeze a little tighter." The pressure increased. My hands flew to his wrist, nails digging into skin as my lungs screamed for air. "I could break you. Right here. Right now." His grip loosened, and I sucked in a sharp breath. "Then do it." I gritted out.

He huffed out a humorless laugh as he pressed his nose to my cheek, and I could feel his smile against my skin. "Oh baby, I'm going to break you." He pressed his hips into mine. "I'm going to do it so slow it's torture watching your life crumble in front of you." His thumb stroked the pulse point in my neck. "And I'm going to enjoy watching it."

"Fuck you." The words tore from my throat, rough and defiant. Even if he broke me, he'd never see the cracks.

His lips pressed against the shell of my ear. "I don't fuck dirty little whores."

My teeth clenched so hard my jaw ached. "Go to fucking hell, Zaiden."

He dropped his hands and stepped back, disappearing. "You should leave town and never come back, or you'll regret it, princess."

I reached out for him, but he was gone.

A shudder shot through me as the darkness felt like it was suffocating me.

"Zaiden?" My voice broke on his name. The silence that answered pressed against my eardrums, worse than his threats had been. The thought of being alone was more terrifying than Zaiden. My hand flew to my chest, fingers splayed wide as panic consumed me.

The lights flickered once, twice, then blazed to life with a harsh electronic hum.

I scanned the room, heart still hammering against my ribs, expecting to see him lurking in some corner. Nothing. Empty tables. Empty chairs.

A wave of relief crashed through me, so intense my knees nearly buckled. He was gone. The air rushed from my lungs in a single exhale, as if I'd been holding my breath since the moment the darkness fell.

But beneath the relief, something else stirred, something I didn't want to acknowledge. A hollow ache. An echo. The same feeling I'd had as a child when the roller coaster ended: terror so acute it circled back around to exhilaration.

I rolled my eyes at my own conflicted emotions, my breath escaping in a shudder. My fingers trembled as I pushed my hair back from my face, the ghost of his touch still burning against my skin.

If Zaiden Knight thought his little intimidation act would drive me out of town, he had seriously underestimated me.

This—whatever game he was playing—was one more thing to endure, to overcome. To win.

The trembling in my hands stilled as determination replaced fear.

Straightening my shoulders, I strode back to my table, ready to pack up and put this whole night behind me. I stopped cold.

"No." The word barely passed my lips as I frantically scanned the empty surface. "No, please, no."

My laptop was gone. With it, hours of work had vanished, the project that had kept me here late, that I'd just finished minutes ago. The project I'd only managed to save to the laptop's desktop.

"Fuck." The word echoed in the empty library, carrying more weight than all of Zaiden's threats combined.

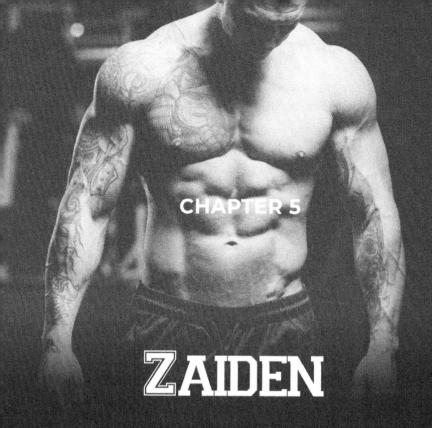

CHAPTER 5

ZAIDEN

M etal scraped against metal as I yanked open my
locker. The bang echoed through the room. I
slung my bag over my shoulder before
throwing it closed again.

Sterling slammed his locker shut at the same time. The
sound rang like a gunshot.

Silent, we moved toward the exit, our footsteps
matching the rhythm of my pulse. Too fast. Too hard.

"I haven't seen Ariella today. Did last night work?"

Rolling my eyes, I shouldered through the swinging
locker room door into Sports Alley - the central tunnel
connecting all the coed locker rooms at Westbrook.

Unlike other schools, Westbrook prioritized athletics
above everything else. You could tell from the moment you
stepped inside, with an entire massive building dedicated

solely to their sports programs. Each team had its own dedicated space, though they all shared a unique arrangement. While the locker rooms were technically coed, they were designed with girls' lockers on one side and boys' on the other, with shared amenities like showers in between. Football players shared with cheerleaders and the dance team. Hockey players with figure skaters. Basketball players had their own dance team and cheerleading squad.

"No." The word came out rough. "Her car was in student parking this morning."

"So you're letting this go?" Sterling asked.

A laugh escaped me. Cold. Empty.

"No." I met his eyes. The plan had been forming all night, each detail clicking into place like the blade of a knife. "I have something better in mind."

"Looks like she already belongs to the football team," Sterling said, and I lifted my gaze, following his line of sight.

The football team's coed locker room was diagonal to the hockey team's locker room.

"Is she on the dance team?" Sterling adjusted his Westbrook Predator's ball cap, and I nodded. "Ah, come on, man, you're not only going to try to start a feud with her. You're going to put the whole hockey team against the football team this year." Sterling warned, his voice dropping. "You know the rules."

I knew them all too well. The invisible boundaries that kept the peace. Hockey claimed the figure skaters. Basketball, the hip-hop dancers. And football? They guarded their half-time dancers and cheerleaders like crown jewels.

I just didn't care.

My gaze followed Ariella in her tight black leggings and white Predator dance team tank top as she walked down the hall next to Elijah, also known as EJ Anderson, the quarterback of the Westbrook Predators, with most of the team surrounding them.

Ariella's hair was pulled up loosely in a ponytail that swayed back and forth as she walked, and my cock stiffened. Apparently, it did not understand the assignment.

"Don't worry," I smirked, not taking my eyes off Ariella as she hiked her bag higher on her shoulder and threw her head back on a laugh. My jaw tightened with annoyance, and I couldn't explain why. Maybe because she was here laughing and Kacie wasn't, or maybe because he made her smile like that. "It will be her decision."

"Yeah, I doubt that." He stepped in line with me as I picked up my speed. "It was her and Kacie's dream to be on that dance team. She's not quitting."

"She doesn't have to," I said. "She just has to tell them she belongs to me."

"Right," he said, drawing out the word.

"I'll catch you later." I waved him off as I bolted for the football team.

"Knight."

Adrian Donovan's voice cut through the hall. The wide receiver's call silenced the group. One by one, heads turned.

The conversation died.

Ariella's bright blue eyes found mine, ice against fire.

"Hockey team showing up this weekend?" Adrian asked, breaking the silence.

"We'll be there." Every year, one of the teams hosted a massive blowout party at the beginning of each season, and we were heading into football season. It was the only party where all the teams participated together. "But I need to borrow Ariella for a minute."

Elijah slid a protective arm around her neck, and my jaw flexed. "Sorry, man, Ari is part of the team."

"Yeah, bro," Kai Morgan, a linebacker for the Westbrook Predators, said. "Maybe you didn't hear, but she's on the dance team."

"And maybe you didn't hear she's my new stepsister."

"We didn't, but now isn't a good time," Elijah said. "We are headed to a meeting on the field. I'm sure you'll catch up tonight at home."

"Yeah, man." Sterling's fingers dug into my shoulder, his grip just shy of painful. His brown eyes flashed a warning. I hadn't realized he'd followed me. "I'm sure you two can catch up later."

"Sure." The words slid between my teeth as our eyes locked. "I'll catch you tonight, Ariella."

Her jaw flexed.

She squared her shoulders and coiled an arm around Elijah's waist. "Go to hell, Zaiden."

"Ohhh," Adrian's voice cut through the tension. "Fighting with the little sis." His laugh echoed down the hallway. "See ya at the party, bro."

Their laughter faded as they moved toward the field. But I caught it—the glance Ariella threw over her shoulder. Uncertain. Wary.

Good. She should be.

"Zaid." Sterling's voice dropped. A warning. "Do you even know what game you're playing?"

I watched until she disappeared around the corner, the memory of her defiance burned in my chest.

"Trust me. After tonight, Ariella Ledger will learn exactly who's in charge." My fists unclenched, one finger at a time. "She will learn exactly who she belongs to."

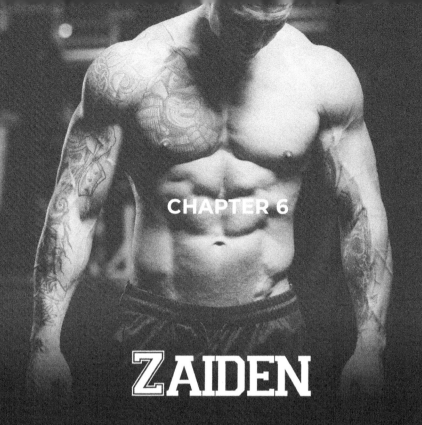

CHAPTER 6

ZAIDEN

The digital clock's red numbers glowed 9:47 PM. 10:13 PM. 10:38 PM. Each minute stretched into an eternity as I sat motionless in my dark bedroom, ears straining for the sound I'd been waiting for. The pipes groaned faintly within the walls. Then, finally, water rushed through them toward the bathroom that connected Ariella's bedroom to mine.

I smiled in the darkness.

Since the library incident the night before didn't scare her enough to make her leave, it was time for us to establish our new relationship. The one where I owned her. The one where I slowly took everything she loved away from her, like she did to me.

The house was empty except for Ariella and me. Her

mom was away for a charity event, and my father was always at work.

Silently, I pushed out of the chair and opened my bedroom door. I knew the bathroom door would be locked, but I had the key. Without making a sound, I inserted the key into the lock, listening to make sure she was in the shower. I pushed the door open and stepped into the steamy bathroom, listening to her hum a song that was low and sweet.

It was a nervous trait. She'd hummed herself to sleep the first night she'd ever spent in this house. She was seven, and it was the first time she'd been away from her parents. It was Kacie, me, Ariella, and Sterling, and we'd decided to watch a scary movie in the dark. She'd hummed through the whole movie. Not loud, but I could hear her fear. I'd ended up holding her hand until she fell asleep because it turned out she was even more scared of the dark. Those days were over, and I'd never be the one to hold her through her fears again because now I planned to terrorize her and become what her fears were made of.

I knew all of Ariella's dreams, knowledge that would make crushing them effortless. I understood exactly what she cherished, making it simple to strip it away. And I was intimately familiar with her deepest fears, the perfect weapons to use against her.

My hand hovered over the light switch. One flick and her biggest fear would engulf us. I needed to move with precision, relying on sound and memory rather than sight. I drew a silent breath and held it.

Darkness.

Her scream pierced the black void. The curtain rings scraped against the rod as I yanked it aside. Then chaos—

water spraying, her hands flailing wildly, desperate to connect with anything. With me.

"No!" Her voice echoed against the tile.

I caught her wrist mid-strike, the impact vibrating up my arm. Cold metal kissed skin as the first cuff locked into place. She twisted violently, her wet body slippery, but I'd anticipated this. Her spine hit the tiled wall with a dull thud.

"Stop—" The word died in her throat as I secured her other wrist.

The handcuffs rattled against the shower rod, a metallic rhythm punctuating her ragged breathing. Only then did I allow myself to acknowledge the heat that spread through me where her skin had brushed mine. The memory of a different time, a different touch.

I searched for the light switch, wanting to see her fear.

"Zaiden." My name emerged from her throat like something feral, halfway between recognition and curse.

I let the silence stretch between us, savoring the ragged sound of her breathing. Water continued to fall, striking her skin before spattering against the tub.

"I always knew you'd put up a good fight." The words came out rougher than I'd intended, betraying exertion I didn't want her to hear.

The cuffs struck the shower rod three times in quick succession. "Zaiden, let me go."

My fingers found the light switch and hesitated, prolonging the moment. When I finally flicked it on, the sudden brightness was almost painful. I blinked, my vision adjusting, to find her staring back at me with eyes like blue flames.

Water beaded on her skin, tracking down her curves. I

brushed my hair back, giving myself time to rebuild the mask of control she'd nearly dislodged.

There was no denying Ariella was hot. She was petite, with curves in all the right places. Her skin was deeply kissed by the sun except for the little triangles of creamy skin around her pink nipples that pulled tight like she was cold and a patch over her bare pussy. I dragged my tongue along my bottom lip as I fantasized about running my tongue along her tan lines, wondering if she still tasted the same as she did back then. "I think it's time we had a chat."

"Can we not have a conversation like normal people?" she hissed. She pulled her leg up, twisting slightly to hide herself from me.

"This was your choice, princess," I smirked, crossing my arms over my chest and leaning against the door frame. "When you let your little boyfriend talk for you."

"What the fuck do you want, Zaiden?" She seethed. She was angry. Good, that was exactly how I wanted her.

"I think it's time we set some boundaries," I smirked. "Or should I say rules?"

"Great," she forced a smile. "Boundaries would be great. Starting with no more leaving me naked, and I want my laptop back."

I laughed. "No, the rules are for you, not me." My eyes held hers. "And if you want your laptop back, you'll have to follow my rules."

She rolled her pretty blue eyes. "Go fuck yourself, Zaiden. I'm not following your rules." She jerked against the shower rod, making her perfect round tits bounce. "If you didn't know how this works, I'm part of the football team. You don't set rules for me."

"I had a feeling you would say that."

I remained against the wall, watching her. Letting her

think she still had some control. Letting her believe her defiance meant something.

I pushed off from the wall when her eyes narrowed with suspicion. My hand slid into my pocket, fingers closing around my phone.

"Let me tell you how this is actually going to go."

Her chin lifted slightly. Defiant still. Good. Breaking her spirit would be so much more satisfying this way.

I swiped through my phone, taking my time, watching her from the corner of my eye.

"I'm going to set the rules," I said, voice dropping lower. "And you're going to follow them."

A short, dismissive laugh escaped her lips. "Or what?"

"Or there will be consequences."

I turned the phone toward her. For one heartbeat, confusion crossed her features. Then recognition. Her smile crumbled, color draining from her face as she stared at herself on the screen—on her knees in front of her dance coach, performing in ways that would destroy everything she'd built.

"Now, you're probably thinking if this video gets out, you could lose your scholarship or even be kicked out of the school for bribing a coach."

"Where the fuck did you get that?" She hissed. "Delete it now." She surged forward, but the cuffs wrapped around the shower bar held tight. "You have no idea what that is."

"I don't care," I smirked, cocking my head to the side. "This video ensures you'll do whatever I tell you to do, doesn't it? My guess is that even more than not wanting to lose your scholarship, you don't want this video to go viral. What would your little football fuck boy think about you blowing your coach." Clicking my phone black, I shoved it back into my pocket.

"Fine, Zaiden, what do you want?"

Reaching out, I brushed a strand of her wet hair out of her face, my gaze locked on her full lips. "I want to own you. I want to ruin you."

"You really think this is what Kacie would want?"

"You really think Kacie would want to be dead right now with you living your best life and moving into her bedroom like she never existed."

"Zaid—"

"Shut up," I ordered. "First, you're going to let your football fuckboys know you belong to me. You'll no longer be changing with the rest of the team. You'll use the hockey locker rooms starting tomorrow."

"I can't do that, Zaiden. I don't have a locker in the hockey room. I have an assigned one in the football room."

"Figure it out," I groaned, turning toward the bathroom door. "Or your video will go viral, and you'll be headed back to your daddy." Stopping, I twisted back to her and stepped forward until my black boots hit the porcelain tub. My gaze raked down her naked, wet body, making her squirm. "The video is the last consequence I'll use." I gripped her jaw and leaned in so she could feel my words against her lip. "You make sure you let them know who you belong to, or I will. "My lips lifted into a sinister smirk. "And I prefer public humiliation." I shrugged. "Just so you know." I jerked her face away from me and ran my tongue up her throat. She tasted as sweet as I remembered, but with a hint of salt. That taste. A new addiction.

Fear.

She tasted like fear, and for some unknown reason, new to me, that fucking turned me on.

I stepped back, hand falling away from her face. Her skin left a damp impression on my fingertips.

"You win, Zaiden." Her voice had changed, softened around the edges. "Now, please let me go."

That "please" hung between us—sweet, desperate. Exactly what I wanted to hear. I reached into my pocket, taking my time, letting her wonder what would come next.

The spy camera was smaller than a matchbox, black, and inconspicuous. Her eyes tracked it as I inserted it into the outlet near the sink.

"What is that?"

The camera slotted into place with a click. A tiny red light blinked once, then steadied.

"Smile for the camera, princess."

Understanding widened her eyes. She pulled against the handcuffs, the metal biting into her wrists. "Zaiden, no." Her composure fractured, panic bleeding through. "Do not leave me here."

I moved backward toward the door, maintaining eye contact. Her fear was intoxicating, better than I'd imagined. Steam continued to rise from the shower, enveloping her.

"Put on a good show for the hockey team for me, baby." My hand found the doorknob behind me. "Make sure you scream my name when you struggle to free yourself."

The door closed between us, inch by inch, her panicked expression gradually disappearing from view. Only when the latch clicked into place did I allow myself to smile.

Through the door, her voice carried, stripped of everything but raw desperation: "Zaiden! Don't do this!"

It would only be a few minutes before she realized the cuffs were fake and there was a safety release on them, but she'd never know that I was the only one watching her struggle right now. Pulling my phone back out of my pocket, I flipped open the app and clicked on the mini camera as I locked myself in my room.

My cock throbbed at the sight of her naked, wet, struggling to free herself and screaming my name. The memories of how she tasted mixed with the feeling of her skin brushing against mine pushed forward, sending blood pumping through my cock, making it beg to be emptied. I was flicking open my pants and setting myself free before I even realized what I was doing.

My gaze raked down her naked body as I wrapped my hand tightly around the base of my dick and stroked from root to tip. Closing my eyes as I continued to stroke, I turned the volume up, listening to her scream my name, the sound the cuffs made when they hit the metal bar, and her tiny little whimpers of frustration.

"Fuck," I grunted as I used the precum from my wide head to quicken my strokes. I tightened my grasp, the muscles in my forearm flexing as I increased my speed as my gaze zeroed in on her perfect round tits thrashing around as she fought to free herself.

"Zaiden," she growled. "Let me go, now."

I closed my eyes, picturing her on her knees in front of me, opening her mouth, ready to take my load on her tongue. "Fuck." My cock twitching and my abs clenched as I exploded into my hand.

Everything went silent, and when I rechecked the camera, she was freeing herself.

My sister's empty bedroom lay across the hall, door ajar. A shrine to what had been taken from us. From me.

I pressed my forehead against my bedroom door, listening to Ariella's muffled struggles through the wall. She didn't deserve the mercy of a quick revenge. No, this would be methodical. Calculated. I would dismantle her life piece by piece, just as she had destroyed mine.

The memory of her skin against mine lingered, unwelcome but persistent. Hatred and desire created a strange feeling, but I would use both. Take whatever pleasure I could from her body, then discard her when I was done.

My fingers traced the door's wood grain, following its natural lines and breaks—like the path I'd mapped for Ariella's destruction—first, her dignity, then her reputation, her relationships, her future.

By the time I finished, no man would recognize what remained of her. That thought alone sent a shiver of satisfaction through me that rivaled the physical release from moments before.

Tonight was only the beginning.

CHAPTER 7

Ariella

Sinking onto the football field grass between Journey and Mila, I glanced up into the stadium seats to see Zaiden sitting in the same spot he was twenty minutes ago. The sun was bright and warm, and the sky was cloudless.

Journey nudged my shoulder and tilted her chin toward the stands. "Looks like you have a secret admirer."

Mila twisted a strand of dark hair around her finger. "With the way he's looking at her, I don't think it's a secret."

I dug my fingers into the turf. "Trust me. The only thing Zaiden admires is the thought of me losing everything."

"I've never seen Zaiden Knight at one of our practices," Journey smirked. Journey was a third-year dancing predator, and Zaiden was a second-year Predator. We all knew each other from high school. Even though Journey was two years ahead of Mila and me in college, she was the same age; she'd just opted to start college earlier than us.

"Then what's he out here for?" Journey asked, using the back of her hand to wipe away a bead of sweat dripping down the dark skin of her temple.

"To ruin my life," I muttered, reaching for my toes to stretch. Journey and Mila's gaze met and narrowed before turning to me. "He still blames me for Kacie and now my mom for breaking up his family."

"Kacie got into a car drunk and drove away from the party," Mila said. "How could that be your fault?"

I shrugged. "I don't know, but to make it worse. He has a video of me—" I lowered my voice. "Earning my scholarship."

"What?" Mila's voice lowered with mine as she leaned in. There wasn't a girl on the dance team who didn't know what I was talking about. Coach Ryan Palmer made it clear from the go what was required to make his winning dancing team with a full scholarship. "Where did he get that from?"

I shook my head. "I don't know."

"Does he have other videos?" Journey asked.

I shrugged. "If he does, I don't think he intends to use them. He wants to torture me for whatever it is he thinks that I did to Kacie."

"If the team finds out he's threatening you, it will cause a war." Mila's voice dropped to a whisper, her eyes scanning the field for eavesdroppers.

I grabbed her wrist. "They can't find out." My fingers tightened. "Not ever. If that video goes viral, I will lose my scholarship. The whole team could be at risk."

"Too bad he doesn't hate me," Journey said, staring up at him. "He's so fucking hot."

My gaze followed her line of sight, freezing on Zaiden. Zaiden was gorgeous, with dark hair and greyish-blue eyes. He was tall and tanned, with tattoos covering both arms, his neck, and one of his legs. I hadn't seen the tattoos on his leg before because he always wore pants, but today, he wore black shorts and a white Predator T-shirt.

"That's a wrap, ladies!" Coach Palmer's voice carried across the field.

Twenty dancers tensed. No one moved. No one breathed.

"Hit the showers." A pause that stretched too long. "And Laken? My office."

The team's collective exhale was audible, relief from everyone except me.

"What do you think will happen if EJ and the team ever find out about Coach Palmer?" Journey asked.

"I don't know," I sighed. "But how they would react would be the least of my worries."

"Let's go shower and change," Mila smiled. "We are meeting up with the team at Hurricane's."

In the stands, Zaiden rose to his feet, his eyes locked on mine with the kind of intensity that made my skin prickle. His hands disappeared into his pockets, but his message was coming through loud and clear: This isn't over.

I needed an out from the locker room, from Hurricane's tonight, from whatever confrontation he was planning. My phone chimed on the grass beside me, and I nearly lunged for it, desperate for any escape.

> Mom: Family dinner at six tonight. Don't be late.

I rolled my eyes because that was the last thing I wanted to do, but it did give me an out for tonight.

"Sorry, guys," I frowned, pushing to my feet. "My mom wants to have a family dinner tonight." My gaze lifted, noticing Zaiden was on his phone. He'd probably gotten the same text.

"Well, you need to tell your mom that you belong to the team during football season."

I chuckled. "Yeah, I'll let her know." I leaned forward, snatching my bag off the ground. "I'll see you guys tomorrow."

"You're not coming back to change?" Journey narrowed her big brown eyes.

I flicked a glance up to the now empty stadium. Zaiden, without a doubt, would be waiting by the hockey locker room. I shook my head. "No, I'm heading home and changing for dinner tonight."

"Call if you need backup tonight," Mila chuckled as they headed towards the tunnel.

Luckily, my mom and his dad were home. I doubted he would do anything stupid with both of them in the house.

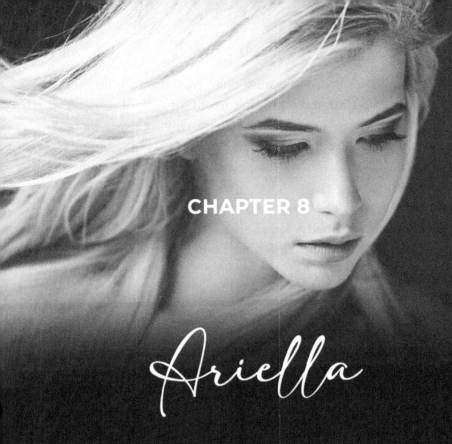

CHAPTER 8

Ariella

Swerving my car into the drive, I pulled to a stop in front of the three-car garage, noting that Zaiden's bike wasn't parked in its usual location. Grabbing my bag, I bolted for the house, hoping to get in, showered, and dressed before Zaiden ever pulled into the driveway.

Throwing open the front door, I stormed inside, dropping my bag in the doorway and bolting for the stairs.

I shrieked when my mom appeared out of an open doorway.

"Oh good." My mom's lips curved into that particular smile, the one that said she'd won something. "You didn't respond to my message, so I was worried you would purposely miss dinner."

"Nope." The word crawled from my throat. "I'm here. I'm going to get a shower and change."

"Perfect, I left you something on your bed to wear tonight."

I rolled my eyes. "I can dress myself."

She smoothed her already-perfect hair. "Of course, you can, dear. I just wanted to do something nice."

I shook my head and forced a smile. "Great." I didn't have time to argue if I was going to be dressed and downstairs before Zaiden got home. "I'll be down for dinner in a few."

I took the stairs two at a time and burst into my bedroom. The lock clicked into place behind me, not that it mattered in this house. Last night's bathroom incident had proven that much.

My gaze landed on the dress my mother had left.

"This is what we wear to dinner?" I shook my head. The dress was beautiful, but it belonged on a beach date, not a family dinner.

It was a short white summer dress with a lacy V-neck top and spaghetti straps. I snatched the dress off the bed, a pair of sandals, and a white lace thong and bolted for the shower.

It took me exactly seventeen minutes to shower, dress, do my hair, add a little bit of makeup, and race down the stairs, and I managed to do it all without interruption from Zaiden. Stopping at the bottom of the stairs, I squared my shoulders with a grin, feeling like I'd won a round. It sounded stupid, but I'd take even the smallest win right now.

I strolled through the living room and stopped in the entranceway to the large dining room. My gaze landed on Zaiden standing next to the eight-person mahogany dining table with only four of the eight chairs around it.

Fuck.

That meant Mommy dearest already had our seats picked out, and I was almost positive mine would be next to Zaiden.

Zaiden stood in black joggers and a white WBU Predators hoodie, casual, like he'd walked in from practice. So my mother only dictated my wardrobe. Great.

His eyes found mine.

I tried to look away. Failed. His greyish-blue gaze held me for a beat, then dropped, raking over me with deliberate slowness.

He licked his lips.

Like he was starving.

Like I was his snack.

He stepped forward but stopped when my mother appeared from the kitchen. "Oh good, you're here," my mother smiled, setting a water pitcher on the table. "You and Zaiden will sit there." She pointed to two chairs side by side, directly across from where my mother and Dennis would be sitting.

He obviously didn't want to cause a scene in front of our parents, so I thought I was safe through dinner anyway. I stepped forward, wrapping my hands around the outside of the chair as my mother disappeared back into the kitchen.

The heat of Zaiden's firm body surrounded me as he pressed his front to my back, and I froze when his hands curled around my hips. His masculine scent wrapped around me, and I breathed him in. "You look like you want to be bent over this table and thoroughly fucked," he whispered against my ear.

"I do," I smirked, pulling my chair out and bumping him off me. "Just not by you." Sliding around the chair, I sank into the seat, pretending to be completely unfazed by him.

"Is that so?" He slid into the chair beside me, one eyebrow arched, mouth curling into a dangerous grin. "Do you have someone in mind?"

"Someone who *can* fuck me thoroughly." I squared my shoulders, meeting his gaze head-on. "So I guess anyone other than *you* would do."

A low laugh rumbled from his chest. "That sounded like a challenge, baby girl."

I rolled my eyes as I reached for the water glass.

"Keep your hands on the table tonight." The command came out in a rushed whisper.

My gaze snapped to his. "Where else would I—"

"Dinner is ready!" My mother appeared in the doorway, her smile fixed in place. "Dennis?" She leaned toward the living room, her voice sharpening. "Dennis?"

Zaiden's father appeared from the living room entrance into the dining room and slid into his seat without looking up from his phone. Dennis was significantly older than my father. He was tall like Zaiden and had similar facial features, but his hair was salt and pepper with more salt than pepper.

Everyone passed around the decorative ceramic dishes, loading their plate with food before taking the next one. My mother was a terrible cook, but there was one thing she'd always made well because it was something that she and my grandmother made once a week: pot roast with mashed potatoes, green beans, and rolls. It was the only meal she made that was edible.

"This is so nice, isn't it?" My mother paused for effect. "Having the whole family together in one room."

Dennis hummed without looking up from his phone.

I rolled my eyes. This wasn't my family, and I wasn't theirs.

My mother's smile brightened. "So, Zaiden. It must be nice having your sister at school with you."

I coughed, nearly choking on the mashed potatoes I was about to swallow as my gaze flashed up, widening on her. She was completely oblivious to what she'd said. I wasn't Zaiden's sister. His sister was dead. I flicked a sideways glance at him to see if he was about to lose his shit or play into my mother's delusion.

"My sister?" he repeated as a question before his gaze shifted to me. "Yeah." His gaze dropped to my chest. "It's nice having my sister around." I froze when his large hand curled around my bare knee.

My gaze flashed to him, glaring in warning.

What the fuck was he doing?

"Oh shoot," my mother said. "I forgot the rolls." She pushed back from the table and disappeared into the kitchen.

My hand sank below the table, wrapping around his wrist and shoving his hand away, but he didn't move.

"Hands on the table." The command slipped under his breath, barely audible but unmistakable.

I gritted my teeth, shaking my head as my eyes darted to his dad, then back.

He held his phone between us—the video of me and Coach Palmer playing silently.

"Hands." His voice dropped an octave. "On the." Each word was as precise as a knife point. "Table."

My chest rose and fell with deep breaths as fear and anger pushed up my throat. The worst thing that could happen was for Zaiden to show my mother that video. It would only give her something else to hold over my head for the rest of my life. I would rather lose my scholarship than have my mom see that video.

Dropping my gaze to my plate, I swallowed my anger as I pulled my hand out from underneath the table and placed it flat.

"That's a good girl," he whispered so only I could hear him. Not that his dad would hear it if Zaiden were hanging upside down from the chandelier, shouting it. "Now spread your legs for me, baby." I shook my head. He laughed, hitting play on the video again.

"Fine," I whispered, stiffening my spine as I spread my legs for him. "Put the video away."

"Here we go," my mother said, setting a basket of rolls on the table. "So where were we?" She slid back into her seat.

My stomach fluttered, and my heart pounded when he trailed his fingertips up my inner thigh and under my dress.

"Is something wrong with the food, Ari?" my mother asked, zeroing in on my plate. I shook my head. "Well, eat, dear."

"Yeah," Zaiden added. "You should eat."

My jaw clenched as I forced a smile and picked up my fork. I didn't want to eat; I wanted to throat punch him. I shoved my fork into the mashed potatoes and then brought the fork to my lips. He groaned as he ran his fingers over the damp material of my panties.

"So, how's the dance team going, Ari?" My mother asked.

"Good," I huffed out, completely focused on what Zaiden's hand was doing.

"Well, tell me about it," my mother insisted.

"Yeah," Zaiden added as his fingers found my clit

making little circles around it. Teasing. Taunting me. The thin material of lace between my legs brushed against my clit with every circle making my breath hitch. "Tell us about it."

My cheeks heated with embarrassment as his hand continued to stroke me, and all eyes except Dennis's were on me. "Um," I cleared my throat, trying to focus on my words and not his fingers. "It's fun, and Journey and Mila are on the team." He added more pressure, and my stomach muscles clenched. A moan pushed past my lips.

"What was that, dear?" my mother asked.

"Nothing," I snapped, gripping the edge of my plate with both hands. "I was just saying I can't wait for the season to kick off."

"Any new boyfriend prospects?" She smiled.

"Yes," I moaned, and he pinched my clit through my panties. It was a warning. "I mean, um, no."

My body vibrated with the effort to maintain composure. One wrong breath and I'd—

Crash!

Zaiden's plate hit the floor. "Shit," he muttered, never pausing his torturous rhythm beneath the table.

"Oh dear." My mother pushed her chair back.

Fuck!

"No." Zaiden's voice hardened. "Stay. I'll get it."

My mother nodded and pulled her chair back to the table as Zaiden sank below the table.

"He's such a good boy," she mouthed, and all I could do was nod. She had no idea.

"Well, don't worry about boys too much, dear," my mother said, picking up the conversation right where we left off. "There will be plenty of time for that."

I nodded, sucking in a tiny gasp as his lips met my

outer thigh. I stared forward as Zaiden shifted under the table. "I like my teachers too," I said, trying to keep her attention on me and not on what Zaiden was doing on the floor. He worked his fingers, adding the perfect amount of pressure that lit my body on fire.

The heat was a slow roll as it swept over me, making my legs tremble and my stomach quiver. I bit down hard on the inside of my cheek, and I bucked my hips forward into his touch, chasing the feeling. He ran his tongue over my thigh, and I dropped my head and bit down so hard on my cheek I tasted blood as I exploded like a rocket at the dinner table sitting across from my mom and his dad.

"Are you okay, dear?" My mother asked. "You look flushed."

My body relaxed, and I nodded as I tried to steady my breathing. His hands were gone.

"Are you getting it, Zaiden?" my mother asked.

"Yep," he said, appearing from underneath the table with his plate. "Just needs to be mopped."

"Well, don't worry about that," she smiled. "I'll have Gisselle get it after we are done." Gisselle was the Knight's full-time housekeeper.

"Are you not hungry, Ari?" My mother asked.

"I thought dinner was delicious," Zaiden smirked, bringing his fingers that just gave me a mind-blowing orgasm to his lips and licked them clean. My stomach fluttered, and I realized exactly what he meant.

"Dinner was great," I said. I needed space from Zaiden Knight. "But I'm tired, and I still have some schoolwork to do. So, I need to excuse myself."

"Of course," my mother said. "I would like to do these family dinners at least once a week if you two could make time." My gaze shifted to Dennis, who hadn't said a word or even looked up from his phone once.

"I think that's a great idea, Claire," Zaiden said. His tone was so nauseously nice that I wanted to vomit. She had no idea that he meant he would love to torture me once a week at the dinner table. He enjoyed seeing me squirm.

"Great," she said, sounding pleased. "You two have a good night."

I pushed out of my chair and bolted for the stairs, hoping to make it to my room, and lock the door before Zaiden was out of his seat. I crossed the doorway into my room and threw the door shut, but I was too slow. Zaiden caught the door before it closed.

"I'll scream." The threat spilled out as he advanced, and I retreated.

"No, you won't." The corner of his mouth hooked upward. "I missed you in the locker room today."

I lifted one shoulder in feigned indifference. "I decided to come home and change."

"The clock is ticking, Ariella," he warned. "If you don't inform the entire football team that you belong to me, I will, and I promise you will wish you did." He turned, walked out of my room, and closed the door behind him.

I had no intention of telling anyone I belonged to Zaiden because I didn't belong to anyone. I was only okay with the football team claiming me because it should have kept Zaiden away from me, and it would have if he hadn't had that video.

I just had to wait him out and hope he got bored.

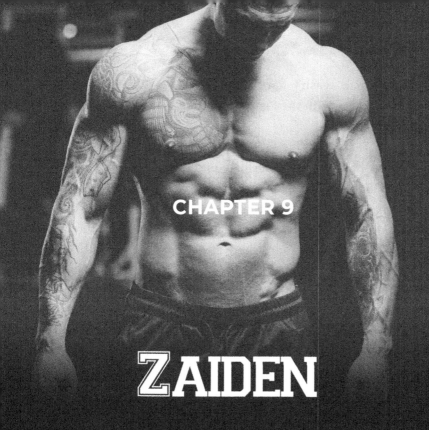

CHAPTER 9

ZAIDEN

Watching Ariella squirm in front of her mother to my touch was not just intoxicating. It was addictive. A high that I was already craving another hit of, and it was more distracting than it should have been.

"Did you hear me?" Sterling stepped in front of me, blocking my path as we entered the parking garage. His eyebrows arched the way they did when he thought I was being difficult.

I could hear him; I just wasn't listening. I shook my head. "Are you going to Trey's place tonight?"

It was Friday night, and Trey, Westbrook Predator's left wing, was hosting a party, but I knew Ariella wouldn't be there. She wouldn't have been invited because she belonged to the football team. She would be wherever they were, which wasn't happening. If my sister couldn't be there to party with the team because of her, then she wasn't going to either.

"No." I avoided his eyes. "I have plans."

"You have plans?" Sterling folded his arms across his chest. "Do these plans have anything to do with Ariella?"

I fixed him with a hard stare. "Don't start with me."

"Come on, man," he groaned. "Don't let this turn into an obsession. Forget about her and come party with us tonight." The corners of his lips curled up. "Lauren Taylor is coming." Lauren, also known as the ice princess, was one of Westbrook's best figure skaters. She was high mainte-nance but incredibly fucking hot, and the best part was that she played hard to get for everyone but me. She was always a sure thing. "A round or two with Lauren, and you'll feel better."

I rolled my eyes. He was patronizing me, but maybe he was right. Watching Ariella come had me all worked up and not thinking clearly. "Maybe—" my words trailed off when a flash of movement from the opposite end of the garage caught my attention. My gaze shifted to see Ariella walking through the dark parking garage by herself without the protection of her team. My lips twitched with excitement. Who needed Lauren when I could force Ariella to her knees on the dirty ground next to her car?

Sterling spotted Ariella and gripped my shoulder. "Come on, Zaid. Let her go, and let's go have some fun."

I nodded mechanically, but my attention had already locked onto Ariella, tracking her movement through the garage like a predator.

She wore tight black leggings and a black sports bra under her old black, red, and white high school dance jersey. She turned down a row of cars, and I gritted my teeth. It wasn't her jersey, it was Kacie's.

Fuck that.

"I'll meet you at the party," I growled. My entire body language changed. I was pissed. Where did she get my sister's jersey from? And actually, that didn't even matter. She had no right to wear that jersey when it was her fault my sister was dead.

I stormed forward, following her to her car. Anger radiated off me. If she knew I was behind her, she didn't let it show. Her pace was slow as she loosely jingled her keys at her side. I stepped up behind her, quickly snatching the keys out of her hand as she stopped in front of her car.

She spun around, keys vanishing from her grasp. "What the—" The words died in her throat when she saw me.

I curled my fingers around her bare upper arm, the warmth of her skin a sharp contrast to the cold purpose in my grip.

"Let me go." She pulled against my hold, each tug stoking something dark inside me.

"Zaiden!"

"Get in the car," I snarled, releasing her arm and jerking the passenger side door open. She didn't move. "Get in the fucking car." She flinched as my command came out in angry, violent waves. Her face twisted with confusion, like she didn't understand why I was so angry, which only made me angrier. "Get in the fucking car, or I'll put you in the trunk."

"Okay." A muscle twitched in her jaw as she dropped into the seat, her movements stiff with defiance.

I slammed the door hard enough to rock the car, circled

to the driver's side, and slid behind the wheel. The interior suddenly felt too small for the anger radiating off me.

"Where are we going?" She adjusted her seatbelt, forcing casualness into her voice.

I kept my eyes on the road, my knuckles whitening on the steering wheel. During our drive, she repeated her question two more times, each attempt weaker than the last, until she finally surrendered to the weight of my silence.

She leaned forward, eyes widening as I swerved into Westbrook Memorial Cemetery. "What are we doing here?" I didn't answer as I drove down the dark, narrow path. The cemetery closed after dark, but the gates had been broken for years, and the city was too cheap to fix them. "Zaiden, what are we doing here?"

I pulled to a stop a few feet away from Kacie's grave. Other than the headlights of Ariella's car, it was pitch black.

"Get out."

"No," she said, bearing down and crossing her arms over her chest. "I'm not getting out."

Grabbing the keys, I shoved open the door, stormed around the car, and jerked her door open. "Get out, or I will drag you out."

"Why, Zaiden? What are we doing here?" When she didn't budge, I leaned down. "Okay." She quickly unbuckled and slid out of the car. My large hand curled around her thin arm, jerking her out of the way as I slammed the car door closed and shoved her into the side of the car.

"Where did you get that jersey?"

Her brows pulled together as her head dropped. She looked at her shirt like she didn't remember what she was wearing. "Kacie and I traded jerseys at the end of every year since 9th grade." Her gaze lifted, meeting mine. "It was our tradition. She gave it to me."

"Take it off," I growled, stepping into her and pressing my body to hers. I dropped my head so our noses were nearly touching. "You don't deserve to wear her jersey."

"Zaiden," she hissed, placing her small hands on my chest. She shoved me backward, and I let her. I needed some space between her and me to think clearly. "I didn't hurt her. She was in a car accident."

The fact that she couldn't accept her part in my sister's death only made me angrier.

"We were all at that party. I didn't kill her."

My lip curled into a snarl. "Take the fucking jersey off."

The wind picked up, rustling through the trees surrounding the cemetery. Moonlight broke through the clouds, casting Kacie's headstone in silver light.

Ariella's eyes flicked to the grave, then back to me. Something shifted in her expression.

"I loved her too, Zaiden." Her whisper barely disturbed the cemetery air. She touched the jersey over her heart. "She was my best friend."

I advanced until the heat of her body mingled with mine, until I could see the pulse racing in her throat.

"You don't get to say that anymore."

CHAPTER 10

Ariella

I released a shaky breath as adrenaline coursed through my veins. Zaiden brought me all the way out to Kacie's grave after dark when the cemetery was closed, and I had no idea what his intentions were, but there was no mistaking he was pissed.

I couldn't figure out why he thought I was responsible for Kacie's death. We'd all been at that party. Kacie left the party by herself in her own car. I wouldn't have been able to stop her any more than he could have or Sterling, or Journey, or Mila. For some reason, he needed to blame me.

"Take the fucking jersey off, Ariella." Zaiden's jaw clenched, a muscle twitching beneath the shadow of his stubble.

My throat tightened. Sweat beaded between my shoulder blades, trickling down my spine. I forced my breathing to steady. Whatever he was planning wouldn't end well for me, but panic would only make it worse.

My only chance was running, but I needed a head start.

"Fine." I raised my hands in surrender, watching his eyes for any shift in attention.

My pulse raced, and my heart pounded as I grabbed the hem of the black, white, and red jersey and pulled it over my head. Sucking in a deep breath, I tossed the jersey at his face hoping it would temporarily distract him and bolted, but he was faster than I was. He kicked his foot out, tripping me. Pain shot through me as I tumbled down, slamming into the hard dirt.

"Shit," I muttered, shifting to push up but froze when his boots squeezed my sides.

"You should know I enjoy the fight." The corner of his mouth curved upward, eyes glittering in the darkness. His hand slid against my scalp, fingers tangling in my hair.

I yelped as he jerked my head back.

He knelt, his breath hot against my ear. "I love the chase."

He released my hair with a small shove. I rolled to my back, my heart hammering against my ribs.

"Zaiden." I forced steel into my voice despite the tremor in my hands. My tone was a warning, a weak one, but still a warning.

"Did you really think you were going to hang out with your friends and party while my sister is dead because of you?"

"Zaiden, I didn't kill your sister." My voice cracked on the last word, betraying me. I swallowed hard. "She was my best friend."

His shadow fell across my face, darkening with each

passing second. When he spoke, his voice was terrifyingly calm.

"You're the one who should be six feet under. Not her."

The words landed like a physical blow. I couldn't breathe for a moment.

I pushed up on my elbows, dirt embedding under my nails. Defiance rose in me, a dangerous warmth.

"You don't think I wish it were me?" Each word was heavy. "Every. Single. Day."

His face remained impassive, carved from stone.

"You don't think I would trade spots with her if I could?" My voice strengthened. "Tell me what I could have done, Zaiden."

I shifted to get up—a mistake.

He moved with predatory speed, dropping his chest and flattening his palms against my shoulders. The force drove me back to the ground, pinned beneath his weight.

My heart jumped. Fear, yes. But something else, too. Rage. Pure, clarifying rage.

Fuck.

This situation was going from bad to worse.

"Why don't you tell me what you did?" My brows pulled together. "Tell me why my sister left that night. Tell me what you did, and I'll take you home."

He was going to leave me here alone in the dark. Panic rose in my throat at his words. "Zaiden, I didn't do anything."

His nostrils flared as he leaned down, wrapping his strong hands around my arms. I had no idea why he was so angry. I had no idea why he thought I was responsible for Kacie's death or what he thought I did, but what I did know was that if I didn't get out of this situation quickly, it was going to end badly for me.

He jerked me, and I raised my knee at the same time, shoving it hard into his balls. He grunted, releasing me as his hands flew to his groin.

I bolted into the darkness. Tombstones loomed, and branches clawed at my face. My lungs burned, but I pushed harder, faster.

Footsteps behind me. Gaining. Even injured, he was faster.

No. I wasn't going down without a fight.

Strong arms locked around my waist. My feet left the ground as he yanked me backward, my spine colliding with his chest.

"Let me go," I screamed, kicking, scratching, and hitting.

"Sure," he whispered against my ear. The evil in his tone sent chills racing up my spine. "Right where you belong."

His arms vanished. A push.

I stumbled backward, arms windmilling against nothing. One step, two, then my heel met empty space.

Time slowed. My body tilted backward, a heartbeat suspended in the air.

Then gravity claimed me.

I plummeted through the darkness, a silent scream locked in my throat. My back slammed against cold, wet earth, a dull, sickening thud. The impact forced air from my lungs in a harsh gasp.

Six feet of vertical darkness surrounded me. The stars above, impossibly distant, framed Zaiden's silhouette.

I was lying in an empty grave.

"Omigod," I cried, scrambling to my feet and staring up at him standing above me. His eyes were dark and evil. "Zaiden. "The panic and terror in my tone was excruciatingly painful. "Please. Please don't leave me here." I was scared of the dark, but even worse, he was leaving me alone in a dark grave.

"Too bad I'm not standing here for your funeral," he said, his tone void of any emotion. He knelt, filling his hand with dirt. "My sister deserved better than you."

I reached up, extending my hand to him. "Zaiden, please, this isn't funny. Please just help me out."

He stood to his full height, staring down at me. "Good night, Ariella." He dropped the dirt in his hand, and I dropped my face to keep it from going in my eyes as it covered my head.

My gaze snapped up, and he was gone. "Zaiden," I screamed. "Zaiden, please, please don't leave me here." I dug my fingers into the dirt, and it crumbled in my hands before I could pull myself up. The grave had to be at least six feet deep, and I was only 5'2". I wasn't sure if I was strong enough to pull myself out, but I wasn't staying here tonight.

The faint glow of headlights faded, taking with it my last connection to the world above. "Zaiden, please!" My voice echoed against the dirt walls. Then—nothing. Complete darkness swallowed me. The cemetery's silence pressed against my eardrums. Tears carved hot trails down my cheeks.

"I didn't hurt her." My voice trembled. "Just tell me what I did." I knew he was gone, but I was overwhelmed with fear and sadness. I was stuck in a grave only feet away from where I'd watched Kacie's casket lowered into the ground.

Panic rose in my throat as I frantically clawed at the ground, but it crumbled in my hands. The fear consuming me made it hard to think straight. I sucked in a deep breath through my nose and slowly exhaled through my mouth. "Calm down and think, Ari." My eyes widened. "My phone." I patted down my pockets and pulled it out. My trembling fingers opened the phone before clicking on Mila's contact.

"Hey!" Mila's voice lilted through the speaker, bright and oblivious. "Where are y–"

"I need you—" I swallowed hard, grit grinding between my teeth. "Come get me."

The darkness pressed down, a weight on my chest. My fingers dug into the dirt walls.

"Now."

"Ari? What's—" Alarm sharpened her tone.

"NOW."

Keys jingled through the speaker. A door slammed. Mila was moving.

"No time—" My voice caught as the battery indicator flashed red. "Phone dying. Sending location."

I disconnected, fumbled with trembling fingers to open messages, and sent my location.

> Ariella: Cemetery. In an open grave next to Kacie's.
>
> Ariella: HURRY

I shook my head. I wasn't thinking clearly. All I needed to say was I was at Kacie's grave.

The screen flickered. Darkness swallowed me as the phone died, its glow vanishing like a snuffed candle.

The silence that followed was absolute—nothing but the sound of my own ragged breathing and the distant cry of an owl. I pressed my back against the cold earth wall, the reality of my situation settling over me like the weight of the dirt Zaiden had let fall on my head.

I tilted my head back and let loose a scream that tore through my throat, rage, terror, and defiance all wrapped into one sound. Let the dead hear me. Let anyone hear me. But when the echo faded, I was still alone—still buried—still waiting.

I had to get out of here.

I ran my trembling hands along the grave walls, inch by desperate inch. Seeking. Hoping. The dirt crumbled between my fingers, each handful another small defeat. My breath came in short, ragged bursts as panic threatened to overwhelm me.

Then, near one corner, something fibrous. Different. Not dirt.

A tree root.

I gripped it, fingers whitening with pressure. Yanked once, gently. Then harder.

It held.

My body went still. One chance. Just this one chance.

I pressed my forehead against the cold wall, gathering strength. I dug my shoe into the dirt, creating a small foothold. I pulled upward, every muscle screaming in protest. The root groaned under my weight.

Please, please, please.

The root creaked, a terrible warning sound as I threw my elbows over the edge, dirt cascading around me.

A choked sob escaped me as I reached for anything to grab onto. There was nothing. Headlights appeared in the distance, and judging by the speed, I guessed it was Mila.

The car skidded to a stop near Kacie's grave, and the car doors on each side flew open.

"I'm here," I shouted to Journey and Mila.

"Oh my fucking God," Mila cried out, racing to me. They each grabbed an arm and pulled me out of the grave.

"What the fuck happened?" Journey's eyes widened as she took in my dirt-covered form, her breath coming in quick gasps.

"Zaiden." The name fell from my lips. I wrapped my arms around myself, shivering despite the warm night air. "Take me home. Please."

I stared at the grave one last time, then turned away. The need to wash away this night burned beneath my skin. Tomorrow. I'd deal with everything else tomorrow.

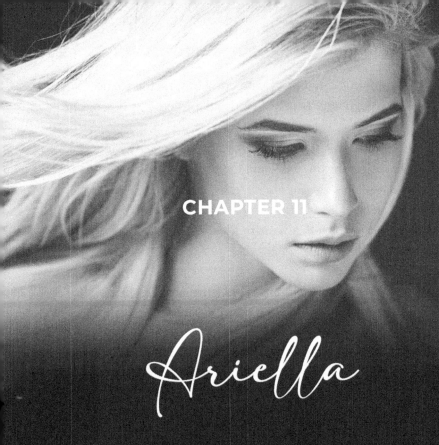

CHAPTER 11

Ariella

Anger boiled through my veins as I stood in the shadows of the school hallway, watching Zaiden laugh and joke with his friends. I wanted to murder him. Any thoughts I'd had that Zaiden had any human decency disappeared last night when he left me alone in the dark, scared and cold, along with any lingering sympathy I'd had because he'd lost his sister.

He'd declared war.

I knew I wasn't as big and strong as him physically, so I'd have to be creative.

"I know you're plotting something." Mila leaned closer, her voice barely audible. "I can see it in your eyes."

I shrugged, tracking Zaiden's movements across the hallway.

"He's psychotic and deranged, Ari." Mila chewed her bottom lip. "You won't win."

She was right, but my rage consumed me, egging me on. Making me believe I was ten feet tall and bulletproof.

"Yeah," I muttered. "I need to figure out what he thinks I did to Kacie."

"Do you really think there's a reason?" Her brows pulled together. "I think he just needs someone to blame."

I shook my head. "I don't think so. I think there's more to it, and we need to find out what it is."

"How do we do that?"

I shook my head. "I'm not sure, but I think we need to get to Sterling." My gaze shifted, meeting Mila's. "Are you two still friends?"

"Yeah, of course." Her gaze twisted to the guys. "But I'm not sure he'll tell me anything. He's loyal to Zaiden and his team, and we aren't on his team. We belong to the football team."

I rolled my eyes. I didn't belong to anyone, but I wasn't going to argue about it either because I needed that protection right now. "Don't ask him straight up. Beat around the bush."

She nodded. "I'll try."

The hockey team dispersed. The hallway emptied except for Sterling and Zaiden, their footsteps echoing as they strolled our way. Memories of last night—dirt filling my mouth, darkness pressing down—surged forward. My muscles coiled. I shifted.

"Ari," Mila whisper-hissed. "Don't do this. You won't win." I didn't know if she was right or not. I couldn't see clearly through my pounding rage. I surged forward. "Ari." She grabbed at my arm, but I was already gone. "Shit."

My fist clenched at my side, and my jaw flexed as I stormed forward, my body tight with anger. Zaiden's grayish-blue eyes lifted, meeting mine, and a slow, sadistic smirk twisted on his lips like he'd won.

Sterling's dark eyes widened on me as I stormed forward, shoulders first.

"Aw, I was hoping you'd drown in that grave," Zaiden sneered.

I stopped. Time slowed. His smirk widened as I reared back and slammed my fist across his jaw.

"Fuck you."

Pain exploded through my hand. Bones grinding against bones. I kept my face blank, fist clenched at my side as I resisted the urge to shake the pain out. No way I'd let him see how much it hurt.

"Holy shit," Sterling and Mila both shouted.

Mila grabbed me, pulling me back as Sterling shifted to grab Zaiden if he needed to, but Zaiden didn't charge me. The corners of his lips lifted as his gaze froze on me. He drew in slow, controlled breaths as he swiped his thumb across his lip, wiping away the blood.

My heart pounded. Uncontrollable breaths rang in my ears. Panic gripped my chest as the realization of what I'd done sank in. Too late now. I squared my shoulders and stiffened my spine.

"You just fucked up, princess." Zaiden's tongue darted out to taste the blood on his lip.

Sterling stepped between us, hands raised. "Why don't we all calm down?"

"Yeah." Mila's fingers dug into my shoulder.

"Fuck that." I wrenched free from her grip, my voice raw. "He left me in an empty grave last night."

Sterling's eyes widened as his gaze shifted back to

Zaiden, who was still shooting daggers at me. "That's what the fuck you were doing last night."

"She deserves to be buried right next to my sister." He stepped forward, puffing his chest out.

"If I deserve to be next to her, so do you." I stepped forward, bumping my chest with his.

His hand moved to grab me, but Sterling hooked an arm around him, jerking him back. "It's not my fault she's dead. It's yours, and you have to live with that guilt for the rest of your life."

"What did I do?" I threw my hands up in the air. "What, Zaiden?"

His lips curled into a smirk. "I'll see you tonight, princess."

He jerked hard, shrugging Sterling off him, and walked away. Sterling gave us a 'what-the-fuck' look before following after Zaiden.

"You just punched Zaiden Knight in the face," Mila squealed once they were gone. "I don't know whether to be proud or scared."

I shook my head.

"He's going to get me back at the party tonight."

"You think he'll show the video to everyone?" Mila's voice bounced off the concrete walls, making the question echo.

My gaze tracked Zaiden and Sterling until they disappeared around the corner, the sound of their laughter lingering in the air like a threat.

"I don't think so. That's the only leverage he has over me. If he uses that, then it's over. I'm ruined, but I'm free."

"No, girl." Mila's voice dropped. She glanced around before continuing. "You'll never be free as long as he thinks you killed his sister."

"Yeah." I rubbed my bruised knuckles, wincing. "See if you can get Sterling alone tonight at the party."

Mila fidgeted with her bracelet. Hesitated. "Maybe we should skip the party tonight." She glanced over her shoulder. "It's going to be so packed that the team probably won't miss us."

"EJ will know I'm not there, trust me," I said. "Plus, I'm not giving that asshole the satisfaction."

"Satisfaction?"

"Of thinking he won." I lowered my voice. "I'm not letting him scare me into hiding in my room."

My gaze shifted to her. "Which, by the way—"

Mila's eyes narrowed. "What?"

"–isn't a safe place either."

"If you're sure."

I nodded. "I'm sure." The sooner we figured out why he was so angry with me, the sooner we could correct it. "Come on, let's get ready for practice."

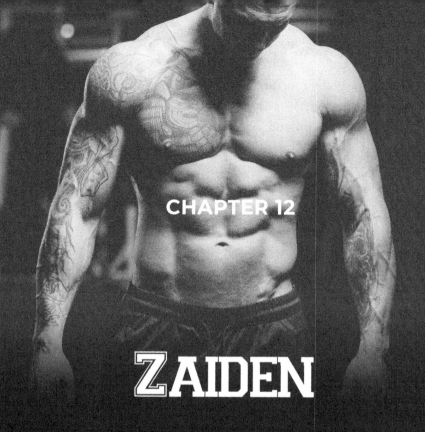

CHAPTER 12

ZAIDEN

"You're giving off stalker vibes," Sterling muttered, stepping beside me outside the football stadium tunnel. "And what's worse is that you're not even trying to hide that you're stalking her."

"I'm not stalking her," I said dryly, my gaze shifting to meet his. "Not yet, anyway."

I pushed off the wall, the concrete rough against my palm. Each step down the stadium stairs brought me closer to my vantage point—and to her. The empty row of seats offered the perfect view of the dance team, of Ariella. Just where I needed to be.

I wasn't opposed to stalking her if I needed to, but it hadn't come to that. I wanted her to know I was there, watching, waiting for her to do something stupid.

"I think you've tortured the girl enough," Sterling said, following me.

"Maybe you missed her punching me in the face an hour ago." I traced the tender spot on my jaw, sliding into a stadium seat with a front-row view of the dance team. My feet kicked up as I settled in like I was watching a movie I'd paid good money to see.

"Yeah, bro." Sterling's laugh grated against my ears. "You deserved that. So let's call a truce and move on."

My fingers curled into fists against my thighs. "My sister can't move on." My voice was flat and void of any emotion. "She's stuck in a grave because of her." I pointed down to the field. "There's no way I'm going to let her live her best life when my sister can't live at all."

"What did she do?" Sterling twisted in his seat. "We were all at that party, and I don't remember her doing anything to Kacie."

I didn't answer; I just stared forward, eyes locked on Ariella. It didn't matter what she did.

"Tell me what she did." Frustration edged into his voice. "Maybe then I can understand this obsession."

My gaze narrowed as the dance coach gave his dismissal speech.

"What are you planning to do to her at the party tonight?" Sterling asked after I ignored his other questions.

"Nothing." That was the truth because she wasn't going to make it to the party.

The coach's voice cut through the afternoon air. "Mila, I need to see you in my office."

I caught the silent exchange between Journey, Mila, and Ariella, eyes widening, color draining from faces, fingers gripping water bottles too tightly. Not disappointment. Not embarrassment.

Fear.

"Why do you think he calls a different girl's name at the end of each practice?"

"What?" Sterling sneered.

I nodded toward the dance coach on the field. "After every practice, he calls one of the girls' names and tells them he needs to see them in his office. Why?"

Sterling shrugged as he shook his head. "I don't know, maybe because they did really bad, and he wants to scold them privately."

"Except all the girls look," I paused as I swiped my tongue along my lips, trying to think of the right word. "like they're praying that their name isn't called, and when it isn't, they look relieved."

"No one wants to be in trouble."

My stomach twisted. "My gut says it's something else." It was no secret that the coach was inappropriate with his dancers, but how far did that go, and was it still a thing between him and Ariella?

"Why don't you ask Ariella?" He smirked. "Oh, you can't because she hates you now." I rolled my eyes. "Ask one of the other girls, maybe Journey or Mila."

"Yeah," I agreed, but I had no intention of asking Journey or Mila, though I probably had a better chance of getting the truth out of them quicker than Ariella. I pushed out of my seat. "I'll see you at the party tonight."

"Seriously, man." Sterling threw his hands up, face flushed with frustration.

I was already walking away.

I made it into the tunnel and was waiting near the football locker room entrance when Ariella finally showed up. She moved toward the open entrance without acknowledging me.

"I wouldn't do that if I were you," I scowled, stepping in front of the locker room and blocking it.

"Haven't you taken enough of a beating for today?" she smirked. "Get out of my way."

"Not even close." The corner of my lips curved into a grin as my gaze lifted to see Journey standing behind her. "What's up, Journey?"

"Yeah," she frowned, holding her hands up. "I'm not getting involved in whatever this," she waved a finger between Ariella and me, "is." She sidestepped me and disappeared into the locker room.

"Get out of my way, Zaiden," she demanded.

"You know the rules," I reminded her.

"Fuck your rules." Her palms connected with my chest, the shove punctuating her words. "And fuck you too."

I grabbed her wrist—one quick motion—and pulled her against me. The sudden collision forced a small gasp from her lips. The bruise forming on my jaw from her earlier punch throbbed with my heartbeat.

"I already owe you for earlier." I dropped my lips to hers, letting my breath fan across hers as her pulse raced beneath my fingers. "Don't make this worse on yourself, princess."

"The entire football team is in that locker room right now, and if you don't move, I'll scream, and you'll start a war."

My lips curled into a smirk. If she thought I gave a fuck she was sadly mistaken, but lucky for her, this isn't how I wanted this to go down. I threw my hands in the air in a sarcastic surrender as I stepped back.

"You're right, I don't want to start a war." And I didn't. I wanted her to submit to me, and she would before I was through with her. She stepped forward.

"What happens when your coach calls your name at the end of practice?"

Her confident stance faltered. "What?"

I stepped closer, watching her pupils dilate slightly. "At the end of every practice, your dance coach calls a name to meet with in his office." My voice dropped lower. "What happens when you meet with him?"

She shook her head. "I—I don't know."

Chatter from the locker room grew louder as the team headed for the exit. She was lying, but I'd have to get it out of her later.

"See you at the party, princess." The lie tasted bitter on my tongue. I strolled away, unhurried, shoulders relaxed.

Now, I was going to stalk her because I needed to get to her before she got to that party tonight.

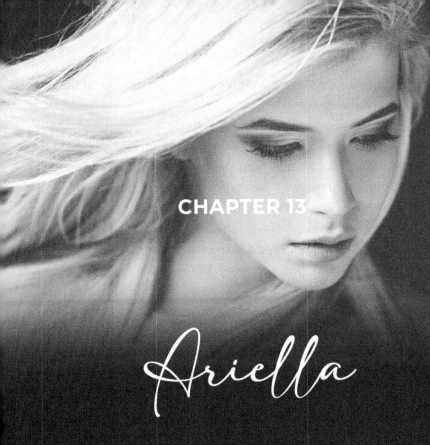

CHAPTER 13

Ariella

"**Y**ou did what?" Journey's voice scraped between her clenched teeth as she followed me through the rows of lockers.

I dropped my towel on the hook. "I punched him in the face." The shower curtain rings screeched against the metal rod. "In front of Mila and Sterling."

"You are playing with fire," Journey warned. I recognized her fear, but I wasn't sure if it was for her or me. "He's going to make that video go viral, and who knows what will happen. You could lose your scholarship." I rolled my eyes but didn't say anything. "What if he has videos of the rest of us, too?"

I glanced over my shoulder and kicked on the water. "He's not going to share that video. It's his only leverage." I stepped toward the shower. "Once it's out there, his power is gone." Steam began to rise. "And his beef is with me. Not you. Not the other girls."

I didn't really want that video to go viral, but there was only so much one person could take before they said 'fuck it' and let him show the video. "He's probably going to share it once he's done with me anyway."

"Let's hope not," she frowned. "I really need this scholarship, and if they shut down the dance team, who knows what will happen."

"They may take away my scholarship, but they have no reason to take away everyone else's."

"We have dance scholarships." Journey twisted her bracelet around her wrist. "If we aren't dancing, there is no scholarship."

I nodded, hoping the cold feeling in my stomach was wrong.

"We need to figure out why he's angry with me and fast."

She nodded. "I'm heading home now, but I'll meet you at the party around ten." I nodded. "We'll come up with a game plan when we get there, but you're going to want to avoid Zaiden if you can."

"I'll stick close to EJ tonight. He won't try anything with the whole team around."

Journey's face darkened. "I think you underestimate him."

She was right. I always did. And I always paid for it.

"Expect everything," she whispered.

"You're right. I'll see you tonight."

She left, and I stripped down and slipped into the shower. The water hitting the tile floor echoed through the silent locker room, and steam filled the space, escaping through the openings in the curtain. I stepped forward, letting the hot water wash away all the stresses of my day for a brief moment before coming up with a game plan for tonight.

I needed a list of everyone who was at the party the night Kacie died, and then we could split up and casually question everyone to see if we could find out why Zaiden thinks I had something to do with her death.

A dark shadow slid under the curtain. I froze. The roar of water seemed distant, muffled by the blood rushing in my ears. A footstep. Then another. Everyone but Mila should be gone by now. The shadow grew larger. Closer.

"Mila?" I called out. No answer.

My heart crowded my throat, making it hard to breathe. Zaiden wouldn't dare come into another team's locker room. It was forbidden.

"Mila?" My voice cracked this time.

The shower curtain ripped open, and I screamed. Not because it was Zaiden, but because it scared me.

"What the fuck, Zaiden?" My arms flew across my chest, a pointless shield. Water dripped between us. "What are you doing in here?"

"I want to know what happens when your Coach calls your name at the end of practice," he said, his tone deep and dark as he reached in and flicked off the water.

"Seriously?"

He moved fast, too fast; he stepped forward, wrapping his large hand around my throat and shoving me into the wall. "Seriously." He pressed into me, dropping his face to mine. His grip tightened around my throat in warning. "I asked nicely. Now I'm telling you I want to know what is happening in that office."

"I don't know."

His grip tightened, and my hands wrapped around his wrist. "I have no problem burying you next to my sister."

"I really don't know," I gasped, and his grip loosened. "My name hasn't been called yet, but if you must know, I imagine it's similar to what is required to make the team." He stepped back, and his hand dropped. "So you do whatever he tells you?" I nodded. "If he tells you to bend over his desk and take it in the ass, you do it?" I shrugged. "You can't tell anyone or interfere, Zaiden." "You think I give a fuck if your Coach fucks you," he laughed. "I don't. I just wanted to know."

"Now you know," I said. "So, can I finish my shower?"

He shook his head, and he narrowed his dark, intense eyes on me. My heart sank, and my stomach turned.

"Get on your knees." His finger stabbed downward, marking a spot on the wet tiles.

I shook my head, hip cocked to one side. "I'm not sucking your dick." My arms formed a barrier across my chest, more for defiance than modesty.

"Yes, you will, but not today," he smirked. "Get on your knees, or I will text Mommy dearest this video of you blowing your coach to make the team."

Fuck. My lips twisted with disgust like I tasted something gross. Why did he have to bring her into this? Because he knew she was the last person I wanted to see that video. I told him that without saying a word, the night of our family dinner.

Blowing out a heavy sigh, I dropped to my knees, squeezing my thighs tightly together and sinking my ass onto my calves.

"That's a good girl." His face said he was pleased with me, and my stomach churned.

My gaze lifted, meeting his as my lip curled. "Fuck you."

He laughed. "I wouldn't fuck that dirty pussy with my worst enemy's dick." That was meant to cut deep, but it didn't because we both knew I was a virgin, or at least he knew I was all through high school.

"Then I guess we are done here," I smirked, moving to get up.

His hands curled around my shoulders as he held me down. "Give me your hands."

"How about a finger?" I scoffed as I lifted my left hand and flicked him off.

His large hand caught my wrist. "Other hand." I didn't move. "Now. Ariella."

My jaw clenched, but I lifted my hand, and he grabbed it, pulling my wrists together. Before I knew what was happening, he slapped a metal band around one wrist, pulled the chain through the metal shower safety bar just above my head, and slapped the other end of the cuffs on my other wrist.

"What the fuck, Zaiden?" He reached into his back pocket and pulled out a black and white handkerchief. My eyes widened as panic clawed at my insides. "No." I shook my head as he knelt, bringing the material closer to my mouth. "Zaiden."

"I need you to shut the fuck up." He raised his brows as his gaze dropped to my lips. "As much as I'm going to enjoy using this pretty mouth. I don't need it today." I jerked my face away from the cloth. "Open." I shook my head. "Open your fucking mouth, Ariella. Or I'll make you."

I thought about it for a minute, and being gagged definitely didn't sound as bad as him using my mouth for other things, so twisting my head back, I slowly opened my mouth. I didn't want him to change his mind if I continued to refuse because he got off on the fight.

He slid the soft material through my lips and tied it behind my head. His heated gaze raked down my body, and an explosion of goosebumps spread over my skin when he forced his fingers between my knees. "Spread your legs."

I squealed through the gag, shaking my head no.

"We both know I'm going to win, and as much as I love a fight, I'm done now. Spread your legs."

I was at his mercy. I didn't know what he was going to do, but I was one hundred percent sure it could always be worse. I let him push my thighs apart, spreading me open. "I bet this pussy is so fucking wet for me right now."

I wanted to say yeah, we are in the fucking shower, but I imagine those types of responses were why he'd gagged me.

His gaze lifted, locking on my lips. His throat flexed on a hard swallow, his nostrils flared, and the muscles in his arm tightened as his hand raised. He pressed his thumb to my bottom lip, tugging it. "This sassy little mouth is going to look so fucking pretty wrapped around my cock."

The hungry look in his eyes and his dirty words did something to my insides that sent a heat through my stomach straight between my thighs, making me want to squeeze them together to alleviate the pressure. It shouldn't do anything to me. I hated him, but it did.

He pushed to his full height, his greyish blue eyes never leaving mine as he flicked open the button on his jeans and lowered his zipper before reaching into his pants, and my eyes squeezed closed.

"Open your eyes, princess," he ordered, his tone low

and commanding. I didn't want to open my eyes, but I couldn't fight my curiosity. My eyes eased open and widened as his hand wrapped around his thick cock. Fisting his dick in his hand, he stroked himself slow and steady as his gaze dropped, raking over my wet naked body.

My stomach fluttered, and I couldn't look away even if I should. He was long, thick, and rock-hard, the complete opposite of the only other dick I'd seen. I blinked, and my mouth went dry as he worked his hand over his length, increasing his speed. Precum beaded at the tip of his head, and he used it to quicken his strokes.

My heart rate kicked up, and I was practically panting as the muscles in his arms flexed and the veins bulged. He bit down on his bottom lip, and his abs tightened.

My nipples pulled tight, and it felt like torture, not being able to touch myself. I whimpered through the gag and thrashed against the cuff, begging to be released, but that only seemed to turn him on more. "Does this turn you on, princess? Do you like watching me?"

Way more than I'd ever want to admit.

His grip tightened. "Do me a favor, make that sound again."

I didn't want to, but I really couldn't help it. It was like I no longer had control of my body.

"Oh fuck," he groaned as his head fell back and his lips parted. He stepped forward, and he exploded, splashing warm sticky ropes of cum on my face and chest. "Fuck," he panted.

He quickly tucked himself back in his pants before stepping back and taking in his cum covered canvas smiling like he was proud of his work.

He stepped forward after a long moment and untied and removed the gag.

"You look so pretty covered in my cum." He swiped his thumb across my cheek, dragging the sticky substance across my lips.

"Please let me go now."

"Yeah, I don't think so." His smile didn't reach his eyes. "I'm headed to the party." He backed away. "Sleep tight, princess."

The distance between us grew with each step. My options shrank just as quickly.

"If you leave me here—" My voice cracked. I forced steel into it. "I will tell everyone exactly who did this." I yanked at the cuffs. Metal bit into my wrists. "This is worse than any stupid video going viral."

The corner of his lip lifted into a crooked, sadistic smirk. He leaned forward, dropping his body so we were face to face.

"You won't."

His finger and thumb pinched my chin, forcing my gaze to his. I tried to twist away.

He tightened his grip. "Do you want to know why?"

My jaw clenched. Silence seemed safer than words.

He leaned closer. His breath was hot against my ear. "Because if you do—"

A pause.

"I'll make your two little friends go viral."

My eyes widened, and my jaw dropped. "You may not care about your video, but my guess is you don't want your friend's videos to go viral because of you."

My gaze flicked back and forth over his face, searching for truth. Had he been listening to Journey and me? Had he been in this locker room the entire time?

"I call bullshit." My voice echoed against the shower walls. "You don't have videos of them."

He laughed, the sound bouncing off the tiles. His shoulders rose in a casual shrug as steam swirled between us. "Then try me. I'll release Journey's audition for the dance team first."

"I want to see the video."

"You will if you're stupid enough to tell anyone who left you."

"What if Coach Palmer finds me?" I was grasping at straws, thinking maybe he would care.

He pushed to his feet, staring down at me with zero emotion. "Then I hope he fucks your throat like the little whore you are." He turned, dropped the key to the cuffs outside the shower stall, and disappeared.

I opened my mouth to scream, but stopped myself because I knew it wasn't going to be him who came back for me. My gaze lifted to the handcuffs, checking to make sure there wasn't a safety release on them like the pair he'd used when he'd cuffed me to the shower rod, but there wasn't. I was stuck unless I could reach the key.

Why did he always have a pair of handcuffs on him?

Anger boiled in my veins as I stared at the key, willing it to move closer. If he hadn't threatened Mila and Journey, I would have told him to show everyone that video, but I couldn't let him ruin my friend's scholarships because he was mad at me.

"Ari," Mila whisper-yelled. "Are you still here?"

"Mila." The name burst from my lungs. My shoulders sagged. Not Coach Palmer. Not the football team. Just Mila. "I'm here."

She rounded the corner of the shower, and her eyes widened as she froze. "What the fuck?"

Swallowing hard, I shook my head, letting her know I didn't want to talk about it. "The key is right behind you. Can you please uncuff me?"

Her gaze dropped as she shifted around until she spotted the small silver key on the floor. She knelt and picked it up before rushing to uncuff me.

"Can you grab me a clean towel and let me shower?" She nodded and left. If I had to guess, the towel I'd left on the hook was gone. I flicked the shower on, scorching my skin with scalding hot water to wash away any exterior evidence that he was there, but the burning anger in my gut reminded me.

"The towel is on the hook," Mila said outside the blue curtain. "What happened, Ari?" When I didn't say anything, she added. "I saw him leave the locker room. I know it was Zaiden."

I ripped the curtain open and grabbed the towel, wrapping it around me. "You can't say anything."

"If you tell EJ, they will handle this."

I shook my head, fingers tightening around the towel's edge. "He doesn't just have videos of me." My gaze dropped to the floor. "He has them of you and Journey, too."

Mila's breath caught, her pupils dilating to dark pools.

"He threatened to use them if I told anyone."

"Oh," she frowned. "Look, it would suck if that video got out of me, but I don't need this scholarship. My family will cover me, but Journey and some of the other girls—"

"I know," I cut her off. "The only way out of this situation is to figure out why he thinks I'm responsible for Kacie's death. If I can prove he's wrong, maybe this will end."

"So, I guess we are getting ready for a party?" She asked with a wary smile.

"Yeah." I nodded. That party would have tons of people from the high school party. "Just try to be low-key about it. We don't want Zaiden getting word that we are asking around."

We exchanged a knowing look, and she nodded. I didn't need to tell her that Zaiden would ruin me if he knew we were asking around and trying to clear my name. I wasn't sure that finding the truth would stop him, but I knew it was my only chance.

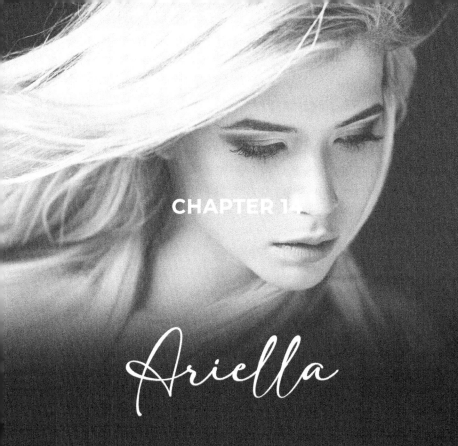

CHAPTER 14

Ariella

I t was after ten when I made it to the party and met Journey and Mila in the driveway.

It was the start of football season, and the fraternity house Alpha Delta Alpha, which was home to most of the football team, hosted the first party of the year.

"Zaiden is here." Journey gripped my arm, her voice dropping. "He's out back with the rest of the hockey team."

"I overheard Hawk say the party was lame with no new pussy." Mila rolled her eyes, fingers tightening around her cup. "So I think they'll leave soon."

Journey shook her head. "Zaiden won't leave if he knows you're here."

I nodded, scanning the crowded hallway. "So, we avoid the hockey team for now."

"I thought you wanted me to talk to Sterling," Mila narrowed her eyes.

"If anyone knows anything, it would be Sterling," I whispered as a group of partiers passed us. "But if we can't get to him tonight, we'll have to wait." I reached into my pocket, pulled out three pieces of paper, and handed them a sheet. "This is a list of everyone I remember seeing at the party that night, even those who have moved away or probably won't be here tonight." They both unfolded the white sheet of paper. "If you think of anyone else, add their name to the paper and let us know so we can add it to ours. We keep questioning until we find out who saw Kacie leave that night."

"We should split up," Journey suggested. "We'll be less noticeable."

We split up, each taking a different area of the house. Mila took the back of the house, Journey took the kitchen and backyard, and I chose the living room and family room, which were as far away from Zaiden as I could get.

As I went through the room, I stopped and talked to anyone on the list, but they were all dead ends. Either they didn't see Kacie that night, or they were too drunk to remember. After two hours of conversation that led to nothing, I sank onto the couch. I knew someone had to have seen something that night. I was starting to think that person wasn't at this party.

The first party to kick off each team's season was always the largest party of the year because it was when the teams came together, where the rest of the year, each sports team kept to themselves. These were always my least favorite parties, not that I really enjoyed any of them anymore. Every room in the house was so packed it was hard to breathe; it was hot and musty, the music was loud, and it smelled like vomit mixed with stale weed.

My phone buzzed in my hand.

> Journey: Heads up, EJ's looking for you.

I rolled my eyes. I didn't have time for EJ right now.

> Ariella: Thanks.

My gaze lifted, scanning the room, and thankfully, EJ hadn't made it to this side of the party yet, but it was only a matter of time. My eyes stopped, landing on Cody Black as he lifted his professional camera and snapped a picture of something on the opposite end of the room.

"Holy shit," I muttered as I pushed off the couch. Cody would have been at the party the night Kacie died. He wasn't on my list because no one ever noticed him. He was always in the background, taking pictures.

He was part of the yearbook team in middle and high school. Everyone got so used to seeing him in the background taking pictures that he became invisible. Now, Cody was some type of social media influencer who shared his photographs with the world, but he was still invisible behind that camera. If anyone saw something that night, it would be him.

"Hey, Cody." I smiled, shouting over the bass that vibrated through the floorboards.

His gaze lifted slowly from his camera. Dark eyes widened with surprise as they landed on me. "Hey, Ari." He blinked twice, adjusting his glasses. Being invisible for so long had left him unprepared for direct attention.

I leaned in, the scent of his cologne replacing the smell

of beer and sweat. "I was wondering what you do with all your old photos?"

"Um." He shook his head, thumb nervously stroking the side of his camera. "I post some things on social media—"

"No." I touched his arm lightly. "Like all the old photos from high school. What did you do with all of them? Do you still have them?"

His posture straightened, shoulders pulling back as his passion overrode his shyness. "Of course." A genuine smile broke across his face. "I keep everything."

"This may sound weird, but do you remember that last party we had at The Myers' house in high school?"

He nodded. "Yes." His smile faded. "The night Kacie died."

Swallowing hard, I nodded. "Yes. Do you have the pictures from that night?"

"Yes. They're all saved on my computer at home, and I have them backed up on a drive."

"Do you think I could get a copy of them?"

"Are you looking for pictures of Kacie?"

"Yes, I was hoping to find something that told me why she got back in her car drunk and left that night. I've asked around, but no one seems to remember seeing her that night."

"I saw her." My eyes widened. "I saw her when she got there, and then I saw her when she left about twenty minutes later."

"Twenty minutes?"

"Yeah, and when she left, she was really upset. I tried to ask her if everything was ok, but I don't think she noticed me."

"Did you see what upset her?" He shook his head.

Kacie wasn't dating anyone then because she'd recently broken up with her ex, and I didn't remember seeing him at the party. "Did she come with anyone that night?"

"Nope. She went through the house and out the back like she was looking for someone, and then the next time I saw her, she was storming through the house and out the front door."

What had upset her? I didn't remember any type of commotion that would have insinuated there was a fight of any kind that night.

"Oh, and she wasn't drunk." Cody's voice lowered.

"Yeah, she was." I frowned, leaning closer. "They told the family that she had high levels of alcohol in her system."

Cody glanced over his shoulder before meeting my eyes again. "I don't know who 'they' is," he murmured, fingers tightening around his camera strap, "but she wasn't drunk when she left. Ten minutes down the road, when she crashed—there's no possible way."

My brows pulled together as a chill ran through me. "How can you be sure?"

"I'm a people watcher." He held up his camera, a shield between us and the rest of the party. His gaze turned distant as though reviewing mental footage. "Been to every party since freshman year. I've seen Kacie drunk plenty of times." He shook his head firmly. "That night? Stone cold sober."

Well, this just got a whole lot weirder. If Kacie had been at the party for only twenty minutes, that was plenty of time to have a drink or two, so if Kacie was trashed when she left, that would mean she'd been drinking before she got to the party, and that wasn't like Kacie. So maybe Cody was right, and she wasn't drunk, but then why did she crash?

"Can I stop by your place and look at those pictures tomorrow?"

"I'm leaving town tomorrow morning, but I can email them to you tonight when I get home."

"Thank you, Cody, and if you think of anything else that you remember that night, will you let me know?"

"There you are." EJ's voice boomed from behind me, words slurring together. The scent of tequila rolled off him in waves.

I suppressed a wince and squared my shoulders before turning. "Hey." My lips stretched into what I hoped passed for a smile. "I've been looking for you."

I opened my mouth to suggest leaving when movement behind EJ made me freeze.

My gaze collided with Zaiden's. He leaned against the doorframe, arms crossed over his broad chest, bluish-grey eyes glittering with amusement—a predator watching prey.

My lip curled involuntarily.

Fuck.

My mind raced through scenarios like flipping cards. Option one: Leave now. Zaiden would follow—I'd bet my life on it. Option two: Stay. Flirt with EJ, which was exactly what Zaiden had warned me not to do.

I shifted closer to EJ, fingertips brushing his arm. With witnesses around, Zaiden wouldn't make a scene.

Probably.

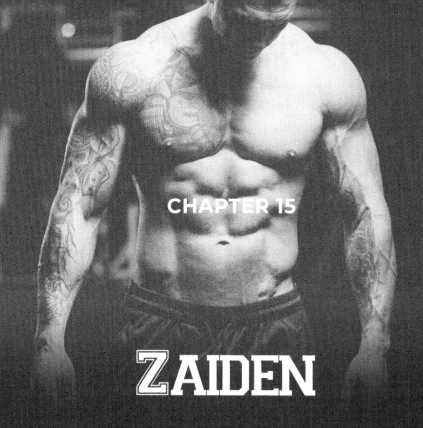

CHAPTER 15

ZAIDEN

Standing in the dark, crowded room, I clenched my bottle of water in my hand so hard it crunched under the pressure. Most of the hockey team had left. The party was boring, but as long as Ariella was here, so was I. I knew she wouldn't stay locked up in the shower long. I knew Mila wasn't far away, but I didn't expect her to show up at the football party tonight. I should have known she wouldn't hide with shame. That wasn't Ariella's style.

She wore tight, low-cut dark, ripped jeans and a white tank top that hugged her feminine curves. The top was short enough to show off the stud sparkling in her belly button. Her blonde hair was pulled off her neck, exposing her delicate little throat. My jaw flexed, and my gaze swayed with her hips as she ground herself against EJ to the music. She was putting on a show for me, letting me know I didn't control her.

She was wrong.

I may have pushed her far enough that she didn't care if I shared her video, which I seriously doubted, but I knew when I mentioned Journey and Mila that I had her by the throat, which was exactly where I wanted her.

My eyes lifted, meeting hers, holding my gaze as she pressed her back into him, letting her head fall back to his chest as she guided his arms around her. His hands raked down her body over her full tits and down until the tips of his fingers slipped into the waistband of her jeans. She cocked her head to the side as his mouth dropped to her neck. Red-hot anger filled me, and I clenched my fists tightly at my side, ready to snatch her out of his grasp.

She broke the rules. And now she was going to pay for that mistake.

I stepped forward, pushing through the crowd. At the same time, Adam Walker, wide receiver for the Predators, interrupted Ariella and EJ, pulling him away. EJ pressed his lips to Ariella's ear, whispering something before disappearing into the crowd.

Ariella turned her back to me without missing a sway of her hips.

Stepping into her space, I pressed my body flush with hers, my large hand curled around her small waist. I dropped my head. "You're playing with fire, Princess," I whispered, letting my breath fan across her cheek. She didn't flinch or fight me; she melted into me. She wrapped her hands around my wrist, pulling them around. My hand flattened on her bare stomach, and the other raked over her dark jeans and down to the curve of her V. My cock grew hard. My hand slipped under her shirt, and her head fell back as her lips parted on a moan.

I froze. Something wasn't right. She wasn't right.

Gripping her hips, I spun her. My gaze searched her face. Something was wrong. The colored lights strobed across her features, giving me glimpses of what I'd missed.

"What did you take, Ariella?"

I gripped her jaw, my fingers pressing into her skin. Her eyes met mine, unfocused, pupils blown so wide the blue of her irises had nearly disappeared. Her pulse hammered against my thumb.

"I didn't take anything." Her words slurred at the edges. She pushed weakly against my hand, and I let go.

"I don't feel good." The confession came out small, vulnerable.

The color drained from her face in one sickening wave. She pitched forward. Time slowed as she fell, her hair swinging forward, her body boneless. I caught her against me, my arm snaking around her waist before she hit the floor.

"Zaid," Sterling whisper-hissed, stepping up behind me. "You have to leave the girl alone, or you're going to get us all kicked out."

"I think someone drugged her." Heat crawled up my neck. I adjusted my grip on Ariella, her head lolling against my shoulder.

Sterling studied my face for a moment before his shoulders relaxed. "That's fucked up." He glanced toward the crowd, where curious eyes were beginning to turn our way.

I pulled Ariella closer, protective despite myself. "I'm taking her home."

Sterling nodded, already scanning the room for the

quickest exit. "I'll cover for you." He wiped sweat from his forehead, then jerked his head toward the kitchen. "Take her out the back. Less people."

"I think you two need to leave." EJ appeared out of nowhere, swaying slightly. His gaze slid from me to Ariella's limp form and back. "Since you seem to be confused about which girls are off-limits to the hockey team."

The bass from the speakers vibrated through the floor, matching the thrum of rage building in my chest. Around us, the crowd sensed the shift, voices quieting as people stepped back, creating a small clearing. My lip curled into a snarl.

Sterling moved beside me, shoulders tensing. "Yeah, we're out." His voice cut through the sudden pocket of silence. "We didn't know the football team had to drug their girls to get lucky."

EJ's gaze shifted from Sterling down to Ariella as I scooped her in my arms. "Drugged?" He rolled his eyes and sucked his teeth. "She took X all on her own."

My gaze narrowed on him. Ariella was a dancer, and like most athletes, she didn't do drugs, or at least the Ariella I knew before my sister's death didn't. My eyes shifted past him to Mila, who was standing to the left of EJ. She gave the slightest shake as my gaze met hers. She told me, without saying a word, that Ariella didn't take anything on her own.

I lifted my chin and squared my shoulders. "That's a fucking lie."

EJ stepped forward, puffing out his chest, trying to intimidate us, but he was so drunk he just looked like a drunk idiot beating on his chest. "Are you calling me a liar?" He slurred, stumbling as he stepped forward.

I narrowed my eyes. He looked like he was on the same thing she was. "I did call you a liar."

"Everyone here knows Ari didn't take anything willingly," Sterling frowned. "So we're going to take her and go."

"We will take her," EJ said, reaching out for her.

I shifted my weight, jerking Ariella out of his reach. "If you touch her, I'll break your fingers."

"How do we know you didn't drug her?" EJ's voice rose, drawing attention from nearby partygoers.

"I'll make sure she gets home safe." Mila stepped between us, her small frame somehow filling the space. She placed a steady hand on EJ's chest, creating distance. "She lives with Zaiden, so he would be the best person to get her home, and I'll go with them."

EJ's jaw worked, a muscle twitching beneath his flushed skin. His gaze darted between Mila's hand and my face before he rolled his eyes. He threw his hands up, stumbling back a step.

"Whatever."

The crowd parted as he walked away, mumbling under his breath. I watched his retreat, the tension in my shoulders barely easing. He may have said whatever, but the look he shot over his shoulder told me this wasn't the end, especially if it wasn't EJ or the football team who drugged her.

"Fuck, man." Sterling's voice dropped to a harsh whisper. He ran a hand down his face, eyes darting toward the hallway where EJ had disappeared. "Now we've started a war."

The weight of Ariella in my arms suddenly felt heavier. Every second we stayed put us all at greater risk, but the need to know burned hotter than my instinct to run.

"Who drugged her?" I asked Mila, ignoring Sterling's warning.

She glanced over her shoulder. Voices grew louder from the next room—multiple voices, angry tones.

Her eyes widened slightly. "I'm not sure," she said, words clipped with urgency. "But we should get out of here before he comes back with the rest of the football team." She grabbed my elbow, tugging me toward the back door. "Now, Zaiden."

"Is Journey here too?" Sterling asked Mila, his voice dropping to a hushed tone.

She nodded, her eyes darting to the staircase. "Outside by the pool."

Sterling's shoulders squared with newfound purpose. "I'll get Journey and make sure she gets out of here safely." He squeezed my shoulder once before disappearing into the crowd.

I shifted Ariella in my arms, her weight slight but present. My chest tightened with conflicting emotions. I shouldn't care what happened to her. Each time I looked at her face, I saw flashes of my sister's accident. She was the reason my sister was dead.

I should have let them pass her around like they wanted.

Ariella's breath whispered against my neck, fragile and trusting. My grip tightened.

No. That wasn't what I wanted. The thought of their hands on her made my stomach turn. If anyone was going to destroy her, it was going to be me.

Ariella Ledger was mine.

Mila followed me out of the house. "Zaiden." I stopped twisting to see her. She opened her mouth like she was going to say something, but then snapped it shut like she chickened out.

"I'm not going to touch her," I said. I had zero intention of touching her half-conscious, but if she threw herself at me like she'd done on the dance floor, I wasn't sure I'd be able to control myself.

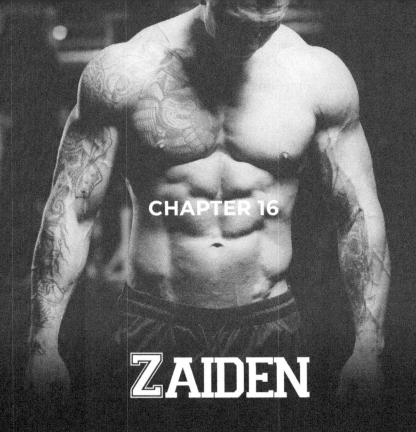

CHAPTER 16

ZAIDEN

When I dropped Ariella into the passenger seat of her car, she was passed out, but that lasted exactly two minutes.

"It's so fucking hot in here?" She whined, wiggling in her seat. I rolled my eyes. It wasn't hot, not even a little bit. "Why is it so hot?"

"It's not hot." I kept my eyes locked on the road, my jaw clenched against the urge to look at her again. "Here," I switched hands on the steering wheel before I pulled my bottle of water out of the cup holder and shoved it in her chest. "drink this." Drugs weren't my thing, but I knew this was a side effect of the drug she was given.

"I can't drink this." Her voice hitched, fingers fumbling with the bottle cap. Sweat beaded along her hairline despite the cool air. "It's hot, and I'm too hot. I need air."

"Then take off your clothes." My words were laced with annoyance. I tightened my grip on the wheel until my knuckles whitened. "But drink the fucking water."

The last thing I needed was for her to end up in the hospital for dehydration.

She shifted in her seat, and I quickly glanced out the corner of my eyes as she pulled her shirt over her head, tossing it to the floor. A smile tugged at the corner of my lips. I wasn't serious about the 'take your clothes off' part, but I wasn't mad either. She popped the button of her jeans open before wiggling out of them, drawing my full attention. I'd seen her naked a dozen times, but that didn't mean I didn't want to see her again.

I hated her, but her body was fire. My gaze raked over her feminine curves as her hands traced over her sensitive skin. She was horny—another side effect of the drug. If what they gave her was ecstasy, every nerve ending in her body was electrified with the slightest touch.

Her head fell back, and her eyes closed as she trailed her fingertips up her inner thigh, spreading her legs wider. A whimper escaped her parted lips, and I let out a shuddering breath as my gaze followed her hand that disappeared between her thighs, making my body awaken with new life.

I was well aware that sober Ariella would never do this, not willingly with me anyway, but I didn't care.

A horn blew, snapping my attention back to the road in time to jerk the car back into my lane. My gaze flashed to Ariella. She hadn't even noticed we'd almost died. There was no way I could focus on the road and driving when she was topless and making the most erotic sounds I thought I'd ever heard. There was also no way I was stopping her.

My knuckles whitened against the steering wheel as I spotted the turnoff ahead. I swerved down the isolated dirt road, tires crunching over gravel and fallen branches. The car jolted as we bumped over the old railroad tracks, and I eased to a stop, positioning us between the heavy tree line and the abandoned rails.

When I killed the engine, the sudden silence pressed against my ears. Not a single car light broke the darkness. Not a single sound besides our breathing disturbed the night. No one used this road anymore, which was exactly why I'd chosen it.

I hit the door lock button, but only my door locked. Ariella drove a Toyota Corolla that was older than she was and had almost a hundred thousand miles on it. Nothing worked, and this was an area where door locks were necessary.

Lifting out of my seat, I reached across the center console and over Ariella, brushing my skin against hers as I reached to lock the door. Her body arched into my touch, and I groaned.

"Touch me." Her whisper contradicted the forcefulness of her grip as she seized my wrist, guiding my hand to her thigh. Her eyes remained closed, head tilted back as she spread her legs wider, begging for the touch of my hand between them. "Please."

It wasn't my touch that she was craving. She was high. She'd be begging anyone around her right now to chase that feeling.

My hand slid slowly up her inner thigh, lightly brushing my fingertips over her heated skin, over her bare pussy, and up to her lower stomach. I wanted to watch her come. Shifting in my seat, I hooked an arm around her waist and jerked her across the seat, over the center console, and onto my lap. She settled quickly, immediately grinding herself against my cock over my pants.

I lifted my back off the seat, pressing my body into hers and sliding my hand into her hair. My grip tightened, jerking her head back as I pressed my lips to her throat.

"Ride my lap, baby, like you're gonna—" The words caught in my throat as she shifted position. My control, already hanging by a thread, began to unravel completely. I forced myself to take a breath to regain some semblance of composure. "Like you're gonna ride my cock real soon," I finally managed, the growl in my voice barely recognizable as my own.

I wanted to pull out my cock and slide it into her. To feel her wet heat wrapped around me and use her body to forget all of my rage, at least temporarily. "I want to watch you ride me until you come."

I nipped at her throat and then kissed that now tender spot. "I want you to soak my lap. Do you understand me?"

Silence answered me, broken only by her shallow breathing. Her eyes glazed over, lost in sensation. I waited one beat, two, before tightening my grip in her hair—just enough to bring her back to me.

The sound she made—half surprised pleasure, half surrender—vibrated through my palm where it pressed against her throat.

"I said, do you understand me?"

"Yes." The word escaped on a breath, barely audible over the pounding in my ears. She swallowed, her throat working beneath my gaze. "Yes."

I wondered, briefly, if she'd even remember saying it tomorrow.

I released my hold on her hair, dropped my back to the reclined car seat, and watched her ride me. My mouth watered, watching her naked body grind against me, and my hands trembled as they eased down the curve of her waist before curling around her hips. I guided her over my length and lifted my hips so every stroke hit her clit.

Ariella had always been sexy as fuck. Her perky tits were small but the perfect handful, her stomach was toned and tanned, and her pussy was bare and glistening from her arousal. I'd had a crush on her from a young age, but it wasn't until high school that I made my first move. She'd played hard to get, and then Kacie died, and that changed everything.

Now, I wanted to use her body like I should have done to begin with.

"Oh, fuck." She caught her bottom lip between her teeth, trying to contain the sounds I drew from her.

I watched the muscles of her stomach contract and felt the tremor building where our bodies met. I could read her approaching release like a book I'd memorized but never truly understood.

I rose slowly off the back of the seat, each inch bringing me closer to her heat. The air between us seemed to crackle with electricity. When I finally pressed against her, the contact sent a jolt down my spine that nearly undid me.

My hand traced the curve of her back, feeling each knob of her spine, before sliding up to tangle in her hair. The strands wrapped around my fingers like silk ropes. I tightened my grip, not enough to hurt, just enough to control, and guided her head down until her mouth angled over mine and our eyes locked. Her pupils were blown wide, leaving only a thin ring of color. In the moonlight, I could see my reflection in them, and for a second, I didn't recognize the man staring back.

My chest rose and fell with deep, ragged breaths as she

ground herself hard against me. Her lips parted on a whimpering moan, and the heat of her breath fanned across my lips.

"Ride my lap until that pretty pussy is so wet and messy it's covering me."

With her eyes locked on mine, her body tensed, her lips parted into an O, and her breath hitched so tightly she wasn't breathing as she exploded in ecstasy.

Her body relaxed, and her breath released in a whoosh of air.

"Fuck, that was hot." I uncurled my fingers from her hair, one by one, savoring the way she melted against me, boneless and exhausted.

I traced the curve of her spine with my fingertips, collecting the beads of sweat that had gathered there.

"The next time you do that," I whispered against the shell of her ear, "I'll bury my cock deep inside that sweet pussy." Minus the drugs, though. "Too bad you probably won't remember most of this in the morning."

My gaze shifted to my phone, sitting in the dash holder I'd set up before we pulled out of the driveway, and it was still recording. I had a crazy feeling she'd do something wild that could be used against her later.

"But don't worry, princess." Moonlight caught on the screen of my phone, and the recording was still running. I reached out, angling it to better capture her face, peaceful in a way she never was when fully conscious around me. My thumb hovered over the stop button. "I'll be happy to remind you."

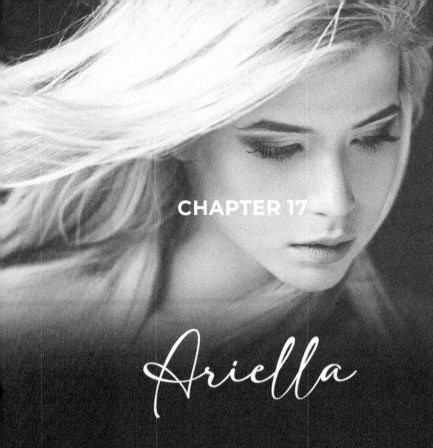

CHAPTER 17

Ariella

I sank into the hard plastic chair and flipped open my laptop, the screen creating a barrier between me and the rest of the world. From the top row, I had a perfect view of every exit and every face.

The classroom buzzed with morning chaos. Professor Adams adjusted his bow tie at the lectern, scanning the room with eyes that seemed to pause a second too long on empty seats.

I slumped lower, aiming for invisibility. Partly because my head still throbbed with each heartbeat—a souvenir from whatever happened Friday night. But mostly because the assigned textbook reading remained untouched in my bag, its pages as mysterious to me as the missing hours from Friday night.

Fragments of the night flashed behind my eyes, but not enough to piece together what actually happened.

I remembered talking to Cody, but I didn't remember he was going to email me pictures until I opened my computer and saw the email at the end of my last class. This was another reason I chose to sit in the back, so I could dig through these photos and see if I could find any of Kacie without anyone looking over my shoulder.

Dipping down a little lower in my seat, I hid behind my laptop as I clicked open the attachments of Cody's email.

"Holy shit," I whispered-groaned. There were two hundred and eighty pictures from that night. It would take me days to sift through these pictures. I clicked through the first dozen, none of which had any images of Kacie, until Professor Adams ended class fifteen minutes early, but I was thankful that I managed to make it through the entire class without being called on.

I closed my laptop and pushed back from the desk. The classroom emptied quickly—everyone eager to escape Adams and his monotone lecture. I joined the surge of bodies moving toward the exit, another anonymous face in the flow.

Classes were done for the day.

"Hey!" Mila's voice cut through the noise as she appeared beside me, slightly breathless. I continued walking because stopping wasn't an option in the crowded halls. For some reason, Hall B2 dismissed all of its classes at the same time. If you didn't move with the flow, you'd either get run over or cause a people jam. Mila managed to strong-arm her way through the crowd and step in beside me, matching my steps. "Where have you been all weekend? You didn't answer any of my calls."

"Apparently, those few shots I did were stronger than I thought." I kept my voice low, casual. "I slept all weekend." Mila's pace faltered. Her brows pulled together, creating that little crease she got whenever something didn't add up.

"Shots?" The word hung between us, heavy with implication. "You don't remember what happened?"

I pursed my lips. Shook my head. Something cold slithered down my spine.

"Zaiden didn't tell you?"

"Zaiden?" My voice pitched higher than I intended, drawing glances from passing students

I lowered my voice to a hiss. "First, why would Zaiden tell me anything? Second, why would I talk to Zaiden? And third—" I counted on my fingers, "—I haven't seen Zaiden all weekend."

Mila's hand found my arm, her grip tightening. "Because you were drugged." Her eyes darted around, checking who might be listening. "And he protected you."

I halted so abruptly that someone behind me nearly slammed into my back. They swerved at the last moment, muttering something under their breath.

The hallway continued to empty around us, voices fading.

A laugh escaped me—high and brittle. "Zaiden?" My lip curled into a snarl. "Protected me?" I touched my fingers to my chest as I shook my head. "Yeah. No. Zaiden doesn't protect me. He wants to ruin me. So, if anyone—" I trailed off as my gaze lifted and zeroed in on Zaiden. "I'll meet you at practice."

"Ari!" Mila's voice faded behind me as I pushed through the thinning crowd.

I knew Zaiden better than anyone. The perfect student.

The charming athlete. The vengeful enemy who had made it his mission to destroy me piece by piece. If anyone had drugged me, it was him—and I'd bet my scholarship he was already bragging about it.

I spotted him at the end of the corridor, his broad shoulders turned away from me. My heartbeat quickened, and each thud was a warning I chose to ignore. The crowd parted unconsciously as I moved through it, perhaps sensing the storm building inside me. Every step forward tightened the coil of rage in my chest until it threatened to spring loose.

He was laughing with Hawk and Creighton outside Professor Wilson's lecture hall, completely at ease as if he hadn't potentially assaulted me three nights ago.

My pulse thundered in my ears. Each step toward him felt like moving through cement, but I forced myself forward.

Creighton Vanderbilt was Westbrook's Hockey team's infamous goalie. He was tall with dark curly hair and dark eyes. His gaze lifted, spotting me storming toward them, warning Zaiden before I got there.

Zaiden twisted in time to see me throw out my hands, shoving them into his rock-hard chest. "Woah," Zaiden laughed. "Someone's mad I didn't call the morning after."

I shoved him again, my palms connecting with solid muscle. He didn't budge an inch. "What did you do to me?"

His eyes, cold and calculating, swept over me. "Do to you?" The smirk formed slowly. "I think you mean, what did you do to me?

"I didn't do anything to you." My voice dropped to a hiss as students slowed around us. "I don't even remember what happened."

"Don't worry, baby." He stepped closer, towering over me. "It was good for you."

The smirk on his face made my palm itch. One swift movement. That was all it would take.

He leaned in, voice just loud enough for nearby students to hear. "Wish I could say the same, but your pussy was a little too loose for me.

Creighton and Hawk's laughter cut through the hallway. A girl with a red backpack covered her mouth. Someone whispered behind me.

My cheeks heated, and my chest tightened with humiliation, and before I even knew what I was doing, my flat palm was flying across the air, but he was faster than me. He caught my wrist and jerked me into him. He dropped his face to mine, our noses nearly touching, and my pulse raced. "Don't ever. Do that. Again." He shoved me away, and I stumbled backward.

"You're a disgusting pig." The words tasted bitter, but not as bitter as the humiliation burning through me.

Creighton leaned against the wall, his perfect white smile spreading slowly. "Is that any way to talk to the man who gave you a mind-blowing orgasm?" Each word landed like a slap.

"If you want another one, you could just ask him." Hawk's eyes gleamed as they darted between Zaiden and me. He lowered his voice, drawing out the moment. "No need to be so aggressive. Or—" The pause stretched uncomfortably. "Is that y'all's thing?"

The circle of onlookers tightened around us. Someone snickered.

My lip curled up in disgust. "I would rather chew my own arm off and eat it than let him touch me."

"That's not what you were begging for the other night, princess."

"If I did anything, it was because you drugged me."

Creighton and Hawk shook their heads, but Zaiden's jaw flexed, and a look of irritation flashed across his face. "I don't have to drug girls, and I didn't drug you, but you should have a chat with your football buddies. EJ informed me you took X."

Confusion spread across my face. I would never take drugs. It wasn't my thing. I was a dancer and an athlete. I worked out four to five times a week, I ate healthy, and I didn't smoke or do drugs, but I did occasionally drink.

"They were going to rape you," Hawk added.

I shook my head. They were wrong. The football team had no reason to hurt me. "You are all so naive," I hissed as my gaze shifted to Zaiden. "The only person who wants to hurt me is you."

He stepped forward, eliminating the space between us in one fluid motion.

"You're right." His voice dropped to a whisper meant only for me. "I want to ruin you."

The eerie seriousness in his tone drained the oxygen from my lungs. The words weren't shouted for an audience or wrapped in his usual sarcasm. They were raw, honest, and terrifying because of it. The heat of his breath fanned across my face, carrying the faint scent of mint. Chills raced up my spine, spreading outward until my skin felt electrified.

Time seemed to stretch between us. Someone laughed nearby, the sound distant and muffled as though existed in our own bubble of hatred. Or something else entirely.

He was so close that our chests nearly touched with

each breath. His blue eyes held mine hostage. The corridor faded away until there was only him, only us, locked in this moment that felt too intimate for enemies.

I should step back. Create distance. Break whatever this was.

Instead, I squared my shoulders, tilting my chin up. His gaze dropped to my lips for the briefest second.

"I want to slowly take away every single thing that you love. I want to own you, but I didn't drug you, and I didn't force you to do anything you didn't want to."

He stepped back, reached into his pocket, and pulled out his phone. After a few clicks, he held it out.

My heart clenched as my eyes widened, and my jaw dropped as I watched myself completely naked, grinding myself over Zaiden. My moans echoed through the still mostly full hallway. I swatted at the phone, but he jerked it out of my grasp. "Stop it," I shouted, embarrassment coursing through me. My gaze flicked around. We had everyone's attention. "Zaiden, please," I pleaded.

"Damn, that's hot," Creighton purred. "I've never heard a girl sound like that before.

"And you never will," I shouted without a second thought about what I was saying. "Because your dick's too small to do anything but tickle a woman." I had no idea what Creighton's dick looked like, but I was angry.

"Ouch," Creighton laughed, clutching his heart sarcastically.

Zaiden increased the volume. My recorded moans echoed through the hallway, growing louder with each second. Students slowed their pace, heads turning our way. Phones appeared in their hands.

He leaned in, his breath hot against my ear. "As you can

see," he whispered, "that was all you. You used me to get off."

My recorded voice climbed toward release. I couldn't move. Couldn't breathe. Couldn't look away from the screen.

Just before the final moment, he cut the video. His eyes locked with mine. "See you later, Ariella."

Something fractured inside me. My hands trembled first, then my arms. Rage and humiliation collided in my chest as tears threatened to spill. Not here. Not in front of him. Not in front of everyone.

"Hey, Ari," Hawk shouted loud enough to draw more attention to us. "Next time you need a lap to get off on, call me."

"Fuck you, Hawk." I raised my middle finger, holding his gaze while conversations died around us.

Then I walked away. One foot in front of the other. Shoulders back. Head high.

Every step felt like walking through fire, but I wouldn't give them the satisfaction of seeing me run.

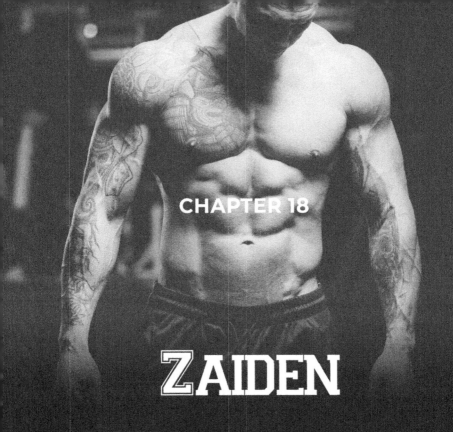

CHAPTER 18

ZAIDEN

"**W**hat the fuck are we doing here?" Sterling's shoulders slumped forward. "I've been at Westbrook for three years, and I've never attended a football game." He twisted to face me, his jaw clenched, hands gesturing wildly. "Do you want to know why?"

I shook my head, not taking my eyes away from the field. I knew why we hadn't attended a football game. I didn't need him to explain it to me, but for the last few years, Ariella hadn't been on that field.

"Because hockey players don't go to football games," he continued. "And football players don't go to hockey games." He raised his voice with each word.

I rolled my eyes. I never understood why we didn't participate in other sports functions. It was all stupid, but it was the way Westbrook had been since my parents attended and probably even before that.

A buzzer sounded, echoing through the stadium, and the game stopped.

"You didn't have to come," I mumbled as my gaze followed the football team off the field.

It was halftime.

"Yes, I did." He pinched the bridge of his nose. "Someone has to keep you from doing more stupid shit."

He turned around, putting his back to the field, staring up into the crowd. "Could we at least go to the top of the stadium? So no one sees us." Being here could be social suicide for someone who gave a fuck. I did not.

We stood at the first level; the metal bars and a short drop were the only things separating us from the field. I'd spent enough time watching her practice to know exactly where she'd be.

"Zaiden." Sterling's voice cut through the crowd noise. I kept my eyes fixed on the field.

Something heavy settled between my ribs, squeezing until each breath came shallow. My gaze fixed on the spot where Kacie should have stood. This had been her and Ariella's dream since they were little girls, practicing routines in our backyard, giggling until sunset.

And now, because of Ariella, Kacie would never get the chance.

My hands curled into fists, fingernails carving half-moons into my palms until the skin threatened to break. The pain was welcome—something tangible to focus on besides the fury pulsing behind my eyes.

Bass thundered through the stadium as the dance team emerged from the shadows of the tunnel, a flash flood of black and red. Their bodies caught the stadium lights—

glittering Predators logos stretched across heaving chests, crimson streaks racing down toned legs as they claimed the field with synchronized precision.

My gaze followed the line, knowing exactly where Ariella would be.

She waved to the crowd, a huge smile plastered on her face, as she found her place. As her eyes swept across the ground-level seats, she froze. Our gazes locked.

Her smile vanished, replaced by something cold and raw.

The corner of my mouth hitched upward, satisfaction spreading through me. Let her dance, knowing I was watching. Let her wonder when I'd appear next. Let her spend the night with that itch between her shoulder blades that comes from knowing you were being hunted.

The music transitioned, and Ariella's head dropped as she got into position. On cue, her head popped up, and her show smile was back in place as her hips moved to the music.

When Ariella was in her element, she owned that field. My chest tightened with a familiar ache.

Suddenly, I was in high school again, leaning against the metal bars of the bleachers, watching her dance. I'd been obsessed with her for as long as I could remember.

But she was my little sister's best friend.

"Stay away from Ariella," Kacie had begged me. "Promise me, Zaiden."

And I tried. God knows I tried.

Ariella leaned forward before flipping her head up, her long blonde hair flying everywhere. If this had been before, her eyes would have met mine, but not this time. Now, she purposefully avoided me. She spun around to the opposite side of the field, and my gaze dropped to her ass, following as it moved with the beat.

My teeth sank into my bottom lip as heat pooled low in my body, the familiar ache of wanting someone I shouldn't. The contradiction twisted inside me—how the same person could simultaneously make my blood boil with rage and my skin burn with desire. Each beat of the music pulled her body into movements that felt like they were designed specifically to torture me.

The crowd cheered the girls on, and something about the fact that other men were watching Ariella triggered something dark inside me.

The music ended, and the girls froze, their big smiles and wide eyes staring up into the stadium.

"Can we fucking go now?" Sterling growled.

The girls ran off the field, and the announcer came over the speaker, announcing the cheerleaders.

"Yeah." I pushed off the metal bars, my gaze lingering on the tunnel where Ariella had disappeared. "Let's get out of here."

"Thank you." Sterling threw his hands up dramatically, eyes rolling toward the stadium lights. "Let's go meet the guys at Hawk's party."

"Nah," I shook my head. "I'm going home."

"To the frat house?"

"No." The bike keys bit into my palm as I gripped them tighter. "To my dad's."

Sterling's "Whatever, bro" bounced off my back as I shouldered through the heavy exit doors. His footsteps veered in the opposite direction.

The cool night air hit my face as I entered the parking lot. My phone chimed in my pocket.

I pulled it out and groaned as 'Mom' scrolled across the screen.

My thumb hovered over the phone, her name flashing like a warning. A year of these calls, and every conversation still felt like moving chess pieces between two kingdoms at war. I took a deep breath and answered, already mentally preparing myself for whatever battle she was recruiting me for this time.

"Hello." I sighed, the cool metal of my bike beneath me.

"Hey, honey." Her voice came through too bright, too chipper, the artificial sweetness crackling through the speaker.

"When are you going to be at your dad's again?"

I blew out a heavy sigh. This was what all our conversations consisted of. She wanted me to tell my dad something or find something in the house.

"I have no idea," I lied. "What do you need?" I stopped in front of my bike.

"I need you to let me know when the house will be empty." I rubbed the bridge of my nose. "I'm missing some of Kacie's things, and I want them back."

"What are you missing, Mother?" I kept my voice steady.

"It's just a few sentimental things that I thought I had, but I don't. They are probably in the garage. I would prefer to come get them."

There was nothing left of Kacie's in the house except a small keepsake box my father kept with pictures, a few things that were special to him, and one picture that still hung in his office. Everything else was gone. I knew nothing was left in the garage, which meant she wanted to start trouble with Ariella's mom and my dad.

I pressed my lips into a tight line as I decided how I wanted to handle this. "Mom, Dad and Claire don't want you in the house anymore." I honestly wouldn't care, except I didn't want to be in the middle anymore. "And I don't plan on going back to the house any time soon. You should call Dad to see if he can help you find whatever you're looking for."

I hoped that put an end to this bullshit.

"Your father ignores my calls." Her voice rose, that familiar edge creeping in. "So just call me next time you're at the house."

The same script, different day.

My shoulders sank. "Mom—"

"Zaiden," she cut me off. "That is my house. I built it from the ground up with your father."

There was no point in telling her it wasn't hers anymore or arguing with her. I would lose. "I gotta go, Mom." I didn't bother waiting for a goodbye before disconnecting because it wouldn't come.

A part of me felt sorry for my mom and her situation. She'd lost her daughter and then found out my dad was having an affair with her best friend. What my dad and Claire did to her was wrong, but I didn't want to be in the middle of it.

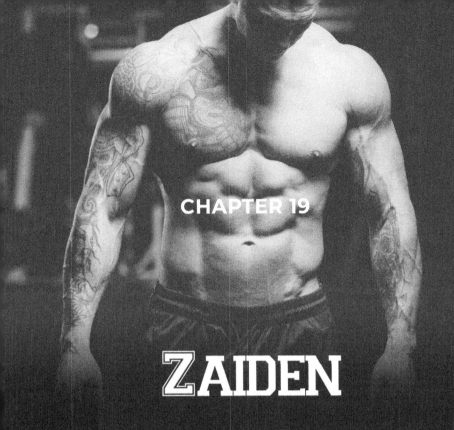

CHAPTER 19

ZAIDEN

Lying in my bed, staring up at the ceiling, I remembered how much I hated this house. I hated it even more now that Ariella was in Kacie's room down the hall from mine.

I rarely stayed there anymore. It had been hard enough to come back after Kacie's death, but the day my mom left and Ariella's mom moved in, I started staying in the frat house more and more.

Pushing up, I threw my legs over the edge of the bed, my hands curling around the corners of the mattress. I'd spent all night waiting for Ariella to get home, and she'd come home trashed, which didn't exactly surprise me since the dance team and the football team went to the local sports bar after the game.

Pushing to my feet, I strolled out of my room, through

the hallway, stopping in front of her door. She'd been home for over an hour now, and my guess was that she was passed out cold. I twisted the knob and smirked when it caught.

"Smart girl," I whispered, my fingers finding the cold metal in my pocket. I turned the key over, feeling its ridges against my thumb. "Too bad the boogeyman has a key."

The locked door gave Ariella the illusion of safety, the comfort of closing her eyes without fear, the ability to drift into dreams, and the feeling that she was protected.

She was so wrong.

I slid the silver key into the hole and twisted as I turned the knob, and the lock clicked open, quiet as a promise.

I stepped through the doorway, silently closing the door behind me before strolling up to her bed.

My gaze swept over her as she slept, the bedside night-light casting a soft orange glow across her face. The gentle light highlighted her features and traced the curve of her shoulder, fading where the thin blanket draped across her tits.

She was naked under that blanket. I was positive.

I stepped forward, my knee slamming into something hard enough to rattle the nightstand. My lips curled around a curse, but I managed to keep it from escaping.

She stirred.

My entire body turned to stone. My heart surged into my throat, pounding so loudly I was certain it would wake her.

Her breathing remained deep and even.

I wasn't worried about her catching me standing over her bed like some midnight predator. The fallout would be manageable—another battle in our endless war. I didn't want the fight tonight. I wanted to watch her.

Her arm shifted above her head. A small sigh escaped her lips.

I didn't dare breathe as my gaze dropped to the drawer hanging open, and my eyes widened on the fluorescent pink vibrator lying next to her black lace thong on the floor. The drawer was opened because that was where she kept her pretty pink toy, and afterward, she'd discarded her panties with the toy.

"Fuck—" The word escaped as barely a breath. My cock strained painfully against my boxer briefs, the thin fabric doing nothing to conceal my reaction. I took a step closer to the bed.

I leaned down. The black lace was soft against my fingers as I lifted it from the floor. I rolled the damp material over my hand, the fabric still warm.

The house fell silent around me. Just the sound of her breathing. The distant tick of the hallway clock.

I brought the panties to my nose. Closed my eyes. Inhaled.

Her scent—sweet and primal, tinged with the unmistakable evidence of her pleasure—flooded my senses. My head swam. The room tilted.

For a moment, I forgot why I hated her.

When my eyes eased open, they froze on her still form, fast asleep. Her hair spread across the pillow, her arms above her head, the soft rise and fall of her chest.

My chest rose and fell with deep, ragged breaths as my hand, still holding her panties, slipped inside my boxers.

Wrapping her soft material around my cock, I stroked her panties over my length. Ariella's legs shifted, but this time, I didn't freeze; I continued to stroke myself. The thin sheet over her twisted in her feet and shifted down.

I released a low groan deep in my throat as her perfect

tits slid out from under the sheet as it continued to move down her tight, toned stomach stopping above her pussy. One of her legs kicked out.

Using my free hand, I slipped my boxers down, releasing my cock. Giving myself more room to find the release I desperately craved. I took the panties from around my cock and brought them back to my nose, inhaling deeply as I pumped harder, faster. My eyes traveled from her full pink lips to the delicate curve of her throat, over her perky tits, down to her stomach. My mouth watered with the fantasy of tasting every inch of her, and my grip tightened, imagining the feel of her.

Wet sounds filled the room as I thrust my hips forward, chasing the orgasm that was so fucking close. I pictured her legs wrapped around me while I unforgivingly pounded into her, punishing her for everything she'd done to me, to Kacie, to my family.

Her nipples pulled tight, and I licked my lips, desperate to taste them.

My balls tightened, and my abs clenched as my breathing turned frantic. Quickly bringing the panties back to my cock, I bit down on my bottom lip as I exhaled a silent breath and came into her panties.

Fuck that was hot.

New kink unlocked.

My chest heaved with exertion. Stars burst behind my eyelids as I came down from a high I'd never experienced before. My mind was filled with dangerous possibilities, like what it would be like to have her. Not just like this, in secret and shadow, but beneath me. Against me. Around me.

I shoved myself back into my boxers, pulse still hammering in my throat. With care, I dropped her panties to the exact spot where I'd found them. Tomorrow, she'd pick them up covered in my cum, never realizing what happened. Never knowing I'd been there, watching her sleep, violating her private space.

The pink vibrator felt warm in my palm as I snatched it from the floor—a trophy.

The door hinges threatened to squeak as I eased it open. I paused, counting the seconds between her soft exhales.

Satisfied she wouldn't wake, I slipped into the hallway. The door closed behind me with a barely audible click.

In the darkness of the corridor, I smiled.

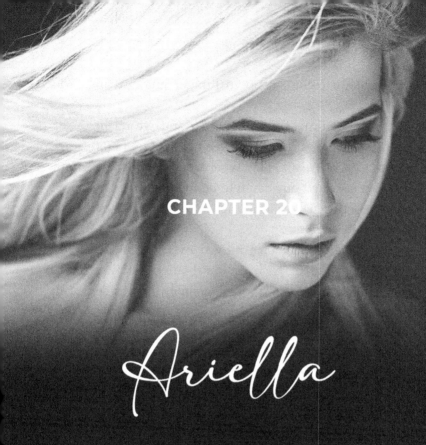

CHAPTER 20

Ariella

Sitting on the field under the bright sunlight, I glanced into the empty stadium seats for the four-hundredth time since practice started. It was the first time all season that Zaiden wasn't sitting there. A huge part of me was relieved, believing maybe he'd finally moved on. Maybe my virginity was all he wanted, but the other part of me felt an overwhelming sense of anxiety, wondering what he was planning next.

Mila leaned in, her voice low. "We can meet at my place after practice. We'll go through pictures and see what we can find."

Journey's eyes lit up. "We should order food."

"Yeah." Mila patted her stomach with a grin. "I'm starving."

I nodded, feeling my own hunger gnaw at me. "Me too."

"That's a wrap," Coach shouted, and we all held our breath as our gazes shifted between each other before stopping on Coach. We all knew what would happen next, and none of us wanted our name to be the one called. "Tomorrow's practice is canceled, so I will see everyone Wednesday afternoon."

He paused as his gaze moved over us, lingering too long as he perused each of our bodies. My heart rate spiked when his gaze stopped on me, the sudden rush making me lightheaded. "Ari, I need to see you in my office." Everyone but me released their breath as they stood and scattered across the field.

But I was frozen.

"It's okay, Ari." Mila's eyebrows furrowed, and her voice lowered to a whisper. "Just don't go."

"I'll be moved to the sidelines or, even worse, kicked off the team, which means I lose my scholarship." Even though my mom recently married into money, none of that money was hers. If I wanted to go to college, I had to do it on my own, and a scholarship was my only option.

"She's right," Journey said, pushing to her feet.

"What does he do to you?" My gaze lifted, flashing between Mila and Journey, each breath feeling heavier than the last.

"He told me to get on my knees," Journey mumbled.

"Me too," Mila added. "Just tell him you're a virgin."

"What?" Journey snapped, shaking her head. "Do not tell him that."

I groaned. I wasn't a virgin anymore. I didn't remember it, but apparently, Zaiden had already taken that from me.

"He's a nasty perv," Journey added. "He will definitely take it."

"I can do this." The lie tasted metallic in my mouth as I pushed to my feet. I raised my chin and squared my shoulders—armor I didn't believe in, but needed them to see.

"Do you want us to wait for you?" Journey asked, her voice dropping to a whisper.

I forced a smile that felt like cracked glass on my face. "No, go to Mila's, order food." I waved them off with a hand I was proud wasn't shaking. "I'll meet you there."

What I didn't say: I couldn't bear for them to see me afterward, to watch me try to reassemble myself in the aftermath. Some humiliations needed privacy.

We walked silently to the locker room, our footsteps echoing against the empty hallway's cinderblock walls. The lights buzzed overhead, casting harsh shadows across our faces. At Coach Palmer's door, we split up. Journey squeezed my arm once before walking away, her eyes not meeting mine.

The door's peeling red paint stared back at me like a warning. I closed my eyes, inhaling the lingering scent of sweat and artificial pine cleaner that never quite masked what happened in this room. My exhale came out shaky as I opened my eyes and reached for the doorknob, the metal warm from previous hands.

He was waiting for me, sitting on the edge of his desk.

"Yes, Coach," I said, trying not to let my voice shake. "You needed to see me."

His face split into a grin, and I refrained from cringing. "I know this is your first time being held after practice, but I'm sure you know how this works." I nodded. "Great, lock the door and bend over my desk."

My eyes widened, my jaw dropped, and I lost my calm and confident persona. "What?"

"Lock the office door and then bend over my desk." He said it slower this time, like I was stupid. "You can remove your leggings if you'd like, or I can do it. Your choice."

"I just thought that—"

"Better if you don't think," he cut me off. His tone was rude and condescending.

I had two choices.

My hand hovered over the lock, trembling. The metal felt cold against my fingertips. Click it to the right, and face what comes next. Leave it unlocked, run, and kiss my future goodbye. Each heartbeat pounded louder in my ears as seconds stretched into eternities. My stomach twisted into a tight knot as the truth settled in my bones. There was no good option—only survival.

I flicked the lock and turned back around, slowly walking to the desk as he worked to free his dick. My heart raced, and my stomach churned as bile worked its way up my throat when I stopped in front of the desk. "Either take off your leggings or bend over."

Remove my own leggings? Like I was a willing participant in my own violation? Like this was some consensual encounter. I wasn't here because I wanted to be. I was here because I didn't have a choice. My throat closed up. Every cell in my body screamed to run, but my feet remained rooted to the floor. One thought kept repeating: Scholarship. Future. Escape. Scholarship. Future. Escape.

Drawing in a breath that felt like inhaling glass, I slowly, inch by excruciating inch, bent over the edge of the desk. The surface was cold against my palms. I focused on that sensation, trying to separate myself from what was about to happen.

"Grip the edge of the desk, and no matter what, do not let go." Swallowing hard, a tear escaped, dripping onto the dark mahogany desk. My arms spread, and my hands wrapped around the edge of the desk. "That's a good girl." Acid burned my throat, and my pulse thrummed in my ears, drowning out his disgusting, heavy breathing. He pushed up the back of my tank top, exposing my back before he hooked a finger into the side of my leggings and panties, and I sucked in a deep breath.

"Get. The. Fuck. Off. Her."

Zaiden's voice sliced through the room. My eyes snapped open, neck craning so fast something popped. His massive frame blocked the entire doorway, turning it into a dark silhouette against the hallway light. One hand gripped the doorframe, knuckles bone-white. The other formed a fist so tight I could see veins standing out along his forearm. His eyes—God, his eyes, had gone from their usual bluish-grey to something feral, something ancient and dangerous. They promised violence.

Coach's hands disappeared, and I shot up from the desk. My chest tightened, relief and rage warring within me. I wanted to thank Zaiden and punch him at the same time. I didn't want to have sex with Coach Palmer, but I also didn't want to lose my scholarship.

"Zaiden," I snapped in warning.

"Go get changed, Ariella," Zaiden said, his tone lethal. "Coach and I need to have a chat."

"You need to leave, boy," Coach Palmer growled, throwing an arm out to prevent me from leaving. "How did you get in here?"

My eyes narrowed. How did he get in here? I did lock the door, didn't I? "Just go, Zaiden," I pleaded.

Zaiden took a step forward. "Move your arm, or I'll break it."

"Are you threatening a Coach?" Coach huffed out a humorless laugh. "I'll make sure you never step foot on this campus again."

"Go ahead," Zaiden shrugged, completely unfazed by Coach's threat. "I'm sure they'd love to hear that you were about to rape a student."

"It's your word against ours," Coach said, sounding so confident in his words.

"Yeah, except for all the video footage I have of you with your students."

Coach's face turned red as he dropped his arm. "You're bluffing."

"Go get dressed, Ariella, and go home."

"Zaiden, please, don't do this."

"Get. Out," he raised his voice.

My jaw clenched, grinding my teeth together as I walked past them and out the door, wincing when the door slammed behind me.

Fuck—

CHAPTER 21

ZAIDEN

T he door crashed against its frame, rattling the glass. Coach Palmer's eyes snapped up from his desk. "What do you want?"

"You don't want to see the evidence first?" I smirked, leaning back against the wall.

He shook his head. "No, tell me what you want and get out."

I leaned in close. "Stay away from Ariella." Anger coated each syllable. "Her name. Never leaves your lips after practice. This office? She's never alone in here with you again." I paused, letting the silence stretch between us. "And if I catch even a whisper of you threatening her scholarship or her place on the team—" My lips curled into a cold smile. "Those videos? They'll go viral faster than you can say 'disgusting coach.'"

"Anything else?" A vein pulsed in his forehead, his words coming out in sharp, clipped tones.

"Ariella no longer steps foot in this locker room. Going forward, you'll ensure she has a place in the hockey locker room."

"How the fuck am I supposed to do that?" He narrowed his eyes. "I have no control over the other locker rooms and—"

"I don't give a fuck how you do it," I hissed, cutting him off. "But you are going to do it."

His upper lip twitched, exposing a flash of teeth as his jaw clenched tight. "Is that it?"

I shook my head. "No, the same goes for Journey and Mila. You don't touch them again, but they can stay in this locker room." Kacie's face flashed in my mind as I spoke Journey and Mila's names. My throat tightened. But when I thought of Ariella, my fists clenched, a familiar mixture of desire and hatred flooding through me.

"Fine," he gritted out through snarled teeth. "Now, please leave, and don't ever come into this office again."

I smirked. "You're not really in a position to throw around orders. So I'll tell you what, I'm going to leave, but if I find out that you look in Ariella's direction, your job will be the last thing you're worried about losing."

I jerked open the office door, stepped out into the football locker room, and slammed the door behind me.

My gaze scanned the locker room as I strolled through, looking for Ariella, but thankfully, she wasn't there. I wasn't in the mood to hear her bullshit because even though she had no idea what I'd just done, she was going to be angry, but my intentions weren't exactly heroic either. They were selfish and malicious. Ariella was mine to ruin.

Exiting the locker room, I strolled through the hall

toward the exit. My ears perked up at the sound of small footsteps echoing behind me, and I inwardly groaned, but I didn't bother stopping.

"What the fuck, Zaiden?" Ariella's words cracked. Rolling my eyes, I ignored her as I continued toward the exit. "Seriously, Zaiden?"

I gritted my teeth, shoulders tensing as her voice carried down the hall. She shoved her small hands into my back, pushing me forward.

I whirled around, and she stumbled. My hand shot out, finding her throat, shoving her back until she hit the wall. Hard. "Don't." My fingers tightened. "Ever." Her pulse raced beneath my palm. "Do that." Her eyes widened. "Again." I released my grip, letting my arm fall to my side.

"Oh, so you're allowed to do whatever the fuck you want, and I'm supposed to sit back and take it?" Her lip curled up. "Fuck you," she spat out.

"You might want to scurry home before that pretty little mouth writes a check your ass can't cash." I spun around to leave.

"Taking my virginity wasn't enough for you," she shouted. "You needed to take my scholarship away, too?"

Virginity?

Shes a virgin?

Wait, she actually thought we had sex?

I stopped slowly, turning back to her. "You were a virgin?"

Ariella's eyes narrowed, a mixture of disbelief and anger flickering across her face as she crossed her arms over her chest. "There was nothing," she said slowly, each word dripping with sarcasm, "that gave that away?"

I huffed out a heavy sigh. "You're not going to lose your scholarship or your spot on the team." I shook my head.

"You're not losing anything but your locker." Her brows pulled together. "You'll have a locker in the hockey locker room by your next practice, so you'll never have to change in front of that pervert again."

Her head recoiled. "You were protecting me?" She shook her head like she was confused. "Why would you do that?"

I stepped forward, invading her personal space. My mouth dropped to hers, hovering over it so she could feel my words. "Because you are mine, princess. My property. If anyone touches you, I will kill them."

My hand wrapped around her throat, holding her in place. My gaze fell to her lips, breath catching in my throat as an overwhelming urge to kiss her surged through me, threatening to overpower every other sense and rational thought, but kissing her wasn't part of the plan. It was far too intimate, too dangerous of a line to cross.

I stepped back as I released her. "And I didn't take your virginity."

"What? But, I saw—"

"What you saw was you riding my lap. You were coming all over my pants." Her eyes widened. "My pants were still on."

"Then why did you—"

A loud pop from the distance startled her, cutting off her words and drawing both of our attention in the opposite direction.

"What the fuck was that?" A voice boomed from near the hockey locker room exit.

Ariella's whisper trembled in the sudden silence. "What was that?"

I opened my mouth to reassure her, to brush it off as

nothing, but the words died in my throat as the air shattered around us.

Then— Pop. Pop. Pop.

Three more shots. My heart raced.

The sounds ricocheted off the walls, each one a hammering blow of realization, each stripping away another layer of denial until nothing was left but the raw, ugly truth.

Another pop. Screams erupted.

"It's a gun," I mumbled.

The world moved in slow motion as chaos broke out around us. Students were screaming and running as I stood frozen, my eyes darting around, trying to comprehend what was happening.

"Zaid." I whipped around. "Let's go." Hawk's voice cracked, his eyes wide and darting.

My muscles tensed, adrenaline coursing through my veins. Despite the chill of fear, sweat beaded on my forehead. Each pop of gunfire echoed through the halls over the panicked screams.

My gaze flashed back to Ariella, who was still frozen in place, exactly like she had been before the second pop sounded. "Come on, Ariella. We need to go." She didn't move. My jaw clenched. "Ariella," I shouted to get her attention."

Nothing.

I turned to leave her, but stopped halfway after two more pops sounded. "Fuck." My body moved to protect Ariella before my mind could object, years of instinct overriding a year of cultivated hatred.

Even if I did hate her, I didn't want her to die because then I wouldn't be able to torture her, or at least that was what I was telling myself.

"Ariella, we need to go." Ariella's jaw hung slack, her gaze fixed on the open hallway that curved, hiding whoever was causing the chaos. Her chest barely moved, as if she'd forgotten how to breathe.

We didn't have time for this. With every wasted moment, the shooter was getting closer, and before long, we'd be in his sight.

"Zaiden," Hawk shouted again. "Now!"

Leaning forward, I threw her over my shoulder and bolted for the open door where Hawk was still standing. I wasn't typically the type to run from danger, but I wasn't stupid enough to think I had a chance against an automatic rifle head on.

I stepped through the doorway into one of the locker rooms. The air hung heavy with the lingering scent of sweat and cheap body spray. Metal lockers lined the walls, their red paint chipped and worn from years of use.

My gaze darted around the room. It wasn't safe here. We were too exposed. "Storage closet," I ordered Hawk, his girlfriend Abby, who was part of the figure skating team, and Trey.

Abby ran for the door to the closet, her blonde hair bouncing with each step, and quickly walked inside. I followed her, finding a table in the back corner with a few boxes to one side to drop Ariella's ass on. I twisted to walk away, but the minute that door closed and we were covered in darkness, Ariella came back to life, her hands curled into my clothes. Her grip was unwavering, stopping me from moving.

"T—turn on the lights," she cried out.

I squeezed my eyes shut and bit down on my bottom lip to keep from cursing out loud. She was terrified of the dark. In the pitch black, Ariella's fingernails dug into my arm. Her breath came in short, ragged gasps, each exhale a soft whimper.

I wrapped my hands around her waist to calm her, letting her know she wasn't alone. "Ariella, there's a shooter out there. We can't turn on the lights," I whispered, keeping my tone low and calm.

"I want out," she raised her voice with each word. "Let me out," Ariella pleaded, her voice cracking. The raw fear in her tone made my chest tighten.

She was so scared of the dark that she'd rather take her chances with an active shooter. She shifted her weight to slide off the table, but I pinned my hips to the table between her thighs, giving her no room to move. "I can't let you go. You put us all in danger by leaving now."

"Shut her the fuck up," Trey whisper-yelled. "She's going to get us all shot."

The air was thick with tension, fear, and desperation that clung to us like a second skin.

"Ariella, please," I said, sliding my hands around her face and pressing my thumb to her chin. "I need you to calm down."

Her breathing increased, and her pulse raced under my fingers, but I knew it wasn't my touch that was doing that to her. Her small hands wrapped around my wrist, pulling softly like she was raging a war. She wanted me to let her go, but she also didn't.

"Please turn on the lights."

"Seriously, man," Hawk growled. "Shut your girl up before she gets us all killed."

"Just let me out, I'll run." She started hyperventilating like the loud crying type.

"Shut her up, or I will," Trey hissed. Typically, that

comment would make me throat punch him, but I understood. If she didn't shut up, we could all die.

"Fuck," I muttered. I needed to calm her down, but I could only think of one way to do that. Her cries died when my mouth captured hers. Her rigid shoulders softened, her body curving into mine as her lips parted, allowing my tongue to explore hers.

My hand dropped to her ass, and the other hand twisted into her hair as I dominated not only the kiss but her.

I hadn't wanted to kiss her, but now I couldn't stop. My hands roamed over her body, desperate for more contact as I moved on autopilot, pressing closer, craving her warmth.

My body screamed for more, a traitorous hunger I thought I could overpower. I was wrong. Tomorrow, I'd hate myself for this moment of weakness. But right now? Right now, with death potentially seconds away, all that mattered was her warmth, her breath, the familiar curve of her lips against mine.

My tongue stroked along hers as my hand gripped her ass hard, pulling her harder into me. If we were alone right now, I'd fuck her right here on this table, but we weren't, and I couldn't. I pressed my raging hard cock into her, letting her know exactly what I was thinking.

"Are we going to have to listen to you two sucking faces the entire time," Abby groaned, her tone laced with disgust.

"Shut up, Abby," Hawk whisper-hissed. "At least she's quiet."

I pulled out of the kiss and released her, our labored breathing filling the small, quiet air. The taste of her lips lingered, a bittersweet reminder of the past when things were good.

My lips hovered over her as I pushed against her chin, tilting her head up and whispering against her lips. "Ari, I need you to focus on my words, okay?" I kept my tone smooth and calming as I let the heat of my breath fan across her lips. "I'm not going to let anything happen to you. They will have to go through me to get to you, but I need you to stay calm, okay?"

My hand dropped to her neck, and my thumb stroked over the pulse point in her throat softly. Her chest stilled, frozen mid-inhale. Against my fingertips, her pulse raced. She was holding her breath. The last thing I needed was her passing out.

"Slow, deep breaths for me, baby." I wrapped my arms around her pulling her into me and sucking in a heavy breath. Her familiar scent hit me like a punch to the gut, memories of that night a year ago flooding back. The last person I'd held like this was her a year ago.

The night Kacie died.

I was a different person then, and she wasn't responsible for my sister's death.

My heart thundered in my chest, each beat a seismic event threatening to give away our location as a loud bang came from right outside the door. Abby squealed but was quickly cut off; I was betting Hawk covered her mouth.

My arms constricted around Ariella, muscles coiling tight enough to tremble. The air caught in my throat, refusing to move as I prayed that whoever it was didn't hear us and Ariella stayed calm.

Time stretched, each second an eternity, as we huddled in our makeshift sanctuary.

In the darkness, my eyes strained uselessly, seeking phantom shapes. The air felt thick, almost suffocating, carrying the sour tang of fear and sweat. Ariella's body trembled against mine, her ragged breath hot and damp on my chest. The gunfire had ceased, leaving behind a ringing silence punctuated by the thundering of my own heartbeat. Every tiny sound - a creak, a whisper of movement - sent icy tendrils of dread down my spine. Was it over, or was the gunman out there, his footsteps masked by the blood rushing in my ears?

I wasn't sure how long we'd been in this closet's darkness, but it felt like an eternity.

"Police!" A deep voice boomed, reverberating through the small space. My knotted muscles uncoiled, leaving behind a dull ache.

"Anyone in here?"

"In here!" Hawk's voice cracked, raw with tension.

The door crashed open. Blinding light cut into the room, searing my dark-adjusted eyes. I winced, tasting copper as I bit my tongue. Hands shot up around me, a forest of trembling limbs. Ariella remained motionless against me, her fingers digging painfully into my sides.

"Everyone okay in here?" The officer's voice was gruff, tinged with barely contained urgency.

"Yeah," Trey said. "We're all good here."

"Let's go," the officer said, gesturing for everyone to follow him.

"Ariella, you're okay," I whispered, my voice rough and unfamiliar to my own ears. I covered her hands with mine, feeling them tremble where they clutched my shirt. The fabric was damp with sweat. "I'm going to carry you out, but I need you to loosen your grip."

Her fingers uncurled slowly as if each movement caused pain. I scooped her up, cradling her in my arms, her small frame surprisingly heavy with tension. Her shampoo, faint lavender, mingled with the sharper smell of fear-sweat.

Ahead, Hawk moved with careful steps, Abby tucked against him. His shoulders were rigid, muscles coiled beneath his shirt. Trey led the way through the locker room, his sneakers squeaking softly on the tile floor.

The SWAT officer's gear clinked softly as he ushered us forward, the sound countering our ragged breathing.

"Follow the crowd out," the officer ordered, pointing forward.

Trey's head snapped around as he stood momentarily frozen in the doorway, his eyes locking first on Hawk, then me. The muscle in his jaw jumped, his usual easy grin nowhere to be seen. He raised a hand, two fingers jabbing toward Ariella and Abby before pressing against his eyelids. For a heartbeat, his eyes screwed shut, his face contorting as if in pain. When they opened again, the message was clear: Don't let them see.

That moment felt like it was so long when, in fact, it all happened in a matter of seconds.

I tucked Ariella's face into my chest, her warm, rapid breaths seeping through my shirt. We merged into the flow of bodies in the hall, a current of trembling limbs and stifled whimpers. Discarded backpacks and scattered papers littered the floor, abandoned reminders of the ordinary school day that had been violently interrupted.

My peripheral vision blurred, narrowing to a tunnel. Focusing straight ahead took every ounce of willpower, my neck muscles aching with the effort not to turn, not to see. Each step echoed hollowly, the sound ricocheting off the walls. Somewhere ahead, a door banged open, the sudden noise causing a ripple of flinches through the crowd.

Minutes stretched like hours as we stumbled towards the exit. The rhythmic thud of combat boots and the crackle of police radios surrounded us, a cocoon of urgency. A gust of cool air hit my face, we were outside.

The sun's glare was jarring after the dim hallways. I squinted, my eyes watering as they adjusted. Police barricades loomed ahead, their red and blue lights pulsing silently against the day's brightness.

We didn't stop until we reached the parking lot's sun-baked asphalt.

"You're safe," I whispered to Ariella, my voice hoarse. As I eased her down, my arms trembled from exertion and fading adrenaline. Her feet touched the ground, but her fingers remained curled in my shirt as if afraid to let go.

"Fuck," Trey's voice cracked as he spun around. "Do they have the shooter?"

I swallowed hard. "I don't know," I said, the words feeling inadequate on my tongue.

"I counted two," Hawk said.

I knew he was talking about bodies. "Could you tell who it was?" I asked, sliding an arm around Ariella's shoulders.

"Oh my God," she cried out. "Journey and Mila."

"They were male," Hawk said, his tone low and somber. "But I couldn't tell."

My gaze scanned the crowds of students coming out of the school, standing around the parking lot behind the barriers law enforcement set up. Everyone was waiting for someone they cared about to appear.

"We should get out of here," Trey said, his voice tight. He ran a shaky hand through his thick, dark hair, leaving it standing on end. "We can start making calls to check on everyone."

Ariella's hands fluttered over her pockets, her movements jerky and uncoordinated. "I don't have my phone," she mumbled, her voice distant, as if coming from underwater. "I must have left it inside." She shifted her weight, swaying slightly on her feet. Her eyes, wide and unfocused, fixed on the school building behind us.

My hand wrapped around her arm, feeling the goosebumps on her clammy skin. "You can't go get it," I said, trying to keep my voice steady despite the lump in my throat.

"I need it," she cried out, her voice rising to a pitch that made my ears ring. Tears spilled down her cheeks. "I need to check on Mila, Journey, and my team." Her chest heaved with each ragged breath. This wasn't about a phone. It was the fear of the day coming to a head.

"We will check on everyone," Trey said. "But right now, we need to get out of here."

"I have Mila and Journey's numbers in my phone," Abby said, reaching into her pocket. "You can call them."

"Call them on the way," Hawk said, ushering us toward our cars.

I knew these next few hours would be the worst as we waited to find out who was injured and who didn't make it out.

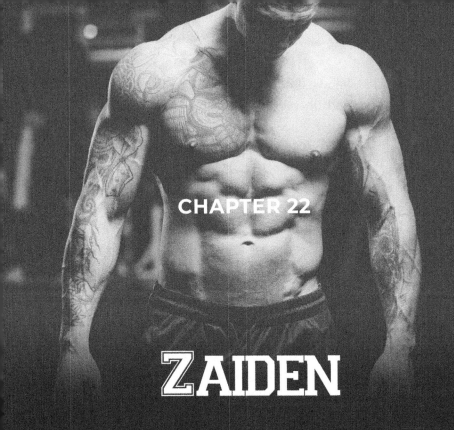

CHAPTER 22

ZAIDEN

S tanding in the darkness, I stared at Ariella sitting at a park table with her feet propped on the bench under a pavilion. A storm of emotions churned inside me. Anger at what she'd done to my sister mixed with the instinctive need to protect her, to make sure she was okay. I hated how easily old feelings resurfaced, and that kiss didn't help the situation.

By the time we made it to my house after leaving campus, we had decided to send out a group invite to meet at a local park so we could accommodate everyone. Apparently, everyone had the same idea because before we knew it, the park was full of ballers, dancers, and cheerleaders.

We'd been here for almost an hour, and most of Westbrook's athletes had been accounted for, but we were still missing Mila and Journey.

Sterling appeared through the crowd, his usually carefree demeanor replaced with a grim determination. He'd volunteered to help account for our team. "Everyone is accounted for on our end," he reported, voice steady despite the worry lines creasing his forehead. "But the other teams—" He trailed off, glancing towards the clusters of anxious athletes still waiting for news. "We're still missing a couple of people from the football team, dance team, soccer team, and a few cheerleaders."

It was possible that others had lost their phones like Ariella and didn't know we were waiting for them, but knowing that didn't make the wait any easier for those waiting to see if their friends were alive or dead.

"Mila and Journey still haven't shown up," Sterling stated. "I saw them heading toward the exit before everything went down. They were probably heading home."

"Yeah," I muttered without taking my eyes off Ariella. "Their practice was over."

"Maybe they both lost their phone," he said. "A lot of people dropped their things in the chaos."

I nodded. "It's a possibility, but it's also a possibility they were hurt or worse. They went out the way the shooter came in."

It wasn't just Ariella who was worried about Journey and Mila. We all grew up together. Ariella, Mila, Journey, and Kacie were best friends. Growing up, I couldn't remember a memory they weren't part of.

"Maybe it's time to send out team captains to see if they can account for everyone else."

"I'm going to take Ariella to Mila and Journey's house to see if we can find them."

"We can split up," Sterling suggested. "You and Ari go to Mila's, and I'll go to Journey's."

I nodded again. "Let EJ know what we're doing, and I'll grab Ariella."

"I'll call you if I find anything," Sterling said as he twisted and disappeared into the crowd.

I strolled to Ariella and climbed up on the table beside her. "Where are they?" Ariella murmured, staring through the crowd like she was waiting for them to appear, her fingers nervously tracing patterns on her black leggings.

My chest tightened with sympathy. "They could have lost their phones like you in the chaos." She nodded softly. "Sterling is headed to Journey's house now. Why don't we go check Mila's?"

"We were supposed to meet at Mila's after—" She trailed off, biting her bottom lip.

"Come on," I urged, already moving to slide off the table. "We'll take my bike. It's faster."

She nodded and slipped my hand into hers as I slid off the table, gently tugging her to follow me. I stopped waiting for her to hop off the bench, and when her feet hit the ground, and I didn't release her, her gaze lingered for a long moment on our tangled hands before lifting to meet mine. A moment passed between us, drawing memories from our past—the past when she was secretly mine, and I was hers.

Clearing my throat, I tugged at her hand. "Let's go."

When we got to my bike, I tossed a leg over and adjusted before jerking my head, silently telling her to load up. I leaned forward to grab my helmet when my phone rang. I shoved my hand in my pocket and jerked out my phone, and a wave of relief washed over me when I saw

Mila's name on the screen. I held the phone out, showing Ariella her leg midair to get onto the bike.

"Answer it," Ariella demanded, her voice tight with anxiety as she abandoned her attempt to mount the bike and pivoted to face me.

I slid right. "Where are you?" I blurted out, my heart racing as I pressed the phone to my ear.

"Journey and I are at my house," Mila rushed out, her words tumbling over each other in barely contained panic. "We saw what happened, and we haven't been able to get a hold of Ari."

"Did you not get the text that everyone was meeting at Barnet Park for a head count?"

"We were getting ready to head that way. I accidentally left my phone in my car, and Journey changed her number last week, so she hadn't updated anyone yet." She sounded winded and rushed. "Have you seen Ari? She was supposed to meet us here and never showed."

"She's fine." I flashed a look at Ariella, still standing at my side, anxiously waiting for me to tell her what was going on. "She's with me. We were actually about to go look for you and Journey."

"Oh, thank God," Mila breathed, relief palpable in her voice even through the phone's tiny speaker. "The news said over twenty people were injured, and one person was dead."

"Do they know who yet?"

"Yes, but they aren't releasing the name until they've informed the family. They did say it was a staff member."

I narrowed my eyes. The only staff members in the sports hall would have been coaches. "A coach," I muttered.

"Yeah," she whispered, the single word heavy with unspoken dread.

"Did they identify the shooter?"

"Yeah," she sighed. "His name was Bradley Fletcher."

Bradley Fletcher. I remembered him - a first-year with a chip on his shoulder. There had been rumors about his grades and behavior. I'd heard he was kicked off the football team and lost his scholarship. I felt sick. "He's also dead."

"Let me know if you hear what coach—"

"Oh, wait," Mila interrupted, her voice suddenly sharp. In the background, I could hear the urgent tones of a news broadcast, but I couldn't understand what they were saying. "Oh shit—" she gasped, the words escaping in a horrified exhale.

"What?" I snapped. "What is it?"

"It was Coach Palmer. My coach."

"Oh." My gaze shifted to Ariella, and I held up two fingers. "Two deaths."

"Who?" she demanded, my patience fraying as I gripped the phone tighter.

"The shooter and Coach Palmer," I reported grimly, watching Ariella's face for her reaction.

Her chin jerked back, but she didn't say anything. I could see the mixture of emotions flashing across her face.

The loss of life was always sad, but I wasn't one bit upset about losing a man who took advantage of the team he was supposed to protect, and I imagined Ariella and Mila felt the same.

"Are they sure that's it?" I asked. "We still have several unaccounted for."

"They're probably at home sleeping or something and

don't know what's going on. Has everyone from the dance team been accounted for now?"

"Yes," I said. "The football and soccer teams are still missing people."

"They could send someone to their house to check on them, but the news said it was only one plus the shooter."

"I'll let EJ and Curtis know," I said into the phone. "And then I'm going to take Ariella home."

"Stay safe," Mila said and disconnected.

"Mila and Journey are safe." I slid off my bike as Ariella visibly relaxed. "We should let everyone know the info we got, and then we'll head home."

Ariella and I took a minute to update EJ, Sterling, and the soccer team captain, Curtis, before we headed home.

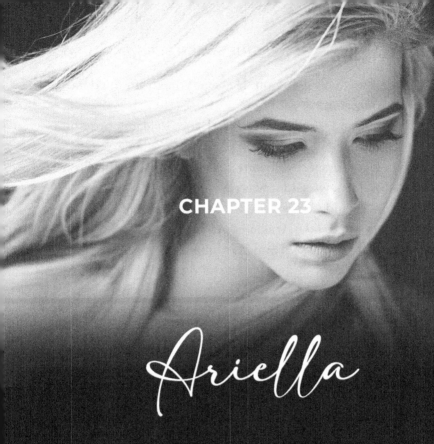

CHAPTER 23

Ariella

My shoulders sagged, each step up the stairwell requiring more effort than the last. The events of the day clung to me like a lead weight, my eyelids fighting to stay open. I followed Zaiden up the stairwell, stopping at my room.

"You should go to bed," Zaiden's words came out more as a command than a suggestion. "I'll be gone in a minute."

"You're leaving?" My gaze shifted around the dark house. I didn't want to be alone, not after everything today.

"I'm staying in the team house tonight." He sidestepped me, his shoulder brushing against mine. The brief contact sent a jolt through my body, a reminder of the electric tension between us. The heat radiated from him as he passed, heading to his room.

"Please don't leave," I pleaded, following behind him. My hands trembled slightly as I reached out, the memory of today's terrors still etched in the lines of my face.

His body went rigid, one foot suspended mid-step. Slowly, he pivoted toward me. His forehead creased, eyebrows knitting together. "Are you asking me to stay here with you?"

I shrugged as I slowly nodded. "The house is empty and dark—"

"Ariella," he snapped, cutting me off. "Nothing has changed. I was stuck with you today, and now I can't wait to get away from you." His words cut through the air like shards of ice, each syllable dripping with venom. The muscles in his jaw tightened, his eyes narrowing to slits. He turned back and stormed through the doorway into his room.

"That's a lie," I said, grabbing a handful of his shirt and jerking hard to stop him. "You kissed me the same way you kissed me—"

He huffed out a humorless laugh as he snapped his body around, pulling his shirt from my hand. His hand shot out, fingers grazing my collarbone before curling around my throat. Time seemed to slow as he closed the distance between us, his eyes never leaving mine. The wall hit my back with a dull thud, driving the air from my lungs.

His grip tightened, not enough to choke, but a clear threat. I could feel my pulse hammering against his palm, a frantic counterpoint to the eerie calm in his eyes. "That kiss," he growled, his breath hot against my cheek, "was to save my life, my teammate's lives." He pressed closer, our noses almost touching. His scent, a mix of sweat and adrenaline, enveloped me, making it hard to think and breathe. "No more, no less. You mean nothing to me, Ariella."

I shook my head, and his grip tightened on my throat. "You don't kiss someone you hate like that," I choked out. "And you protected me from Coach Palmer."

"That wasn't protection for you," he muttered. "That was protection for me. You are mine," he whispered, the words sliding like ice down my spine. His grip on my throat loosened, but his other hand came up to cage me against the wall. "And no one," he continued, his voice dropping even lower, "will touch you until I'm done destroying you." The last word hung between us, heavy with promise and threat. I didn't know if I wanted to run from him or stay, the line between fear and something else blurring dangerously, and I knew I'd officially lost my mind.

My lip curled into a snarl. "You're really going to pretend like you feel nothing for me."

"I stopped feeling anything for you when you killed my sister."

My chest tightened with anger. "Tell me," I said, my voice low and dangerous. My hands clenched at my sides. "Tell me what I did, Zaiden." His chest rose and fell rapidly, matching my own ragged breathing. "What," I hissed, shoving hard at his chest, "did I do to Kacie?"

"Why don't you tell me?" He scowled. "You are the reason she left that night."

I blinked rapidly, my brows furrowing as I sifted through the hazy recollections of that night. "What?" I shook my head. "Zaiden, that's not true."

"It is true." He released me, taking a step back.

"I didn't even see Kacie that night."

"Stop lying," His voice erupted like a volcano, its force

making me flinch. Veins stood out on his neck, his face flushing a deep crimson as he leaned in, eyes blazing with a mix of fury and desperate denial.

"Who told you that, because I never saw her that night?" I squared my shoulders, not backing down. He was wrong, and I needed him to know it. "I didn't know she'd ever shown up to the party until after the accident."

"What did you argue about, Ariella?" He ignored me. "Did you tell her about us?" My eyes widened. "I told you it wasn't the right time—"

"I didn't tell her anything because there was no us, Zaiden," I growled, shoving my finger into his chest. "I told you there wouldn't be an us until you told her, but I didn't tell her anything because I didn't see her that night." I thought back to that night. I had only been at the party an hour before we found out about the accident. "I was with Journey, Sterling, and you all night."

He shook his head. "You're lying."

"Who told you she left because of me?"

"Samantha Morrison," he said. "She saw Kacie leaving that night. She asked her what was wrong because Kacie was so upset. Kacie said it was you."

"Is that all she said?"

"That's all she had to say. My sister left that party drunk that night," his voice cracked. "And got behind the wheel because of whatever you said or did to her."

"Kacie was my best friend—"

He surged forward, using his body to slam me back into the wall. "You never deserved her friendship."

This wasn't getting us anywhere. I needed Zaiden to remember that night, to remember how he felt for me and how close Kacie and I were. "That night at the party," I whispered. What did you say to me?"

"When?"

"When you pulled me off to the side, and you kissed me so hard I couldn't breathe."

"You pushed me off of you."

"Because I didn't want to be your dirty little secret."

"You weren't."

"I was as long as you kept us and our feelings a secret. I agreed to let you tell her because you asked to be the one, but the last thing I ever wanted to do was hurt Kacie, and you know it. It's why I pushed you off of me."

Our eyes locked, the air between us crackling with unspoken words and suppressed emotions. For a fleeting moment, the mask of hatred slipped, revealing a glimpse of the pain and confusion swirling in the depths of his gaze. "Tell me what you told me."

"I was drunk."

"That didn't make it any less true."

"Maybe not, but I don't feel that way anymore. I lost those feelings when I lost my sister."

The realization settled over me like a suffocating blanket. He was never going to believe me. No matter what I did, he was never going to believe that I had nothing to do with his sister's death. I was stupid to think the trauma of today changed anything.

"Let me go," I ordered, my voice eerily calm despite the storm raging inside me. I placed my hands flat against his chest, feeling the rapid beat of his heart; I shoved him until he stepped back. "I'm going to bed."

I shifted my weight to step around him, but he stepped in front of me. His large frame blocked my way, and he swung his foot behind him, shoving his bedroom door shut, covering us in darkness. "Zaiden." I reached out for him.

His voice dropped to a whisper, each word dripping with menace. "You want to go to bed?" The question slithered through the darkness, and a beat of silence followed, heavy with anticipation. My heartbeat thundered in my ears, feeling the weight of his gaze even in the pitch black. "Then get in the bed." The words hung between us, a challenge, a threat, and something else I didn't dare name.

My eyes strained against the inky blackness, searching for any hint of movement, any sign of where he was. The silence pressed in, broken only by our ragged breathing. I took a hesitant step forward, then another, my hands outstretched.

The darkness seemed alive, pulsing with unspoken tensions and buried emotions. Each second stretched into an eternity as I waited for his touch, his voice, anything to break this unbearable suspense. "Zaiden—Turn on the light."

I instantly regretted following him, for thinking something had changed between us because he was about to make me wish I'd locked myself in my room.

CHAPTER 24

Ariella

The room was a void, darker than pitch. My pulse quickened as my eyes strained, every nerve on high alert. "Zaiden."

The walls seemed to press in, my chest constricting as if trapped in a vise. Each shallow breath felt like a struggle against the weight of anticipation and fear.

I sucked in a sharp breath when his large hands curled around my hips, jerking me into him—my back to his front. For a split second, I was transported back to the first time he kissed me, his soft, full lips, the heat of his body against mine, the gentleness in his touch. Those days were long gone.

Burying his nose in my hair, he inhaled deeply. "You don't want to be alone tonight, Ariella." His hot breath tickled my ear, sending chills rippling over my skin. His hands tightened on my hips as he turned us. My chest tightened, each breath a struggle as panic and desire stirred within me. He brushed his lips over my ear, his teeth grazing my earlobe. "Then get in the bed." He shoved my hips forward, and I stumbled forward into the bed, my body bending over the bed.

"What the—" My words were cut off when his fingers curled into the thin material of my black leggings covering my hips and hoisting the bottom half of me onto the bed. "Zaiden." I pushed to my hands and knees, scrambling to get across the bed. It was my only chance to escape, but he was faster than me.

His hand wrapped around my ankle, jerking hard enough to pull my hands and knees out from under me. My breath came in short, ragged gasps, each inhale a struggle against the tightness in my chest.

The bed sank in as he crawled over me, and I flipped to my back. I couldn't see him, but I could feel him.

Part of me wanted to give in, to let Zaiden take control. It would be easier than fighting. "What do you want, Zaiden?"

The heat of his breath fanned my face, his lips mere inches from mine. "I want you naked and cuffed to my bed."

A lump formed in my throat, choking off my words. My mouth went dry, my tongue sticking to the roof as I struggled to form coherent thoughts, let alone speak to them.

If he cuffed me to this bed, I would lose any chance of control, even though I doubted he was going to give it to me willingly anyway.

"No cuffs," I mumbled. "But I'll take off my clothes." I shifted my hips, trying to push him off me.

He huffed out a menacing laugh as his thighs tightened, holding me in place. "That's not how this works." His lips brushed across mine as they trailed over my jaw and down to my throat. My heart pounded against my ribcage, its frantic rhythm drowning out all other sounds in the room as I lost all rational thinking at the feeling of his mouth on me. His hands raked up my side, brushing his knuckles over my skin as he dragged the hem of my shirt with it, sending goosebumps racing over my skin. I arched my body into him as he tugged my shirt over my head and tossed it to the floor.

"Zaiden, what are we doing?" I whispered, a hint of fear mixed with excitement laced in my tone.

"Don't worry," he breathed against my skin as his large hands wrapped around my wrists, forcing them above my head. "You don't have to worry about my sister finding out anymore." The spell I was under evaporated, and I jerked against his grip. "Because she's dead."

I thrashed against his grip, disoriented in the darkness. "Zaiden. Let me go."

"Where would be the fun in that?" Cool metal slapped around one of my wrists, and panic set in. I thrashed my body around underneath him, bucking my hips and jerking my uncuffed arm, but it was no use. His chest dropped to mine as all of his body weight pressed me hard into the mattress, suffocating me. The metal slapped around my other wrist before the sound of metal hitting metal echoed through the quiet room.

Fuck.

I was cuffed to the bed.

And then his weight was gone. "Zaiden." I sucked in a deep breath holding it as fear and panic wrapped around me, making it hard to breathe. It was dark, and I realized he was the only thing keeping me from losing it, which was completely irrational. I knew he'd protect me from whatever was lurking in the darkness, but the problem was that there was no one to protect me from him.

The soft glow of a nightlight kicked on, and I released my breath in a whoosh. Zaiden stood beside the bed wearing nothing but a pair of low-hanging black joggers. The light was only bright enough to see him. My gaze raked over every curve of his tanned and toned chest down to his perfect abs, and my heart rate spiked. His dark tattoos scrolled across his broad shoulders and down his arms, covering his chest and back. His body was the perfect canvas, and yet I couldn't understand how someone so beautiful could be such a massive dick.

His lips curled into a cocky smirk. "Like what you see, princess?"

Busted—

A flush crept up my neck, flooding my cheeks with warmth. I could feel the heat radiating off my skin, grateful for the dim light that might hide the signs of my body's betrayal.

I shrugged, but there was no point in lying. "Yes, too bad it's all wasted on an asshole like you."

"Asshole?" He raised his brows. "Me?" He touched his fingers to his chest. "You mean the asshole that saved your life today?"

"And yet here I am, handcuffed again." I jerked against the cuffs, making the metal clank against metal just in case he forgot. It looks like you're the one I need saving from." I nodded toward him. "If you could do me a favor and give me a heads-up on what personality I'm going to be dealing with, that would be great."

He huffed out a laugh. "Which personality?"

"Yeah, the psychotic version, which always has a pair of handcuffs, then the I don't give a fuck version that avoids me, or the protective and possessive version that seems like he might still give a fuck."

He cocked his head to the side. "Let's not pretend like this doesn't turn you on." His gaze lifted to the handcuffs. He was talking about before. Before the accident. Back when I trusted him. "If I remember correctly, this shit turns you on, right?"

"If you're referring to the one time we fooled around," I scowled. The one time we made out while he tied me to the bed before using his fingers to give me my first mind-blowing orgasm when I was drunk. An orgasm I hadn't been able to match myself. Well, other than the orgasm he'd given me at the dinner table. It did make me wonder what else he could do. "Then yes, I was into it, but you weren't such a dick then."

"I was the same person then." He shifted his weight and leaned over to the nightstand, and I raised my head, trying to see what he was doing. "And if I remember correctly, all of this makes your panties wet." He stood to his full height, and my eyes widened on the eight-inch pink vibrating dildo.

It was mine.

"You stole my fucking vibrator?"

He held down the button, filling the quiet room with a low buzz. "If you want to get off in this house, you're going to have to beg for it." His gaze dropped. "Why don't we see how wet your panties are?" Lifting his leg, the bed sank in as he pressed his knee into the mattress and hooked his fingers into the waist of my leggings, tugging them down my legs until I was wearing nothing but my black sports bra.

Even though I knew I should tell him to stop, I didn't want to. This wasn't the Zaiden I was scared of. I wasn't afraid of the Zaiden threatening another earth-shattering orgasm; I craved this Zaiden. I shouldn't want this. I shouldn't want him. I was seriously fucked up in the head, but it didn't matter because my body was desperate for his touch.

He brought my panties to his face as his eyes closed, and he inhaled deeply. I squeezed my thighs together to alleviate the pressure building deep in my core. His eyes open, locking with mine. "Fuck, you smell so sweet when your soaking wet for me, baby."

Gripping my ankles, he spread my legs as he climbed on the bed, shoving them wider with his knees as he crawled over me, finally settling between my thighs.

Butterflies erupted in my stomach, a dizzying cocktail of desire and dread. My muscles tensed, caught between the urge to pull him closer and the instinct to push him away. Well, if I wasn't tied to the bed.

His gaze dropped to my lips and slowly moved down my body, stopping on my pussy. My legs clenched against his thick thighs, desperate to close them, to hide myself, but his knees spread, forcing me to open wider for him.

"You're so fucking wet, your pussy is glistening for me." He shifted, grabbing the vibrator off the bed. My eyes followed the pink toy as he brought it down to just above my bra, softly pressing the vibration to my skin. He slid his free hand under the band of my bra, placing it flat against my sternum.

"Your heart is racing," he smirked, his voice a low rumble of seduction. "Are you scared or excited?" I didn't bother answering. He already knew the answer. He shoved my bra up, and my tits bounced free, his breath rasping harshly as his gaze trailed over me. He dragged the vibrator over my bra, bunched over my breast. I arched into him, and the corner of his lip tipped up. "You want more?" I did, but I wasn't going to beg. He circled my right breast with the vibration before moving to my left and circling it.

Fuck, I needed more.

He moved back to the right, dragging the vibrator over my nipple, slowly circling the tight bud. My back arched off the bed, and my eyes closed as my lips parted with a soft moan. "What do you do with this toy?" he breathed. "Do you tease your body, or do you use it to make yourself come?"

"Come," the words came out in a rush as he circled my other nipple.

"What a waste." He dragged the toy down my stomach before sliding it over my pussy.

"Oh, my—" My words cut off when he pressed the head to my clit and slid it down before pressing the tip to my entrance. The vibration made my legs tremble.

"Zaiden," I moaned, bucking my hips forward, desperate for more.

"You want more," he breathed, pushing the tip in, and I nodded.

He stopped and pulled the vibrator away. "You use this plastic toy on this virgin pussy?"

"No," I shook my head. "Stimulation."

"Has anything been inside this pussy?"

My eyes narrowed, my face twisting with confusion and frustration. I didn't want to talk; I wanted to come— just you."

"And you want me to fuck you with this toy right now?"

"Yes," I breathed.

"Beg."

I clenched my jaw, frustration building. "Just make me come, Zaiden. Or let me do it myself."

"Nice try, but I'm sure you can do better." His mouth dropped to my chest, and my head rose off the pillow following his every move. "Beg for me, baby." His hot breath fanned across my nipple before his tongue darted out, striking the taut bud.

I didn't want him to stop, but I wasn't going to beg. He pressed the vibrator to my clit, pinning it there with his hips as he rocked into me. His other hand cupped my other breast, pinching my nipple and rolling it between his finger and thumb.

"Zaiden," I cried out, my body vibrating with pleasure.

"Beg," he hummed against my nipple. "Or it all stops."

I was close, so fucking close. I rocked my hips into him, finding the perfect rhythm with the vibration. I was at the edge. My abs tightened, my head fell back—And he stopped.

"No," I snapped.

"I warned you," he said, tossing the vibrator to the floor. "Sleep tight."

"Zaiden," I hissed as he lifted and shifted until he was lying on his back beside me. "What the fuck?"

He fake-yawned. "Next time, you'll listen like a good girl instead of being a stubborn brat."

"Fuck that." My gaze lifted to the cuffs and back to him. My hands curled around the chain of the cuffs, and I pulled myself up, twisted, lifted my leg, and landed on his chest.

"Either you're going to make me come, or you're going

to let me go so I can do it myself." My jaw flexed. "It's okay if you're not up for the challenge."

His lips curved up as his arms wrapped around my thighs. "We both know I'm the only one who's ever made you come. Not much of a challenge."

"Then let me go."

"You really want to come?" He asked like we didn't have a whole conversation about it. I nodded. "Okay. You can ride my face if I can ride yours."

He didn't give me a chance to agree. He grabbed my ass, hiking me up as he slid down until my clit was pressed to his soft, warm lips.

"Come all over my face, princess." His tongue licked across my clit, and I rolled my hips over his face as his hands gripped my ass tighter, slowly guiding me over him back and forth.

My hands tightened around the bars as my muscles clenched and my body shook. I increased my speed, taking control. I was already so worked up that it wouldn't take much. I wanted to dig my hands into his hair and smother him, but instead, I stroked myself harder and faster over his tongue until I found a rhythm that set every nerve ending in my body on fire.

My head fell back, and I cried out as I exploded in an earth-shattering, mind-blowing orgasm.

"Holy fuck," I moaned as he released me, and I fell back to the bed.

He shifted to his side, his face, mouth, and chin covered in the evidence of my orgasm. "You taste a lot fucking sweeter than I remember." His mouth crashed against mine, forcing me to taste myself, my orgasm, the orgasm he'd given me. His tongue tangled with mine, swallowing my mouth, literally sucking the air from my lungs.

Jerking my mouth from his, I sucked in a harsh breath, desperate for air. He reached for the nightstand, grabbing the key before releasing me.

"Get your clothes and go to bed, Ariella."

"But I thought—"

"I'll let you know when it's time to return the favor." His lips turned up into a sadistic smirk, and I knew I had just really fucked up.

CHAPTER 25

Ariella

Mila's eyes widened as I pushed through the door. "Oh my God, Ari!" The relief in her voice hit me like a wave, and my chest tightened. I hadn't realized how much I needed to see them, to be somewhere that felt normal.

As Mila rushed towards me, nearly tripping over her own feet, I fought the urge to break down right there in the doorway.

"We were so worried." Journey's voice cracked with emotion as she threw her arms around me, and Mila embracing us.

"I'm glad you guys weren't there."

"What happened?" Journey asked as we pulled out of the embrace.

I shrugged. "Everything happened fast, even though it

felt like it was moving so slowly." I strolled through the entryway and into the living room. "I was standing in the hall arguing with Zaiden, and then we heard a loud noise. When we realized, or well, when Zaiden realized, because I was already in shock, he rushed us into a closet. We stayed there until the police came."

Journey's eyebrows shot up, her mouth hanging open slightly. "Zaiden saved your life?"

I nodded, my fingers absently tracing the hem of my shirt. The irony wasn't lost on me. The guy who hated me most in the world had become my unlikely savior. Part of me wanted to laugh at the absurdity of it all, while another wanted to cry. Instead, I felt numb. "Have you heard when we go back to school?"

Mila and Journey exchanged glances, then shook their heads in unison. Mila's shoulders slumped as she spoke. "The entire campus is closed while they investigate."

"Well, I'm not in a hurry to go back," I said, sinking onto the couch. The thought of walking those halls again made my stomach churn.

A shiver ran down my spine as memories of gunshots echoing down the hall filled my mind. "What do you think is going to happen now that Coach Palmer is dead?"

"Hopefully, they don't shut down the dance team," Journey said. "I need that scholarship."

Mila waved her hand dismissively, trying to inject optimism into her voice. "I'm sure they'll just find a new coach."

The room fell silent for a moment. I fidgeted with my sleeve, then looked up, my voice barely above a whisper. "Have you heard anything about the students who were injured?"

Mila's eyes clouded over. She pulled her legs onto the

couch, hugging them to her chest. "We know that most of them have been released from the hospital, but—" She paused, swallowing hard. "Ashley Barker, a cheerleader, is still in critical condition. And Lucas Ramirez, from the soccer team—" Her voice trailed off for a moment. "He's critical, too. I think everyone else had minor injuries."

"Is Ashley and Lucas going to make it?"

Mila shrugged. "Hopefully."

"If Zaiden hadn't pulled me into that locker room," I said. "It would have been me in that hospital."

"So, did you and Zaiden make up?" Journey asked.

"No, but I did find out why he blames me for Kacie's death," I muttered. "We need to find Sammy from high school."

Mila's brow furrowed. "Sammy M?" I nodded, my jaw clenching involuntarily. "Why?" Mila leaned forward, her curiosity piqued.

"Sammy is the reason he believes I'm responsible."

Journey's frown deepened, her forehead creasing. She leaned forward, eyes intent. "Wait. What did Sammy tell Zaiden?"

I exhaled slowly. "That Kacie left upset, and she was upset because of me."

Mila's brows knitted together, her head tilting slightly. "You didn't even see her, did you?"

"No." I shook my head, my hair falling into my eyes. I brushed it back impatiently. "He thinks we had a fight, but we didn't. I didn't even know she was there yet."

"That doesn't make any sense," Mila said. "You two never fight. Why would she think that?"

I shrugged. "I don't know, but I'm going to find out. We need to find Sammy first."

Mila jumped to her feet. "I'll grab my computer." She

disappeared down the hallway, her footsteps echoing from her bedroom. Journey eased onto the couch beside me, her leg brushing against mine in silent support. Moments later, Mila reappeared, her MacBook tucked under her arm. She plopped down on my other side, flipping open the lid with a grin. "Got it."

I snapped my fingers, suddenly remembering. "Search Instagram. Her full name is Samantha Morrison."

Mila's fingers flew across the keyboard, her brows furrowed in concentration. The room fell silent except for the soft tapping of keys. Minutes ticked by, feeling like hours. Finally, Mila released a frustrated sigh, pushing her dark hair back from her face. "I don't see anything on her Instagram other than she's attending Brigham University in Texas, but—" Her eyes widened, a smile breaking across her face. "Wait! I found her phone number on her Facebook page."

"Fuck yes!" I practically leaped off the couch, my heart racing. My hands shook slightly as I fumbled to pull my phone from my pocket. I unlocked the screen, my finger hovering over the keypad. "What is it? I'll call her and find out exactly what Kacie said and what she told Zaiden."

"It is 865-873-0921."

I punched the numbers into the phone and pulled it to my ear." I held my breath as it continued to ring, only releasing it in a rush of air when her voicemail picked up.

"Shit," I muttered.

I knew that was too easy.

"Maybe leave her a message," Journey suggested. "She probably doesn't answer numbers she doesn't recognize."

I shook my head. "If she knows it's me, she definitely won't answer." I'd just have to keep trying.

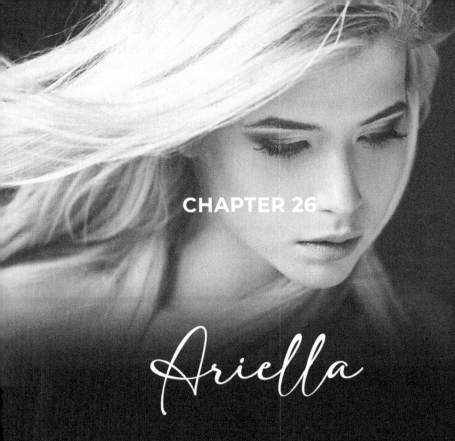

CHAPTER 26

Ariella

"Still no answer?" Journey asked as we trudged up the weathered frat house steps, our phones glowing in the dark—another failed call. We'd been calling every thirty minutes all day, and still no answer.

"Still nothing." I pocketed my phone with more force than necessary.

Mila fidgeted with her phone case, peeling at the corner. "Maybe you should leave a message."

"Or send her a text." Journey paced the creaking porch boards behind us.

If she saw my name pop up, she'd probably ignore it, especially after lying to Zaiden. "I'll keep trying until she answers."

The porch railing groaned as Mila slumped against it. "What if she never answers?"

"Then I'll—" A car door slammed somewhere in the darkness, making me jump. "I'll show up at her school."

Journey's keys jangled as she stumbled back. "In Texas?"

"Yes." The word came out sharp. I uncurled my fingers, finding half-moon marks where my nails had dug into my palms. "The longer this goes on, the more time Zaiden has to ruin my life."

We all stood side by side on the porch of the old wooden house. "I can't believe we are having a party tonight." My gaze scanned up the house. "Feels a little morbid to celebrate after what happened."

"I think everyone is just trying to find a way to move on." Journey touched my arm as we crossed the threshold, the bass vibrating in our chests.

"Plus, we have a lot to celebrate," Mila smirked. "We don't have to get on our knees anymore to keep our spots on the team."

"Yeah, and at least you don't have to worry about Zaiden here." Journey added.

"Yeah," I shrugged. Journey was right. After the first party of the year, the teams usually didn't co-mingle. "I guess." I didn't want to go out tonight, but it was kind of an unspoken requirement.

I tugged at my sleeve, already planning my escape. "I think I'm going to make a quick appearance, and then I'm bailing."

"What?" Mila's brows furrowed as she spun toward me. "EJ isn't going to like that."

The mention of his name sent a wave of irritation through me. "Not my problem. Plus, I need to keep calling

Sam, and if she doesn't pick up, I'll have to figure out another way to get a hold of her."

Mila cocked an eyebrow. "Like what?"

I shrugged. "I don't know." A plan formed as I said it. "Maybe she'll come home for Thanksgiving Break, and I can catch her then."

"That's several weeks away," Mila scowled.

"It's the only plan I have right now."

They both nodded.

"You want us to leave with you?" Journey caught my eye, her lips twitching.

I shook my head. "No, I think I'm going to make it an early night. Honestly, I'm exhausted."

"Just let us know when you're leaving," Mila shouted over the music as we strolled through the entryway into the dark living room.

"Hey, baby." EJ's voice cut through the bass, bringing with it the sharp smell of beer and cologne. My skin crawled at the pet name, one of the many unwanted "perks" of belonging to the football team.

I spun to face him, muscles aching from holding my fake smile. "Hey!" The false cheer in my voice made my throat hurt.

"You want a drink?" He was already holding a red cup.

Journey caught my eye, her lips pulling into a mischievous grin. "We're going to go mingle." Traitor. She melted into the crowd before I could grab her sleeve, leaving me stranded in EJ's orbit.

"No," I offered a polite smile. There was no way in hell I was taking a drink from anyone after what happened last time. "I'll get one later."

EJ leaned closer, his breath hot against my ear, and my

stomach curled. "You wanna get out of here and go up to my room and—"

My phone vibrated in my pocket, and I reached back, pulling it out. The screen lit up with an unknown number. "Sorry, E." I stepped back, creating space between us as I raised the phone. "I need to take this."

EJ's jaw tightened, but he backed away with a practiced casualness. "Come find me later." He disappeared into the crowd, and my shoulders finally relaxed.

"Hello?"

Bass thundered through the floorboards as I shouldered past sweating bodies. The line crackled—empty static or careful breathing, I couldn't tell.

"Hello?" I wedged into the bay window alcove, pressing one palm against my free ear.

The music pulsed around me, but the phone line remained dead silent. My reflection stared back from the dark window as I tried again: "Anyone there?" The line hummed, empty but somehow expectant.

Sighing, I pulled the phone from my ear and looked at the screen again. The call timer kept ticking up: 1:42, 1:43, 1:44.

"Okay, last chance, and I'm hanging up." A huge part of me hoped it was Sam, and we had a poor connection, but it was probably a stupid prank call.

I disconnected the call, hit my last called number again, and listened to it ring until Sam's voicemail picked up.

I hit the end-call button, and frustration burned in my chest. "Fuck," I muttered. My best friend was dead, and her brother thought I was responsible because of something this freaking girl said, and now I can't get a hold of her to say it to my freaking face. "Ugh."

A familiar cologne wrapped around me half a second before he did, and my spine stiffened.

"Something wrong, princess?" Zaiden's breath ghosted across my neck.

"What do you want?" I tried to step forward, but his arm snaked around my waist, palm spreading across my stomach. The party seemed to disappear, leaving us and the darkness beyond the window.

My heart slammed against my ribs as his grip tightened. "You're not supposed to be here." The words came out in a whisper, fear closing around my throat. "What the fuck are you doing here?"

If Zaiden was there, that only meant one thing. He was there to ruin my life just a little more.

"You shouldn't be here." I shoved at his arm, but he didn't budge. "You need to leave."

His lips brushed the shell of my ear. "It's time to repay the favor."

The heat of his breath sent chills raging over my body, but his words made my stomach clench because there was no way he was talking about the favor I was thinking about. "What favor is that?" I shoved at his arm again, and he released me.

The steady thrum of music seemed to fade, replaced by the sound of my own ragged breathing. "The one where you get on your knees for me." His chest vibrated against my back, his words reverberating through my ribcage. "And take this dick like the good girl we both know you can be."

Rage surged through me, hot and sharp. "Fuck you." I twisted, fighting against his grip until I could face him. The look in his eyes made me falter. "You're fucking crazy."

I shoved at his chest, desperate to put space between us. My palm burned where it met his body. "I'm not sucking your dick in a hall closet so you can fulfill some disgusting fantasy."

His lips twisted – not a smile, something darker. Something that made my blood run cold. "My fantasy has nothing to do with a hall closet."

My brows pulled together as he leaned in so close his minty breath ghosted across my face, making my nose twitch. "I'm more into public humiliation."

My eyes widened as understanding crashed over me. Oh God. "You wouldn't." But even as I said it, I saw the truth written in the cruel curve of his mouth, in the predatory gleam of his eyes. "Zaiden, if you do this—" My voice cracked. I swallowed hard and forced the words out. "I will be disowned by not only my team but the football team."

"It's over, Ariella," he sneered. "I'm ruining your life the same way you ruined my sisters."

My chest constricted. "I. Did. Not. Kill. Your. Sister."

Hard eyes held mine, unblinking. Searching. For what? A crack in my armor? A hint of guilt? He wouldn't find it because I wasn't responsible for her death.

"Did you even ask Sam what I did?" My voice rose, desperation clawing at my throat. "Or just took what she said and ran with it?" His silence screamed louder than any answer. The muscle in his jaw ticked. "No, you decided I was guilty because you needed someone to blame."

"It doesn't fucking matter." The casual shrug of his shoulders felt like violence.

He reached into his pocket. My heart stuttered. A

phone. Just a phone, but the sight of it made my blood freeze. The video. Oh God, the video. "You have two choices. Either I ruin your life or your friends." My chest tightened as the video flashed through my thoughts. "What do you think the grieving wife would think?" His thumb hovered over the screen. "When the videos go viral?" A pause. "And the school has painted him as a hero. What will they think?"

"Call Sam." The words burst from me, one last desperate scramble. "Ask her what she saw, Zaiden. I never talked to Kacie that night."

"Make the choice, Ariella." His voice dropped low, intimate, like we were lovers sharing secrets instead of enemies trading threats. "You or your friends."

My lip curled into a snarl even as defeat settled heavily in my gut. The choice was already made. Had been made the moment he pulled out that phone. We both knew it.

"Fine, Zaiden. You want me on my knees?" I threw out my hands, a hollow gesture of surrender. "I will." My voice dropped to a whisper. "But I will find out the truth, and when I do—"

His large hand shot out, wrapping around my upper arm. The sudden movement cut off my words as he dragged me forward. He stopped in the center of the room, jerking me against his chest.

"I know the truth." His breath was hot against my ear, but his words were Arctic cold. "Now, get on your knees."

My heart hammered against my ribs as I scanned the room—faces everywhere—the football team, cheerleaders, dancers, and football groupies.

"Zaiden, please."

His fingers flexed against my arm. "Get. On. Your. Fucking. Knees." He jabbed a finger toward the ground, the gesture almost casual. Almost. "And make it look good, princess." His voice pitched lower, meant for my ears alone. "Make it look like my cock is the best thing you've ever tasted."

The floor was cold through my leggings as I sank, wincing when my knees hit the hardwood floor. My eyes locked on his, defiance burning even as shame crawled up my spine. "You will regret this." Venom laced every syllable. "I hate you."

His hand moved too fast to dodge, pinching my chin between thumb and forefinger. His grip was deceptively gentle, like handling fine china before shattering it against a wall.

"Good." The corner of his mouth twitched. His thumb traced my bottom lip, the touch almost reverent. Almost tender. It made my skin crawl. "Now open your mouth and suck my cock like you fucking hate me." His eyes darkened, pupils blown wide. "You're going to look so pretty, gagging on my dick."

"What's going on?" EJ's voice cut through the heavy air like thunder. The crowd shifted, parting. But Zaiden's grip on my face tightened, holding me in place and forcing me to stare up at him.

"Eyes on me, princess." He didn't even glance at EJ. Didn't need to. He had his audience exactly where he wanted them.

"What the fuck are you doing here, Knight?" EJ's voice was closer now. Confused. Angry. "Why are you on the floor, Ari?"

"Tell him, Ariella." Zaiden released my jaw, but the phantom pressure remained. His hand settled on my head, fingers threading through my hair. A lover's caress twisted into something cruel. "You want me to tell him, baby?"

My throat worked against a hard swallow. The music cut out abruptly, leaving only the sound of my ragged breathing and the rustle of dozens of bodies shifting closer. The silence pressed in like a physical weight.

"Tell me what?" EJ's voice cracked. "Baby, get off the floor."

"Baby?" Zaiden's eyes widened with mock surprise. A humorless laugh bubbled from his throat. "I think we should show him." His fingers tightened in my hair. His gaze flashed to EJ. "Ariella is mine." His entire body tensed as his jaw flexed. "Now open your mouth for me."

My teeth clenched so hard, it ached. His eyes held mine.

He leaned down, lips brushing my ear. The warmth of his breath made me shudder. "Play stupid games, get stupid prizes," he whispered, the words slithering into my brain. His hand twisted, forcing me to look toward the TV, where Hawk stood waiting. "I'm only going to tell you once before Hawk shows your friends' videos to everyone."

Something inside me cracked. Splintered. Shattered.

"Fine," I ground out.

Zaiden pressed two fingers against my bottom lip. The touch was rough. "Open your mouth."

My lips parted. His fingers slid in, cold against my tongue. His thumb dug into my jaw, a silent warning.

"Good girl."

"What the fuck is going on?" EJ's shout bounced off the walls, but no one moved. No one spoke; just watched, a sea of faces hungry for the show.

For my destruction.

Zaiden bent over me, his hand shifted, gripping my cheeks until they hurt. The party lights caught his eyes—

something dark swimming in them that made my pulse spike. My heart slammed against my ribs so hard I thought they might crack. The hushed whispers of the crowd faded to white noise as I waited, suspended in this moment, for whatever cruelty came next.

He positioned his mouth above mine, and I prepared myself to kiss him, but he spit in my mouth.

He'd just laid his claim.

Time stopped. Fractured. Reality narrowed to this single point of humiliation. The hot slide of his saliva down my throat triggered a violent gag reflex. But that wasn't the worst part. The worst was knowing this was only the beginning. He'd taken my reputation and my dignity, and there was nothing I could do. Not if I wanted to protect them.

The football team would turn their backs on me now. Social suicide, executed with surgical precision. Which was exactly what he wanted.

"Unbutton my pants."

My fingers trembled as they found his zipper. The metallic sound of it lowering felt obscenely loud in the thick silence. His bulge strained against the fabric, and bile rose in my throat. This turned him on – the power, the control, the audience. The sick bastard was getting off on every second.

A movement caught my eye. Mila was in the corner, her face twisted with horror. Her body half-turned toward me, ready to intervene. I gave a tiny shake of my head against Zaiden's grip. No. This was my problem, not theirs, and I wasn't going to let them take the fall for this.

"Eyes. On. Me." His fingers dug into my cheeks, snapping my head forward. Then his hand dropped and – oh my God. The sight of him, thick and hard, made my vision swim. This was really happening. Here. Now. In front of everyone.

"Open wide for me." His fingers twisted in my hair, the sharp pain bringing tears to my eyes as he yanked me into position. His other hand gripped his cock at the base, guiding himself toward my mouth slowly. Making me wait. Making me dread.

"Just get this over with," I snarled under my breath, a final act of defiance.

He didn't hesitate. Didn't warn me. Just shoved past my lips straight to the back of my throat in one brutal thrust. The crowd erupted—whistles, shouts, cheers. Men egging him on like this was a fucking sport. My hands clenched into fists against my thighs as my eyes squeezed shut, fighting against the invasion.

But he didn't move. He held himself there, deep, cutting off my air. Panic clawed up my chest as seconds ticked by. My eyes flew open, meeting his. The wild look there made my blood run cold, he was enjoying this. The struggle. The fight.

My vision started to blur at the edges. Spots danced in front of my eyes. My hands shot up to his thighs, nails digging through denim as I fought for a breath. For control. For anything.

The edges of consciousness started to fade, and still, he watched. Still, he waited until the last possible second when my body was on the verge of collapse.

He jerked back, leaving me gasping. My lungs burned as I sucked in air around the thick head of his cock. Stars burst behind my eyes.

"And now," his voice carried across the silent room, "I'm going to ride your face like you rode mine, princess," he said loud enough so the entire room could hear him.

His grip tightened in my hair until tears pricked my eyes, but my hiss of pain drowned beneath the wet sound of him slamming back into my throat. Deep. Hard. Brutal. There was no mercy in his violent strokes.

No time to breathe. No time to think. Only the relentless rhythm of him fucking my mouth. Each thrust forced a desperate gasp between strokes. Survival instinct took over–counting seconds, timing breaths, fighting the urge to panic.

Tears streamed hot down my face, pooling on my thighs. Drool trickled past my stretched lips, dripping onto the floor. The physical humiliation was complete. But then I made the mistake of looking up.

His eyes. God, his eyes.

Something electric passed between us. Something that made my thighs clench together involuntarily. Wrong. So wrong. My body's betrayal felt worse than anything else he'd done.

The crowd disappeared. The room faded. Nothing existed except the savage rhythm of his hips, the burning in my throat, the ache of my jaw, and that scorching gaze that seemed to see right through me. Hatred and arousal twisted together until I couldn't tell them apart.

His abs tightened. His breathing turned ragged. "Fuck." The word came out strangled as he drove deep one final time. Hot spurts hit the back of my throat, forcing me to swallow or choke.

Then—emptiness.

The violent sensation of him pulling out. The sound of him zipping up as I collapsed forward, lungs heaving. The room spun as oxygen rushed back to my brain.

Through tear-blurred eyes, I saw the crowd. All guys. All cheering. For him. My gaze found EJ's face, the disgust there cut deep. I wiped desperately at the mixture of spit and tears on my chin, but the damage was done.

Zaiden's breath was hot against my ear again. His words were soft. Intimate. Devastating. "And now you belong to me."

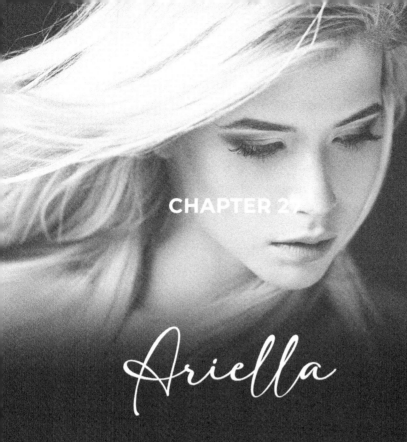

CHAPTER 27

Ariella

"**G**et. On. Your. Knees."
My eyes flashed open, heart hammering against my ribs, each pulse point throbbing beneath sweat-slicked skin. I kicked off the blanket, its weight suffocating. My gaze darted to each shadow in the corners, to the barely open closet door, to the closed bedroom door, searching, expecting Zaiden to be somewhere lurking in the dimly lit room.

Silence. Empty space. Nothing but my own ragged breathing.

It was just a dream.

The phantom sensation of his command still vibrated in my ears, my skin still electric with goosebumps. It should have felt like a nightmare—my rational mind insisted it should—but the flush spreading across my chest, the dryness in my throat, and the damp fabric between my thighs portrayed it as something else entirely: a fantasy.

I breathed a heavy sigh of irritation as my eyes shifted to the bedroom window. Moonlight filtered through the half-drawn blinds, casting zebra-stripe shadows across my rumpled sheets.

The digital clock's red numbers—3:42 AM—mocked my unsuccessful attempts at sleep after everything that had happened earlier that night.

I'd been so humiliated when I ran out of the party, all eyes following my hasty retreat. But what twisted my stomach even more was realizing that beneath the shame burned something so much deeper, something so unex-pected—arousal. The same man who had publicly humili-ated me had awakened something I hadn't even known existed.

My eyes closed, and the image of the dark ink above Zaiden's cock that was standing at attention flashed through my memories.

"Fuck," I groaned, rolling to my back as my eyes flicked open. "What the fuck is wrong with you?"

Zaiden blackmailed me into doing something I never would have done on my own, or at least I don't think I would have, but the way my body was reacting to the entire thing made me realize I didn't know much about myself when it came to sex, fantasies, and desire.

Sighing heavily, I closed my eyes, realizing there was only one way I was going to ease this sexual frustration building within me. Unfortunately, Zaiden still had my vibrator, but truthfully, that wasn't what I wanted. I wanted to feel skin-to-skin, even if it was mine and not his.

I stroked my fingertips across my collarbone slowly, sensually. I shouldn't be doing this. Not while thinking of him. Not after what he did.

And yet.

My fingers continued their path downward, each touch a silent rebellion against my better judgment. I tried summoning outrage, disgust, anything to drown out the want. But with each passing second, my resistance weakened.

My hand lowered, trailing between my breasts. My nipples tightened as cool air hit them, mixing with the erotic thoughts I couldn't stop. Didn't want to stop. My hand continued down my stomach and dipped below the elastic band of my panties.

I sucked in a slow breath letting my body relax as I let my new fantasy play without interruption. The one where Zaiden pinned me down, taking whatever he wanted from me. My fingers slid through my already soaking wet flesh, finding my clit.

This was a whole new experience. I'd masturbated before, but only with a vibrator, and it was always a quick release. I'd never used my fingers or savored the moment, the feeling of what I remembered his touch felt like.

My fingers moved in tight little circles over my clit, first slow, teasing. I pulled back each time the sensation intensified, prolonging the moment and torturing myself with restraint.

Would he be patient or demanding? Would he savor or devour?

I was pretty sure I knew the answers to those questions.

I increased pressure gradually, my body begging for more even as my mind tried to maintain control. The last remnant of power I had was choosing when to surrender. I imagined Zaiden's breath on my neck, hot then cool as he exhaled against dampened skin. His tongue traced lazy patterns across my nipples before suddenly taking one between his teeth. His fingers—God, his fingers—pushing inside me, curling forward in a beckoning motion while his palm pressed firmly against my pubic bone. All while I remembered the perfect weight of his hand around my throat, how instinctively he'd known exactly how much pressure to apply.

My back arched off the bed, spine curving, my lips parting with a gasp that seemed to echo in the darkness. Every nerve ending sparked and tingled as the feeling brought me to the edge of ecstasy, my toes curling against the cool cotton sheets.

I pictured his weight pressing me firmly into the mattress. The pressure against my chest. The heat of his skin. His breath against my neck. And then—his cock slipping inside, filling me completely.

That was all it took.

A bolt of pleasure ripped through me as my entire body tensed, and I let the orgasm take hold of me, holding my breathing hostage until I cried out his name in a violent exhale of air.

My body went limp against the mattress, the momentary bliss already giving way to a complicated knot of emotions. My cheeks burned not just from what I'd done but from the realization that I'd surrendered completely to the fantasy of him and how loud I'd been doing it. The pleasure had been undeniable, but now shame crept in.

Since he wasn't busting down my door, I assumed he wasn't home or hadn't heard me anyway.

I rolled to my side as exhaustion washed over me, my limbs heavy, my mind finally quieting. Sleep approached like a merciful friend, and I surrendered to it gratefully.

CHAPTER 28

Ariella

Click. Click. Click. Each photo from the party blurred into the next as I hunched in a dark corner of the library. Three days of searching, and still no sign of Kacie in any of them. Still no clue as to what really happened that night. The lights hummed overhead, a sound that had become the soundtrack to my obsession.

I pulled my feet into the chair, wrapping my arm around my legs. I hit the enter button over and over, flipping through all the pictures from the party the night Kacie died, but nothing stood out.

It had been three days since Zaiden publicly humiliated me, and I hadn't seen him since I ran out of the party with mascara streaked down my cheeks, more determined than ever to prove I had nothing to do with Kacie's death. I'd spent every day since I left that party flipping through pictures, looking for anything that might explain what actually happened, but so far, nothing.

A shadow fell across my screen. I flinched, expecting another whispered accusation from a passing student, but it was Journey's concerned face peering down at me. Mila hovered behind her, scanning the library like a lookout. "We've been looking everywhere for you," Journey whispered.

I shrank deeper into my seat, feeling the familiar tightness in my throat, the one that came whenever someone pitied me. "You shouldn't be here." The words came out rough, sandpaper-raw. "Being seen with me is—"

"Social suicide?" Mila cut in. Her bag hit the table with a thud that made me flinch. Not from the noise but from the fierce loyalty behind it. "Yeah, we don't give a fuck, and I can't believe you think we would."

"If you need a few days to recover from whatever the fuck that was the other night," she shrugged, "fine but don't ghost us. We're still your friends."

"Plus, we know there had to be a good reason you did it." They both raised questioning eyebrows. "So if you want to talk about it—"

"If I didn't do it, he was going to make the videos of all of us with Coach go viral."

"Oh," Journey's eyes went wide. "Not a good time for that, considering he's a town hero right now."

"Yeah," I muttered as my gaze dropped back to the computer, and I hit the enter button again.

"What are you doing?" Journey asked, pulling out a chair and sliding in before setting her laptop on the table in front of her.

"Flipping through those pictures Cody sent me," I

shook my head, "but there's nothing. I haven't seen Kacie in any of them."

"Well," Mila smirked. "We've been calling and texting because we think we might have found something."

"What?" I dropped my feet to the ground as my spine stiffened.

"We figured what happened the other night had something to do with this whole revenge thing because of Kacie. So, we decided to go back through everyone's social media posts the night of the party. There were thousands of photos, by the way."

"Okay, but what did you find?"

"This." Journey's laptop screen cast a sickly blue glow across the table.

At first, my tired brain registered only the surface details: another party selfie, another grinning classmate smiling for the camera. Just one more dead end in an endless search.

Then I saw it.

In the shadowy background, half-hidden by a red Solo cup, Kacie's face was frozen. I knew exactly what she was looking at, even before my eyes tracked her sightline across the frame.

Me–

And Zaiden.

"Oh my God." The words escaped in a whisper as my hand flew to my mouth. "She saw us that night."

The truth crashed over me. She hadn't disappeared; she'd run. Run because her best friend had betrayed her, or that was what she thought she'd seen that night.

"So it was your fault?" Mila's brows twisted, her voice sharp with accusation.

"No." The word came out hard, certain. I slammed my

laptop shut, the crack of plastic on plastic echoing through the library's quiet. "It was Zaiden's."

My hands shook as I reached across the table, but I forced them steady enough to screenshot the photo. One-click to email it to myself. Evidence.

"I didn't kiss him." The words tumbled out now, urgent and raw. "He kissed me. I told him no, I wasn't going to do it behind Kacie's back." My voice cracked. "But he kissed me anyway."

"Wait?" Journey frowned. "So you and Zaiden were dating?"

"No, but—" The memory of stolen glances and almost-touches burned in my throat. I swallowed hard. "We both liked each other, and we wanted to."

My fingers traced unconscious patterns on the table's surface, mapping out the maze of good intentions and bad choices that had led us here. "I told him I was going to talk to Kacie and do things right, but he said no."

The bitter laugh that escaped surprised even me. "He said he wanted to tell her himself. Another lie to add to the collection." My nails dug into the wooden table. "Instead, he kept pushing. Testing limits. Playing games."

"When I finally stood up to him, I told him I wasn't going to sneak around behind Kacie's back. I tried to walk away." The memory rolled through me like thunder. "But he grabbed me. Pulled me back. Kissed me, and I kissed him back."

"Woah," Journey said. "So he's been blaming you this whole time, and it's actually been his fault?" She shook her head slowly. "He's not going to take that news well."

"I don't care how he takes it," I snarled, pushing out of my chair. "I need to go find him and put an end to this nightmare."

"Actually," Mila said. "There's more." My brows pulled together, and she nodded to the chair, signaling I should sit back down for this. "The night of Kacie's accident, my brother was doing a ride-along with the officer who was first on the scene. I knew this, but it never dawned on me until this morning to ask him what happened that night. Well, I didn't want to know details about how she died, but—" She paused briefly, adjusting in her seat. "But I thought maybe he could tell us if she was drunk or not."

"And?"

"And he said—" Mila's voice wavered, and something in her tone made my skin prickle. "She was alive when they arrived."

The world tilted sideways. My chest tightened until each heartbeat felt like it might crack my ribs. Kacie, alive. Conscious. Speaking. Every word bringing us back to the moment I found out my best friend was gone.

"He said she told them she wasn't drinking."

"Well, that matches Cody's story," I managed, though my tongue felt numb and clumsy with the weight of the implications.

Mila's fingers fidgeted in front of her. "She told them her brakes quit working."

The words hit like ice water.

"Failed?" My mind raced back to the official story, the one everyone knew. "But the police report—"

"Said she was drunk." Mila leaned forward, her chair creaking under the shift of weight.

A pause.

"Except," Mila's voice dropped so low I had to lean in to hear, "my brother swears she was sober when they found her."

The implications hit me one by one, each realization a fresh shock.

The official report twisted it into a lie.

My fingers dug into the edge of the table. "Someone," I said slowly, tasting each word, "wanted everyone to think this was just another drunk driving accident."

The truth of it settled over our little group. There was some reason that the officer wanted everyone to think Kacie was drinking and driving that night. But what?

My chair scraped against the floor as I stood. I finally had my answer. I knew what Kacie had seen that night that made her run, but now there were even more unanswered questions. "First," I pushed back out of my chair. "I'm going to deal with Zaiden, and then I'm going to find out what really went down that night."

CHAPTER 29

ZAIDEN

Pushing off the weight bench to a sitting position, I swiped my white towel across my sweaty forehead. I met my gaze in the mirror, realizing I no longer recognized myself. Who'd I'd become since Kacie's death was someone completely different.

I thought back to Ariella on her knees. It felt good to see her submissive to me. To ruin her. To humiliate her. It felt like retribution for my sister's death, but something about her last few words haunted me. She'd asked me if I'd asked Sam what she actually saw. I hadn't, and I couldn't explain why. It wasn't like me to take someone at their word, but I did, and I wasn't sure why. Did I need someone to blame so much that it didn't matter who it was or what actually happened? Or was it something else?

When our parents' affair became public after Kacie's death, my mother moved out, and her mother moved in; it made it so much easier to hate her.

The door to the gym flung open, banging against the wall as Ariella appeared in the doorway.

Fuck.

I hadn't seen her since everything had gone down at the football party, and I wasn't in the right headspace to deal with her yet.

"I need to talk to you." Ariella planted herself in the doorway, her shoulders squared like a boxer entering the ring.

Pushing off the weight bench, I tossed the white towel over my shoulder. "Not now, Ariella," I said dryly as I circled the bench, already reaching for my gym bag. "I'm busy."

"Too fucking bad." Her palms slammed between my shoulder blades, the force of her shove making me stumble slightly.

Every muscle in my back coiled tight. I spun to face her, using my height to loom over her small frame, a move that usually had people stepping back and looking away. But Ariella's chin tilted up, her eyes hard, and something in my chest twisted at how small she looked and how fucking fearless she stayed.

"What is it, princess?" I stepped into her personal space, a cocky smirk pulling at the corners of my lips. "You miss my cock in your mouth?"

Her lip curled into a snarl. "You will never do that to me again."

I huffed out a humorless laugh. "Let's not pretend you didn't love it, princess." I took a step forward, bumping my chest into hers. "Let's not pretend it didn't make your panties wet." Her cheeks flushed. "On your knees, under my complete control, claiming you in front of everyone. It turned you on, didn't it, baby?"

"You're a psychopath." Ariella's hands trembled against my chest as she shoved me, the shake in her voice betraying everything her fierce expression tried to hide.

My heart hammered against my ribs as I leaned down, close enough to catch the faint scent of her shampoo, close enough that my breath stirred the loose strands of hair around her face. I waited for her to back away, to show even a flicker of the fear I wanted to see. Instead, she held her ground, and I felt the steady rhythm of her breathing brush against my skin—too controlled, too calm, like she knew exactly what game we were playing.

"Next time," I let the heat of my breath fan across her skin, "I'll bend you over and fuck you from behind."

She shoved her hand into my chest, and I let her push me away, snickering, knowing how I got under her skin. "You will never touch me again."

I rolled my eyes and turned away from her, slowly strolling towards the treadmill. "I think you've forgotten who holds all the power here."

"It's me," she said so confidently that it stopped me in my tracks, and I turned to look at her. "Do you want to know why?" I raised my brows but didn't answer. "Because of this."

My gaze followed as she held up her phone, zoning in on the picture. My brows pulled together in confusion. It was a selfie of some girl we'd gone to high school with. My eyes shifted back to hers, amusement dancing in them. "I don't even know who that is."

"Her name is Sarah, and we went to high school with her." My brows raised. "And she captured the real reason your sister left the party early that night." My gaze flashed back to the picture. "If you look in the background behind Sarah, you'll see Kacie, and if you keep looking, you'll see what she saw that night that made her leave."

I leaned in to get a better look as I scanned the picture, trying to take in exactly what I was looking at. Kacie's strawberry blonde hair should have stood out the first time I looked, but it didn't. I followed Kacie's line of sight, and my breath caught. She saw me kiss Ariella that night.

My head started to spin, and my pulse raced as it sank in. Kacie thought I'd betrayed her. She was angry with me, not Ariella.

"I guess you're realizing that it wasn't my fault." She pushed a finger into my chest. "It was yours." I shook my head as I struggled to accept that my sister was dead because of me, and on top of it, I'd punished Ariella for it. "This was the reason I wanted you to tell her. She thought we were sneaking around behind her back."

"We weren't." I dragged a hand down my face, tasting the bitter truth of what I'd really wanted back then. Ariella had been the only one with enough sense to stop it, but I'd wanted her so fucking bad I was willing to risk it.

"But that's not what it looks like in that picture." She thrust the phone in my face, her knuckles white around the case. "If you had just told her—"

"I couldn't, Ariella—" The words ripped from my throat as I cut her off, pacing like a caged animal. "I couldn't tell her."

Her brows pulled together as her arms dropped to her side. "Why not?"

I shoved my hand through my sweaty hair. "Because she made me promise not to ever mess with you."

"What?" Her forehead creased, eyes narrowing to dark slits. "When?"

"After the sleepover, when we kissed after playing spin the bottle." My fingers traced the edge of the bench as the memory surfaced, sharp and clear. "The next morning, after everyone left, we were sitting in the kitchen, and she brought it up and asked me if I liked you."

"We were kids—"

"Yeah." A humorless laugh escaped me as I met Ariella's gaze in the gym mirror. "She told me I could have anyone I wanted. Just not you. You were important to her, and she didn't want to share you with me. At that time, it didn't matter, but then, it did."

"I had no idea she ever said that." Ariella's voice dropped to a whisper as she closed the distance between us. The anger in her stance softened for the first time. "But do you know what she said to me?" Another step forward. "Three days before she died." I shrugged. "It was Kacie, Mila, Journey, Kayla, and me, and we had to pick who we thought would be perfect for our friends."

"Okay?"

"Kacie picked you for me. She liked the idea of me being her sister-in-law someday."

"I don't understand."

"She'd been trying to hook us up, and I said no, but then we hung out that night when Kacie fell asleep early, and I thought we had a connection. I didn't want to sneak around."

"I promised her."

"When she was thirteen, Zaiden." Her lip curled up into a snarl.

"This was all my fault."

She blew out a heavy sigh before slowly shaking her head. "This wasn't your fault. It wasn't my fault."

"It was an accident, right?"

"Actually—" Ariella wrapped her arms around herself, something dark flickering across her face. "I'm not sure."

CHAPTER 30

Ariella

My fingers uncurled from their fists, one joint at a time, as the familiar rage ebbed away. Damn Zaiden. Damn him for destroying my life, and damn me for the unwanted sympathy that crept in whenever I saw that haunted look in his eyes. He'd thrown blame around like weapons, desperate to make someone—anyone—responsible for Kacie's death. Only to end up cutting himself deepest when he learned the truth: she'd left the party that night because of him.

But that didn't change the fact that he wasn't responsible for her death.

I had a gut feeling that someone else was, but I had to figure out who, and I wasn't even sure where to start.

"What are you talking about?" Zaiden's voice cut

through the humid gym air. He dragged the towel across his face, but his eyes never left mine, sharp, predatory.

My jaw ached from clenching, a physical reminder to keep my mouth shut. Looking at him now made my stomach twist—part disgust, part that old, traitorous pull that refused to die. Getting involved with Zaiden again would be like reaching into a tiger's cage, especially after everything he'd done to me.

"Nothing." The lie tasted bitter as I turned toward the door, measuring each step like I was walking on glass. "I have to go."

I'd almost made it to the door when a strong arm hooked around my waist, jerking me back. I winced when the door slammed shut.

His arm tightened, molding me against the hard planes of his body. Sweat dampened his shirt where it pressed to mine, and the heat of him seeped through the thin fabric, a phantom caress that sent electricity dancing across my skin.

"Let me go." I meant it. I did. But my body remembered other times he'd held me like this–times when his touch had been welcomed, addictive. Dangerous. The slight tremor in my voice gave me away, and his knowing smirk told me he hadn't missed it.

"If you know something, start talking." His hands lingered a heartbeat too long before he released me. I spun to face him, hating how my skin burned where he'd touched me, hating more how much I wanted him to do it again. "Do you want to do this the hard way?" I stepped back. "I like the hard way."

The wall hit my back, knocking the air from my lungs, the truth about Kacie's brakes burned in my throat, demanding to be spoken. But working with Zaiden meant letting him back in, and after everything he'd done to me, I didn't want him anywhere near me.

"Ariella." The way he said my name—low, rough, almost a growl, sent heat curling in my stomach. His hands bracketed my head, his body forming a cage of muscle and barely-leashed control. "What are you hiding from me?"

Slowly shaking my head, I made the mistake of meeting his eyes, wide with something that wasn't just anger. My breath caught, drawing in the scent of him— clean sweat and pure male. His gaze dropped to my lips as I pressed them together, and the temperature between us spiked. The smallest movement would bring us together or could shatter everything.

"Liar." He moved closer, each inch between us crackling with electricity. His breath fanned across my lips, and memory flooded my senses—the taste of him, the way he'd once made me forget everything but his touch. "Your pulse is racing, baby. Is that fear—" His fingers ghosted over my throat. "Or something else?"

I shoved my hands into his hard chest as I averted my gaze. "No, I'm not lying."

He grabbed my wrists, slamming them into the wall above my head. "Yes, you are." His grip tightened around my wrist as he pushed his pointer finger into my palm. "You want to know how I know?" I bit down on my bottom lip but didn't answer. "Because you chew the corner of your lip when you lie."

A chill crawled down my spine as recognition hit. He was right, and the fact that he still knew me made my skin prickle. I forced my teeth to release my lip, tasting the faint impression they'd left behind. "It's a nervous tick."

He shook his head. "No, when you're nervous, your hands fidget."

I met those infuriatingly knowing blue eyes, trying to forge my unease into something sharper, safer, like annoyance. But my racing pulse betrayed me. A year apart, and he could still read me like a book he'd memorized.

"You don't know me," I breathed. Heat bloomed where his chest nearly touched mine.

"You're wrong, baby." His voice roughened as he traced his nose along my jawline. "I've made you my life's study. Every reaction—" His lips brushed mine, making me shiver. "Every emotion—" His eyes darkened as they tracked the movement. "If they'd offered a degree in Ariella Ledger, I would've written the textbook." My breath hitched. "So I know when you're lying, and right now you are lying."

"I think someone tampered with Kacie's brakes." The words came out in a rush.

Zaiden went still, the deadly stillness of a predator processing a threat. His fingers tightened on my wrists for one burning moment before he released me and stepped back.

"Explain." The command was barely more than a whisper, but it filled the space between us.

I gulped in air, my lungs finally remembering how to work. "A walk." My hand trembled as I gestured toward the door. "I can't, I need air."

"If you try to run—" The threat coiled beneath his words.

"I won't." We both knew the truth—he was faster, stronger, and far more ruthless. Running was just another way to lose.

I followed him out of our home gym, through the house, to the backyard. "Now talk."

"Mila's brother was there that night. He was doing a ride-along when they found Kacie. She wasn't drunk, Zaiden. Before she—" The word 'died' lodged in my throat. "She told them her brakes failed."

"No." Zaiden's face drained of color. "The police report —" His fingers curled into fists. "The official report said—"

"The official report lied." I wrapped my arms around myself as a cool gust of wind swirled around me. "Which makes me think something is off. I think someone might have been trying to kill her."

He shook his head again. "Who would want my sister dead?"

"I don't know, but that morning, she told me she'd found something out and needed to talk to me, but she didn't say what. She wanted to talk in person." My gaze darted around as I tried to piece everything together. "Your dad is a powerful man. Maybe someone killed her to get to your dad."

Zaiden's eyes widened. "She was driving my mom's car that night. Maybe it was my mom who was the target."

Zaiden's mom and sister drove the same car, right down to the interior and exterior colors. So it would be hard to tell the difference if you didn't know. "Why?"

"It was a last-minute change. Kacie went out to her car, and it wouldn't start, so my mom tossed her the keys to her car."

"But if your mom was the target, then why did they never go after her again?"

He shook his head. "I don't know, but I'm going to find out."

"It's too bad we don't have the car so we could check the brake line to see if it was cut."

"We do." Something dangerous flickered in Zaiden's eyes. "Dad 'inherited' a junkyard a few years back."

"Inherited?"

"Trust me." His smile didn't reach his eyes. "Some questions are better left unasked."

I swallowed hard, remembering exactly who I was dealing with—not just Zaiden, but the entire Knight family and their empire of carefully buried secrets.

"Do you know how to tell if a brake line's been cut?"

"No, but I know someone who would. I'll call him and see if he can meet us there."

"Zaiden." My voice cracked on his name, and I hated myself for it. "This changes nothing between us. We find out who hurt Kacie, and then—" I forced steel into my spine, ice into my words. "I don't want to be your friend. We will work together this one time, but after that, I don't ever want to talk to you again."

His eyes softened in that dangerous way I remembered —the calm before the storm. "We can discuss that when this is over."

I shook my head. "There's nothing to discuss. You did exactly what you wanted to do. You wanted to humiliate me, to isolate me from not only my school but my friends and team, and you did. All for something I didn't do. I want nothing to do with you after this."

Holding my gaze for a long moment, he finally nodded. "Okay."

CHAPTER 31

ZAIDEN

My boots sank deeper with each step, the ground soft from yesterday's rain. Stacks of crushed cars loomed on either side, their jagged edges catching the moonlight. Ariella's footsteps fell in perfect rhythm with mine, almost like she was afraid to let the distance between us grow.

A loose piece of metal creaked somewhere to our left. Ariella's breath caught. The sound of her stumbling closer was exactly what I'd been waiting for.

"How much further, Zaiden?" She quickened her pace, nearly stepping on my heels.

My lips curled into a grin. Ariella's fear was intoxicating. I'd always loved how scared she was of the dark, and that I was her safe spot. It wasn't Ariella's fear specifically that was intoxicating. It was how she held on to me when she was scared. It was how I made her feel safe. Even now, when I'd been the monster of her nightmares, she still trusted me to protect her.

"It's right up here." The brush of her fingers against mine sent a familiar jolt through my arm. She fell into step beside me, close enough that her shoulder bumped mine with each step. "My dad had them put it in the back so he wouldn't have to see it every time he came here."

Ariella's head swiveled left, then right. "It's really dark out here." Her voice had that slight tremor she always tried to hide.

My head lifted, taking in the glow of the full moon. "Don't worry, I'm the only big bad wolf out here." Glancing out of the corner of my eye to Ariella. Her fear of the dark was greater than her fear of me, and that piqued my curiosity. "Why are you scared of the dark anyway?"

"I'm not scared." Ariella lifted her chin, but her fingers twisted the hem of her shirt.

I cut her a look. "Seriously?" She said that like I'd never met her before, like I didn't know her better than, well, I'd bet on anyone.

"Even if it were true, why would I tell you anything?" She wrapped her arms around herself, creating a barrier between us. Her eyes were fixed on a point somewhere in the distance. "Like I would give you anything else you could use against me."

Fuck.

Blowing out a heavy breath, I stopped and twisted into her path, stopping her, and her spine stiffened. "I'm sorry for blaming you for Kacie's death."

"If you think that I'm going to forgive you—"

"I don't."

"Then why are you apologizing?"

"Because—" I trailed off. I'd spent a year hating Ariella. I'd spent months planning how I was going to destroy her, only to find out it wasn't her fault. It was mine. If I'd listened to Ariella, to begin with, Kacie wouldn't have left the party that night upset. "Because I am sorry." My hands curled around her waist. "I blamed myself after Kacie died, and then when Sam pointed the finger at you, I didn't even need proof. I needed to blame you."

"Well," she shoved my hands off her, "that doesn't change the fact that you ruined my life."

"Did I, though?" The corner of my mouth lifted in that way I knew made her blood boil.

"What? Yes." Ariella's hands balled into fists at her sides. Her voice cracked between fury and something rawer. "You isolated me from my team, EJ won't even look at me, and you—"

"I what, Ariella?" I hooked an arm around her waist, drawing her against me. Her pulse hammered where my fingers pressed against her skin, betraying everything her glare tried to deny. "I made your panties wet. I got rid of the dick that drugged you at the party."

She shoved at my chest, but I didn't let her go. "You don't know that."

"True." I traced my thumb along my bottom lip, watching her eyes track the movement. "But it doesn't matter. You're not into him."

"I'm not into you either." Ariella's voice wavered on the last word as she bit down on the corner of her lip. Some things never change.

"Liar." The grin spread across my face as her pupils dilated. I leaned closer, close enough to see the pulse jumping in her throat. "Tell me something, did you go home and touch yourself that night?"

Her hands slammed into my chest. I let the impact separate us this time, but not before catching the way her breath quickened. "You can say whatever you want, Ariella, but I did you a favor."

"Whatever, Zaiden." The words came out as a hiss between clenched teeth. She wrapped her arms around herself, shoulders hunching against the night air—or maybe against the truth. "Can we just get this over with so I can go home?"

"Tell me why you're scared of the dark."

She shook her head.

"No."

"Okay," I crossed my arms over my chest. "Then tell me this: Do you feel safe from the dark when you're with me?"

"I'm not answering that." She sidestepped around me and started walking forward.

I spun around, a huge smile spreading across my face. "Isn't that odd?" I followed behind her. "The person you hate most in this world is also the one person you feel safe with."

She stopped whipping around and shoving her finger into my chest. "You're a massive dick, and I do hate you, but," her hand dropped to her side, "I know you won't let anyone else hurt me." She was right. It didn't matter what I said about her or did to her. If anyone else even looked at her wrong, I would kill them. "So yes, I feel safe from the darkness with you, but I do not trust you, and I know I'm not safe from you."

"And why are you scared of the dark?"

She blew out a heavy sigh. "It's stupid."

"Tell me anyway."

"There's absolutely no reason," she said. "It's a completely irrational fear, but it doesn't matter how many times I tell myself that I can't control it. I guess it's kind of like someone who's scared of heights. I'm scared of the dark."

Something about her answer relaxed me, knowing that something traumatizing didn't happen to her to cause her fears.

"You weren't safe when I wanted revenge. I don't want revenge anymore." I wanted her the same way I wanted her before Kacie died. I guess I never really stopped wanting her, except I wasn't sure she'd ever forgive me.

I shifted to remove my jacket. "Here." I held it out. "You're cold. Wear this."

"I would rather eat my own toes for dinner."

"It's just a jacket, Ariella, not a marriage proposal."

"We both know what wearing that letterman's jacket means."

I huffed out a laugh. "What does it mean?"

She shook her head, ignoring my question. "Can we please find this car so we can get out of here?" She twisted back around and started walking again. "Where is this guy at?"

"The car's over this way." I slipped my hand into hers, and for the first time, she didn't fight me. I led her through a pile of stacked cars. On the other side was Kacie's, or, technically, my mom's car.

The hood slammed against the frame with a metallic crack that echoed through the junkyard, but it didn't click closed because of the damage. Kevin's flashlight beam swept over us. "Bout time you get here." The light lingered on Ariella. "Who's that?"

My shoulder angled slightly between them. "This is Ariella. She was Kacie's best friend."

Ariella raised her hand in a small wave, but her other hand squeezed mine a little tighter.

Kevin stood by the car's crumpled front end, his fingers tracing the damaged metal. He wiped his hands on his oil-covered white shirt, leaving more dark smudges. "Can't be one hundred percent sure because of the damage and the amount of time it's been sitting here, but—" His jaw tightened. "If I had to put a bet on whether or not it was or wasn't. I'd bet my entire pot on it was."

My gaze shifted, catching Ariella's and holding for a long minute. Ariella didn't know Kevin like I did. She had no idea he was a car expert. While everyone was getting ready for college, he was working in his dad's shop. When we all left for college, he was taking tech classes to learn everything he could about the ins and outs of a car, and if he was willing to bet the brakes were tampered with, then they definitely were.

"I took a few pictures and sent them to your phone, showing you exactly what I saw so you'd have them if you needed them."

I shoved my hand into my pocket, grabbing a wad of money. "Thanks." Pulling my hand out, I shoved the money toward him.

He shook his head. "Nah, this one was on the house. Your sister deserved better than this. I hope you figure out who did it and give them exactly what they deserve." Shoving the money back in my pocket, I nodded. When I found out who did this, I was going to bury them. "I parked at the back gate." He threw a thumb over his shoulder. "Let me know if you need anything else."

We stood silently for a long minute, watching until Kevin disappeared into the darkness.

"So she was murdered."

"Looks that way." The truth about Kacie's death had been here all along, rusting away in my father's junkyard while I'd spent a year plotting and planning how I was going to destroy the wrong person. "Listen carefully. We can't tell anyone about this."

"Journey and Mila—" She moved to reach for her phone in her back pocket.

I caught her wrist before she could reach it. The touch sent electricity through both of us, and she jerked away like she'd been burned. "We can let them know tomorrow when we meet up." My voice dropped to barely above a whisper, paranoia creeping in with the shadows. "But no text. No phone calls, and we don't bring anyone in that we don't trust."

Ariella's eyes widened as understanding dawned. She gave a sharp nod.

My fingers drummed against my thigh as pieces started clicking into place. "If someone was after my mom, then it probably had something to do with my dad, and he's been in bed with some bad people."

Ariella stepped closer, her eyes scanning the darkness beyond the car. "So you think they were for sure after your mom?" The question came out soft as if she was afraid the wrong ears might hear it.

I raised my shoulders. "No one knew that my mom and Kacie switched cars that night except me, Kacie, my mom, and my dad."

"True," she said. "I didn't even know."

A roll of thunder echoed through the silence. "We should get out of here before it rains."

A branch snapped somewhere in the darkness. Ariella's whole body jerked, her shoulder ramming into mine. "What was that?"

The rustling grew louder, dry leaves skittering across the pavement. Before I could open my mouth, she launched herself at me, fingers clawing into my shirt. "What the fuck is that?"

Her body molded against mine, every curve finding its familiar place. My arms locked around her automatically as she buried her face in my chest, her racing heart echoing through both our bodies.

"It's probably a raccoon." A laugh bubbled up before I could stop it. It was not because of her fear—it was because of how perfectly she still fit against me, how her body remembered what her mind wanted to forget. The familiar scent of her shampoo, vanilla, and something floral filled my lungs. Every tremor that ran through her body echoed in mine.

"It's not funny." The words vibrated against my collarbone, her lips brushing my skin through my shirt.

"No, it's not." My hands found their way to her hips. One smooth motion, and she was up, legs wrapping around my waist like they belonged there.

Ariella's breath hitched. Her fingers clutched my shoulders, caught between pushing away and pulling closer. "What are you doing?"

"Protecting you from the big, bad animals running around out here."

She opened her mouth like she wanted to argue, but she must have been scared enough to decide against it. Instead, she wrapped her arms around my neck and hooked her legs around my back. "Let's get out of here, please," she hummed against my neck, and my dick twitched against the denim of my jeans, reminding me how badly I wanted her, and I knew she wanted me too, even if she wasn't willing to admit it yet.

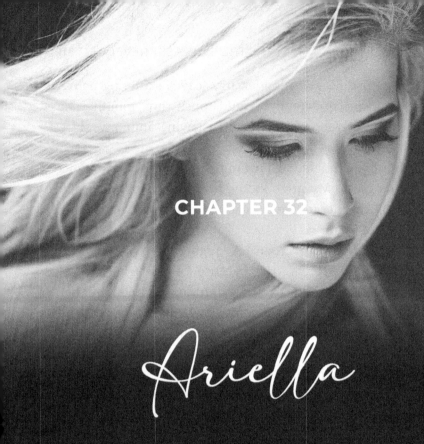

CHAPTER 32

Ariella

One a.m. The red numbers on my alarm clock pulsed like a warning. Sleep should have come easily after everything that happened, but every time I closed my eyes, all I could see was Kacie's car, and all I could feel was Zaiden's warm arms wrapped around me. I hated that the grief of losing my best friend kept tangling up with memories of him, the one person I'd sworn to never trust again, but I couldn't stop thinking about Zaiden and the way my body reacted to him even after everything he'd done to me.

Shoving a hand through my hair, pushing it out of my face, I squeezed my eyes closed. This room felt like the walls were closing in, and it was suffocating. My eyes flashed open, staring into the darkness beyond my bedroom window. I needed fresh air, but it was so dark outside.

I stepped up to my bedroom window and stared down at the empty driveway. I hated being in this house without Kacie, but even more, I hated being alone. Zaiden had come back with me, but he must have left afterward because his bike wasn't where we'd left it. I should have felt relieved that he was gone, but I wasn't.

My chest tightened to a suffocating level. "Fuck it," I groaned, spinning and storming out of the room. If I didn't get some air, I was going to die. I pounded down the stairs through the kitchen and burst through the back door leading to the patio. Closing my eyes, I sucked in a deep breath of the humid air. My shoulders relaxed. This was exactly what I needed.

A splash shattered the night's silence, and my eyes flashed open. Zaiden rose from the pool like something from a nightmare—or a dream—water streaming down his bare chest, the moonlight reflecting off the dark ink covering him.

"Can't sleep?" His trademark smirk appeared. "Or are you following me?"

"I didn't know you were—" The words died in my throat as he sank into the water. He was teasing me. "I needed air." My eyes followed a droplet of water as it trailed down his chiseled jaw. I forced my gaze to meet his. "What are you doing out here?"

"Swimming, I couldn't sleep either." His confession stopped me in my tracks. "Between this mess with my sister and you, I was wide awake." I turned slowly back to him.

"Me?" I touched my fingers to my chest.

The corner of his lips lifted in a cocky grin. "Are we still pretending there's not something between us?" I shook my head, but before I could respond, he continued. "Are you going to tell me you weren't in your room, pacing the floor, thinking about me?"

He was always so infuriatingly blunt. He'd always been like that, but it only bothered me now that he was calling me out. "I couldn't sleep because I was thinking about Kacie." I crossed my arms over my chest and cocked my hip. "It had nothing to do with you."

"We both know that's not true..." I opened my mouth to argue, but there was no point. He was right. I was thinking about him and how fucked up I was for it after everything he'd done. "But what did you come up with?" My brows pulled together, questioning him. He chuckled. "What were your thoughts on Kacie?"

"Oh, right." I stepped forward until I was standing at the pool's edge. "I was actually wondering what happened to her phone?"

He leaned back, looking up at me. "We never found it."

My gaze lifted, staring off into the darkness surrounding the patio. Kacie didn't go anywhere without her phone. "I wonder what happened to it."

My gaze dropped as Zaiden's hips floated behind him. "Are you fucking naked?" I stepped back, immediately redirecting my eyes.

He laughed. "I don't swim with clothes." Water sloshed as he moved in my peripheral vision, and I realized he was getting out of the pool.

"What are you doing?" I turned my back to him. "Our parents—"

"Aren't home." He finished for me. His bare feet slapped against the concrete deck.

"I'm going to go." I stepped forward, but his strong arm

hooked around me, jerking me back against him. The water from his skin seeped through the thin layer of my tank top.

"So modest," he breathed against my ear. A drop of water hit my shoulder, and a shiver ran down my spine. "Like my cock hasn't been in your mouth."

"What the fuck?" I jerked away from him, turning and shoving him away. "What is wrong with you?" My lip curled into a snarl. "Why are you acting like we are going to be anything more than frenemies?" I shook my head, keeping my eyes locked on his. "After we figure out what happened with Kacie, I don't ever want to see you again."

"We both know that's not true."

My eyes narrowed. "You are delusional."

He stepped forward. "Come swimming with me."

I stepped back. "Are you not hearing me?"

"I hear you, but I'm not listening because you're not talking to me. You're talking to yourself." He invaded my personal space. I shook my head, holding out a hand like I thought that might stop him. "Because there's no way you're going to convince me you're not into me." He pinched my chin between his thumb and finger, holding my face in place.

I shoved him hard. "I never said that I wasn't into you, Zaiden. I *was* into you. I *was* attracted to you." I blew out a breath, pausing for a moment. "I am attracted to you, and I hate that my body reacts the way it does when you're around, but you ruined any chance of anything ever happening between us." I took another step back to put more space between us. "Let's just figure out what happened to Kacie so we can end whatever this is." I ripped the towel off the table and tossed it to him.

He wrapped the towel around himself but didn't say

anything. He obviously didn't believe me. Hell, I wasn't even sure I believed myself.

I rolled my eyes and shook my head. "I'm going to bed." I didn't wait for him to say anything or try to stop me before I stormed into the house, closing the door between us.

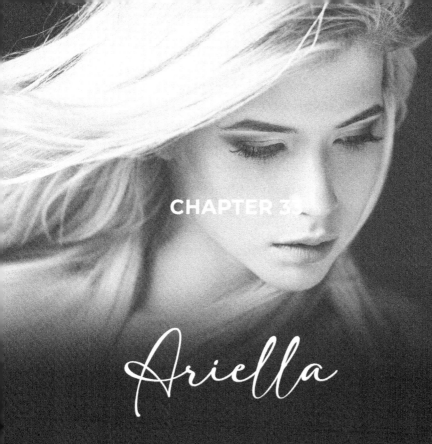

CHAPTER 35

Ariella

Sliding the coffee holder with three iced caramel Frappuccinos on the small round table outside the school cafe, I dropped into the chair. It was our first day back on campus since the shooting. The athletic hall was still closed until further notice, and all practices except football were canceled, but all classes resumed as normal today, and even though the campus had a different, almost eerie feeling, I was happy for things to get back to normal.

"Oh, thank God." Journey collapsed into the chair across from me, dark circles shadowing her eyes like bruises. She reached for her cup with grabby hands, dramatic as always. "Coffee."

"I was getting used to sleeping in." Mila snagged her drink, then slumped down. Her fingers drummed against the cup in the same rhythm they used for warm-ups, betraying her anxiety beneath the casual tone.

I flipped open my laptop, the screen reflecting my own exhausted face. "Twenty minutes till class." The login cursor blinked accusingly while I tried to remember my password. "And my brain's still in break mode."

Journey's forehead met the table with a soft thunk. "Same."

"So." Mila leaned forward, elbows on the table, voice dropping to that conspiratorial tone that usually preceded gossip. "What happened last night? Did you guys—" Her spine snapped straight, eyes widening at something over my shoulder.

Metal screamed against tile, the sound of a chair dragging closer.

Before I could protest, Zaiden's presence materialized beside me. The conversations around us died one by one, like candles being snuffed out.

Heat radiated from him, along with his familiar scent. My stomach clenched. I kept my eyes fixed on my coffee, but couldn't ignore how the air seemed to change when he entered it.

Heads turned. Whispers rippled across nearby tables.

"What are you doing?"

His lips curved into that infuriating half-smile. "Sitting with what's mine." He settled into the chair, each movement a claim to the space. To me.

My chair squealed against the tile as I shoved back, but his knee was already there, a solid barrier blocking my escape. Around us, a dozen pairs of eyes darted away, pretending not to watch our drama unfold.

"I don't belong to anyone." The words felt weak against the certainty in his expression.

He leaned closer, voice dropping to a murmur that scraped against my nerves. "Keep telling yourself that, princess."

"Do you two need a minute?" Mila asked. My gaze snapped to her, giving her a 'what-the-fuck' look. "Because we only have a few minutes to figure out our day before we have to go to class."

"She's right." Journey twirled a strand of hair around her finger. "And you decided to bring him into this."

My eyes widened. He was her freaking brother. How could I exclude him?

"Plus, he's right." Journey shrugged one shoulder, loyalty to her brother winning out. "Everyone here thinks you are his. So, can we get back to what we were doing?"

"I'm good." Zaiden leaned back in his chair, victory written in the relaxed set of his shoulders.

My teeth clenched together hard enough to send pain shooting through my jaw. "Fine."

"Mila." Zaiden's tone shifted, suddenly all business. "Ariella said your brother was at the scene that night."

She nodded, lifting her coffee to her lips.

"Did he say anything about Kacie's phone?"

"No, but I'm having dinner with him tonight. I could ask him if he knows anything about it."

"You're having dinner with your brother?" Journey asked. Mila's brother rarely had time for her since he moved out of the house. They chatted on the phone often, but dinner together meant something was up.

"Yeah," she scowled. "I was supposed to meet his newest girlfriend, but they broke up. We're still having dinner."

"Is your brother a cop now?" Zaiden asked.

"Yep," she smiled. "That's why he started questioning

what happened with Kacie. He read the final report, which didn't match what happened."

"We can meet up tonight," I suggested. "After your dinner."

"There's a party at Delta Gamma Phi tonight.

"Yeah, like a back-to-school thing," Journey added.

"I'm not going to another party." My gaze flicked to Zaiden, who was pretending to be absorbed in his phone. I rolled my eyes. "I don't want to run into anyone from the football team yet."

"You don't have any classes with any of them?" Journey leaned forward, elbows on the table, her protective-friend mode activating.

I shook my head, twisting a paper napkin between my fingers.

"Well, that shouldn't be an issue." Mila tapped her manicured nail against the table decisively, like she was marking the end of a debate. "They're all leaving this morning for an away game. So the only people you may run into from the last party are dancers from our team."

"Come on, Ari." Journey's hand covered mine, squeezing gently. "You can't hide forever."

The truth was, I didn't care about what happened at the football party with Zaiden anymore. I'd done what I had to do to protect my friends from feeling the same humiliation I had. I wasn't ready to face E.J. and the team's rejection.

"I'll be there around nine." I traced a circle on the table with my fingertip, already regretting the commitment.

Zaiden's chair scraped back. "I gotta go." He stood in one fluid motion, slinging his backpack over his shoulder.

My gaze lifted, betraying me before I could stop it, following the line of his shoulders as he towered above our table.

"I'll meet you guys at the party tonight." He addressed the air somewhere above Journey's head, not bothering to check if they agreed.

Mila nodded, suddenly fascinated by something in her coffee cup. Traitor.

His focus shifted, locking on me like a predator spotting prey. "Ariella." My name in his mouth sounded like a command. "Walk me to class."

It wasn't a question; it was an order, delivered with the certainty of someone unused to hearing "no."

"No thanks." I turned back to my friends, shoulder angling to create a barrier, dismissing him.

"Hey—" My words dissolved into an undignified yelp as strong fingers circled my upper arm, lifting me from my seat with effortless strength. My coffee rocked in its cup.

"What the fu—"

"I said," his lips brushed the shell of my ear, voice dropping to a register that vibrated through my bones, "walk me to class."

"We'll see you at the party, Ari." Mila pushed back her chair, exchanging a look with Journey that lasted a beat too long.

My fingers dug into the strap of my bag as Zaiden steered me toward the exit. "You guys are terrible friends," I hissed over my shoulder.

Journey's laugh bubbled up. Mila covered her mouth, but her eyes danced above her fingers. They waved with synchronized innocence, co-conspirators in whatever game they thought was happening.

The heavy door swung shut behind us with a dull thud, sealing us into the empty corridor. My arm burned where he'd gripped it, but I refused to rub the spot— refused to show weakness.

"What is your problem?" I backed away until concrete pressed cold against my spine. "You have a really weird way of convincing me to forgive you."

The lights caught the dangerous edge of his smile. "Forgive me?" Each slow step he took forward echoed in the hollow space. "For what exactly?"

"Don't play stupid. For destroying my life. For turning everyone against—"

His laugh cut through the air. One hand pressed against the wall beside my head, and the scent of him surrounded me. His thumb traced his lower lip, a gesture that drew my gaze.

"Ariella." My name in his mouth was both a curse and a caress. "I never asked for your forgiveness."

The truth of those words hit harder than any accusation. I started to turn away, but his fingers caught my chin. Gentle, yet relentless. The contrast made my breath catch.

"I apologized for Kacie." His voice dropped lower, intimate in the empty hallway. "Only Kacie." His eyes searched mine, looking for something I wasn't sure I wanted him to find. "The rest?" That dangerous smile returned. "I meant every word, every action. And you?" His thumb brushed my jawline, feather-light. "You're mine. Take all the time you need to accept that." His lips dropped to my ear, the heat of his breath sending chills coursing over my body. "I licked it, so it's mine."

The worst part wasn't his arrogance. It was the way my traitor pulse jumped at his touch, betraying me with every beat. "I'm a patient man, but make no mistake, you're mine."

I shoved his hand away and squared my shoulders. "I don't belong to anyone." My jaw flexed.

"You are mine, and I can prove it again if you want me

to." His eyes challenged me, dark with memories of whatever moment he believed had staked his claim.

I narrowed my eyes, mind racing to decipher his meaning while my body remembered something my brain couldn't, or wouldn't, access. Heat crawled up my neck. "Whatever, Zaiden. What do you want?"

He stepped back, satisfaction written in the relaxation of his shoulders. He'd gotten the reaction he wanted.

"I think I've made myself clear." A slow grin spread across his face, the kind that made girls write his name in their notebooks surrounded by hearts. "See you tonight."

My jaw clenched as I watched him walk away. He was so infuriatingly aggravating and hot, and I wanted to hate him so badly, but a small part of me had already forgiven him even if he didn't ask for it. Everyone had their own way of dealing with grief, and his was tormenting me because he thought I was responsible for her death. Or at least that was what I was telling myself, and there was no way I was going to ever admit it to him.

My brain shouted all the reasons to stay away from him: dangerous, manipulative, cruel. But my traitorous body remembered things my mind couldn't access, the weight of his hand at my waist, the heat of his skin, something else just beyond memory's reach. Logic against instinct, and instinct was winning. Again.

CHAPTER 34

Ariella

The floor beneath my feet vibrated as I stood on the old wooden front porch of the frat house. My gaze dropped to give myself one more glance before I went in. I wasn't typically the type of girl who took hours to get ready. In fact, it usually took me ten minutes to throw on a pair of jeans or skirt, a tank top or sweatshirt, shoes, and lip gloss, but tonight was different. If all eyes were going to be on me, then I was going to give them something to look at.

And—

It may also have had a little to do with Zaiden.

I ran my hand over my short skirt, continuing up to my bare, tanned stomach. I tugged slightly on the small white crop top, which was held together in the middle by a tiny string, creating an alluring gap that accentuated my cleavage.

My phone buzzed, and I reached into my back pocket, pulling it out.

Mila: Where are you?

I smiled at my phone.

Ariella: Walking in now.

Twisting the doorknob, I shoved open the door and walked through the entrance into the darkened house.

Mila: We are in the kitchen. Meet us there.

Bodies pressed in from all sides as I shouldered through the crowd. Cologne mixed with spilled beer and sweat, the air thick enough to taste. Red solo cups bobbed above heads, silhouettes swaying to the music in the blue-black darkness. In this press of strangers, I was just another shadow.

I stepped into the brightly lit kitchen, smiling when I spotted Mila and Journey.

"Holy shit," Journey said, her eyes scanning me up and down. "You look fucking hot."

"Who did you get dressed up for?" Mila teased as I stopped on the opposite end of the kitchen island.

"Myself." I bounced my eyebrows as I reached across the counter and grabbed one of the lined-up solo cups in front of the bottle of clear 1800 tequila. I needed to feel the burn. I threw back the cup and winced as the hot liquid slid down my throat.

"What the fuck are you doing?" Journey scowled, snatching the cup out of my hand. She tipped it towards her, staring into it. "Do you not remember what happened the last time you took red solo cup shots?"

I shook my head, a grin spreading across my face. "Must have been a good time."

She rolled her eyes. "Yeah, so much fun, Zaiden carried you out of the party."

I reached for another cup filled with a different liquor. "Well, that's a chance I'm willing to take." If I was going to deal with Zaiden being part of my friend group tonight, I needed all the alcohol.

"Anyways," Mila said. "So I talked to my brother—"

"We should probably wait for Zaiden," I cut her off. "Otherwise, you're going to have to repeat yourself."

"I don't think he's going to make it," Mila said. "I have a few hockey players in my Eco class, and I overheard them say that their coach called a mandatory meeting tonight."

"Yeah," Journey agreed. "And I ran into Sterling this afternoon, and he said a couple of players got caught doing shit they weren't supposed to, and he thought the team would be doing suicide drills until their legs bled."

"Ew," I scowled.

"I think they'll pass out after that kind of torture," Mila added.

I should have been excited he wasn't going to be there, but a small part of me was disappointed. "Okay, well, I can tell him when I get home."

"My brother said they found her phone in her car, and that was how they contacted her family, but he has no idea what happened to it. He wasn't sure if it left with Kacie or was bagged as evidence."

I blew out an exasperated sigh. "Well, at least we know

she did have it, but there's no way now to figure out where it went."

"We could try getting into her iCloud," Journey suggested.

My gaze held hers. "That's a great fucking idea." I wasn't sure why I hadn't thought about that yet. "We can meet early tomorrow morning. I'll bring my laptop and see if we can get into it. I'll let Zaiden know. He might know her password."

"Hey," a deep voice shouted from the doorway. "It's game time, ladies."

My lip curled into a snarl. "This is why I don't come to frat parties."

"Oh, come on," Journey laughed, strolling around the counter. "It will be fun."

"Making out with a stranger while he tries to stick his hand down your pants is not fun."

Mila and Journey both laughed, and I rolled my eyes.

"Live a little," Mila chuckled. "Unless it's true and you do actually belong to Zaiden."

She'd just said the one thing that ensured I played all the games, kissed all the boys, and pushed myself far past my comfort zone to prove Zaiden Knight didn't own me. "I'm in."

I followed them out of the kitchen and into the dark living area. My gaze lifted to the tall, thin man standing on the coffee table.

"Game one," he shouted. "Meet me at midnight." I rolled my eyes. These were games made up so the guy who wouldn't normally get the girl stood a chance. "Everyone pulls a ticket out of the hat. Each ticket has a time and location somewhere inside the house on it. Every room has one ticket in the pink hat and one in the blue hat.

Ladies, you'll pull from the pink hat and guys from the blue. Make sure you make it to your location before your time because it gets pretty dark once the lights go out."

"What does he mean, the lights go out?" I whispered, and a wave of panic settled in my gut.

"I think he means it will be dark," Journey whispered.

"Fuck."

"It will be fun," Mila added.

"Yeah, so much fun." I groaned, and it probably would have been fun if I hadn't been scared of the dark. Actually, who was I kidding? I had no interest in kissing some random boy. Not in the light or the dark, but I was in it now.

"This game is first come, first served, and we'll play again for those who don't get to play the first round."

"What do we do in the dark?"

Oh, come on... I hated stupid questions. All eyes turned to me. Fuck, I'd said it out loud. Might as well finish my thought. "If you don't know what to do in the dark, then you should go home; it's past your bedtime."

A roar of laughter echoed through the large room.

"Why don't you pick first?" My eyes followed him as he jumped off the table and strolled toward me, as the crowd parted for him. I really wanted to say no and go home, but maybe this was what was needed to show Zaiden he didn't own me. Or it could be what gets the mystery man killed. It was a chance I was willing to take for freedom.

He held out the pink hat, and I reached in and pulled out a ticket. I closed my fist around the small paper and forced a smile as my gaze met his. "Midnight is in twenty minutes."

Pursing my lips, I nodded, ignoring the chill racing down my spine. "Thanks."

Mila and Journey pulled next before he disappeared into the crowd.

"Have I mentioned how much I *hate* games?"

They both laughed again. "Yeah, a few times."

"I'm going to get a drink." I was going to need a lot more alcohol to kiss a stranger.

The floor beneath my feet vibrated as I stood on the old wooden front porch of the frat house. My gaze dropped to give myself one more glance before I went in. I wasn't typically the type of girl who took hours to get ready. In fact, it usually took me ten minutes to throw on a pair of jeans or skirt, a tank top or sweatshirt, shoes, and lip gloss, but tonight was different. If all eyes were going to be on me, then I was going to give them something to look at.

And—

It may also have had a little to do with Zaiden.

I ran my hand over my short skirt, continuing up to my bare, tanned stomach. I tugged slightly on the small white crop top, which was held together in the middle by a tiny string, creating an alluring gap that accentuated my cleavage.

My phone buzzed, and I reached into my back pocket, pulling it out.

Mila: Where are you?

I smiled at my phone.

Ariella: Walking in now.

Twisting the doorknob, I shoved open the door and walked through the entrance into the darkened house.

Mila: We are in the kitchen. Meet us there.

Bodies pressed in from all sides as I shouldered through the crowd. Cologne mixed with spilled beer and sweat, the air thick enough to taste. Red solo cups bobbed above heads, silhouettes swaying to the music in the blue-black darkness. In this press of strangers, I was just another shadow.

I stepped into the brightly lit kitchen, smiling when I spotted Mila and Journey.

"Holy shit," Journey said, her eyes scanning me up and down. "You look fucking hot."

"Who did you get dressed up for?" Mila teased as I stopped on the opposite end of the kitchen island.

"Myself." I bounced my eyebrows as I reached across the counter and grabbed one of the lined-up solo cups in front of the bottle of clear 1800 tequila. I needed to feel the burn. I threw back the cup and winced as the hot liquid slid down my throat.

"What the fuck are you doing?" Journey scowled, snatching the cup out of my hand. She tipped it towards her, staring into it. "Do you not remember what happened the last time you took red solo cup shots?"

I shook my head, a grin spreading across my face. "Must have been a good time."

She rolled her eyes. "Yeah, so much fun, Zaiden carried you out of the party."

I reached for another cup filled with a different liquor. "Well, that's a chance I'm willing to take." If I was going to deal with Zaiden being part of my friend group tonight, I needed all the alcohol.

"Anyways," Mila said. "So I talked to my brother—"

"We should probably wait for Zaiden," I cut her off. "Otherwise, you're going to have to repeat yourself."

"I don't think he's going to make it," Mila said. "I have a few hockey players in my Eco class, and I overheard them say that their coach called a mandatory meeting tonight."

"Yeah," Journey agreed. "And I ran into Sterling this afternoon, and he said a couple of players got caught doing shit they weren't supposed to, and he thought the team would be doing suicide drills until their legs bled."

"Ew," I scowled.

"I think they'll pass out after that kind of torture," Mila added.

I should have been excited he wasn't going to be there, but a small part of me was disappointed. "Okay, well, I can tell him when I get home."

"My brother said they found her phone in her car, and that was how they contacted her family, but he has no idea what happened to it. He wasn't sure if it left with Kacie or was bagged as evidence."

I blew out an exasperated sigh. "Well, at least we know she did have it, but there's no way now to figure out where it went."

"We could try getting into her iCloud," Journey suggested.

My gaze held hers. "That's a great fucking idea." I wasn't sure why I hadn't thought about that yet. "We can meet early tomorrow morning. I'll bring my laptop and see if we can get into it. I'll let Zaiden know. He might know her password."

"Hey," a deep voice shouted from the doorway. "It's game time, ladies."

My lip curled into a snarl. "This is why I don't come to frat parties."

"Oh, come on," Journey laughed, strolling around the counter. "It will be fun."

"Making out with a stranger while he tries to stick his hand down your pants is not fun."

Mila and Journey both laughed, and I rolled my eyes.

"Live a little," Mila chuckled. "Unless it's true and you do actually belong to Zaiden."

She'd just said the one thing that ensured I played all the games, kissed all the boys, and pushed myself far past my comfort zone to prove Zaiden Knight didn't own me. "I'm in."

I followed them out of the kitchen and into the dark living area. My gaze lifted to the tall, thin man standing on the coffee table.

"Game one," he shouted. "Meet me at midnight." I rolled my eyes. These were games made up so the guy who wouldn't normally get the girl stood a chance. "Everyone pulls a ticket out of the hat. Each ticket has a time and location somewhere inside the house on it. Every room has one ticket in the pink hat and one in the blue hat. Ladies, you'll pull from the pink hat and guys from the blue. Make sure you make it to your location before your time because it gets pretty dark once the lights go out."

"What does he mean, the lights go out?" I whispered, and a wave of panic settled in my gut.

"I think he means it will be dark," Journey whispered.

"Fuck."

"It will be fun," Mila added.

"Yeah, so much fun." I groaned, and it probably would have been fun if I hadn't been scared of the dark. Actually, who was I kidding? I had no interest in kissing some random boy. Not in the light or the dark, but I was in it now.

"This game is first come, first served, and we'll play again for those who don't get to play the first round."

"What do we do in the dark?"

Oh, come on... I hated stupid questions. All eyes turned to me. Fuck, I'd said it out loud. Might as well finish my thought. "If you don't know what to do in the dark, then you should go home; it's past your bedtime."

A roar of laughter echoed through the large room.

"Why don't you pick first?" My eyes followed him as he jumped off the table and strolled toward me, as the crowd parted for him. I really wanted to say no and go home, but maybe this was what was needed to show Zaiden he didn't own me. Or it could be what gets the mystery man killed. It was a chance I was willing to take for freedom.

He held out the pink hat, and I reached in and pulled out a ticket. I closed my fist around the small paper and forced a smile as my gaze met his. "Midnight is in twenty minutes."

Pursing my lips, I nodded, ignoring the chill racing down my spine. "Thanks."

Mila and Journey pulled next before he disappeared into the crowd.

"Have I mentioned how much I *hate* games?"

They both laughed again. "Yeah, a few times."

"I'm going to get a drink." I was going to need a lot more alcohol to kiss a stranger.

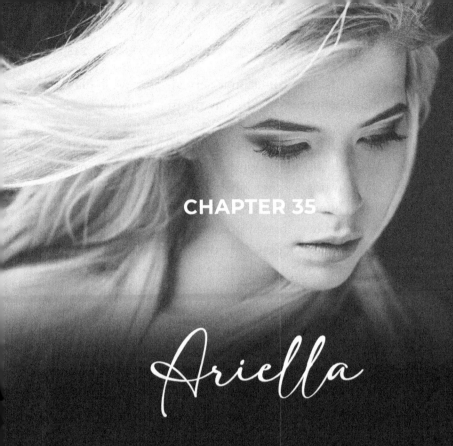

CHAPTER 35

Ariella

The liquor burned through my veins, turning fear into liquid courage. One shot, two, three, I'd lost count, but now the idea of kissing a stranger in the dark didn't seem so terrifying. What made my heart race was imagining Zaiden's face when he found out, when I proved him wrong.

I scanned the crowded room, watching bodies shift and separate like schools of fish, everyone finding their designated dark corners. Journey and Mila had already disappeared into the shadows, leaving me alone with my terrible decisions.

My fingers trembled as I unfolded the paper, the white slip somehow heavier than it should be.

Room 25 closet.

"Fuck my life."

Closets. Of all the places in this massive house, it had to be a closet. One way in, one way out, no windows to offer even a sliver of moonlight. Just four walls pressing in and darkness so thick you could choke on it.

The paper crumpled in my fist as my gaze lifted to the staircase in front of me and then shifted to the front door. No one would know if I left. No one but me, and for some reason, I felt like I had something to prove, not only to myself but to everyone at this party. Realistically, I knew no one cared, but it didn't change the way I felt.

"You better hurry, Ledger." The tall man's shadow stretched across the wall as he passed, his voice dropping to a whisper. "It's going to be dark soon, and who knows what evil will be lurking down here."

My skin prickled at his tone as my gaze followed his retreating figure. "What the fuck does that mean?" The question hung in the empty hallway, unanswered.

Rolling my eyes, I shook my head before sucking in a deep breath as I strolled up the stairs and searched the floor for room 25. This frat house had three floors, and the "2" indicated the bedroom was on the second floor.

Room 25 waited at the end of the hallway. Each step down the corridor made the floorboards creak, marking my approach. The doorknob was cold under my palm, resisting for a moment before giving way.

The smell hit me first, a suffocating mix of stale cologne and something distinctly male. Shadows stretched across rumpled bed sheets and discarded clothes, turning familiar shapes into lurking monsters. Everything about this room screamed warning, but the alcohol in my system translated fear into reckless courage.

The closet door creaked as I pulled it open. One step inside. Another. The lights died as I clicked it shut, plunging me into absolute darkness. The air felt thick, pressing against my chest, squeezing tighter with each shallow breath. "You can do this," I whispered, but the blackness around me swallowed my words. My fingertips found the wall behind me, anchoring me in place as I waited. "You can do this," I mumbled as I stood completely still, trying to steady my breathing.

A creak pierced the silence. My heart slammed against my ribs as I held my breath. "Hello?" The word disappeared into the void, unanswered.

Click.

The door sealed shut, and the air felt different—heavier, charged. Someone else was here, breathing the same thick darkness. Usually, company in the dark meant comfort. But this wasn't Journey or Mila or anyone else I trusted. This stranger with unknown intentions shared six square feet of pitch-black space with me.

"Hello?" Nothing. It was too dark to see anything. "Um—"

I instantly regretted my choice to play this stupid game.

Deep, measured breaths cut through the silence, each exhale controlled. Too controlled.

"I'm Ari—Ariella Ledger." My voice sounded small in the darkness. "And you are—?"

Large hands found my waist, fingers spreading possessively against my ribs. My pulse jumped wildly, a trapped bird beating against my throat. "Um—okay. If you want to just kiss and get it over with—"

His grip turned to iron, and before I could process what was happening, he spun me like a rag doll. My back slammed against his chest, the impact forcing a yelp from my throat. This wasn't how someone moved for just a kiss.

This was something else, something that made my blood run cold.

Panic raced through my veins. I had no idea who this was or what his plans were, but I had no intention of going any further than a kiss, and I honestly didn't even want to do that. I wanted to piss Zaiden off. Prove I wasn't his. To prove I didn't belong to anyone.

It seemed stupid now that I was in a dark closet with a stranger, and Zaiden would probably never even know I was there or what happened.

Sometimes, I had the stupidest ideas.

His large hands circled my waist, holding me in place as his lips dropped to my shoulder.

"Uh, hey," I tried to keep my tone calm, "I think I'm going to go." I pulled against his grasp, but he didn't budge. His grip only tightened. His hand wrapped around my throat as the other one slid lower to the waistband of my skirt.

"What are you—" The question trailed off as his hand slid over my waist, over my stomach to the waistband of my skirt, a new point of contact that made coherent thought impossible.

My chest heaved with fear, and I knew I only had one possible way out of this, and it was going to kill me to say it out loud.

"I belong to Zaiden Knight." The words tumbled out, desperate and raw. "And he will kill you."

He froze. His fingers retracted from my skirt, but his grip remained iron-tight around my throat. Seconds stretched into an eternity as I stood there, barely breathing, waiting for his next move. Then his chest shook—once, twice—with silent laughter, and my stomach dropped.

I was fucked.

"Just let me go," I growled, but my voice trembled at the edges.

His lips brushed my cheek, breath hot against my skin as his grip tightened around my throat. "I told you I'd prove it."

That voice. My blood turned to ice as recognition hit, followed by a dizzying rush of emotions: anger blazing through my veins, fear clawing at my chest, and adrenaline making my hands shake. And underneath it all, a traitorous flicker of relief.

"Fuck you, Zaiden." I jerked my body against his, but his grip only tightened. "I thought you weren't here."

"You belong to me, Ariella Ledger." His breath fanned across my jawline and up to my ear. "If you thought I would ever let anyone else in this closet with you, you seriously underestimated me."

His hand slipped past my waistband, dipping into my panties. "You're soaking wet for me," he breathed against the shell of my ear. "Your pussy is begging for my cock to fill it." His fingers slid through my slick flesh, and I moaned. "You want to give me your virginity, Ariella?"

My body screamed yes, but the stubbornness inside me that was still so angry with him was screaming fuck no. "I don't want to *give* you anything, Zaiden."

He froze, his hand stopped slowly withdrawing from my waistband, and I immediately regretted my answer.

And then the heat of his body was gone.

I whipped around, wishing the lights would come back on. "Zaiden?"

"You don't want to *give* me anything," he repeated, his tone a low rasp.

My face twisted with confusion, but I didn't dare say

anything. The small closet was silent except for my rapid breathing.

"Zaiden?"

And then he was there.

His body crashed into mine, driving me back until the wall stole what little breath I had left. The wood bit into my shoulder blades, his weight an inescapable force pinning me in place.

"You don't want to give it to me." His lips ghosted across mine, each word a spark against my skin. The heat of his breath made me shiver despite the inferno burning between us. "Because... You want me to take it." I sucked in a harsh breath as his hands raked down the sides of my body. "Is that it, Ariella?"

His nails curled into the bare skin of my outer thighs, and I literally couldn't form a coherent thought. He pressed his hips into mine, the evidence of how turned on he was pressing into my lower stomach. "Do you want me to pin you down and take it?" His lips grazed over my jaw and down my throat. "Do you want it rough? Do you want me to fuck you hard and fast? Or slower? Do you want to fight me? Or will you give in?"

"Zaiden—" His name escaped as a desperate plea, hanging in the darkness between us.

"Does this turn you on, Ariella?" His words ghosted across my skin, making me shiver. My fingers twisted into his shirt, caught between pushing him away and pulling him closer. "Is it the fear that gets you? Or the adrenaline rushing through your veins right now?"

His hands slid around my thighs, rough palms against bare skin, and my breath hitched when his grip tightened, and he lifted me off the ground, wrapping my legs around his waist.

The closet door burst open. And we were quickly moving through the darkness.

There was a couple standing at the end of the bed.

"Get out," Zaiden roared, and they rushed out of the room.

With me still wrapped around him, he crawled onto the bed, and my heart began to race.

"What are you doing, Zaiden?"

The room was dark except for the moonlight seeping through the window, giving me enough light to see him.

"Taking what's mine." He pressed my body into the mattress with his. "Put your arms over your head." He pushed up, leaning back on his knees as his hands worked to unbuckle his belt.

"Why?"

He froze, jaw muscle ticking. "Because," he ripped his belt from his pants, "I said so." He didn't wait for me to obey him as he grabbed one of my wrists and then the other, looping his belt around them before securing it to the rod iron headboard.

I pulled against the restraints as he shifted lower on the bed. "Zaiden—" The words died in my throat when he pressed his lips to the skin above my waistband as he worked my skirt up. His mouth dropped lower, pressing his full lips to my inner thigh as he spread my legs, settling between them.

"What are you doing?" I was desperately fighting a war within myself. I shouldn't have wanted this, but I did.

"I'm getting you ready," his breath was hot against my skin, "to take my cock." Chills raced over my body despite the warmth spreading through me.

He ran his nose up my length over my panties, inhaling

deeply. "Fuck." His chest rumbled with a groan. "I love the way you smell when you're turned on."

Jerking my panties to the side, his tongue swiped up me striking my clit, and my lips parted on a moan as my head tilted back and my eyes closed. "Oh my God," I purred as the heat of his breath mixed with the pressure of his tongue made my body start to tremble.

"Fuck," I groaned. I wanted to slide my hands into his hair and ride his face, but he was in control.

I was already so fucking close. His tongue flicked over and over again, finding the perfect rhythm with just the right amount of pressure. He slipped a long, thick finger inside of me, and my eyes widened at the feeling. "Oh—" was all I could manage.

"I need you to come all over my fingers, baby," he hummed against my pussy. "I need you soaking wet to slip my cock inside this tight pussy."

My back arched off the bed as his finger and tongue moved in sync, finding a rhythm that set my body on fire. He paused, adding another finger. The feeling so exquisitely foreign. He held them deep and still, letting me adjust around them for a moment, but I wanted more.

My hips lifted, grinding against his hand.

He slowly withdrew his fingers. "You want my fingers to fuck you?"

"Yes," I panted, and his finger slid back. This time, there was no pause as they pumped in and out of me. His tongue found my clit as he increased speed, and that was all it took for me to fall over the edge.

"Zaiden," I screamed out as I came all over his hand. "Holy shit," I breathed as he withdrew his fingers and shifted on the bed.

Hooking a finger in each side of my panties, he

dragged them down my legs before quickly shoving down his pants and crawling up to me.

"I'm going to take what's mine now," he purred against my lips as he settled between my thighs.

The sound of foil tearing echoed through the room, and I leaned up, the silver foil of a condom wrapper reflected off the moonlight.

I swallowed hard and sucked in a harsh breath holding it as I prepared for what was to come.

He slid his cock through my slit, coating himself with the orgasm that he'd given me. "Breathe, Ariella." I exhaled. "If you stop breathing, I stop fucking you." My gaze held his as I nodded.

The tip of his head nudged my entrance, and my hands tightened around the leather belt. Fuck, I wanted this.

He moved his hips, and I bit down hard on the inside of my cheek.

He slowly worked himself deeper inside me. "Fuck," he grunted. "You're so fucking tight." He was big, and I was a virgin.

He stilled with only the head of his cock inside me, and I willed myself to relax and breathe.

"More," I ordered. I wanted to rip that band-aid off. "Get it over with."

With one powerful snap of his hips, he thrust inside, filling me, and I cried out. A burning, stinging pain enveloped me, and I forgot to breathe.

His lip curled into a teasing grin as his hand closed around my throat, and he slowly withdrew from me. His fingers tightened around my neck as his hips jutted forward, filling me again, but this time, there was no pause as he started fucking me hard and fast. It was a mixture of pain and pleasure as his fingers tightened enough that I struggled for a breath.

His pace grew harder and faster. Each of my moans was a tiny gasp for air. "You're taking my cock so fucking well, baby."

I sucked in a sharp breath as white dots formed in my vision, and my entire body clenched. His grip around my throat tightened until I couldn't breathe as his hips snapped harder against mine, continuing to fuck me through my orgasm.

He released my throat, and my breaths came fast as he pulled out of me before flipping me over. The leather from the belt biting into my skin. He tugged my hips up so I was on my knees, and before I had a second to process everything, he slammed back into me. I cried out again, but this time, there was no mercy in his thrust, each one more brutal than the last.

"Oh fuck," I moaned.

"You are mine." He pushed himself deep, grinding his hips against my ass. "Say it, Ariella."

"I am yours."

With one more hard thrust, I cried out, and he buried himself deep inside me, stilling as he came.

"Holy fuck," I mumbled as Zaiden crawled off the bed. "Let me go."

He didn't say a word, his eyes locked on me with my ass in the air as he slowly dressed and panic set in. He was going to leave me like this. "Zaiden."

"Relax," he teased. "I'm not going to leave you. I'm just admiring the view."

My cheeks heated as I felt self-conscious. A thud echoed through the room, and my head shot to the door. "Fuck."

Zaiden climbed onto the bed and quickly released me. I flew off the bed and corrected my skirt as the lights exploded to life, reality crashing in like a wave of cold water. Coralee Mathers shoved open the door and stood in the doorway, her perfectly lined mouth forming an O of surprise. I scrambled to straighten my skirt.

"Holy shit," Coralee breathed, her eyes gleaming with the kind of hunger that made my skin crawl. "No one told me Zaiden Knight was an option tonight."

"I'm not." His eyes cut to mine, dark and unreadable. "Let's go." His fingers wrapped around my wrist, not the bruising grip from before, but something more calculated, a public display of ownership that made Coralee's smile falter.

She pressed herself against the doorframe, refusing to yield. "You don't have to be rude about it. We're all just playing a game here."

Zaiden moved past her like she was nothing more than furniture, pulling me in his wake. The party seemed to part around us, or him, really. Even drunk college kids recognized a predator in their midst.

The night air hit my flushed skin.

"Where's your car?"

Zaiden's pace never slowed as he led me toward my car, his grip on my wrist a constant reminder of what happened in that closet.

"Keys," he demanded, palm out. When I fumbled them from my pocket, his fingers brushed mine, sending aftershocks through my system.

He took them, pushing a button and unlocking the doors. "Get in." He jerked open the passenger side door and practically shoved me inside the car.

"Where are we going?" I asked, watching him slide behind the wheel.

"Home."

The car's interior filled with unspoken words, the heat from the closet crystallizing into something harder, colder. Each streetlight we passed painted shadows across his clenched jaw.

"What did Mila find out about Kacie's phone?"

The question hit like a bucket of ice water, dragging us back to reality. The monster under Kacie's bed was still out there, waiting, while we played games in dark closets.

Sucking in a deep breath, I exhaled slowly. "Her phone was on the scene, but he had no idea what had happened to it after they contacted her family."

"It wasn't with her things at the hospital."

"Maybe your parents—"

"They don't have it." He cut me off, voice clipped. "It's the only thing we didn't recover."

"Maybe we don't need it." The alcohol made me bold, or maybe it was the lingering adrenaline from the closet.

His eyebrow arched as he glanced at me. "What do you mean?"

"Kacie used the same passwords for everything." I could feel a plan forming through the fog of alcohol. "Her MacBook—"

Our eyes met, realization hitting him. Her MacBook would have almost everything that was on her phone. "I can get it and charge it tonight. I'll bring it to school tomorrow."

CHAPTER 36

Ariella

Why couldn't anything ever be easy?

The sharp crack of hockey sticks against ice echoed through the empty arena, making me flinch. The familiar glow of Kacie's MacBook login page mocked me as I tried her third password combination.

Access denied.

Again.

Zaiden and Sterling's skates carved violent figure-eights into the ice as they fought over a puck. I wasn't a regular at the ice arena, but currently, it was the only place I knew I wouldn't run into anyone from the football team. I knew I'd eventually have to face them, but I'd already been disowned. I wasn't sure how they'd react when they saw me again, and I wasn't ready to find out.

I shifted in my seat, the laptop wobbling on my knees as I keyed in another password attempt. The rhythmic scraping of blades against ice had become almost hypnotic over the past half hour, but it couldn't quite drown out the voice in my head asking why Kacie would suddenly change her password after using the same one for years.

Today was the first day since the shooting that they'd opened the rink and the sports hall where everything had gone down. I wasn't ready to go back into the sports hall yet, but thankfully, the rink had an exterior entrance, so I didn't have to.

"Still playing digital detective?" Mila dropped into the seat beside me, immediately pulling one knee up to her chest and wrapping her arms around it. Her dark hair was tied in a messy bun, and her baggy sweatshirt hung below her cutoff shorts, making it look like she wasn't wearing anything but the hoodie. "Any luck?"

I shook my head, running a finger over the laptop's edge. "Kacie used the same password for everything. Like, literally everything." I glanced at Mila. "Why would she decide to be security-conscious with her cloud?"

"Maybe because—" Mila trailed off, her usual quick comebacks absent. She slumped lower. "I don't know. But if anyone can crack Kacie's mind games, it's you. You were her person." Her voice caught on the past tense, and she quickly pulled out her phone, hiding behind her screen.

Sighing, I sank back in my seat, letting the laptop teeter on my lap. "Have you heard anything about practice?"

"Yeah," she said, scrolling through her phone. "We are meeting with the sports director in about an hour on the field."

"What do you think he's going to say?"

She shrugged. "He's either going to tell us they found a new coach, or we are taking the rest of the season off."

"Honestly, if it weren't for my scholarship, I'd be okay with taking the rest of the season off."

"Is that because you've been banished from the team?"

"Pretty much," I nodded.

Movement on the ice drew my attention to where Zaiden was "practicing" with Sterling – if you could call it that. Zaiden circled Sterling like a shark, all fluid grace and predatory focus. Each stolen puck came with a flourish meant for the empty stands - meant for me. I caught him watching between plays, that familiar smirk playing on his lips. The same smirk he'd worn at the party, right before he'd grabbed my wrists and said those three words: "You're mine now." Sterling might think they were practicing, but Zaiden was performing, showing off his power. His control.

"So, what's going on with you and the hockey God down there?" Mila's eyes narrowed like I was a puzzle she needed to solve. "Everyone saw you leave the party with him."

I gripped the MacBook harder, the plastic edge pressing into my palms. "According to him, I'm 'his' now."

"His?" Mila's whole body stiffened. "Like his girlfriend?"

"No..." My phone chimed with a new email, distracting me. My gaze narrowed to see that it was my school email. My eyes zeroed in on the name. Scott Hillard. Coach Hillard was not only the head football coach, but he was also the sports director. "Coach Hillard just emailed me."

Mila perked up. "What does it say?"

"He wants me to meet him in his office—now." My gaze

lifted, meeting hers. "Why would he want to meet with me before the meeting?"

She shook her head. "I don't know. Do you want me to go with you?"

"No," I shut the laptop, "I'll meet you at the meeting." I pushed out of the seat. "If Zaiden asks where I went—" My eyes lingered for a long minute on the ice. "lie." The last thing I wanted was for Zaiden to show up and stick his nose where it didn't belong.

I held up the computer. "I'll take another crack at this after practice today."

"I'll see you on the field," Mila said, gathering her things. "I'm gonna meet Journey at the smoothie cafe, grab a smoothie, and head to the field."

"Bring me back a strawberry lime?" I tried to keep my voice light, but my eyes were already fixed on the heavy metal door at the top of the stairs. The same door we'd been standing near when everything went down.

The MacBook felt like lead in my arms as I climbed. Each step brought me closer to the door that led to a hallway filled with memories of fear.

Behind this door, sneakers had squeaked against polished floors, and voices had echoed off high ceilings. Behind this door, those ordinary sounds had been replaced by screams and gunshots and—

I pulled my hand back, wiping my palm against my jeans. The shooter was dead. The hallway was just a hallway now. I repeated these facts like a mantra, but my heart still hammered against my ribs.

Three deep breaths. I forced air into my lungs once, twice, three times, then pushed the door open before I could change my mind. The lights hummed overhead—a sound so normal it felt wrong. My footsteps echoed in the empty corridor, each one a reminder that I was alone here. That I was safe. Yet my shoulders remained tense, my body ready to run, as if it remembered something my mind was trying to forget.

"Ms. Ledger." Coach Hillard's voice cut through the empty hallway. He stood in his office doorway, shoulders rigid, lip in a tight line instead of his usual easy smile.

"Hey, Coach." The words stuck in my throat. Every instinct screamed at me to turn around, but my feet carried me forward anyway. "I got your email."

"Come in." He didn't step aside right away, his massive frame blocking most of the doorway. When he finally moved, it felt less like an invitation and more like a trap closing.

"Is something wrong?" I asked over my shoulder, but froze when my gaze shifted forward and landed on Dean Sweeney sitting behind Coach's desk. "What's going on?" I flinched when the door slammed behind me.

"Ms. Ledger," Dean Sweeney forced a smile. "Why don't you have a seat?"

I shook my head. "No, thank you." I crossed my arms over my chest. "What's going on?"

Dean Sweeney pushed out of her chair, pressing her hands flat on the desk as she squared her shoulders. "A video that's been circulating on campus was brought to our attention."

Video.

I pressed my lips into a tight line, and my eyes closed on an exhale. There was only one video she could be talking about, the one of Coach Palmer and me.

"Unfortunately," Dean Sweeney's manicured nails tapped against her desk, "This kind of behavior is unacceptable. It reflects poorly on our institution." Each tap felt like a countdown.

My brows slammed together. "Behavior like what?" In my peripheral vision, Coach Hillard shifted his weight. "Being forced—" I stopped myself because Coach Palmer hadn't technically forced me. I knew what was required to make the team, and I knew what was required to get a full scholarship. Even though I didn't want to, I'd willingly gotten on my knees because if I hadn't, college was off the table for me. The dance team I'd dreamed about being part of since I was a little girl would be gone.

"Are you saying Zaiden Knight forced you?"

"Zaiden?" I shook the confusion out of my head. "What are you talking about?"

The photo slid across the polished mahogany. My fingertips went numb as the image came into focus. Me—on my knees in the dim light of the football party. The grainy quality didn't hide what was happening, didn't blur the shame that rose like bile in my throat.

It didn't surprise me that someone had videoed it, but until then, I'd been able to pretend there wasn't video evidence of Zaiden forcing me to my knees in front of everyone. Of him claiming me as his, in front of my entire team.

"Where—" My voice cracked. I tried again, tasting copper where I'd bitten the inside of my cheek. "Where did you get this?" My hands shook as I flipped the photo over, but the image was already burned into my retinas.

The memory rushed back, the weight of Zaiden's hand on my head, the feel of him deep in my throat, the taste of his cum on my tongue, the music thumping overhead where the party continued without us as everyone watched.

"It doesn't matter." Dean Sweeney's voice cut through my spiral. "Now that it's been brought to our attention, we have to deal with it."

A laugh bubbled up in my chest, high and hysteric. Deal with it? Like this was a missed homework assignment or a dress code violation. Since when did a blow job become a concern of the school?

"I don't understand." My voice sounded distant, like it belonged to someone else. "Why is this a school issue?"

"You are a dancer." Coach Hillard said, squaring his shoulders. "You represent this school."

Represent. The word echoed in my head.

My vision blurred as I stared at Dean Sweeney.

"You're off the team, Ms. Ledger, and you're suspended pending further investigation."

Dean Sweeney's words hit like physical blows. Off the team. Suspended. Possible expulsion. Each pronouncement drove another nail into the coffin of my future, the dance scholarship I'd spent years earning.

"What do you mean by further investigation?" My voice came out smaller than I intended, a scared kid's voice, not the confident dancer I was supposed to be.

Dean Sweeney's face remained unfazed as if she hadn't just blown up my entire life. "At best, your suspension will be lifted. At worst—" She let the words hang there, heavy as storm clouds. "You will be permanently expelled."

"And what about Zaiden?"

"Mr. Knight is fortunate that we can't see his face."

A laugh bubbled up in my throat, sharp and bitter. "Are you fucking serious?"

"Ms. Ledger." Dean Sweeney's voice cracked like a whip. "Do not make this worse than it already is."

"Worse?" The word tore from my throat, raw and

ragged. My vision blurred, but I refused to let them see me cry. "You've taken everything from me, but Zaiden, the God of Hockey, can do no wrong." I spat his name like a curse, remembering his smirk when he'd told me I was 'his.' I pursed my lips. "What if he had forced me? What would you have done?"

"That's enough, Ms. Ledger," Coach Hillard snapped.

"No, really?" Anger radiated off me. "Would you have kicked out your star hockey player? Or would I have been punished for that, too?"

She squared her shoulders, lifting her chin. "We will contact you once a decision has been made."

"This is such bullshit," I growled, whipping around and storming out of the office. My chest was heaving with anger.

This was all Zaiden's fault.

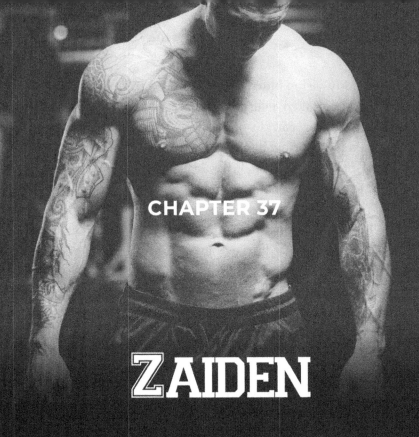

CHAPTER 37

ZAIDEN

I t felt good to be on the ice again.

I was so ready for hockey season to start.

The cool air hit my face as I glided around the rink before skidding to a stop and throwing up shaved ice.

My gaze lifted to the stadium seating, narrowing when I realized Ariella was gone. I spun on the ice, scanning the entire arena. She'd left.

Sterling slid to a stop beside me. "She left about fifteen minutes ago." He tapped his hockey stick against my shin pad. "So you can stop showing off now."

I traced the path she would have taken through the empty seats. "Where did she go?"

Sterling twisted his stick between his palms, that knowing smirk spreading across his face. "How the fuck would I know that?"

"I meant, did you see which way she went?"

"Oh." He planted his stick on the ice, using it to pivot toward the upper level. His free hand gestured to the doors. "She went into the sports hall."

My gaze locked on that door, remembering how she'd hesitated to even come into the ice arena. The slight tremble in her fingers. The way her breathing had shortened.

Ariella could wear anger like armor and wield sadness like a shield, but fear was different. It consumed her to a level that was overwhelming, which made her such an easy target.

"Where would she have gone?" The question came out casual, but Sterling's expression made my stomach twist. The sports hall reopened today, and it was mostly empty. There were no practices or team meetings.

He leaned on his stick, that shit-eating grin spreading wider. "Oh, I don't know." The pause stretched. "Maybe cleaning out her locker? You know, since you torpedoed her life."

I forced my lips into a smirk, ignoring the sudden chill that had nothing to do with the ice. "I didn't ruin anything. I improved it."

"Would she agree with that?"

"She will eventually see things my way."

Sterling's gaze lifted over my shoulder. "Oh, yeah," he raised his brows. "I think you're wrong." He nodded behind me, and I spun.

My smile faded as my eyes narrowed on Ariella, storming towards me on the ice without skates. "He—"

Her fist connected with my jaw, cutting off my words. "Fuck you, Zaiden." Her voice shook with fury.

"Yeah," Sterling said. "I'm gonna head out." I didn't bother turning to tell him goodbye. I had bigger problems. Ariella spun around like she was going to hit me and leave.

"What the fuck?" I growled, throwing my hockey stick to the ground as I pushed off the ice, sliding up to Ariella. My arm looped around her waist, and I lifted her off her feet, holding her against me as I slid to a stop.

"Let me go, or we'll both hit the ice."

I stopped at the edge of the rink, dropping her to her feet. "What is your fucking problem?"

She spun, pressing her finger into my chest. "You." Her lip curled into a snarl. "You are my fucking problem."

I backed her into the glass, close enough to feel the heat radiating between us despite the chill of the rink. Her breath hitched—barely perceptible, but I caught it.

"That's not what you were screaming last night." My voice dropped lower, watching the flush creep up her neck.

"Get out of my way." But her pupils dilated, betraying the fury in her voice.

My palms pressed flat against the glass on either side of her. She tilted her chin up in defiance, but I noticed how her eyes dropped to my mouth for a fraction of a second.

"No." The word came out rough. "Tell me what your problem is." The space between us crackled with something darker than anger.

Her jaw flexed as her gaze challenged mine. "You got what you wanted."

"I usually do."

She dipped under my arm, and I let her go. "I hope you're fucking happy."

"You're going to have to be a little more specific, Ariella." I followed her, gliding on the ice as she slipped and slid towards the exit. "Because I usually am happy to get my way."

She slipped, tumbling backward and hitting her butt. "Ahhhh," she screamed out as she worked to correct herself. She rolled to her knees, and I skidded to a stop in front of her. Her gaze lifted, meeting mine, and I could see the hatred flicker in her eyes. "Fuck you." She shoved her hands against my thighs, pushing me back. "I got kicked off the team today because of you."

My head recoiled in confusion. "Because of me?"

Her angry facade cracked, and her voice trembled. "Not only did I lose my entire team, but I also lost my spot on the dance team. The only thing I ever wanted is gone because of you." Tears filled her eyes, and my chest tightened. "Now, I've lost my scholarship, so it doesn't even matter that I'm being investigated for possible expulsion because I can't afford to go to school without a scholarship."

I slid forward, hooking my arms under hers, and pulled her to her feet.

"Ariella, what are you talking about?" My words came out soft. The familiar surge of satisfaction at seeing her hurt had vanished, replaced by an unfamiliar ache in my chest. This wasn't what I'd wanted—not anymore.

She cleared her throat. Her spine stiffened as she lifted her chin, that same stubborn pride I both hated and admired. "Dean Sweeney and Coach Hillard told me my behavior was unacceptable." Her voice cracked on the last word. "I'm off the team."

"What behavior?"

"Because someone sent them the video." Her tone dropped to a whisper, shoulders curling inward. "Of me—

and you. At the football party." Each word seemed to cost her something. When she looked up, a single tear carved down her cheek. "The perfect revenge for killing your sister, right?"

The rink fell silent.

Her next words hit like a blade between my ribs: "Except I didn't kill her."

Those five words echoed in my head, a truth I'd only recently accepted after months of burning hatred. Each time she'd tried to tell me, I'd refused to listen. Now, seeing her destroyed by my revenge, the guilt was suffocating.

Each tear tracking down Ariella's face carved away at the certainty I'd carried for months. I'd orchestrated her isolation, convinced she deserved to lose everything for what happened to my sister. I'd been wrong. It wasn't her fault. It was mine. The only problem was that what happened that night, at the party, had to happen.

In the history of Westbrook University, girls belonged to their team. Dancers and cheerleaders belonged to the football players, and figure skaters belonged to the hockey team. It was just how it worked here. Ariella Ledger was mine. I wasn't going to share her with the football team or EJ. So what happened would have happened regardless of my revenge plot or not.

The plan had always been to destroy everything good in Ariella's life. I wanted to isolate her from the football team, to claim her as my own. I never once regretted those intentions—until I discovered the truth. It honestly never crossed my mind that she might be kicked off the team for what happened. Now, I had to fix this.

"Go to practice," I said, voice rougher than intended. When I reached to brush a strand of hair from her face, she flinched away from my touch. "I will handle this."

"Oh," she huffed out a humorless laugh. "You have nothing to worry about. You're not losing your spot on the team because it's completely acceptable behavior from you." My eyes widened as the realization that she was being punished, but I wasn't for something that was ultimately my fault, sank in.

"Ariella—"

"Leave me alone," she growled. "I'm going home to pack my things, and then I'm going back to my dad's."

"You can't go back to your dad's because you have class this afternoon."

"Are you not freaking hearing me?" Each word came out razor-sharp. "There are no more classes." Her laugh was brittle, dangerous. "No more team. No more scholarships." With each statement, she advanced another step. "No more anything." I held my ground on the ice. "I'm suspended pending further investigation, which I'm sure will end in expulsion. I don't have classes anymore." She pressed both palms against my chest before shoving me. "Get. Out. Of. My. Way."

I let myself slide back, allowing her to pass. She could leave now. Go home and calm down because her suspension would be lifted before she made it home.

CHAPTER 38

ZAIDEN

My fingers trembled against Coach Hillard's door, not from fear, though. Rage had a way of making everything sharper, clearer, like the first time I'd stepped onto fresh ice at dawn. Everyone in this school preached about integrity while dealing in favors and secrets. I'd learned that lesson freshman year, watching them break their own rules whenever it suited them. Now, at least, I played their game better than they did.

I stood silently listening as muffled gasps and the sound of skin slapping together echoed through the door. A smile twisted my lips. How convenient that giving a blow job off campus was grounds for suspension, but apparently screwing someone's husband during school hours was perfectly acceptable.

If it had been anyone else in the school other than Dean Sweeney, this might have been a different situation, but I had plenty of dirt on her, and I knew she'd reverse her decision.

Digging through the pocket of my jeans, I pulled out my keys.

My fingers traced the cold metal. The master key had been my first real conquest at Westbrook. Freshman year, while everyone else memorized locker combinations, I memorized the janitor's schedule. Three months of careful observation, two weeks of strategic friendliness, and one staged emergency later, every locked door on campus became mine. Back then, I'd only wanted late-night access to the ice arena, a place to practice when no one was watching. Now, as the key's familiar weight settled in my palm, I appreciated how power rarely stays small once you get a taste for it.

Pulling my phone out of my back pocket, I slid it open before clicking on the camera button and switching it to video. I eased the key into the lock, careful not to make a sound. I didn't want to disturb the lovebirds before I got the footage I needed. Not that I didn't have plenty of other things to hold over Dean Sweeney's head. This just simplified everything.

I inched the door open, wide enough for my phone's lens. The ancient hinges stayed silent as I steadied my hand. Through the screen, I watched Dean Sweeney arch her back, her usually pristine blonde hair wild across Coach's desk. Last year, when she'd cornered me after practice with hungry eyes and whispered suggestions, I almost took her up on her offer. Almost. Now, watching her squirm under Coach Hillard, I was satisfied with my decision.

Dean Sweeney was fairly young for her position and incredibly hot. She had long wavy hair that was typically pulled back, and black framed glasses covered her dark brown eyes. She was thin and had decent curves, but she couldn't even hold a candle next to Ariella.

Dean Sweeney's cry of pleasure cut through the air, then choked into silence as her eyes met mine. For one perfect moment, time crystallized: her lips still parted in ecstasy, the realization dawning in her widening eyes, the blood draining from her face. I let my smirk build slowly as she scrambled to push herself up from the desk, dignity scattering like the papers beneath her.

"What are you—" The words died in her throat.

"Get the fuck out!" Coach's voice pitched high, his authority crumbling faster than his reputation was about to. The man lecturing his team about discipline couldn't keep his pants up.

I leaned against the doorframe, savoring the moment. "Please, don't let me interrupt." My tone dripped with honey-sweet venom. "Though I have to say, Coach, your form needs work."

"Knight." He spat my name like a curse, jabbing a trembling finger toward the door. "Out. Now." Coach's voice cracked between rage and terror, the mighty authority figure reduced to a man with his pants around his ankles. Each second of their panic was delicious.

"Well, okay then," I sauntered into the room, ending the video and shoving my phone in my pocket. I rounded the chairs in front of Coach's desk as they scrambled to find their clothes. "I think we need to talk." I dropped down into the chair.

"If this is about—" Sweeney's hands trembled as she searched for her clothes scattered across the office floor.

"That's exactly what it's about." I settled deeper into the chair, enjoying how she flinched at my relaxed tone.

"Well then," she managed, yanking her shirt over her head. The silk caught on her necklace. "You have nothing to worry about. You won't be punished." Her fingers smoothed her skirt compulsively, again and again. "Though I would suggest being more discreet in the future."

I huffed out a laugh. "I could say the same."

Coach zipped his pants. "If that's all, please see yourself out."

"Actually," I leaned forward, the chair's leather creaking beneath me. Their eyes snapped to mine. "We're not done." I let the silence stretch, watching them squirm. It was amazing how quickly power shifts; just minutes ago, they'd been the ones making all the noise.

"Ariella isn't going to be punished either."

"Unfortunately, that's not an opt—"

"Stop." The word felt soft but sharp. "Let me paint you a picture, Dean Sweeney. It's dinner time. You're sitting across from your husband, Thomas, right? He's asking about your day. Meanwhile, his phone buzzes. Then, your daughter's phone. Then every phone in every home of everyone of your colleagues." I pulled out my phone, turning it slowly in my hands. "How long do you think it would take for this video to reach them? Twenty minutes? Ten?"

The sounds of her early moans filled the small office, and the color drained from her face. Beside her, Coach Hillard's hands had curled into useless fists.

"So yes, Dean Sweeney. It is an option. In fact, it's your only option."

"That's blackmail, Zaiden." Sweeney crossed her arms

over her chest, trying to summon the authority that had crumbled the moment I opened that door.

Blackmail. It's such an ugly term for such a useful tool.

"Yeah," I finally said, tasting the power in my pause. "It's what I do best." My phone felt heavy in my pocket, warm with secrets. "But we can skip the moral outrage, Dean Sweeney. We both know you can't afford to let this video see the light of day. And maybe I'll share how you've propositioned most of the hockey team. Or how your dance coach was forcing dancers to suck his dick to make the team."

"Don't make claims you can't prove." Coach's voice had found its authority again, that same self-righteous tone.

I let my smile widen slowly. My phone slid across his desk. A video that had been passed through every player on the hockey team of Sweeney getting rammed by two hockey players last year. "I never do."

His eyes dropped to the screen, then snapped to Sweeney. "Are you—" The words seemed to stick in his throat. "Are you fucking students?"

Sweeney's silence filled the room. Her perfectly manicured nails dug crescents into her palms as she glared at me, but beneath the rage, I caught it, that flicker of fear.

The leather chair breathed as I rose, taking my time. No need to rush now, the game was already won. "Fifteen minutes, Sweeney." I checked my watch, an unnecessary gesture that made her flinch. "That's how long you have to reverse Ariella's suspension. With a formal apology, of course."

I moved toward the door with unhurried steps. I paused, not bothering to look back. "Oh, and Dean? Make it convincing. Think of it as a performance." My hand rested on the doorknob. "Maybe with less moaning this time."

The door clicked shut behind me with the softness of a whispered threat. In the empty hallway, I finally let myself smile. Sweeney would do exactly as she was told, as people always did when their carefully constructed lives hung by a digital thread.

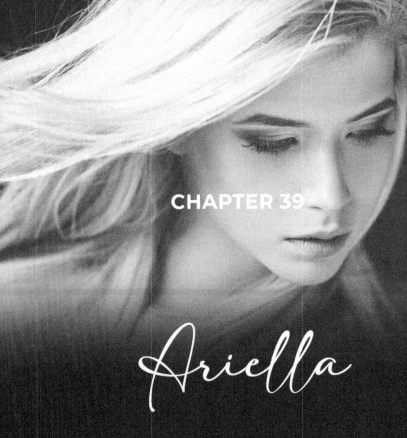

CHAPTER 39

Ariella

When it rained, it poured—And right now, it felt like a monsoon.

Everything I'd worked so hard for was gone.

I was four years old the first time I saw the Westbrook University dancers perform on the massive field, and I was eight the first time I got to tag along for a day. I knew I wanted that. I'd spent years in dance practicing, training, and dancing to be the best, and now it was all for nothing.

All because of Zaiden and his stupid plan to ruin me for something I didn't do.

I stared at the empty suitcase standing closed at the end of my bed. I didn't want to go back to my dad's house, but I also didn't want to be here. I'd never wanted to be here.

My gaze shifted, freezing on Kacie's MacBook sitting

on my desk, and I released a slow breath as my shoulders sagged. I couldn't leave without trying to figure out what happened to Kacie. I knew there was a big chance we'd never figure it out, but I had to get into that laptop. The fact that it had a different password than all her other devices told me that there was something she didn't want anyone to see. But what? I was her best friend, and I had no idea what it could be.

I leaned forward, jerking the laptop off my desk and onto my lap. Flipping it open, I stared at the login screen, gently tapping the keys.

"Okay, Kacie," I mumbled. "What is your password?"

I thought back over the passwords she used for everything else. Her bank and school logins were the first love of her life, Bella, her four-pound dachshund who passed away when she was twelve, and Kacie's birthday. Her social media logins were her best friend's initials and the date we met, but neither of those worked for her laptop. She always used something that was most important to her. My mind raced through the things she loved.

My phone buzzed on the bed beside me, pulling me from my pity party.

It was Mila. Again.

I'd ignored all her texts and phone calls because I didn't want to explain what happened again.

> Mila: We're at the front door. Let us in.

I started typing out a text telling her to go home, but an email chimed.

My heart knocked against my ribs when I spotted Dean Sweeney's name in my inbox. Already? The board never moved this quickly.

> Mila: Okay, well, we are coming in.

I barely registered Mila's text. My finger hovered over the email, trembling slightly. One click separated me from knowing whether I'd be packing my life away or staying. I closed my eyes, drew in a breath, and tapped the screen.

The first line blurred as my eyes raced ahead, searching for the only words that mattered.

> Ms. Ledger,
> The school board has determined that your actions were in poor taste, however—

My gaze stumbled, caught on the word "however." The kind of word that pivots futures.

> —They do not call for harsh actions since the incident occurred off campus. Your spot on the dance team will be reinstated, and your suspension will be lifted.

I gasped, the air rushing from my lungs as if I'd been holding my breath underwater. Staying. I was staying.

But then, at the bottom:

> We do apologize for misspeaking before we had all the details.

I froze, rereading the line. Dean Sweeney had never apologized to a student in the history of Westbrook. My eyes narrowed as understanding clicked into place—Zaiden. This had his fingerprints all over it.

My lips curled up into a grin. I didn't care as long as I could dance. As long as I didn't have to leave school and go back to my dad's.

"Ari," Mila burst through my bedroom door, freezing, as her gaze scanned the room. "Wow." She paused. "I haven't been in here since..." Her words trailed off.

"Yeah," I sighed. "It's a constant reminder that she's not here anymore."

She stepped into the room. "She loved you. If she would want anyone to move into her old room, she'd want it to be you."

I forced a smile as I nodded, my chest squeezing tightly as a hint of sadness hit me.

"Are you okay?" Journey asked, pushing past Mila. "You didn't show up to the meeting."

"It's a long story, but yeah, I'm good." I tucked my hair behind my ear, avoiding their concerned looks. "How was the meeting? Did they introduce a new coach?"

"No." Journey leaned against my desk, idly spinning a pen between her fingers. "They said they're working to find someone, but for now, they put the captain in charge."

My eyes widened as realization dawned. "You're the captain." I straightened, grabbing Journey's shoulders with both hands.

"Yep." Journey tried to look nonchalant, but the slight lift at the corner of her mouth betrayed her pride. She crossed her arms, rocking back on her heels. "And we're dancing at the home game this week."

"That's freaking awesome!" I bounced on the edge of my bed, my body automatically moving to an imaginary beat. Some part of me was already choreographing in my head.

Mila's smile faded as she sank into the desk chair. "As exciting as that is," she leaned forward, voice dropping, "we may have a problem."

Something in her tone made my stomach tighten. "What kind of problem?"

"I was in the athletic building earlier." She glanced toward the open door and back. "EJ and some of the guys were in the weight room. They didn't see me."

I waited, the silence stretching uncomfortably.

"They were talking about revenge. For what happened at the party between you and Zaiden."

I waved dismissively. "Zaiden's a big boy. I'm sure he can—"

"They're not coming after Zaiden," Mila cut in, her eyes holding mine. "They're coming after you."

A shadow fell across the floor. "Who's coming after Ariella?"

The temperature in the room seemed to drop ten degrees. Zaiden stood in the doorway, his frame blocking the exit completely. His knuckles whitened against the doorjamb; the only visible sign of the rage I knew was building beneath his controlled exterior.

"It's nothing." I shifted in my chair. "Just team drama."

He stepped into the room, his gaze never leaving Mila's face. "Who. Is coming. After. Ariella?"

Mila's eyes flicked to me, silently asking permission. I shook my head slightly, mouthing "no". The last thing I needed was Zaiden starting a war over something I could handle myself, especially when we both knew how his wars ended.

"Who?" Zaiden's voice cracked, making all three of us flinch.

Mila broke. "EJ and the football team," she blurted, the words tumbling out like she couldn't hold them back anymore.

I groaned.

"What did they say?"

"Their exact words—" Journey hesitated, glancing at me.

"What?" Zaiden pressed, taking a step toward her. "What exactly did they say?"

Journey swallowed. "They said they were going to—" Her voice dropped to nearly a whisper. "—ruin that pussy for you." She looked at the floor. "They talked about passing her through all of them."

The room went silent.

Zaiden's face remained perfectly still—too still. Only the muscle ticking along his jawline betrayed any reaction. His head tilted slightly as his eyes narrowed, processing this information with the cold calculation of someone planning a war strategy.

"They're all talk," I said quickly, stepping between Zaiden and Journey. "They're pissed about what happened at the party. Give it a week, they'll find something else to obsess over."

"I wouldn't be so sure," Journey muttered. "EJ seemed pretty—"

I shot her a look that could have frozen hellfire, and her mouth snapped shut mid-sentence.

"Everyone is overreacting." I kept my voice light, as if discussing tomorrow's weather instead of threats against me. "The football team is harmless. They're just boys with bruised egos."

I squared my shoulders and met Zaiden's gaze directly. The temperature in his eyes had dropped to something arctic.

"I'm not worried about any of them." My chin lifted, the lie smooth on my tongue. "Don't make this worse than it already is."

I held his stare, refusing to blink, silently pleading with him to let it go.

"Any luck getting into Kacie's MacBook?" Mila asked, effortlessly changing topics like she always did when tension rose too high. Zaiden finally broke eye contact, and I blew out a quiet sigh of relief.

"No." I shifted back to the laptop, running my fingers along its closed edge. "There was something in there she didn't want anyone finding. She never changed passwords unless—" I trailed off, the implications hanging in the air.

"This would be easier if we had her phone." Zaiden's voice was clipped, matter-of-fact, his problem-solving tone.

"But we don't." I met his eyes, matching his bluntness. "So, I'll keep working on her laptop."

"Let me know if I can help with anything." Mila gathered her bag, always the mediator. "But we have to go, like, now."

"Right." Journey checked her watch. "Tutoring in an hour." She curled her lip and flicked her dark hair over her shoulder. "God, I hate tutoring. Professor Martinez makes us explain the same concept, like, twenty different ways."

"Want to meet up after?" I asked.

"Yeah," Mila said. "Let's all meet at the library."

Mila led the way out with Journey following her.

My gaze shifted to Zaiden, still standing in my room, and my smile faded. I knew he had something to do with that email from the Dean, but that didn't change the fact that it all happened because of him.

"So, does that mean you're staying?" Zaiden asked, his eyes dropping to my empty luggage and then back to me.

I pushed off the bed and took a step toward him. "This was all your fault." I shoved my finger into his chest. "If it wasn't for you," I shoved it harder, "I wouldn't have been kicked off the team to begin with—"

"But." His lips curved into a grin as he caught my wrist, squeezing tightly.

"But—" The words caught in my throat as he pressed his body against mine, trapping me between him and the wall. "Thank you. For whatever you did to fix it."

His hands found my hips, his touch deceptively gentle at first before his fingers dug in, just enough to make me wince.

"So you forgive me?" The question floated between us, soft as a caress but sharp with danger underneath.

I met his gaze. "No." I twisted away, shoving his hands off with force. "You're still the reason all this happened."

One step toward the door. Two.

The air shifted behind me, the only warning before his hand shot out, catching my throat and spinning me around. My back slammed against the wall, the impact forcing the air from my lungs in a quiet gasp.

I blinked, suddenly aware of how close he was, feeling the heat radiating from his skin, and the smell of the mint on his breath.

"That's okay." His thumb traced an agonizingly slow path along my jawline, the unexpected gentleness making my skin tingle in contrast to the unyielding grip at my throat. "I like it better when you hate me."

The pressure at my neck increased by fractions, just enough to make my pulse leap beneath his fingertips.

I refused to look away, to surrender even the smallest victory in this twisted game between us. "You make it so easy," I gritted out.

Something darkened in his eyes then, a shadow passing over deep water. His lips curved into that smile I hated, the one that said he knew exactly what effect he had.

"You don't really hate me," he breathed, so close now that the heat of his breath brushed against my lips. "You want to hate me—" His free hand skimmed up my side, leaving goosebumps in its wake. "But you don't."

My lip curled into a defiant snarl, but the betrayal came from within—heat flooding my body, pooling low in my belly and between my thighs.

His gaze shifted momentarily toward my bed before returning to me, now lit with cruel intentions. "You want me." Each word fell like stones dropping into still water. "You want me to fuck you."

The worst part wasn't that he was wrong.

The worst part was that he was right.

His fingers squeezed, and I felt the contact everywhere. "You want me to make you come."

I was about to argue, to tell him to fuck off, but I was spun around so fast I hadn't fully processed what was happening when he pressed his hips into my ass, pinning me against the wall. His hand tunneled into my hair, ripping my head back and to the side, giving him better access to my neck.

A deep groan rumbled through his chest, vibrating against my skin as his teeth scraped the sensitive spot where my neck met my shoulder. My body betrayed me instantly—back arching, pressing harder into the rigid length of him. The rational part of my brain screamed to push him away, to hold onto my anger, but it was drowning in a flood of want.

"I hate you," I whispered, the words lacking any real conviction.

His only response was a dark laugh against my throat, his hands tightening on my hips.

The world tilted as he spun me away from the wall. One moment, I was standing; the next, I was bent forward, the mattress edge catching me at the waist. My heartbeat thundered in my ears, blood rushing hot beneath my skin as his fingers hooked into the waistband of my leggings. The soft fabric slid down my thighs, taking my underwear with it in one smooth motion.

Cool air kissed my exposed skin, raising goosebumps in its wake. I heard the soft thud of cloth hitting the floor, followed by the sound of him stepping between my feet.

"Spread your legs." His voice had dropped an octave, rough with desire but deadly calm.

The metallic rasp of his zipper sliding down seemed to echo in the silence of the room. Time stretched, suspended in that moment of anticipation, of choice.

My hands flattened against the mattress. Some last flicker of resistance made me push upward, an instinctive attempt to regain control, to remind myself I wasn't a puppet dancing on his strings.

His response was immediate. One large hand wrapped around the back of my neck, pressing me down with unmistakable authority, not hard enough to hurt, just enough to remind me who was in control. Just enough to make my stomach tighten with a shameful thrill.

"Spread. Your. Fucking. Legs."

I hesitated for one heartbeat—two—before surrendering to the inevitable. Slowly, I shifted my feet apart until my hips lay flat against the bed, exposing myself completely to him.

Behind me, I heard his sharp intake of breath, the smallest victory in this power struggle between us.

The distinct sound of a foil wrapper being ripped open echoed through the silence as his free hand curled around my hip. "Take this dick like a good girl." His hips snapped forward, and I cried out as he filled me with one brutal thrust.

My hands curled into the comforter. There was no chance to adjust to his massive cock before he started fucking me. He withdrew before driving back into me harder and faster each time.

The way his cock filled me, stretched me felt so good, I couldn't think straight. My hands reached back, my nails digging into his thighs. "Oh fuck," I cried out as my belly clenched and my blood heated, sending me spiraling closer and closer to what I craved.

The wet sounds of his hips slapping against my ass filled the room.

He wound my ponytail around his fist and tugged, forcing my back to arch. "Oh—My—God."

His speed increased, thrusting faster, hitting a spot that set my body on fire. Every ruthless snap of his hips sent another jolt of pleasure coursing through me until I hit my peak.

My body tensed. "Zaiden!" I exploded around him, my orgasm so severe I couldn't breathe.

He doesn't stop fucking me hard and fast. With a harsh grunt, he withdrew one last time before slamming into me and holding himself deep as he came.

He collapsed on top of me for a long moment as we caught our breath.

"See," he breathed, his lips brushing against my ear. "You don't hate me as much as you think you do."

The satisfaction in his voice cut through the lingering haze of pleasure, a cold reminder of what happened—of my weakness, my surrender.

I placed my palms against the mattress and shoved hard enough that he rolled off me with a grunt. The sudden absence of his weight and warmth left me feeling exposed in ways that had nothing to do with my nakedness.

"Fuck you," I said, each word precisely shaped and delivered with quiet venom.

His laugh followed me as I slid off the bed, my legs still trembling slightly. I felt his eyes tracking me as I crossed the room, forcing myself to walk normally despite the pleasant ache between my thighs.

I didn't look back as I entered the bathroom and closed the door with a softness. A slam would have shown him he was right. Instead, I turned the lock with a soft click that said more than any shouted curse.

Only then, with the barrier between us, did I let my forehead rest against the cool wood of the door, eyes closed, breath unsteady.

I hated that he was right.

I stepped into the shower and turned the water as hot as I could stand it, as if I could wash away not just the evidence of him on my skin but the knowledge that some broken part of me would welcome his hands on me again.

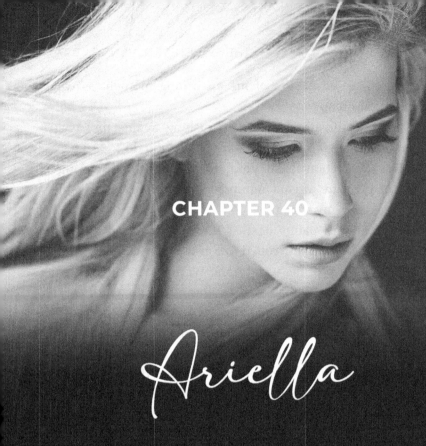

CHAPTER 40

Ariella

The harsh blue glow of the locked computer screen taunted me as I clicked my pen against the library table, the sharp tapping echoing in our corner of the hushed room. My fingerprints smudged the edges of the keyboard, evidence of hours of failed attempts.

"Any luck?" Zaiden asked, the wooden chair creaking as he sank into the seat across from me before sliding an iced caramel macchiato across the table. The ice clinked against the plastic.

Shaking my head, I gnawed my bottom lip raw. The cursor blinked on the password screen, mocking me. Each failed attempt felt like the truth was slipping further away from us.

Staring at the screen, I zoned Journey, Mila, Sterling, and Zaiden out as they quietly chatted around the square table. I had to get into this computer. It was our only hope of figuring out what really happened to Kacie.

"Focus," I mumbled, sipping my coffee. "What were the most important things in Kacie's life?"

Her friends.

Me.

Her family.

Her dog.

And at one point, her ex—

Oh my God. Her ex. That would be the last password I would try.

My fingers hovered over the keys before typing: Dayton.

ACCESS DENIED flashed back.

His birthday—12/04. The screen remained locked.

His first and last name—DaytonMitchell.

Nothing.

"Shit," I groaned, slamming my palm against the table. The library's quiet amplified my frustration. Three students at a nearby table glanced over, then quickly looked away. "When did they meet? Does anyone remember exactly?"

"What?" Mila's gaze narrowed.

"Do you remember when Kacie and Dayton started dating?"

"I do," Journey said. "It was two days before my seventeenth birthday."

I typed the date into the MacBook. Wrong.

"Fuck." My last chance. My fingers trembled as I tried his initials, followed by the date: DM-05172020.

The screen paused. One second. Two. Three.

The desktop blossomed open.

"I'm in," I whispered, then louder: "I'm IN!"

Chairs scraped against the floor as everyone crowded around, their shadows falling across the screen, their breath hot on my neck.

"Where do I start?" My mouse hovered, uncertain over the sea of folders and icons that contained Kacie's digital life.

"Pictures," Mila suggested.

I moved the mouse toward the pictures folder when something caught my eye—a folder simply labeled "evidence?" My hand froze on the trackpad.

"What's that?" Mila leaned in, her finger tapping the screen.

"Only one way to find out." Zaiden's voice was steady, but his knuckles whitened as he gripped the edge of the table.

The folder opened, revealing dozens of subfolders. Each click revealed more photographs meticulously organized by date, screenshots of conversations, and voice recordings labeled with initials.

"Oh my God," I whispered, opening the first image file. Coach Palmer's face filled the screen, his arm around a dancer I recognized from last year's competition team. The next photo showed him with another student, their positions too intimate for comfort.

"Keep going," Sterling urged, his earlier casualness completely gone.

I clicked through more images, the pit in my stomach growing heavier with each new photo. Journey gasped when she appeared in one of them—Coach's hand on her head as she kneeled in front of him. Then Mila in another. Then me.

"There are text messages, too," I said, opening a document filled with screenshot after screenshot. Kacie had been systematic in gathering evidence for months. The conversations between her and Coach started professionally but gradually revealed his pattern of manipulation.

"She was done being his victim," Journey said, her voice barely audible. "She was building a case."

Mila sank back into her chair. "And he knew it." She pointed to a message where Kacie threatened him.

> Kacie: You have two options. You can resign, or I will turn everything I have over to the police and the school.

He never responded.

I stared at the screen, connections forming like constellations in my mind. "This is why she was acting so strangely those last few weeks. She was protecting all of us while gathering evidence."

"And it got her killed," Zaiden said, the words hanging heavy in the library's hushed atmosphere.

"Even if he was the one who cut her brake line," Zaiden said, "That doesn't explain how he knew what car she was driving."

"Maybe it was a good guess," Sterling said. "I mean, think about it, if the brake line was cut at the party. He could have followed her or seen her get out of the car."

"Or maybe," Mila said. "It was a lucky guess. It was the only black BMW at the party that night. I was Kacie's friend, and I would have thought that was her car."

We spent the next hour in tense silence. The only sounds were our breathing and the soft click of the trackpad. Photos of Kacie smiling at parties. Class notes. Social media drafts that were never posted. Each file was a piece of her, but nothing else that explained what could have happened that night.

The brightness of the screen burned my eyes when Journey slumped back.

"This folder's just more dance routines."

Mila sighed. "Everything else is just part of her normal life."

I closed the laptop with a quiet click of finality. "I don't think we're going to find anything else."

"I guess we got our answers," Mila said. "It was Coach trying to stop her from outing him and all his dirty little secrets."

It felt surreal finally knowing what really happened to Kacie, even if we'd never get the full truth because Coach was dead.

"So what do we do now?" Journey asked.

"We could finish Kacie's mission and make all this go viral," Mila said. "Or…"

"We can let it die knowing Kacie got her revenge," Zaiden finished for her. Everyone's gaze locked on Zaiden because this felt like it should be his decision.

"I think we all took in a lot of information that needs time to settle," Sterling said. "Why don't we meet up after school tomorrow?"

We all nodded in agreement.

I pushed out of my chair and slid Kacie's MacBook into my messenger bag. The weight of it—and everything it contained—felt heavier than before. "I guess it's finally over," I mumbled. "We finally know the truth." Though I still had more questions than answers, I was pretty sure we'd never get those answers. We could only guess what else happened, and that would have to be good enough.

CHAPTER 41

Ariella

"Your choice." Zaiden's shoulder pressed against my car door, casual as a predator sizing up prey. "We can do this the easy way, or we can do this with zip ties." A switchblade smile played on his lips.

"Move." My keys bit into my palm, metal warm against my skin. "I mean it, Zaiden. I'm done playing your games."

"Games?" He uncoiled from the car. "Baby, if I were playing *games*, you wouldn't be standing here arguing."

A chill raced up my spine. "Zaiden," I growled, squaring my shoulders. "Get out of my way. I'm taking my car without you in it."

I thought we'd moved past the whole fear of the football team gangbanging me but apparently not.

"No, you're not," he said. "You're getting on this bike with me, and it's up to you how you get on."

My lip curled into a snarl. "I liked it better," I snatched the helmet off the bike, "when you didn't care what happened to me."

He huffed out a laugh as he grabbed his helmet and leaned into me. "I've always cared what happened to you." The corners of his lips curled into a devilish grin. "No one is going to touch you but me. Not for any reason." He shrugged. "That's always been the rule. Why do you think no guys talked to you in high school?"

My brows pulled together. "Because of you?" He nodded. "You're a dick."

"College." He rolled the word like it tasted bitter. "Different crowd, same game. Which is exactly why I had to put you on your knees in front of everyone. EJ wasn't getting the message."

"Don't." My nails dug crescents into my palms, fighting back the hot sting of humiliation. "You did that because you wanted to ruin my life."

"I did that because you are mine, and there was only one way to make that happen." His knuckles whitened around the bike's handlebars. "I just didn't anticipate EJ and his pack going after you instead of me."

"You're being ridiculous." I shifted away from the intensity rolling off him in waves. "EJ isn't going to do anything. You're seeing monsters where there's just—"

"Just the guy whose specialty drink had you stripping out of your clothes?" Zaiden's voice cut like glass. "That kind of harmless?"

My stomach turned. "You don't know if it was him or anyone on the football team."

"It's not a risk I'm willing to take, princess." His breath ghosted across my cheek, warm against the morning chill. "Get on the fucking bike. Before we are both late to class."

He released me.

I stood there, keys still digging into my palm.

With a heavy sigh that felt like surrender, I climbed onto the bike.

I honestly didn't know what EJ was capable of, but having Zaiden shadow my every move felt like trading one cage for another. I wanted him gone, needed him gone, except for those traitorous moments when his presence made me feel untouchable. Safe. The way he used to before everything imploded. Those moments were the most dangerous of all.

The bike vibrated to life before we both pulled on our helmets. I sat up straight with my arms crossed, pouting that he'd won, but there was nothing new about that.

Zaiden always won.

"Hold on," his voice crackled through the helmet speaker. I kept my arms crossed, the cool air biting through my jacket. His hands found my knees, one sharp tug erasing the space between us. "You really like to do things the hard way, don't you?" My lip curled even though I knew he couldn't see it. "You can admit it. You like it when I tie you up."

"I do not. I don't even want to be on this bike with you."

"Would you prefer rope or handcuffs?"

"For—What?"

"To secure your hands around me."

I rolled my eyes. "Whatever, Zaiden. Let's go." I wrapped my arms around his waist, hating how familiar it felt.

"That's better." Satisfaction coiled off him in waves, thick enough to choke on.

"Let's just go." The words came out clipped, brittle.

The bike lurched forward—tires catching gravel, spinning, then finally gripping asphalt. I hadn't meant to, but my fingers betrayed me, digging deeper into his jacket with each acceleration.

At the red light, the bike idled. "When is your first class?" Zaiden asked, his voice unnaturally casual.

I stared at the back of his helmet, seeing only my own reflection. "Why? Planning to escort me to my desk, too?"

His shoulders tensed beneath his leather jacket. "I'm going to drop you off, and then I'll be back before you get out."

"Come on, Zaiden." The morning sun caught his visor, turning it mirror-bright. "Even if I thought EJ might try something, it's not going to be at school." A black truck with windows tinted midnight black crept up beside us, the diesel engine's low growl making my skin prickle. "There are too many people around."

The light flashed green, and Zaiden surged forward, the bike's engine purring beneath us. "Doesn't matter. This is just how—" His voice cut off, head snapping left. "What the—"

I saw it before he did, the black truck's tires angling toward us.

Time stretched. First came the sound—rubber screaming against asphalt. Then movement—the truck lunging into our lane like a beast claiming territory. The bike bucked beneath us, a wild animal fighting for balance as we veered off road.

My fingers clawed desperately at Zaiden's jacket for one breathless second before the force ripped me away. And then—nothing beneath me. Only my body spinning through empty air.

The world tumbled in fragments: sky, grass, concrete, sky again. The truck's engine roared in triumph as it disappeared, leaving behind only the stench of burnt rubber and diesel.

My body slammed into the ground. The impact rippled through me, each wave bringing fresh pain. My lungs seized, trapped between inhale and exhale. Each heartbeat pulsed against my bruised skin.

"Ariella!" Zaiden's voice cracked through the fog of pain. Gravel crunched under his hands and knees as he crawled to me. I'd never heard that edge of raw panic in his voice before. His fingers fumbled with my helmet clasp, trembling in a way that didn't fit with the Zaiden I knew. The helmet lifted away, and cool air kissed my face, carrying the metallic tang of blood from where I'd bitten my cheek.

"Ari, are you okay?" His hands cupped my face with a gentleness that felt foreign, like being touched by a stranger wearing Zaiden's skin. His palms were warm, but his fingers were ice-cold with fear.

"I'm okay," I managed, my words scratching past my throat like lies usually do.

My chest finally remembered how to expand. Air rushed in too fast, making the world tilt, or maybe that was the aftermath of flight and impact still spinning through my head. The truth was simpler: nothing felt broken, but everything hurt.

"Are you sure?" His eyes met mine before dropping to catalog every scrape, every future bruise, every place my body had met the ground.

The mask of arrogant control had shattered, leaving behind something raw and real that scared me more than our near-death experience. Because Zaiden showing fear meant we were in deeper trouble than I'd imagined. "What hurts?"

"Is everyone okay?" A shadow fell across us, belonging to a man hovering at the edge of the grass.

"We're good." Zaiden's body shifted, angling between me and the stranger.

Pain spiderwebbed through my ribs as I pushed myself up, grass staining my palms.

"Good." The dark-haired man's gaze darted between us, and the skid marks scarring the road. "Because that almost looked intentional." It felt intentional, but at the same time, why would anyone want to hurt Zaiden or me? "Should I call the cops?"

Zaiden's jaw ticked. "No. We're good here. Thank you." Steel wrapped in velvet—a tone that discouraged further questions.

"Okay, if you're sure." The man made his way back to his white car, still running on the road. Thankfully, we'd been moving at a slow speed, and he merged us into grass and not concrete or asphalt.

"Are you sure you're okay?"

"I'm a little sore, but I'm okay." My eyes lifted, meeting his. "Are you okay?"

"I'm good."

My back pocket vibrated at the same time Zaiden's phone chimed. He dug into the pocket of his jacket, and I shifted my weight to pull my phone out of the back pocket of my jeans.

"It's Mila," Zaiden said, staring at his phone.

> Mila: I need everyone to meet me in the library before class.

My gaze lifted, locking with Zaiden, holding for a long

moment. "She must have found something she doesn't want to text," I said, and he nodded.

"Do you trust me enough to get back on my bike?" I wrapped my hand around the opposite arm that was still throbbing.

I swallowed hard as my gaze shifted from Zaiden to the bike still on its side. I was terrified.

"Ariella," he extended his hand. My eyes lifted from his hand to him. "I promise I will get you to school safely, and I'll get my truck after, so no more bike."

"Tell me the truth," I whispered. "Do you think that was an accident?"

He sucked in a heavy breath as his gaze shifted in the direction the truck disappeared and shrugged. "I don't know."

"But if it wasn't, we are safer on the road than sitting here waiting for a ride."

I nodded, putting my hand in his. "Okay." He tugged me up, and I grimaced as pain shot through my arm.

"You're hurt."

"It's nothing." My voice stayed steady. "Just bruised."

His jaw worked, gaze fixed on my shoulder like he was seeing a different injury, a different day. "Zaiden." The name fell softly between us.

"Kacie," he breathed. My chest ached. This triggered something for him. Something bringing back Kacie's death. His breathing increased, and for the first time since I'd been back, I saw that Zaiden was human. He was hurting like the rest of us.

"Zaiden." My voice came softer than intended as I reached for his face. His skin felt cold beneath my fingers as I forced him to look at me. "I'm fine."

My gaze dropped. Without thinking, I grabbed his

hand, the same hand that had threatened me with zip ties less than an hour ago, and pressed it flat against my chest. Beneath his palm, my heart hammered out the steady proof: alive, alive, alive.

His breathing synchronized with mine. Gradually, his pulse slowed beneath my fingertips, his eyes clearing as they lifted to meet mine.

"I'm okay," I whispered.

His throat bobbed on a hard swallow, and he nodded as he slowly came back from where he'd been.

"We are both okay, Zaiden."

"I'm okay." He said more as a question than a statement.

I nodded, and he pulled his hand away, twisting to get his bike.

He guided the bike back onto the asphalt. Thankfully, this was a back road that was usually pretty slow unless there was an accident on the main roads. I swiped my helmet off the ground and followed him to the road. He kicked the stand down, holding the bike up.

Strolling up, I stopped behind him. "Do you—" He spun around, his hand gripping my face, and his mouth slammed against mine, swallowing my words. After the initial shock wore off, my eyes closed as I melted into him. His hand dove into my hair, gripping tightly as he tugged my head back, giving him better access to my mouth.

This was what he needed, and maybe I did too.

He pulled out of the kiss, his ragged breath fanning across my face as his forehead dropped to mine. "I thought you were dead."

"I'm not. I'm just a little sore." He nodded. "Let's get out of here."

CHAPTER 42

ZAIDEN

My breathing finally started to steady as I stepped into the library with Ariella's small hand in mine. The purple-blue mark on her left cheek was already darkening beneath the fluorescent glare near the entrance.

The heavy wooden door swung shut behind us with a soft click, sealing out the chaotic world beyond. Students hunched over laptops or sprawled in armchairs, their faces illuminated by blue screen light. Whispered conversations and the occasional page turn punctuated the stillness.

We spotted Mila, Journey, and Sterling sitting at a square table tucked in the back of the library, surrounded by towering shelves of medical references no one had ever touched. It was the perfect place for secrets.

A student passed too close to our table, and Sterling fell

silent mid-sentence. His easy smile remained fixed until the footsteps faded.

His gaze lifted to us as his smile vanished. He shoved out of his chair, the legs screeching against the floor. "Woah, what the fuck happened?" His voice, though hushed, carried enough force to make a nearby student glance our way.

Mila and Journey's eyes followed Sterling's line of sight, having a similar reaction.

"We're okay," Ariella said, stopping at the table. She flashed me a look.

My mouth went dry. "We were run off the road this morning."

Journey's hand flew to her throat. Sterling's water bottle thudded onto the table.

"On purpose?" Mila's voice dropped to a hiss, her face contorting into a scowl that transformed her features.

Ariella shrugged, but I caught the slight tremor in her shoulders.

"I don't know," I sighed, the throb of my bruised ribs pulsing with each breath. "It seemed intentional, but it could have been an accident." The memory flashed again—the swerve across the center line. "It's hard to say."

"Did you go to the hospital?" Journey leaned forward, concern etching her features.

Ariella shook her head, wincing as the movement aggravated her bruised cheek.

"No." I ran a hand through my hair. "We're both a little sore, but we're okay. Everyone should be extra vigilant of their surroundings right now." My tone made it clear this wasn't merely a suggestion.

Sterling, Journey, and Mila adjusted their seats as they

slid back into them, and Ariella and I found a chair to slip into.

"So what are we doing here?" My fingers drummed against the polished wood.

The library's ventilation system clicked off, leaving us in sudden silence. Mila glanced over her shoulder before shifting in her chair, the scrape of wood against the floor unnaturally loud. She leaned forward on her elbows, close enough that I could smell her coffee-tinged breath.

"So last night after we got into the laptop," Mila started. "I started trying to put puzzle pieces together, and I did a little digging on the officer who was first to arrive at Kacie's accident." Her voice dropped so low I had to strain to hear. "He died three months after Kacie's accident."

My fingers froze mid-tap.

"Okay?" I finally managed, my throat suddenly dry as sand.

"The paper said it was an overdose, but it was considered a suspicious death."

"He was murdered?" Ariella's voice dropped to barely above a whisper, the word 'murdered' hanging in the air between us.

I caught Sterling's eye across the table. His jaw tightened.

"I couldn't find anything else on him after the initial article," Mila continued, leaning closer, "but what if it was the coach cleaning up his mess?"

I sank back in my chair, the wood creaking under my shifting weight. The table's worn surface blurred as my mind raced through implications.

If that was true, it didn't matter; everyone involved was dead.

"I can ask my brother to dig into it a little more," Mila started.

I shook my head. "No." My gaze lifted, meeting Mila's. "Coach Palmer is dead. He cut the brakes. The cop covered it up, and now they are both dead. They got their karma, and that's enough for me."

"Then who ran us off the road?"

"I think we are paranoid right now," I sighed, not entirely believing my own words. The memory of the truck veering toward us flashed behind my eyes—the way it had corrected course, aimed right for us. But none of it made sense. Who would want to hurt us?

"The driver was probably on his phone or something and swerved into our lane." My voice sounded hollow even to me.

I pressed my lips into a tight line as my gaze held Ariella's. Her eyes—always so expressive—searched mine for reassurance I wasn't sure I could honestly give.

"It's time for all of us to move on," I said finally, choosing the comfort of denial over the terror of truth. "Kacie's gone, and I have to believe she got her revenge."

Ariella leaned forward. "But what if it wasn't Coach?"

Sterling's head snapped up. "Who else would it be?" His voice had an edge I hadn't heard before. "Think about it. Who else had a reason to want Kacie dead?"

We all sat silently, the clock on the far wall ticking. Names and faces flickered through my mind—classmates, teachers, friends. With each mental image came the same question: Could they have done it?

Journey's pen tapped against her notebook. Once. Twice. Then stopped.

Mila cleared her throat. "No one," she finally said, but her voice wavered. "Everyone loved Kacie." She straightened her shoulders. "She wanted to stop Coach from what he'd been doing for years, and he wasn't willing to go out like that."

Ariella's brows pulled together as her gaze lifted to mine. "How did you get the videos of me and Coach?"

I scowled, thinking back to when I found the emails. "Someone sent them to me anonymously."

"When?"

I shrugged as I pursed my lips. "I don't know. They were sent to an email I almost never check." I flipped open my phone using my thumb to scroll through emails.

"Did the email say anything?"

I shook my head, my eyes locked on my phone as I continued to scroll. "No, just had the videos." I found the email and clicked on it. My eyes widened as I noticed the date and time. "It came in a few hours before Kacie's car accident."

"She knew he was coming after her," Ariella said.

Journey tucked her hair behind her ear. "That was all she sent you?"

"That was it." I traced the edge of my phone case.

"We should all dig through old emails." Ariella leaned forward, wincing as her bruised ribs protested the movement. Her voice took on the determined edge that had made her debate team captain three years running. "Make sure she didn't send anything else. Make sure you check your jun—"

"No."

My voice cut through the air like a blade. Everyone froze. Journey's thumb hovered mid-search. Sterling's water bottle stopped halfway to his lips.

Four pairs of eyes narrowed on me, a synchronized

reaction that would have been comical in any other circumstance.

The silence stretched. One second. Two. Three.

"This is over. Coach is gone, it's not like we need to collect evidence to get him fired or arrested. He's dead."

"But don't you want the truth exposed?" Journey asked.

I shook my head. "No. I don't want those videos getting out because that's what will happen if we expose everything."

Ariella sucked in a deep breath. "So it's over."

"Kacie wanted us all to know the truth," Journey said. "And we do, and I think Zaiden is right. Kacie's looking down, smiling, knowing she got her revenge and we're all okay."

A tear streamed down Ariella's cheek.

My back lifted off my chair, and I spun to her. My large hand wrapped around her knee, and I spun her toward me before pulling her closer so her knees slid between mine. "Kacie can finally rest in peace." I brushed my thumb across her cheek, wiping away her tears.

Her eyes closed as she melted into my touch. "Okay."

"Shit," Sterling muttered, checking his watch. He stood abruptly, chair legs scraping. "I have five minutes to make it to the opposite end of campus before Professor Harmon locks me out." His movements became a blur, backpack grabbed, water bottle capped, notebook shoved inside.

"Yeah," Journey said, rising. "I have to go." She smoothed her skirt. "I'll text you later."

Mila glanced between them, then at her phone. "Shit," she echoed, but made no move to stand. "Time went by fast." She closed her laptop with a decisive click. "I gotta go too."

One by one, they peeled away from our circle. The library seemed enormous around us. Too quiet. Too empty. "Come on," I said, grabbing Ariella's bag off the floor. "I'll walk you to class." We had plenty of time before our first classes. Maybe enough time to breathe, to process.

As we crossed the library threshold into the morning sunlight, a weight lifted from my chest. We knew who was responsible for my sister's death. We knew he had paid the ultimate price. Justice served cold but complete.

My hand slipped into Ariella's, her fingers cool against my palm. For the first time in months, I could imagine a future beyond grief, a chance to forgive myself for not being there when Kacie needed me.

Ariella's fingers tightened around mine, but her eyes remained fixed ahead. I knew she hadn't forgiven me yet.

But she would, in time.

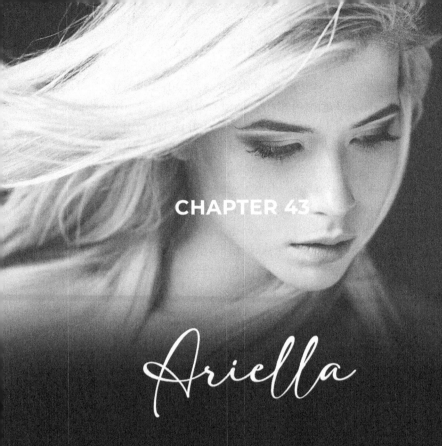

CHAPTER 43

Ariella

It was pouring rain by the time we made it home.

He'd never admit it, but I could see how much everything was weighing on him. He'd lost his sister, and it turned out it wasn't an accident.

"Hey." I perched on the arm of the couch beside him, my fingers fidgeting with the hem of my sleeve. His gaze turned, freezing on me like he'd just realized I was in the room. "You okay?"

He sucked in a heavy breath as his arms dropped to his side, and he moved into my personal space. "I'm good."

I shouldn't care after everything he'd done to me, but a small part of me understood, understood the need to hurt the person who hurt Kacie, and he truly believed that person was me. The loss of Kacie was still so raw for everyone, but especially Zaiden, and no one helped him mourn her because after she died, his entire family fell apart. I'd spent the last year trying to make sense of her death. I'd blamed myself even though I knew it wasn't my fault.

"It's okay not to be okay," I whispered.

His gaze held mine for a long minute. "I'm—" He shook his head, a muscle working in his jaw. "I don't know."

Silence stretched between us. Rain drummed against the windows, punctuated by distant thunder. I watched his hands curl into fists, then release, curl, and release—a rhythm of restraint.

"Today was a lot," I finally offered.

"You could have been killed."

I swallowed. "I wasn't. And neither were you."

The distance between us on the couch felt both too vast and not nearly enough. He stared at his hands, voice dropping.

"I can't lose someone else," he whispered.

I closed my eyes. "I know."

He sucked in a deep breath. "If I didn't know any better, I'd say you cared about me," he breathed as he reached out, brushing a loose strand of hair out of my face and sliding it behind my ear. His touch was so gentle that I almost forgot this was the new Zaiden—the one after Kacie's death.

I did care. I shouldn't, but I did. "I don't want to lose anyone else either." The thought of standing graveside and watching another casket lowered into the ground made my stomach churn.

His fingertips brushed over the bruise on my cheek. "No one is going to hurt you." Everything in his words and his touch made me believe him.

"Zaiden," I whispered, the name caught somewhere between prayer and a curse.

His knuckles dragged down my jaw, so gentle from hands I'd seen curled into weapons. His thumb pressed against my bottom lip, tugging slightly downward.

He leaned closer, his breath warming my mouth without touching it. "I want you more than I've ever wanted anything."

My lungs seized. The rain-soaked air thickened between us. This was the Zaiden I'd fallen for—before accusations, before graves, before hatred. But things had changed—hadn't they?

"I've always wanted you."

His lips hovered over mine, not quite touching. The scent of him filled each shallow breath I managed. My eyes fluttered closed, memory and desire waging war within me.

"Could have fooled me." My fingers spread across his chest, and I shoved gently.

He stepped back. "Really?" he smiled. "You couldn't tell that as much as I wanted to hate you, I couldn't. If you had been anyone else, I would have buried you in that grave alive."

"Zai—"

"Let me finish," he cut me off. "I didn't tell Kacie about us because if she'd said no, I couldn't have you, I thought I might never forgive her. I hate myself for that, but I was as obsessed with you then as I am now. Even through all the hate, I still loved you." I sucked in a sharp breath. "I would have died before I let EJ or anyone else have you, and it had nothing to do with ruining your life. It was all selfish. I wanted you, and I wanted everyone to know you were mine."

"If this is your way of apologizing—"

"It's my way of telling you that I'm in love with you, Ariella, and I know you are too. Even if you're still mad at me, you still love me."

The corner of my lips curled into a grin. "You seem pretty sure about that."

He shrugged. "I'm positive."

He was the only boy I'd ever loved, but I honestly didn't know how I felt now. "If you need time to come to the realization, I can wait."

My gaze held his as my chest rose and fell with deep breaths. His confession pushed away all the bad and reminded me of all the good; protecting me during the school shooting, his tenderness after the motorcycle accident, the fear in his eyes when he thought I was hurt, the way he'd carried me out of the party protecting me from whoever drugged me, the way he'd held me after we found out Kacie was gone in the middle of the hospital. He hadn't even cried; he'd been strong for me, only to be told she left because of me.

I pushed to my feet, moving as though drawn by an invisible thread between us. Standing toe to toe with him, I could feel the heat radiating from his body, smell his cologne clinging to his skin. My chest heaved against his.

Fear and desire tangled in my throat. Hurt battled against the magnetic pull between us. I could push him away, preserve my pride. I could forgive him, release us both from this limbo.

"Kiss me," I breathed.

His brows pulled together, uncertainty replacing the usual confidence in his eyes. He leaned closer, questioning.

"Kis—"

The word dissolved as Zaiden's lips crashed against

mine. The gentleness from moments before vanished. His hand dove into my hair, fingers tangling at the nape of my neck, tugging and angling my mouth where he wanted it. The kiss was possession, apology, and demand all at once, a physical manifestation of everything unsaid between us.

Part of me wanted to resist, to show him I wasn't so easily won. But another part, the part that had never stopped loving him, even through the hatred, surrendered completely.

Spine stiffening, my fingers curled into his shirt, the material bunching between my fingers as I pulled him tighter to me, and he sucked my bottom lip between his teeth. A moan escaped my lips as he captured my mouth, swallowing every sound.

His tongue thrust beyond the seal of my lips and met mine, tangling together.

A flash of light bleached the room white—one second, two seconds. Then came the boom, a crack of thunder so close it rattled the windows. The lights flickered once, twice, then surrendered to darkness.

And for the first time since childhood, I wasn't afraid of the dark.

As crazy as it sounded, with his arms around me, the darkness felt like a cocoon rather than a threat. The man who had terrorized me had somehow become my sanctuary. When I was with him, I felt safe. The irony wasn't lost on me.

He pulled back from the kiss, both of us gasping as though we'd been underwater. In the darkness, I could only make out the silhouette of his face, but I felt the rapid rise and fall of his chest against mine.

"Are you okay?" he breathed, his words warm against my lips, concern evident even in whispers.

The rain intensified outside. The house creaked and settled around us. In this moment of darkness and storm, I made a decision I couldn't unmake.

"Take me to your bedroom," I whispered, my voice steadier than I felt.

His hands curled around my hips, holding me steady. "Does that mean you forgive me?"

"I thought you didn't care if I forgave you."

"No," his lips pressed to my neck below my ear, "what I said was I'm not apologizing for making you mine because I'm not sorry." His teeth grazed my throat as he kissed and licked from one side to the other. "You are mine, Ariella." His lips traced my jawline. "So you can tell me you hate me. Tell me how angry you are. Punch me in the face. Whatever makes you feel better, and when you're done, we can move on because you. Are. Mine."

"I don't hate you," my fingertips traced the curves of his abs through his shirt, "and I'm not angry. Anymore."

The lights flashed back on without warning. In the sudden brightness, we blinked at each other, momentarily disoriented. My gaze lifted slowly to meet his. The vulnerability I'd glimpsed in the darkness remained unmasked by the light.

"And I've already punched you in the face."

We both smiled, a strange, genuine moment of connection over shared violence. The absurdity wasn't lost on either of us.

"I want to move on." The words felt like release and risk at once.

"Then we move on." Simple. Final. His certainty almost made me surrender.

Almost.

My lips pressed into a tight line as I slowly shook my

head. The rain drummed harder against the windows. I pushed my pointer finger into the center of his chest, feeling his heartbeat.

"Not," I tapped once, "until you say: 'I'm sorry, Ariella. I'm sorry for throwing you in an empty grave in the dark.'"

The memory of dirt beneath my fingernails flashed through me. The power shifted between us.

His lips quirked up—that familiar, infuriating half-smile. "Is that what you need?"

I squared my shoulders, summoning courage I wasn't entirely sure I possessed. The room felt warmer, the air charged. I pointed to the ground between us, the gesture both ridiculous and deadly serious.

"On your knees." I pointed to the ground.

"You want me to get on my knees for you?" With his hands on my hips, he slowly lowered to his knees, his eyes holding mine, "and beg for forgiveness." He tugged me closer to him.

I bit down on my lip, and my head slowly nodded as a million butterflies fluttered in my stomach.

The lights flickered, and thunder boomed again as his thumb tugged down a small section of the waistband of my pants. "Does this make it better?" He pressed his full lips to my hip bone. "Or how about this?" His lips traced from one side of my lower stomach to the other before pressing his lips to the other hip bone.

My lips parted slightly as my gaze followed his every move, and my pulse thrummed in my ears. Zaiden Knight, the man who bows to no one, was on his knees for me. He'd hurt me, humiliated me, damn near fucking broke me, but he'd also made me feel safe, protected me, pleased me, and now was begging for my forgiveness.

He pressed his lip below my belly button, staring up through long, dark lashes. "Tell me you forgive me, Ariella."

I shook my head, and he grinned against my skin as his fingers slid into the waistband of my pants and slowly glided them down my legs, dragging my panties with them.

I moaned as my head fell back, and my fingers slid into his hair, unable to form words as he mapped kisses along my inner thighs and pussy. He slid his tongue up my length, and I nearly came undone when he struck my clit.

Our gaze collided as my fingers tightened in his hair. The intensity in his eyes made my breath catch, and the lights went out again. My body immediately tensed.

"I'm here, Ariella." The heat of his breath feathered across my pussy as his hands tightened around my thighs, proving he was here and he wasn't going to leave me. "You're safe. No one will ever hurt you again."

"Promise?" My words were barely above a whisper. "Not even you?"

"I promise."

His hand curled around the back of my thigh before lifting it over his shoulder. I gasped when his wet, heated tongue glided up and down my slit tracing my clit and then moving down to my entrance. His tongue dipped inside, teasing and tasting me before sliding back up, flicking my clit.

My fingers tangled in his hair as my hips bucked into his face.

He resisted. "Tell me you forgive me," he hummed against my pussy.

"Say I'm sorry," I ordered. "The words, Zaiden."

He slid a finger inside me, slowly thrusting in and out

as his tongue swiped over my clit, and my knees nearly buckled. "I'm sorry." He added another finger, and I gasped, biting my lip. "Now, forgive me so I can make you come."

"Oh God," I moaned. "I forgive you."

"Tell me you're mine."

My teeth sank into my bottom lip as my muscles spasmed, and my pussy pulsated around his fingers.

The lights flashed back, painting the room in stark white for a heartbeat before darkness swallowed us again. In that brief illumination, the sight of Zaiden on his knees before me seared into my memory.

"Tell me you're mine, Ariella." His voice vibrated against my most sensitive flesh.

Lightning flickered again. His eyes locked with mine, waiting.

"I'm yours." The confession escaped me just as thunder cracked overhead, as though the storm itself acknowledged my surrender.

His arm snaked around my other leg in one fluid movement. Strong hands gripped my waist, and I was weightless. My squeal of surprise was lost beneath another roll of thunder as he lifted me effortlessly. My back arched, hands scrambling to dive into his hair. The intimacy was dizzying, vulnerability and power exchanging with each ragged breath.

Darkness. Light. Darkness again as the storm played with the electricity. Every flash revealed us in a new position, like frames of a film reel jumping forward in time.

With my hands tightening around the back of his head, my pussy swallowed his face as my thighs clenched around him. He shifted, holding me as he lowered my back to the ground.

My muscles relaxed as my back flattened on the floor, and he gasped for air when I released him. His large hands wrapped around my inner thigh, forcing me to spread wider for him.

"Fuck, you taste so sweet." His words vibrated against my flesh, each syllable a new sensation.

He slid a finger inside me, a slow invasion that made my back arch from the floor. The rhythm he established started lazy, hypnotic, building like the storm outside. The windows rattled with thunder as his mouth covered my clit, the suction precise and merciless.

My thighs trembled uncontrollably. The air grew too thick to breathe properly, each inhalation shallow and desperate.

"Oh, my fucking God," I cried out, the words barely recognizable even to my own ears.

Lightning flashed, illuminating his face between my legs for a split second—his eyes locked on mine, watching, gauging every reaction. In that brief brightness, the intensity in his gaze undid me.

He added another finger, the stretch burning in the most exquisite way.

"Soak my fingers, baby," he commanded, voice rough with desire, "and come for me."

The darkness returned, heightening every sensation. Each thrust went deeper than the last, my body yielding to his relentless rhythm. His tongue circled with precision, creating patterns that made my consciousness splinter. Every muscle in my body contracted, preparing for release, the pressure building at the base of my spine like a gathering storm.

"Zaiden," I screamed as my entire body seized, pleasure blurring my vision as my back arched.

He removed his fingers as his tongue moved to my entrance, darting in and out of me, lapping up every bit of my orgasm. He shifted to his knees, and I pushed up on my elbows to see him. He was already shoving down his pants and boxers, releasing his massive cock before he ripped his shirt off, tossing it.

His body was a fucking masterpiece created by the Gods who obviously favored him.

He wrapped his hands around my thighs and jerked me to him, pulling my thighs over his, positioning himself between my legs.

"Condom?"

"No, baby," he groaned, fisting his cock before he dragged his head up and down the length of me, coating himself with my arousal. "I want to ride you raw." I shivered as goosebumps broke out over my skin. He nudged my entrance, and I held my breath as my heart pounded, anticipation sending it into overdrive.

Our gazes locked, and I sucked in a sharp breath as he sank inside me, filling me inch by inch. He dropped to his hands before lowering to his elbows, hovering over me. This time was so different. It felt like love and not like a punishment.

I liked both versions of him. The revelation should have troubled me more than it did.

I liked seeing the softer side of the beast—the vulnerability, the care, the tenderness I once thought lost forever. But I also craved the beast itself—the possessiveness, the intensity, the sharp edges that had cut me open and left me bleeding.

What did that say about me?

On a low, strangled groan, he withdrew slowly, painfully slow, before pushing back in. My hands flattened against his back, feeling the play of muscles beneath sweat-slicked skin. Each thrust went deeper than the last, a gradual claiming that felt like surrender and victory simultaneously.

His lips brushed mine, surprisingly gentle amidst everything else. "You are mine."

Three simple words that should have enraged me after everything, but instead sent heat spiraling through my core. He captured my mouth, devouring it with an intensity that matched the storm still raging outside.

I kissed him back with everything, every tear I'd shed because of him, every night I'd spent hating him, every moment I'd secretly loved him. Love and hate tangled together until they became indistinguishable, pleasure and pain blurring at the edges. His speed increased with my response, as though he could feel my emotional surrender.

The complexity of wanting someone who had hurt me so deeply should have given me pause. Instead, it pulled me under like a riptide.

His hips snapped forward, and I broke on a gasp. "And I am yours." Our heavy breathing mingled with his words. "Come for me, baby."

My heart rate spiked as my eyes closed and my back arched into him. "Harder." I wanted more.

His deep voice rolled over me, a hint of amusement wrapped around the edges. "You like it rough, don't you, baby?" The question hung between us, both of us knowing the answer. "You like it dirty."

He grabbed my wrists in one fluid motion, pinning them above my head against the cool floor. The gesture was commanding but not cruel, the perfect pressure to make me yield without fear. His mouth descended on my throat, not kissing but claiming, teeth and tongue marking territory.

The shift in power was electric. I could fight it, maintain the control I'd reclaimed earlier. Or I could surrender to this, the pleasure of letting go.

"Yes," I breathed, the single syllable carrying more honesty than any speech could.

Something dangerous flashed in his eyes: satisfaction, desire, and something deeper I couldn't name. The lights flickered momentarily, catching the sheen of sweat on his chest and the intensity of his focus.

His hips snapped forward without warning, and whatever thoughts I had scattered like birds. He set a rhythm designed to unravel me, quick, brutal strokes that left no room for pretense or pride.

"Take my dick like a good fucking girl," he growled, the crudeness of his words contrasting with the almost reverent way his free hand cradled my face.

A sharp breath left me as every muscle in my body tensed in response. The sensations, the roughness of his movements, the tenderness in his touch, created a contradiction my body understood better than my mind. It felt so good I couldn't think straight, couldn't remember why I'd ever resisted this, resisted him.

My pussy clenched around him as I focused on the way his massive cock filled me, the heat of his breath on my skin, his rough greedy moans mixed with the wet sounds of our sweat slick bodies sliding together, and the way we fit together so perfectly.

He ground himself hard against me, hitting that spot that made me cry out as I wiggled against him, desperate for more.

I was so close. So fucking close.

Every vicious snap of his hips sent me soaring closer and closer to the edge until I was teetering over, and with one last deep, hard thrust, I was soaring over with an orgasm so powerful it stole my ability to breathe.

"Fuck," he grunted with a harsh breath. His hands tightened around my wrists, and his abs clenched as he held himself deep before he exploded.

His body collapsed against mine. Our labored breathing filled the quiet room as we stayed still for what felt like forever.

He rolled to my side, and I shifted to sit up. "I forgive you, but if you—"

"I won't." His tone was so sincere that I believed him.

CHAPTER 44

Ariella

"**L**et's go, Ariella," Zaiden shouted up the stairs. It was six in the morning, and I didn't want to be up this early, but he had an early practice and refused to leave me home alone.

"I'm coming," I yelled back. "It's freezing outside. I need a jacket." I hadn't packed any of my winter clothes because I wasn't expecting it to get so cold so fast. Pushing open the door to my mom's room, I rushed to her closet.

Even though my mom and Zaiden's dad were married, they had separate rooms, though I assumed they shared a bed when they were both home. I slid open the closet door and walked into the massive walk-in closet that used to be Zaiden's mom's.

I remembered being a little girl standing in this closet with Kacie, mesmerized by all the sparkly clothes, shoes, and handbags, but now it was my mom's, and I hated that.

I ran my fingertips over the clothes, past silk blouses and designer dresses that whispered of a life I barely recognized. The closet smelled of her expensive perfume, Chanel, not the drugstore brand she used to wear. Each garment testified to how far she'd traveled from who she once was.

In the back corner, almost hidden in the shadows, my gaze caught on something grey and ordinary, a lone hoodie, exiled to the highest shelf. Of course. Casual comfort didn't fit her carefully curated image anymore. This single forgotten item was perhaps the last remnant of the mother I'd once known.

The sleeve was just out of reach, so I jumped up, grabbed it, and ripped it off, ducking as something flew off the shelf.

"Shit." I turned to see if whatever fell was broken.

A medium-sized black box was open on the floor.

Kneeling, I set the hoodie on the floor and froze, my breath catching sharply in my throat. The room tilted beneath me as recognition slammed into me.

It wasn't my mom's hoodie.

It was Kacie's.

I knew it instantly—our high school dance team logo in the center with her name embroidered in red. My stomach lurched violently.

"How fucking sick?" Cold sweat broke out across my forehead as revulsion crawled up my spine. She stole a hoodie from Kacie's room. From a dead girl's room.

I grabbed the black box and searched for the stuff that had fallen out of it and sucked in a sharp breath when just out of my reach was Kacie's phone.

"Oh my God." My voice came out as a whisper. I stared at the phone, my fingers hovering inches away, afraid to touch it as if it might disintegrate—or worse, explode with secrets. "Why did you have this, Mom?"

The walls of the closet seemed to press in. Each breath became shallower than the last until black spots danced at the edges of my vision.

"Zaiden," I called out, my voice breaking. Then louder: "ZAIDEN!"

I scrambled to my feet, legs unsteady, and lurched toward the door. It swung open as I reached it, and I collided with the solid wall of his chest.

"What's wrong?" I pointed to Kacie's phone on the floor.

"Is that..."

"Kacie's phone," I nodded, "yes."

"Where did you find that?"

I pointed to the spot. "I was looking for a hoodie, and when I pulled it down, it was Kacie's, and," my finger pointed at the black box on the floor, "that fell, and her phone fell out of it."

Zaiden stood silently, staring at the phone for a long moment. "Why would your mom have Kacie's phone?"

"Could your dad have..."

"No," he cut me off. "My parents said it was never recovered. They both said they never got her phone back." He shook his head. But why would your mom want to hurt Kacie?"

"Maybe she found out about my mom and your dad? Maybe she was going to tell your mom."

"How would she have known Kacie had my mom's car?"

"Oh my God." The words escaped as barely a breath.

The pieces clicked into place, a terrible puzzle

completing itself in my mind. The blood drained from my face as the truth crystallized with horrifying clarity.

"She didn't mean to kill Kacie." I met Zaiden's eyes, seeing my own horror reflected. "She was trying to kill your mom."

My chest constricted as if caught in a vise, each heartbeat a painful thud against my ribs. Acid surged up my throat while the room tilted dangerously.

Zaiden grabbed my shoulders, steadying me. His face had gone white, but his voice remained controlled. "Okay, listen carefully," he said, each word measured and precise. "Put everything back exactly how you found it. We'll take the phone and charge it to see what's on it, but first, we need to get out of here until we figure out if your mom was involved somehow."

"Where do we go?"

His eyes flicked around the closet like he was searching for the answer. "You can't stay at the frat house; it won't be safe for you, but we can crash at my mom's house. She's out of town until next week. Once you're done packing a bag, meet me at my truck."

"So you're not angry with me?" The question escaped before I could stop it, fragile and uncertain.

He stopped mid-stride. His eyes found mine, searching, questioning. "Why would I be mad at you?"

The gentleness in his voice nearly broke me. I wanted to believe him, needed to, but doubt coiled inside me.

"My mom—" How could he not see it? The blood might as well be on my hands, too.

He rushed forward, invading my personal space, his hands gripping my face. "We don't know why your mom has Kacie's phone. There could be a reason." I couldn't think of one reason for her to have it. None.

"And even if your mom was somehow involved, that's not your fault, but—" He paused, dragging in a ragged breath. His eyes hardened. "If she was involved, there will only be two options for her."

He didn't need to say them out loud.

Jail.

Or death.

The truth hung between us, cold and unforgiving as steel.

"Get everything put back and pack a bag. I need to let Sterling know I'm going to be late. Don't tell anyone where we are staying. Not even Mila and Journey."

I nodded, and he reached down, swiping Kacie's phone off the ground before disappearing.

I ran a hand down my face. My mom was a lot of things, but a killer?

She wasn't the same person I knew anymore, and I couldn't put anything past her.

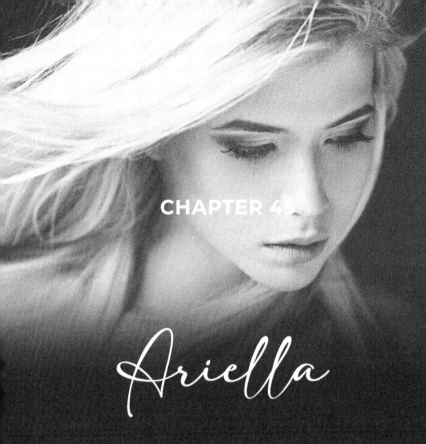

CHAPTER 45

Ariella

Sitting behind the protective glass, I pulled Zaiden's jacket tighter around me and pulled my feet into the seat. My gaze followed Zaiden as the team moved in unison during warm-ups before running drills on the ice. The sounds of their skates scraping the ice together filled the quiet arena. Each player dropped on all fours. The frog stretch. Leaning on their elbows, they let their knees slide wide on the ice, stretching their groin muscles.

The weather was shifting from summer to fall, and it was colder than usual for this time of year, but inside the ice rink, it was freezing. My chair shook as Journey and Mila dropped into the seats on opposite sides of each other.

"Please tell me I had to get up this early for something

good." Journey dragged her beanie lower over her ears, sinking deeper into the seat until only her eyes were visible above her scarf. "Like Mark Matthews professed his love for me last night on his live, and I missed it."

A laugh bubbled up before I could stop it. Journey shot me a glare, which only made me laugh harder. Mark Matthews was a famous vlogger from the UK who didn't even know Journey was alive. "No, but we found Kacie's phone this morning."

The scrape of skates on ice suddenly seemed deafening in the silence that followed.

"What? Where?" Mila's voice cut through the sudden tension.

I gripped the cold metal of the bleacher seat, the chill seeping through my jeans. "My mom's closet."

Journey's gasp formed a larger vapor cloud. Mila went still, her normally expressive face frozen in shock, like the very ice beneath the players.

Journey's fingers curled around the sleeve of my borrowed jacket. "Why would your mom have Kacie's phone?"

"Zaiden's dad told him they never recovered the phone, but—" I paused, my throat dry. Each word felt like stepping further onto a frozen lake, testing which truth would hold my weight.

"So, unless they found the phone after he told him, I can only think of one reason."

Journey shook her head, eyes locked on mine. "Your mom is something sometimes, but I can't see her wanting to hurt Kacie."

I shrugged. "Yeah, honestly, I can't either, not even if Kacie found out about my mom and her dad, but I could see her going after Anne."

"Holy shit." Mila's voice dropped to a whisper, her eyes wide. "Kacie was driving Anne's car that night."

The pieces were falling into place—a puzzle I never wanted to complete.

I nodded, tracing a slow pattern on the arm of the chair. "I just can't figure out how she got Officer Tanner to help her."

Mila chewed her lower lip the way she always did when working through a problem. "Maybe everything that happened with Officer Tanner was a coincidence."

The puck skidded across the ice as Zaiden lined up his shot.

"Maybe."

The crack of a stick against a puck echoed through the arena. The goal light flashed red.

"Or maybe she paid him."

"Do you think she was responsible for his overdose?" Journey leaned in, her breath fogging between us. "Because that seems like a bit of a stretch, even for your mom."

I pinched the bridge of my nose, eyes closed. "Maybe he really did overdose."

Journey's hand landed on my shoulder, gentle but insistent. "So, what are you going to do?"

"If Zaiden finds out it was actually my mom—"

My voice died as I watched him on the ice—the weight of unspoken words pressed against my chest.

A defender lunged. Zaiden slammed into him—no hesitation, no mercy. The player sprawled across the ice, a tangle of limbs and wounded pride.

He was a beast on and off the ice.

Another skater approached from behind. In one fluid motion, Zaiden pivoted, his body a weapon of calculated precision. My stomach tightened as #45 Hawk clutched empty air where Zaiden had been just a heartbeat before.

I remembered the look in Zaiden's eyes when he talked about Kacie, his little sister, his responsibility. The rage that simmered beneath his careful control.

"He'll probably kill her," I whispered, the truth of it hollowing me out.

Their eyes widened. "How do you feel about all this?" Journey asked.

"You know she's left me questioning everything about who she is this last year, but this—" I shook my head as I swallowed back the tears threatening to fall. The cold air burned my lungs with each breath. "This is insane that she would kill—"

"Wait." Mila cut me off, her voice sharp enough to slice through the chill.

The arena seemed to grow quieter as if the very air was listening.

"What if Zaiden's dad was part of it?"

I narrowed my eyes, the implication hitting me like a body check. My gaze drifted to Zaiden on the ice, to the embroidered name on his jersey. The same name that opened doors all over town.

"Zaiden's dad has the power and money to influence a cop to brush something under the rug."

"Why would he—" My voice trailed off as I realized maybe he wanted Anne dead too, then immediately shook it off. "He knew they switched Kacie's car that night. He would have known that he was cutting the breaks to the car Kacie was going to drive. He's a lot of things, but Kacie was his little girl. He wouldn't hurt her on purpose."

Mila tapped her fingernails against the metal bleacher. "Yeah, maybe you're right."

"I think I need to confront my mom." The words tasted bitter in my mouth. "Ask her why she had Kacie's phone."

Journey's eyebrows shot up. "You really think she'll tell you the truth?"

I tugged at a loose thread on Zaiden's jacket sleeve. "I can tell when she's lying." A chill that had nothing to do with the rink crawled up my spine. "But I can't take Zaiden with me. He won't let me out of his sight because of everything going on."

"You probably shouldn't go by yourself." Journey twisted her scarf tighter around her neck, her eyes never leaving mine.

"My mom wouldn't hurt me." I swallowed hard. "Or at least I don't think she will. Especially if she knows I have no proof." I glanced between my friends. "You two can ride with me. Wait outside in case I need you."

Mila exchanged a look with Journey before leaning forward. "Okay."

"Zaiden has early practice every day this week. I need to convince him to leave me at his mom's one morning."

Mila's forehead creased. "His moms?"

"Oh, yeah." I raised my brows, realizing I'd forgotten part of the story. "We are staying at his mom's for now because he doesn't think it's safe to stay at his dad's."

Mila nodded, her shoulders relaxing slightly. "Probably a good idea." She drummed her fingers against her thighs. "So what's the plan then?"

"I will try in the morning to get him to let me stay at his mom's," I whispered. "If it works, then I'll text you both."

"And if it doesn't?"

"Then I'll try again the next day until it does work."

Journey checked her phone, thumbs flying over the screen. "Okay." She glanced up. "So, we'll pick you up and take you to your mom's once you get him to leave you."

I pulled my knees tighter to my chest and nodded, watching Zaiden score below. "But not a word to Zaiden." My voice hardened. "Or anyone else."

Down on the ice, Zaiden caught my eye and flashed a quick smile before Coach called him back to the drill. I attempted to return it, but the gesture felt foreign on my face.

I didn't know if this was the best idea. The weight of Kacie's phone, now hidden in my backpack, seemed to burn through the fabric. But I needed to know the truth even if the words didn't come directly from her mouth.

CHAPTER 46

Ariella

Zaiden and I fell into a routine over the next week. He woke me up every morning and dragged me to his practice whether I wanted to go or not.

Today was different, though. I didn't have classes or practice, so unless he forced me to follow him all day long, he had to leave me here alone.

"Zaiden." I pulled the covers tighter around me like armor. "I'm not going. I want to sleep in and do nothing today."

"Ariella." His voice dropped an octave, that familiar warning growl that made the hair on my arms stand up. He leaned against the doorframe, his posture casual. "I can't miss practice, and I'm not leaving you alone."

"No one knows that I'm here." That wasn't exactly the truth, but he didn't know that. Plus, it was only Journey and Mila that I told. I pushed up to a sitting position, the sheets pooling around my waist. His jaw tightened. The muscles in his forearms flexed as he crossed them. "And I won't go anywhere," I lied. He narrowed his eyes.

The silence stretched between us, taut as a tripwire.

"When you leave, I'm going back to sleep, and when I get up, I'm going to order Door Dash and watch TV."

"Fine," he groaned. "But, Ariella, if you leave this house, I will zip-tie you to the bed for the rest of your life."

"Where would I go?" I lied.

He stood shirtless in a pair of jeans, open at the fly. The beads of water dripping from his damp hair onto his shoulders were slightly distracting.

I pushed off the bed and strolled to him. "I'll be fine, I promise." I flattened my palm on his chest.

"You keep touching me like that—" The alarm on his phone alerted, letting him know he needed to leave now or he'd be late for practice. "Shit."

"Go." I smiled. "I'll be fine."

"If I text you and you don't answer, I will be here in minutes."

"I will answer your texts."

He kissed my forehead. "Go back to bed."

I gave myself a mental high five as I practically jumped back into the bed.

Zaiden had practice until 7:30 and classes until noon. That was plenty of time for me to confront my mom and get back without him ever knowing I left. I curled into bed and closed my eyes, pretending to sleep, until I heard the door click closed. A few minutes later, his motorcycle pulled out of the driveway.

I forced myself to wait, counting out five full minutes

after the sound of Zaiden's motorcycle faded completely. Just to be safe. Just to be sure.

The red numbers on the digital clock blinked: 6:15 AM. Finally, when the house settled into true emptiness, I rolled over and snatched my phone off the nightstand, my fingers already finding Mila's contact.

One ring. Two rings. Each one stretched into eternity.

"Hello?" Mila's voice finally came through, thick with sleep and confusion.

"We're a go this morning," I whispered, though there was no one to hear me. Something about speaking at full volume felt dangerous, as if the walls themselves might report back to Zaiden.

"Shit," Mila mumbled, followed by the rustling of sheets. I imagined her sitting up, suddenly alert despite the hour. "How long do we have before he gets back?"

I glanced again at the clock, mentally calculating. "He should be back around 12:30.

The magnitude of what we were about to do settled over me.

"Okay." I could hear her bed rustling on the other end. "My parents are forcing me to have breakfast with them this morning, but I should be there to get you around nine."

"Perfect. I'll get ready now and wait in case you can slip out early."

"I'll text Journey to meet me there," Mila added.

"Journey has an early class this morning," I reminded her. "It's just you and me."

"Ok, I'll be there as soon as I can."

I disconnected, texted her my location with shaking fingers, and set my phone back on the nightstand. It looked so innocent there, a sleek rectangle hiding plans that could get us all in trouble. My gaze shifted to Kacie's phone sitting on the table next to mine. The screen was still dark despite being on the charger for a week, reminding me why I needed to talk to my mom.

We'd been trying to break free for a week. Plotting. Waiting. Watching Zaiden for any opening. And now that I'd finally convinced him, the universe seemed determined to throw obstacles in our path. Mila was trapped at a family breakfast. Journey was locked in early classes.

Nine o'clock. That was our window. If Mila arrived by then, I'd have three hours to confront my mom and return before Zaiden suspected anything. Three hours to uncover a truth that might shatter whatever was growing between us.

I glanced at the clock: 6:23 AM. The minutes ticked by with excruciating slowness, each one a reminder that I was alone in this house with nothing but my thoughts.

As much as I wanted to go back to bed, I knew I was too overwhelmed to go back to sleep, so I took a quick shower instead.

As the hot water pounded against my skin, scenarios played through my mind. What if she admitted every-thing? The thought alone made my stomach twist. Or worse, what if she lied, and I could see right through it? The steam clouded around me as I spun, letting water saturate my hair.

My thoughts shifted to Zaiden. His face appeared in my mind, not the soft expression he sometimes wore with me, but the cold, calculating one I'd glimpsed when he talked about justice for Kacie. What would he do if we proved my mom was responsible? The words "make her disappear" floated through my mind, and I shivered despite the scalding water. I'd seen enough to know it wasn't an empty phrase in his world.

The pipes gave a sudden groan, making me flinch. Even the house seemed to be warning me.

I stepped out of the shower and wrapped a big, dark green towel around me before strolling into Zaiden's bare room. The only thing in the room that made it look like someone lived there was the messy bed. His walls were bare, and his dressers were empty. I strolled around the bed and pulled open the closet floor.

The closet, on the other hand, was obviously used as extra storage space. It was filled with empty suitcases and brown moving boxes. My eyes caught Kacie's name scribbled across a few of them, and my heart ached.

This was where everything in Kacie's room had gone— a mausoleum of memories, boxed and sealed away from the world.

Even though I knew I shouldn't, my fingers betrayed me. They hovered over a box labeled "DESK" in thick black marker, my mom's handwriting. I peeled the tape back, the ripping sound unnaturally loud in the empty house. Each movement felt like trespassing, and yet I still couldn't stop myself.

The cardboard flaps surrendered, revealing treasures I'd thought were lost forever. The box was filled with items that had once cluttered her desk and dresser. My breath caught as I lifted out a silver frame. Us, grinning at the 8th-grade dance, captured forever in our ridiculous glittery dresses and too-high heels. We'd spent hours getting ready, convincing ourselves that adulthood was just around the corner.

My chest tightened, remembering our moms together

that morning, working together to make sure everything was perfect.

I put the picture back and closed the box. "I can't do this right now," I muttered as my gaze searched the closet for the bag of clothes I'd brought, but I froze when my eyes spotted a heart-shaped floral keepsake box, and I couldn't help but smile. That was the box that Kacie kept everything that ever mattered to her in. I'd given her that box filled with gifts for her eighth birthday.

Grabbing a shirt that still had the tags on it, I pulled it over my head, dropping the towel before ripping the tags off. I reached up, grabbed the box off the top shelf, and carried it out of the closet, setting it on the bed. I strolled to the tall dresser with a flat-screen TV on it, opened the top drawer, grabbed a pair of Zaiden's boxers, and pulled them on.

I strolled back to the bed and sank onto the mattress. Every year, we would put new items inside this box, memories we never wanted to forget, and our secrets.

I knew I shouldn't go down memory lane right now, but I couldn't stop myself from opening the box. I pulled out a picture of her and her ex and smiled. He'd loved her, but she wasn't ready to fall in love.

I set that picture on the bed, pulled out a folded paper, and opened it. My eyes narrowed. I didn't remember this being in there. It was her birth certificate.

I set it to the side and pulled out a handful of pictures. The first three were of her and me, and the next few were a mixture of Mila, Journey, Kacie, and me. I pulled out two friendship bracelets and a white envelope that felt like it had more photos.

I set the bracelets to the side and opened the envelope. As I pulled out the first photo, the floor seemed to tilt beneath me. My fingers went numb, nearly dropping what I held.

"Holy shit," I mumbled, my voice barely audible even to myself.

It was Anne with Coach Palmer. The intimacy in their posture was unmistakable. A chill crawled up my spine as I stared at the image, a sense of dread building like a thundercloud. Something about the house felt different—like the air had grown heavier, watching me.

I scrambled to find my phone on the bed, quickly hitting Mila's name.

"Hello," she whispered. "I'm still at—"

"I found something."

"Hold on," she said, still whispering.

"I'm going to add Journey to the call." My finger trembled slightly as I hit the plus sign, then Journey's name. My heart pounded against my ribs as the phone rang once, twice—

"Hey, what's up?" Journey's voice broke through, sunny and oblivious to what I'd discovered.

"Okay, what's going on?" Mila's voice had changed, dropping to a cautious whisper. I could picture her, probably huddled in some corner of her parents' house, shoulders hunched protectively around the phone.

I swallowed hard, suddenly aware of how empty the house felt around me. How vulnerable. "I was looking for my clothes in Zaiden's closet at his mom's and found Kacie's keepsake box."

"Okay," Mila drew out the word with a hint of impatience. "We all know what's in that box." A dismissive edge colored her tone. We'd all seen the mementos, the friendship bracelets, the notes passed in class.

I glanced down at the evidence in my lap, the photo

that changed everything. "Yeah, except there's also pictures of Kacie's mom with Coach Palmer."

The line went so silent I could hear the static of the connection: no breathing, no background noise, nothing. The silence stretched, becoming its own kind of warning. When I couldn't stand it anymore, I added, "They were intimate pictures."

Something creaked in the house behind me. I whipped around, heart in my throat, but saw nothing. Just shadows. Maybe.

"What the fuck?" Journey said.

"Do you think Zaiden is involved?"

I shook my head like they could see me. "No. It's pretty clear he doesn't stay here. I don't even think he realized the stuff from Kacie's room is in his closet."

"Something else weird that she'd never kept in there before is her birth certificate," I paused, twisting to grab the paper and looking it over. There had to be a reason it was in the box.

"Hang up the phone."

The voice sliced through the room like ice. For one heartbeat, I froze, hoping I'd imagined it. Two heartbeats. Three.

Slowly, I raised my eyes to the doorway.

Anne stood perfectly still, her posture almost casual, except for the small black handgun aimed directly at my face. The barrel looked impossibly dark, a perfect circle of nothing, that promised everything would end. My heart slammed against my ribs as though trying to escape what my brain was processing.

With fingers that felt disconnected from my body, I removed the phone from my ear. The screen glowed bright as I pressed "end call" with a trembling thumb. The soft thud of the phone hitting the bedspread seemed deafening in the silence between us.

"Put everything back in the box."

Swallowing hard, I slowly put everything I'd found back. "I was just—"

"Save it."

"I knew when Zaiden called me to tell me you two were staying here that you wouldn't be able to help yourself. I knew you'd put your nose where it didn't belong, and it looks like I made it back just in time."

"I'm not going to—"

"Shut up," she mumbled. "You've already told your stupid little friends, and now I'll have to kill them too."

"You killed Kacie." It came out before I could stop it, and when she didn't deny it, I knew I was right. "Why would you kill your own daughter?"

"She was going to ruin everything." She took a step closer. "She was going to give those pictures to her dad, and I would lose everything."

"What the fuck could be more important than your daughter."

"Dennis had it put in the prenup that if I was caught cheating, I would leave with nothing, and I couldn't let that happen."

"What the fuck?" I threw up my hands. "She was your daughter."

She huffed out a humorless laugh. "Let's not pretend like you weren't just looking at her birth certificate." Anne's voice lowered, taking on an almost conversational tone that was more terrifying than her anger.

"Kacie wasn't my daughter. Dennis knocked up one of his whores, and she dropped her on our doorstep."

The words hit me in waves, each one more impossible

than the last. My brain rejected them, then scrambled to rearrange everything I thought I knew. The room seemed to pulse around me. Kacie—not her daughter?

I opened my mouth, but no sound came out. My throat had closed around questions I couldn't even form.

"I was so young and stupid then." Anne's voice shifted, a false nostalgia creeping in that made my skin crawl. "I let him convince me to raise her as my own, and he'd made everything in her past disappear. Including her mother." Her lip curled slightly at the word. "No one would ever know she wasn't mine."

She waved the gun, the metal catching the light. The casual way she handled it—like it was an extension of her hand—told me this wasn't her first time holding one.

"Except he didn't get rid of the original birth certificate, and Kacie found it."

The world seemed to tilt on its axis. Kacie had discovered this bombshell and kept it from all of us. Even me, or maybe that was what she needed to talk to me about the night of the party. What else had she been carrying alone? How many secrets had died with her?

"So, you killed her." The words fell from my lips, simple and devastating. Not a question.

Anne's eyes met mine, and what I saw there froze the blood in my veins. No remorse. No grief. Just cold calculation, as if she were discussing a business transaction gone slightly awry.

"I didn't have a choice."

Four words. Four simple words to justify destroying a life, her daughter's life, biological or not. The room seemed to shrink around us, the air growing thinner with each breath.

Everything sank in all at once, and everything made

sense. "So you and Coach worked together to kill Kacie." It wasn't a question.

She shrugged. "He wanted her dead as much as I did." She rolled her eyes. "Kacie was trying to expose him, and while she was digging into him, she found out about us."

"Did you know what he was doing to us?" Anger colored my tone. "What he did to her?"

"Yes," she shrugged. "Well, I mean, I didn't at first, but it didn't take long to figure out, and let's not play the victim here. You didn't have to do it. He didn't force you."

"Are you serious?" My voice cracked as disbelief collided with rage. "For some of us, that dance team was our only chance at affording college. We didn't have a choice."

She rolled her eyes—actually rolled her eyes like we were discussing a trivial disagreement over lunch plans. "Well, Kacie could. If you didn't notice, her daddy's rich." The word 'daddy' dripped with contempt. She waved the gun in a dismissive gesture that made my stomach lurch. "But I put an end to Ryan anyway."

My brain struggled to process her words, rearranging them, searching for a meaning that wasn't the obvious one.

"You were responsible for the school shooting?" The question emerged as barely more than a whisper. My lungs seemed to have forgotten how to draw breath.

The edges of my vision darkened as the implications cascaded through my mind. This wasn't about Kacie. This wasn't about an affair or a prenup. This was systematic. Calculated.

Anne's smile, small and satisfied, confirmed everything before she spoke another word.

"He was supposed to kill you and Ryan, but that didn't work out." She said it like she was discussing a minor inconvenience, a delayed delivery, or a scheduling conflict. Not the planned execution of people.

The room tilted around me as my brain struggled to process her words.

My mouth went dry. "Why me?" The question scraped against my throat. "I didn't know anything." A humorless laugh bubbled up, edged with hysteria. "In fact, this morning, I thought my mom was responsible."

Something shifted behind Anne's eyes, a flicker of surprise, quickly masked. She tilted her head, studying me with the detached curiosity of a scientist observing a specimen. After a moment, she nodded toward the box on the bed.

"And if you hadn't gone snooping through things that didn't belong to you." Her voice dropping to a near whisper that somehow felt more threatening than any shout, "maybe I wouldn't have to kill you now."

The way she said it—'have to'—as if my murder was an unfortunate obligation. As if she were the victim in this scenario, forced into violence by my curiosity. The casual inversion of morality made me dizzy with rage and terror.

The gun in her hand caught the light, the barrel, a perfect black circle, that seemed to grow larger with each passing second—a portal to nothingness.

"The truth will come out."

She shook her head. "No, it won't, thanks to you. Even Zaiden thinks it's your mom. All I have to do is make it look like your mom was here, and he'll take care of the rest."

"Did you run Zaiden and me off the road the other day?"

"Fucking idiot," she growled. "They were supposed to

run you off the road, but apparently, my son is always with you."

This woman was insane, and if I didn't get out of here, I was going to die in this house.

"Get up," she shook the gun at me.

"Why?"

"I said get the fuck up."

I held my hands up as I slowly pushed to my feet. "Okay." My voice trembled with fear.

She shifted out of the path of the doorway. "Walk—" She shoved the gun forward. "To the bathroom."

I slowly eased past her toward the door, close enough to smell her perfume—the same scent Kacie used to wear. The realization turned my stomach. "You don't have to do this." My voice emerged steadier than I felt, a final attempt at reaching whatever humanity might remain in her.

The cold press of metal against my spine was her answer. The barrel of the gun dug between my vertebrae, a precise point of pressure that sent terror shooting down my limbs. A single tear escaped, tracing a hot path down my cheek.

"Shut the fuck up and walk." Her breath hit my ear, warm and mint scented. The mundane detail seemed obscene against the nightmare unfolding.

Swallowing hard against the desert my mouth had become, I stepped into the hallway. Each floorboard creaked beneath my weight, marking what could be my final steps. My eyes locked forward on the path ahead— thirty feet of polished hardwood that seemed like miles.

My mind split in two: one part calculating survival, the other accepting death—two options crystallized from the chaos of my thoughts. I could make a run for it—a desperate sprint toward the front door, gambling that surprise might give me the seconds I needed before she pulled the trigger. Or I could move with excruciating slowness, dragging out each step, buying precious time for someone, anyone, to arrive.

The weight of the silence pressed against my eardrums. No cars on the street. No neighbors mowing lawns. No salvation approaching.

Just me, Anne, and the gun that connected us.

"Don't even think about running," Anne snarled. "There will be a bullet in the back of your head before you make it out of the hallway."

My plans evaporated. She was right. I'd be dead before I managed to turn and run. My chest rose and fell with frantic breaths.

"Walk." She shoved the cold metal barrel against my spine, the pressure just enough to bruise.

I stepped forward, each footfall deliberate and slow. My heartbeat counted down the seconds I had left. One step. Two. The hallway stretched in front of me like a tunnel to my execution, each shadow on the wall a silent witness. My mind churned through scenarios, each one ending the same way—with me dead.

I paused at the threshold, sweat beading along my hairline despite the chill settling into my bones. The bathroom loomed ahead, dark except for a weak rectangle of sunlight struggling through the small window. The light illuminated dust particles floating in the air, making them look like tiny stars in a void. I knew with absolute certainty that if I stepped across that line, it would be the last doorway I'd ever cross.

The irony of the entire situation hit me hard. I'd been punished by Zaiden for the last few months for being responsible for Kacie's death, only to find out it was his mom, and now she was going to kill me, too. The only thing that made this a little easier was that there was no way she was going to get away with this. Zaiden would be back before she could clean everything up.

Sucking in what might be my last deep breath, I hesitated at the edge of darkness. Anne's patience snapped. She shoved me hard, her strength fueled by desperation, and I tumbled forward. The world tilted as I crashed to my knees, the impact shooting pain up my legs. I rolled instinctively, finding myself sitting, vulnerable and exposed.

When I lifted my gaze, time seemed to suspend.

Zaiden stood in the shadows, a statue carved from tension. His finger rested against his lips—the universal signal for silence. But it was his eyes that stopped my breath cold with a fury I'd never seen before, even during his worst moments, blaming me for Kacie's death.

My pulse roared in my ears, nearly drowning out Anne's harsh breathing. I forced my eyes to slide casually back to her, fighting every instinct to keep staring at my unexpected salvation. One wrong look, one flicker of hope on my face, and we'd both be dead.

"Get in the shower," she ordered, sticking her hand holding the gun through the doorway, shaking it loosely from me to the shower. "Hurry up."

I nodded, slowly shifting. Zaiden pointed to the ground, and I assumed he was telling me to stay low.

Everything after that happened so fast. Zaiden threw his hand up underneath the gun, snatching it out of her hand so fast that it took her a minute to realize what happened.

"Zaiden," Anne breathed. "Thank God you're here. She was—"

"Stop," he growled. "I heard everything." He reached for his phone on the bathroom counter. "And it's all recorded."

"What's recorded?"

"Everything." He squared his shoulders. "How you killed Kacie, how you were involved with the school shooting, how you ran Ariella and me off the road."

I shifted to my feet, hiding behind Zaiden.

"Zaiden," she whispered, her voice transforming into something small and placating. The predator trying to sound like prey. "That's not—"

"Shut up." The two words sliced through the air, delivered with such intensity that even I flinched. This wasn't the Zaiden who'd kissed my forehead this morning. This was someone carved from granite and fury, someone I came to know all too well these last few months.

He raised the gun with a steady hand. "You and I are going to take a walk." The barrel aligned with her chest, unwavering. "Turn around and move."

Anne's face drained of color as she stepped backward, deeper into the shadow-filled hallway. Her eyes darted between Zaiden and me, calculating even now.

Zaiden moved forward with the controlled grace of a hunter, following her retreat. "Ariella," he said without looking back, "stay here and do not open this door no matter what."

The cold certainty in his voice crystallized the moment into terrible clarity. The gun. The walk. The finality in his tone.

He was going to kill her.

The realization landed like a stone in my stomach. This wasn't justice. It was an execution.

I stepped out of the bathroom. "Zaiden," I grabbed his

arm before stepping between them. "She's your mom. You don't want to do this." If he killed her, then he was going to jail, too.

"I'm your mo—" Anne started.

"Shut the fuck up," I yelled, my lip curling into a snarl. "There's nothing I'd like more than to end your life." I turned back to Zaiden. "But she's not worth you going to jail, and this isn't what Kacie would have wanted."

"Let me call the police." I place my palm flat on his chest. "Let them deal with her."

His gaze dropped to mine.

"Zaiden," Sterling's voice echoed through the house a minute before appearing in the hallway.

"Sterling," Zaiden called out. "Get Ariella out of here."

"Zaiden, no." I shook my head. "Don't do this."

"Let's go, Ari." Sterling grabbed me around the waist.

"No." I shoved at his arms, trying to fight against his strong grip. "Sterling, don't let him do this."

Sterling ignored me, dragging me down the long hall as my arms flailed, trying to grab anything to stop him. "Don't do this, Zaiden."

It wasn't until we were outside that Sterling released me.

"Oh, thank God," Journey breathed. "You're okay."

"Where's Zaiden?" Mila asked, looking back at the house.

"He's going to kill her." I sidestepped Sterling to get back to the house. "And then he's going to go to jail." But he was too fast and too strong.

The gunshot ripped through the quiet neighborhood, a single, definitive crack that seemed to stop time itself. Birds scattered from a nearby tree, their panicked wings flapping in the sudden silence that followed.

"Fuck," I whispered, the word inadequate against the finality of what happened. My legs threatened to give out beneath me. It was too late. Zaiden had crossed a line he could never come back from.

Sterling's face hardened as he squared his shoulders, a soldier preparing for battle. "No matter what happened," his voice was low and steady as he pointed from the house to each of us, "we have each other's back."

The front door's hinges gave a long, agonizing creak as it opened. My lungs seized, refusing to function, my vision narrowing to the doorway where Zaiden's silhouette appeared.

One second stretched into eternity as my mind cataloged every detail: no blood on his hands, his expression unreadable, his movements measured rather than frantic. As he stepped fully into the light, the breath I'd been holding escaped in a rush that left me dizzy.

"Call the police," Zaiden mumbled, completely void of any emotion.

"Are you sure that's what you want to do, man?" Sterling's gaze flashed from the house back to him. "We can make this disappear."

"She's not dead," Zaiden said. "She's handcuffed and waiting for the police." His gaze shifted, meeting mine. "But if the police fuck this up—"

I nodded. He didn't need to finish that sentence. I knew what he'd do if she didn't spend the rest of her life in prison.

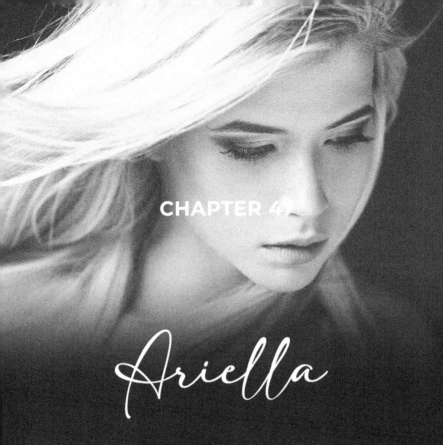

CHAPTER 47

Ariella

I sat wedged between Sterling and Mila on the cold metal tailgate, our shoulders touching, but no one speaking. Journey perched on the opposite side of Sterling, her face ghostly in the pulsing blue and red lights.

Dozens of police officers swarmed the front lawn like uniformed ants, their radios crackling with static and clipped codes. Twenty feet away, two officers huddled with Zaiden, heads bent toward his phone, their faces hardening as the recordings played.

It was finally over, though the metallic taste of fear still coated my tongue.

I imagined this was something that would haunt Zaiden for a long time.

Time seemed to slow as Anne emerged from the house. Two officers flanked her, one gripping each elbow, her hands cuffed behind her back. No one spoke. The only sound was the crunch of gravel under their boots as they marched her toward the waiting police car. I held my breath until the car door slammed shut behind her.

My gaze shifted to Zaiden as he approached, each step measured, controlled.

"They're charging her with attempted murder for now." He shoved his hands into his pockets, knuckles visible through the denim. "But they're reopening the investigation of Kacie's death. And the school shooting."

"Are you okay?"

I already knew the answer. His sister was his half-sister. His mother, a killer. His family, a lie. For a year, his life had crumbled piece by piece, and now, this final, devastating collapse.

"I'm fine." His voice hardened as his gaze shifted to Sterling. "Can you make sure Ariella gets home safely?"

I narrowed my eyes. "Wait, you're not coming with me?"

"No." His voice was hollow. Empty.

"I'll be home later." He paused, gaze fixed on some distant point. "I need to be alone."

I slid off Sterling's tailgate, bare feet hitting gravel. "No, you don't." My voice was steel as I stepped into his space. He stared past me, through me, his gaze fixed on nothing. "You need to be with friends. The last thing you need is to be alone with this."

"Take her home." He pivoted away.

I lunged, fingers catching his arm. "Zaiden—"

He wrenched free. "Go home, Ariella."

"I'll get her home." Sterling's large hand wrapped around my arm, stopping me from chasing after him.

He stormed off, hopping on his bike and zooming off.

"What the fuck is wrong with you?" I shoved his hand away, heat rushing to my face. "He doesn't need to be alone."

"He's going to his sister's grave." Sterling's voice remained maddeningly calm.

I glared at him, pulse hammering in my throat. "How can you be so sure he's not going to jump off a bridge?"

"Because I know him." He tossed me the keys to his truck, metal flashing in the air between us. I snatched them mid-arc, fingers closing around cold metal. "Give him a few minutes and go to the grave site. He'll be there." I looked down at the keys in my hand. "I'll get a ride with Journey, and we can meet up later."

"Thanks." I rushed to the driver's side of his truck, pulled open the door, and slid in. Even though Sterling seemed sure that was where Zaiden would go, I needed to know he wasn't going to do something stupid.

The truck roared to life. I jammed it into drive and swerved into traffic, my eyes darting between the road ahead and the rearview mirror where Journey, Sterling, and Mila stood watching. My heart raced with the engine, knowing if they hadn't acted so quickly, I'd be dead.

The cemetery was only a few miles from his mom's house. Dark clouds gathered overhead as I eased through the massive wrought iron gates. In the distance, a solitary figure stood motionless. Zaiden.

I pulled the truck to the side and killed the engine as I watched him.

I couldn't imagine the storm brewing within him. The wind picked up, sending dead leaves skittering between gravestones. For months after Kacie's death, I'd blamed myself, each night reliving the what-ifs until they wore grooves in my mind. Maybe if I'd ridden with her. Maybe if I'd called one minute sooner. Now Zaiden stood at ground zero of his grief, the earth torn open beneath him again.

I sat in the truck for fifteen minutes, hand on the door handle, watching him stand motionless at his sister's grave. What if he pushed me away again? What if this was the moment he decided he couldn't bear any of it, me included? I swallowed hard and pushed the door open. Each step toward him felt like walking through quicksand.

"I told Sterling to take you home." He didn't turn, his words carried on the cemetery breeze.

I stepped up beside him, eyes falling to Kacie's head-stone. "I beat him up and stole his keys."

He huffed out a small laugh, a sound so unexpected it made my heart skip. "I'm sure that's what happened." A ghost of a smile touched his lips, the first I'd seen since everything fell apart, before vanishing.

I shrugged, nudging his arm with mine. "It is," I teased. "Mila and Journey are taking him to the hospital now."

"What are you doing here, Ariella?"

"You don't need to be alone right now," I whispered. "We don't have to talk, and I can stand back at the road, but I'm here if you need me."

We both stood silently for what felt like forever before he finally said. "I came out here to apologize to her. To apologize for failing her."

"You didn't fail her," I said. "I know it feels like that, but Anne failed her. Regardless of what happened, she was supposed to protect her, but she didn't. None of this is your fault."

He didn't say anything, but I knew he heard me.

"What happened after we left you and your mom in the house?"

Without taking his eyes off his sister's grave, he drew in a deep breath that expanded his chest, then let it whistle slowly between his teeth. "Nothing."

He lifted his shoulders before dropping them, a puppet with cut strings, and finally turned to meet my gaze. "You were right. She deserves to rot in a jail cell. Death was too easy." His voice hardened with each word. "But I wanted to kill her. For what she did to Kacie. What she almost did to you." His gaze skittered away, dropping to the damp grass between us. "I shouldn't have left you—"

"None of this is your fault."

He reluctantly nodded, but it was obvious he didn't believe that.

"Did she say anything to you?"

Zaiden's jaw tightened. "She reminded me that she was still my mother." His laugh was bitter, barely a sound at all. "That I didn't truly understand what my father did to her." He kicked at a rock, sending it skittering across the cemetery path. "That he never wanted to marry her. That he was forced to because—" He stopped, swallowed. "Because they got pregnant with me."

"There are always three sides to every story: his, hers, and the truth." I tucked a strand of hair behind my ear, my voice gentle. "Your dad may have seen things completely differently. You should talk to him."

"I'm done talking about this." He glanced back at Kacie's grave, shoulders hunched against an invisible weight. "My dad seems happy with your mom, and my mom is going where she belongs."

Zaiden's gaze shifted, something dangerous flickering behind his eyes as he stepped forward, erasing the space between us. "And I'm obsessed with you." His hands found my hips, fingers pressing into the fabric as he pulled me against him.

My lip curled into a grin, heart racing beneath my ribs.

"Like how obsessed?" I tilted my head, voice light.

"Like insanely obsessed," he breathed, forehead touching mine. His words ghosted against my lips. "Like I'd kill for you."

"How did you get to me so quickly?"

"I knew you were going to confront your mom."

My brows shot up. "You did?" Heat crawled up my neck as my eyes narrowed. "How?"

He shrugged, too casual, too rehearsed. "It's what I would have done." His gaze held mine, unflinching. "And I let you because I knew it was the only way we might get a confession from her."

"But you left."

He shook his head. "No." A muscle twitched in his jaw. "I drove the bike out of the driveway and parked just down the road. Waited." His voice dropped. "I was going to follow you to the house."

"So, you saw your mom come home?"

His eyes darkened. He looked away, then back at me.

"No." The word hung between us. "She was already in the house." The implication settled over me like a shadow. She'd been waiting. Planning. All along. "I don't know when she got in the house or how long she'd been there, but she'd been waiting for the perfect opportunity to go after you. She thought you knew more than you did, and it somehow got back to her that you were digging around into Kacie's accident."

"How?"

He shrugged. "I don't know, and I doubt we'll ever

know because after we appear to testify against her in court, I don't ever want to see her again."

"How did you find out she was in the house?"

"You didn't hang up the phone, so they knew you were in trouble, but the call was muffled when you put the phone on the bed. So, they didn't know exactly what was going on. Journey didn't have my number, so she called Sterling, and he called me. I didn't know until I was in the house that it was my mom, but I was inside long enough to record most of her confessions."

"I thought I was going to die." My voice cracked. My hands still trembled with the memory of cold metal against my temple.

"She was never going to shoot you." His voice dropped to a whisper. "Too messy."

My throat went dry. "Then how—?"

"A needle." His fingers trembled slightly as he mimed the motion. "Filled with something. If I had to guess—" He met my eyes, his dark with anger. "The same thing that killed Officer Tanner."

"She'd been working her way through killing off any loose ends," I muttered, the reality of it washing over me in cold waves. "And I was a loose end."

He nodded, expression grim.

"Mila and Journey would have been next." My voice quickened with the terrible logic of it.

"Yeah." The single word carried the weight of how close we'd all come.

Silence stretched between us, filled with all the terrible what-ifs. Finally, I forced myself to ask, "So what happens now?"

Zaiden looked up at the darkening sky, a few stars beginning to appear between the clouds. His posture shifted, some of the tension draining from his shoulders. "Now, we go home."

He reached for my hand, his palm warm against mine. "And we live our lives knowing Kacie got the justice she deserved."

I smiled, feeling a tiny spark of hope ignite somewhere deep in my chest.

Zaiden's thumb traced circles on my wrist. "And you move out of Kacie's room."

My brows pulled together, the spark dimming as I thought we were taking steps backward. Before I could speak, he continued.

"And move in with me."

"Where?" My face twisted with confusion as I pulled back slightly to study his expression. "Your bedroom? The frat house?"

The corner of his mouth curled upward, and he huffed out a laugh. "No." His eyes held a gleam I hadn't seen in months. "I just inherited a house."

I narrowed my eyes, scanning his face for signs he was joking. "Your mom's house?"

"Technically, it's not my mom's." His voice took on a strange formality as if reciting something he'd only just learned himself. "My dad was letting her live in the house. It's mine now."

"Your dad!" The realization that he had no idea about what was going on. "Are you going to tell him?"

"I called him already." He swallowed hard. "He's going to help make sure Anne never sees the outside of a prison again." He shoved his hands into the pockets of his jeans.

"Do you want me to give you some time alone?" I gestured toward Kacie's grave, the flowers someone had left already beginning to wilt.

"No." Zaiden shook his head, fatigue etching lines around his eyes that hadn't been there months ago. He reached for me, fingers twining with mine. "I want to crawl into bed with you and sleep for three days."

"How about one day?" I chuckled, the sound strange but welcome in this place of silence. My thumb brushed across the dark circles under his eyes. "You have a game."

"Sounds good."

He leaned down, his lips soft against my forehead. I closed my eyes, breathing in the familiar scent of him.

I smiled as we walked hand-in-hand back toward our vehicles, the gravel path crunching beneath our feet. The cemetery's iron gates creaked as we passed through them, like a final chapter closing.

It was hard to believe that after all that had happened over the last few months between us, this was where we were, but everything about it felt right. The weight on my shoulders seemed lighter with each step we took. Kacie's real killer was getting the justice she deserved, and Zaiden and I were exactly where we were always meant to be— even if we took a really weird way of getting there.

CHAPTER 48

Ariella

It had been a few weeks without a word from EJ, and it was starting to look more and more like he was all talk, but I decided I was done waiting. Ariella made it clear every day that I couldn't be everywhere with her, and she was right. So, there was only one way to ensure she was safe, and that was to make sure he knew the consequences of even looking sideways at Ariella.

I didn't know a lot about EJ, but I knew he was usually the first to the gym every morning. Since he was always with his friends and I needed to get him alone, that was probably my only chance.

Leaning against the wall in the dim hallway, I patiently waited for EJ to show up. I was done waiting for them to make a move. I was putting an end to it today.

A whistling echoed through the empty hallway, and I

knew it was EJ. Crossing my arms over my chest, my gaze dropped to the floor as I reminded myself that I didn't have to kill him.

He rounded the corner, and the whistling stopped, replaced with a groan. "What the fuck do you want, Knight," he said as he strolled up to me.

I shoved off the wall with my foot. "Rumor has it you're planning on hurting Ariella."

He huffed out an exaggerated sigh of annoyance. "That's the thing about rumors, Knight," he smirked. "They're usually not true." He rolled his eyes as he moved to sidestep around me like the conversation was over.

My vision narrowed to a pinpoint, blood rushing in my ears. My muscles coiled tight before releasing in one explosive movement. Before he could register what was happening, my forearm was pressed against his windpipe; his back slammed into the cold cinderblock wall. Each panicked heartbeat in his throat pulsed against my skin.

My gaze held his. "That's the thing, Ethan, usually isn't good enough."

He thrashed against my grip and clawed at my arm. "If you or anyone on your team even uses her name, I will kill you." I added more pressure, and his eyes widened. "You won't find me waiting for you. By the time you see me, it will be too late. You'll be dead." And I meant every fucking word.

The color drained from his face, replaced by an ashen gray that deepened to a dusky blue around his lips. His eyes bulged, bloodshot and watering, silently pleading where his voice couldn't.

"Do you understand me?"

He frantically nodded, and I released him, taking a step back. He fell forward, gripping his knees as he sucked in air, drool trailing down his chin. "What." Breath. "The Fuck." Another breath. "Is wrong with you?"

"Me." I touched my finger to my chest, a humorless laugh escaping my lips. Something raw and desperate clawed at my insides. "Are you really going to deny saying you were going to ruin Ariella for me?"

For a moment, I hated how my voice betrayed me, how obvious it was that she wasn't just another girl to me.

He groaned, recognition dawning in his eyes. "Man, I was just mad." He rubbed his throat, voice raspy. "Truthfully, I never really even liked Ariella. I liked someone else, but because of the stupid rules, I couldn't date her."

"Who?" I narrowed my eyes skeptically.

EJ hesitated, rubbing his neck. "Lauren Taylor."

"The skater?" The name caught me off guard. Lauren was the ice queen. She only dated hockey players, but maybe that was because of the rules.

He nodded, a flash of vulnerability crossing his face. "We met last summer during a community service thing for the school. Your little stunt with Ariella—" His voice lowered. "It made everyone realize how stupid the team-dating rule was. So thanks for that, I guess."

I studied his expression, looking for any sign of deception. The way his eyes met mine wasn't the look of someone constructing a lie.

I didn't respond, but I believed him, plus he knew the consequences of hurting Ariella now.

"If we're done here," he panted. "I would like to get my workout in before everyone gets here."

"As long as we're clear." I held his gaze, unwavering.

He nodded a single sharp movement. "Then we're done."

EJ backed toward the locker room, eyes never leaving mine until the door swung shut between us.

I waited, counting my heartbeats as they slowed. Ten. Twenty. Thirty. Only then did I allow myself to turn away.

My footsteps echoed against the polished floor. The adrenaline that had fueled me moments ago began to recede, leaving behind a hollow satisfaction. A small smile tugged at my lips. EJ was many things—arrogant, impulsive, and desperate for approval, but he wasn't stupid. The fear I'd seen flash in his eyes told me everything I needed to know.

Ariella was safe now.

At least from him.

As the tension drained from my shoulders, I rounded the corner and froze. There she was, leaning against the wall, echoing my earlier stance.

A slow smirk spread across my face, masking the chaos of emotions beneath. "How did you know I'd be here?"

"I told you he was all talk," she said, ignoring my question.

"Whether he was or not," I forced a cocky smile and tilted my head. "I wasn't willing to take a chance." I stepped forward into her space. My hands curled around her hips. "But I don't think we have to worry anymore. His attention is on someone else."

"I was never worried," she smiled, but the slight quiver in her voice betrayed her.

My hands trembled slightly as I cupped her face. My thumb traced her bottom lip, and I watched her eyes soften.

"The thought of anyone touching you, frightening you, hurting you—" My voice broke. I couldn't finish the sentence. It left me raw and exposed in a way that terrified me more than any confrontation ever could.

"I will never take the chance," I whispered, forehead pressed to hers, my breath mingling with hers, "when it comes to someone hurting you."

What I didn't say: I'd already failed at this once. I wouldn't fail again.

There was a long pause, and we both knew I wasn't just talking about EJ anymore. The thought of what my mom could have done still made my stomach churn.

"Did you decide if you were going to go see your mom?" Ariella's voice softened, her fingers gently squeezing mine.

I dropped my hands, feeling the familiar tightness in my chest whenever my mother was mentioned. The hallway suddenly felt too small, too confining.

A week ago, I got a message from my mother that she wanted to see me. She wanted the chance to explain herself.

When I saw her handwriting on the envelope, something calcified inside me. Each word I'd read had turned the key in that lock one more turn until it was sealed shut. I'd watched my hands tear the paper into confetti, each piece falling into the trash. Some doors weren't meant to be reopened.

I'd decided at that moment that I never wanted to see her again.

It was bad enough that we'd all have to face her again in court.

"No," I said, slipping my hand into Ariella's as we slowly headed to the exit. "There's nothing she can say to me at this point that would change how I feel about her."

Even though I still had lots of unanswered questions,

like how my mom was connected with Officer Tanner, how she was connected with the school shooter, and how she got Kacie's phone after the accident. I knew I would never get the real answers from her. In her mind, she was the victim. She was a narcissist. She'd lied about everything.

After everything happened, Claire and my father answered the majority of Ariella's and my questions. Our first question was how Claire ended up with Kacie's phone.

She explained that she had no idea what was in the box. She'd found the black box wrapped in Kacie's sweater in what used to be Anne's closet. She shoved it to the top of the closet and forgot about it, and I realized that was what my mother had been looking for the whole time. By the end of the conversation, we had a clearer picture, and it turned out nothing was what it seemed. Not even my dad and Claire's relationship. Both of them swore there was never an affair. Anne made it all up to turn me against them, and I'd fallen for it.

I couldn't say exactly what the future held for any of us. The road ahead was uncertain, full of court dates and painful reminders. But for the first time in a long time, I felt something unfamiliar settle in my chest: peace.

Even though there'd always be a missing piece where my sister should be, an absence I would carry forever, I could breathe now. The weight of her death no longer pressed down on my shoulders, crushing me with every step. Some part of me would always wonder if I could have saved her, but that question no longer defined me.

We'd all finally gotten the closure we needed. Not an ending, but a way to carry our grief forward instead of being buried beneath it.

And Ariella. The way she looked at me now, like she

could see past all my broken pieces to something worth salvaging, it humbled me. I wanted to spend the rest of my life making up for everything I'd done to her. Not because I owed her, though I did, but because loving her made me want to be better than I was.

I slid my arm around Ariella's shoulders, drawing her close. "Come on," I said softly, "I'll get you a coffee before class."

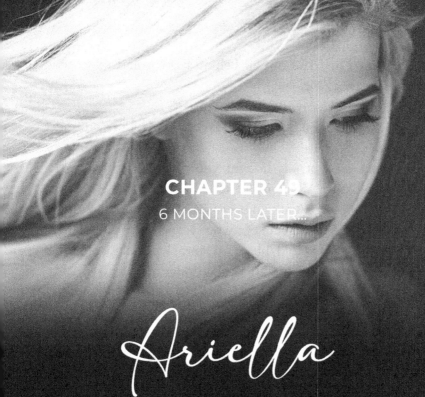

Ariella

The numbers were beginning to blur together on page 394. Probability distributions had started to look like abstract art. I'd been staring at the same problem for what felt like hours.

I rubbed my eyes and checked my phone—9:42 PM. The library would close in less than one hour and twenty minutes, and I was no closer to understanding conditional probability than when I'd sat down four hours ago.

"Just one more problem," I whispered, the sound of my voice echoing through the university library's third floor. I'd claimed this secluded desk behind the dusty linguistics section specifically because nobody ever came back here. Perfect for focusing or for talking to yourself like a crazy person when statistics broke your brain.

I tucked a strand of hair behind my ear and refocused on the textbook.

"How did I know I'd find you here?"

My heart stuttered in my chest as I spun around. "Zaiden?"

"What are you—I thought you weren't coming back until tomorrow." Zaiden left four days ago for an away game that I couldn't attend because of finals.

I was suddenly aware of my unwashed hair pulled into a messy bun, my old black Westbrook Predators dance team tank top, and the dark circles under my eyes.

"Got an earlier flight," he smirked. "I guess I missed you."

This had been the first time since everything went down that we'd been apart for this long. It was funny how Kacie's death tore us apart, only to bring us back together, and I could only think she had something to do with that.

"You 'guess' you missed me?" I raised an eyebrow, fighting the smile that threatened to break through my feigned indignation.

He took another step closer. Then another. Each footfall echoed in the empty library, matching the rhythm of my pulse. The air between us seemed to thick, making each breath more difficult than the last.

"Let me think about it," he said, close enough now that I could smell his cologne. His eyes dropped to my lips for a moment before meeting mine again. "Yeah, I definitely missed you."

I rose from my chair, narrowing the remaining distance between us. "Well," I said, my voice barely above a whisper, "I guess I missed you t—"

The rest of my words dissolved as his mouth found

mine. Four days of absence concentrated into a single point of contact.

I threw my arms around his neck, and his circled my waist as he lifted me off the ground, spinning us as my legs wrapped around him. He dropped my ass on the corner of the square library table.

The kiss told me exactly how much he'd missed me. It was so intense, so all-consuming, that I lost not just the ability to breathe but the ability to think.

My hand dove into his hair, pulling his mouth harder to mine as his tongue slipped past my parted lips. He groaned, and I swallowed it before ripping my lips from his, sucking in a harsh breath of air.

"I had a fantasy that started like this," he breathed, his thumb tracing my jawline. His hand slid to my throat, not tightening, just resting there, a promise of what might come.

I kept my eyes open, watching his pupils dilate. "Tell me about this fantasy."

His mouth hovered a whisper away from mine, not touching.

"It was right here." His voice dropped lower. "This desk."

A distant door clicked shut. We both stilled, listening.

Silence.

His gaze flicked to my statistics textbook, then back to me. "But you were wearing that tight blue skirt. The one with the—"

"I know which one," I interrupted, heat climbing my neck. The memory flashed vivid and sharp: his hands pushing that skirt up against our bedroom door, the cool surface against my back, the warmth of him against my front.

He smiled, the corner of his mouth lifting in a way that made my stomach drop. His lips brushed, not my mouth, but the sensitive spot below my ear. "And in my imagination," he whispered, his breath raising goosebumps down my neck, "you weren't nearly this patient."

I tilted my chin up, offering more of my neck while my fingers curled into fists to keep from grabbing him. "Maybe," I breathed, "your imagination doesn't know how much I enjoy making you wait."

He spread my legs wider, the movement showcasing his strength without hurting me.

The library's lights cast harsh shadows across his face as he settled between my thighs, highlighting the sharp angle of his jaw, the intensity of his gaze, and the slight sheen of sweat at his temples.

His free hand curled around my outer thigh, fingers splayed, possessive, as his lips traced a burning path down the side of my throat. Each point of contact was a separate flame.

"Tell me," I whispered, my head falling back to grant him better access, "what happens in this fantasy?"

The vibration of his groan against my collarbone sent shivers racing across my skin.

"That's the thing," he murmured. His hand trailed upward with tantalizing slowness, leaving heat in its wake as it disappeared under my skirt. The fabric rustled softly, the sound obscenely loud in the library's silence.

His fingers paused at the juncture where thigh met hip —close, so close, but not touching where I needed him.

Our gazes met, his mouth lingering over mine, our breaths mingling together. "I'm more of a show than a tell type of guy."

He continued his slow exploration.

"Your panties are soaked, baby." His voice dropped to a rough whisper and I sucked in a sharp breath as his knuckles brushed over the damp fabric, a ghost of pressure exactly where I needed it most.

I fought to keep my voice steady. "Was that part of your fantasy?"

His mouth dragged across my face, stopping at my ear. For several heartbeats, all I felt was his breath.

"In my fantasy—"

His lips brushed against the shell of my ear, sending electricity racing over my body.

"—your pussy soaked my fingers."

His teeth captured my earlobe, tugging gently, making me gasp.

"My face." Those two words, spoken directly against my ear, sent a violent shudder through me. "My cock."

My heart thudded against my ribs, and warmth pooled between my thighs. Zaiden's fantasies were so much more vibrant than mine, but I couldn't say that I hadn't had a library fantasy once or twice with all the late nights I spent here while he was away.

His fingertips skimmed the edge of my panties, then withdrew. I made a small sound of protest.

"What was that?" he asked, his voice deceptively casual.

I pressed my lips together, refusing to beg. This was our game, seeing who would break first. It was almost always me.

His fingers returned, hooking into the sides of the thin fabric.

But he didn't pull.

One second stretched into two. Into ten.

His eyes locked with mine, challenging. Waiting.

"Should I stop?" His expression remained serious, controlled, but the darkening of his eyes betrayed him.

My body screamed for release, for movement, for anything.

"No," I whispered, the word catching in my throat.

The corner of his mouth lifted, just barely. A victory.

"Then beg me." His voice dropped, the command gentle but unmistakable. His thumb traced small circles against my hip, so close to where I needed him, yet deliberately avoiding it. "Beg me to take off your panties. Beg me to fuck you right here, surrounded by all these books, where anyone could potentially walk by."

"Please," I whimpered, hating and loving how he reduced me to this state. "Please take off my panties."

I raised my hips slowly, a silent offering.

His eyes never left mine as he worked the fabric down. Every millimeter of retreat exposed another nerve ending to the cool library air.

First, past my hips, where he paused. The pad of his index finger traced the indentation the elastic had left on my skin. I bit my lip to keep from whimpering.

Down my thighs, where goosebumps rippled in the wake of his touch.

Past my knees, which trembled not from cold but from restraint, from the effort of not grabbing him, pulling him, demanding more.

His movements were methodical. Worshipful. Torturous.

The lights seemed too bright, too revealing. Yet I couldn't look away from his face, from the raw hunger barely contained behind his careful motions.

When the panties reached my ankles, he removed them

with excruciating slowness, maintaining eye contact as he folded them neatly and placed them in his pocket.

He stepped back just enough that we no longer touched.

The absence of contact left my skin burning.

"Now," he said. His gaze traveled over my body with such intensity that it felt as tangible as hands. A physical weight. A promise.

My mouth went dry.

"Beg," he whispered.

The library's silence pressed against us, a third presence in our forbidden corner.

The words caught in my throat, not from embarrassment but from the raw need behind them. From knowing once I said them, there would be no going back.

"Please—" My voice broke. I swallowed and tried again. "Please fuck me."

His expression remained unmoved, waiting for more.

"Fuck me hard," I continued, my voice growing stronger with desperation. "Right here on this table. Where anyone could see us."

His pupils dilated.

"Until I come," I finished. "Until I can't remember my own name. Until all I know is you."

The air between us seemed to thicken, making each breath an effort. My heart pounded so loudly that I was certain it echoed off the library walls.

His large hands wrapped around my waist, lingering for a long moment before slowly lifting my black tank top and sliding it over my stomach. He hooked a finger underneath the built-in bra, tugging it as he pulled it over my breasts, but he didn't remove it. Just in case we had to redress quickly.

He stepped back. His gaze raked over me, slow, hungry, as if I were his masterpiece.

"Let me see that pretty pussy."

My chest heaved. Blood rushed to my cheeks. I slid back inch by inch, my pulse quickening with each movement. I pulled my feet up onto the wooden table, knees bent.

The library's silence pressed against us, broken only by our breathing.

"Spread them wide for me, baby," he purred as his tongue swept out, wetting his lips. "I want to see all of you."

My heart pounded as I leaned back, using my hands behind me to hold myself up. Lifting my heels and pointing my toes, I slowly slid my feet apart until I was spread wide for him. His gaze zeroed in on my bare pussy, and an overwhelming feeling of both vulnerability and exhilaration surged through me. It was intoxicating like a drug, and I was riding a high. An addiction I couldn't break. I wanted more, and every time we did something like this, it only made me want to push the limits a little further.

Goosebumps raced across my exposed skin as the air conditioning whispered against places usually hidden. I shivered, not from cold.

"You are so fucking beautiful." The words came out strangled. His teeth dragged across his bottom lip, leaving it reddened. The metallic sound of his jeans button popping free seemed impossibly loud in the library silence. "Touch yourself." His pupils were so dilated that his eyes appeared nearly black in the dim light.

Shifting my weight to one hand, I hesitated.

If anyone walked around that corner—

My reputation. My position on the dance team. Everything I'd worked for.

Gone in an instant.

And yet—

My pulse quickened at the thought. The risk. The possibility. The forbidden nature of it all.

I shouldn't want this.

But I did.

God help me, I did.

My body made the decision before my mind could, fingers sliding through slick flesh as my gaze locked on his face. I watched him watching me, the power between us shifting like a current.

Sinking two fingers inside myself, I let my head fall back, a moan escaping before I could catch it. The sound seemed to echo, and panic fluttered in my chest even as pleasure built.

"Rub your clit," The command rasped from his throat.

"Keep your eyes open. I want you to see exactly who's making you come."

The danger sharpened everything, colors more vivid, sounds more distinct, sensations multiplied.

I forced my heavy eyelids up, my gaze connecting with his as I withdrew my slick fingers. The movement drew his attention downward, his breathing visibly changing as he watched me find my clit.

I moved my fingers over myself, rubbing in tight little circles, fighting the instinct to close my eyes against the overwhelming sensation.

The vulnerability of being watched, being studied, while touching myself made every nerve ending hypersensitive. Each circle of my fingers carried shockwaves through my system.

And then I saw him—fully.

Standing flush against the table, his hand wrapped around himself, stroking with controlled movements.

The sight of him, his restraint, his intensity, his absolute focus on me, sent a rush of heat flooding through my body.

I licked my lips, unable to help myself.

"I want—" The words caught. I swallowed and tried again. "I want you inside me."

He stepped closer, his hand never stopping its rhythmic motion. "Not yet."

The desk creaked beneath me as I shifted, impatient. "When?"

A slow smile spread across his face. "When I decide you've earned it."

With my gaze hyper-focused on his hand, I moved my fingers over my clit, rubbing in a measured rhythm.

"Eyes on me, baby."

Each word was a command I couldn't disobey.

My gaze lifted, reconnecting with his.

The raw hunger I found there stole my breath.

This was Zaiden, the boy I'd known for years, the man who'd held me through the awful news of Kacie's death, my antagonist turned lover, but in this moment, he was something else entirely. Something primal. Dangerous.

Mine.

I gasped, fingers faltering as he slipped two of his own inside me without warning. The sudden fullness made my back arch involuntarily.

"Don't stop. Find your rhythm and come all over my hand."

The crudeness of his words contrasted with the admiration in his expression, creating a conflict that heightened everything.

I realized that he needed this as much as I did. This wasn't just about a physical release; it was about reclaiming something we'd nearly lost, about proving we were still alive despite everything.

I added just the right amount of pressure as I continued to work my clit. He withdrew his fingers before thrusting them back inside me. He increased his speed, and I rubbed a little harder and faster.

The wet noises of him pumping into me seemed obscenely loud in the library's silence.

I bit the inside of my cheek hard, trying to contain the sounds building in my throat.

"Let me hear you," he demanded, curling his fingers inside me toward that spot that made coherent thought impossible.

"Someone will—"

"Let me. Hear you." Each word was punctuated by a deeper thrust of his fingers.

The oxygen caught in my lungs, trapped. My vision tunneled, narrowing to only his face above me. The lights created a halo effect around his head, an angelic framework for the devil's own expression.

Stars sparked at the edges of my awareness as my pussy clamped down around him. The pressure building inside me reached a critical threshold, unbearable, unsustainable.

I fought it, trying to prolong the exquisite torture.

"Don't you dare hold back," he whispered, his voice threaded with both command and plea. "Give it to me. Now."

My control shattered like glass.

My stomach muscles contracted, and my spine bowed. A tremor started in my thighs, spreading outward like ripples in water, gaining force with each wave. The ceiling tiles above me blurred, sharpened, and then disappeared completely as something inside me fractured.

When my lungs finally remembered their purpose, his name tore from them, a sound so raw it barely resembled language, echoing off the book spines surrounding us.

He withdrew his fingers, holding them in front of his face, glistening with my orgasm. "I love the sounds you make when you're coming." He brushed his them over his mouth before sucking them between his lips and licking them clean. I swallowed hard, the action so erotically hot. "I love the way you taste."

He hooked his hands under my knees and jerked me to the end of the table.

His hand moved slowly up my collarbone, leaving goosebumps in its wake. His palm curved around my throat, large enough to encircle it completely.

For one heartbeat, he simply held me there.

His thumb found my pulse point, pressing gently, measuring my reaction.

Finding it racing.

The corner of his mouth lifted slightly, satisfied at my body's reaction.

With careful pressure, he pulled me forward, an inescapable force I couldn't, didn't want to resist.

When our faces were inches apart, he paused again. His breath mingled with mine. His eyes challenged me to close the final distance.

I remained still, trapped in the exquisite tension of anticipation.

His mouth captured mine, not the gentle exploration of earlier, but something savage. Suffocating. Messy. His fingers tightened fractionally around my throat, just enough to remind me of their presence. Of his control.

Our tongues tangled together, and oxygen became more of a luxury than a necessity.

I tore my lips from his, head falling back as I gasped desperately for air.

His eyes devoured my reaction, pupils so dilated they eclipsed color entirely.

"Take my dick like a good girl." His hips snapped forward, filling me with one pleasurably painful thrust, making me hiss. He stilled for a moment, a very brief moment, letting me adjust before he started fucking me in quick, brutal strokes. Pleasure built, and I moaned louder than I wanted to.

It felt so good, I didn't want it to end. He withdrew and slammed back into me. Each time more powerful than the last until my legs were trembling.

I was already so close.

He leaned forward, his hands flattening on the table, pressing his forehead to mine, our labored breathing mingling in the space between us.

"Come on my cock, baby," he ordered, and those words sent me over the edge.

"Zaiden." His name escaped my lips, not a moan or a whisper but something rawer. More revealing. A confession disguised as ecstasy.

With one final, almost brutal thrust, he followed me, and a shudder ran through him.

Each creak of the building, each distant sound of footsteps on the stairs, had heightened every sensation. Danger and pleasure had intertwined until they became a single entity.

But in this moment of shared vulnerability, another

element revealed itself: the truth we'd both been circling since Kacie's death.

We needed each other.

Not just physically.

In every way that mattered.

My body still pulsed with aftershocks, sensitive in ways I'd never experienced before, as if my skin had been replaced with something thinner, more receptive.

We stood breathless for a long moment, the library's silence settling around us. My fingers trembled slightly as I adjusted my clothes.

Zaiden slid his zipper up, his expression softening from intensity to something more vulnerable. "Are you hungry?" he smiled. "We could try that new twenty-four-hour diner before heading home."

"Yeah," I matched his smile, studying the familiar lines of his face. Four days had felt like forever. "I really missed you."

Six months ago, I couldn't have imagined saying them, not after the torment, the blame, the way Kacie's death had shattered everything. But now, watching him gather my scattered notes and textbook, I realized the truth of it. He was my safe place, somehow, still despite everything, or maybe because of it.

"Come on," he said, offering his hand. "Let's get out of here before they lock us in."

I laced my fingers through his, feeling the steady pulse in his wrist against mine as we walked away from the secluded desk that had witnessed both my academic struggles and our reunion. Tomorrow, I'd face probability distributions again. Tonight belonged to us.

Ariella

2 *years later...*

I burst through the arena doors, my heart pounding as I checked the time on my phone—7:54 PM. I was so freaking late, and the game was nearly over. Yesterday, my flight was delayed, and then I missed my connecting flight, and I couldn't get another plane until today, which also ended up being delayed.

I sprinted down the corridor, lungs burning.

"Excuse me! Sorry!"

A wall of bodies blocked my path, fans already leaving, thinking the night's excitement was over. I ducked under elbows and slipped between families, my shoulder bag catching on someone's jacket.

After graduation, Zaiden signed with the Atlanta Hurricanes and moved across the country to Georgia. I stayed behind with three years of school still ahead of me.

It hadn't been easy, but we'd made it work. During hockey season, I flew to him whenever possible. During the off-season, he lived with me back home.

The distance had one silver lining: I'd packed in extra classes to graduate early. And secretly, I hoped that after graduation, he'd ask me to move with him to Georgia.

But the best part of all of it was not only that I'd forgiven Zaiden but that he'd learned to forgive himself. He no longer blamed himself for what happened to Kacie or what almost happened to me.

He was finally free, and because of that, he was a completely different person. The one I'd fallen for before.

Six months ago, Anne was sentenced to life without the possibility of parole for the murder of Kacie and twenty-five years to life for the attempted murder of me. She still hadn't been charged for her part in the school shooting or Officer Tanner's deal, but we were all happy to know that we'd never have to see her again. She'd gotten what she deserved.

The sound of the buzzer echoed through the building as I finally emerged into the stands. I usually sat in a suite, but this time, Zaiden got me glass seats, which was so much better. I spotted Journey, Sterling, Hawk, and Mila all cheering along with the crowd. It was our first time all together in over a year.

Journey graduated with Zaiden and moved to New York to pursue a career on Broadway. Sterling was drafted into the NHL the same year, but an injury ended his career early. Now, he was a high school coach, and Mila was graduating with me.

The scoreboard showed less than a minute left in the third period. Zaiden's team was up by one goal. I scanned the ice, spotting him in his number 54 jersey as he skated into position for a face-off.

"I made it," I whispered, collapsing into my seat beside Journey. My lungs still burned from the sprint.

Journey's eyes widened as she spun toward me, her black hair whipping around her shoulders. "Oh my God!" She grabbed my arm, her silver bangles jingling. "You're actually here!"

Across the row, Mila caught my eye and elbowed Hawk, both of them breaking into relieved grins and offering enthusiastic waves.

"We didn't think you were going to make it," Sterling said, leaning forward with his elbows on his knees.

I pushed my hair from my face and exhaled shakily. "I didn't either." The sounds of skates scraping ice and sticks clacking brought me back to the moment. "How's he doing?" I asked, nodding toward the rink where Zaiden's number 54 darted between opponents.

"They're winning," Journey said. "And Zaiden only got put in the box once."

I laughed. "That's definitely a win."

Zaiden took control of the puck, gliding across the ice as he spun and dodged several players on the opposing team.

"At this point," Journey said, pointing to the score-board. "They just need to keep the puck from the other team."

He shot the puck to a teammate as they moved closer and closer to the goal.

The final buzzer sounded, and the entire arena went wild. The Hurricanes won. We all shot out of our seats, jumping up and down and cheering along with the crowd. The arena lights dimmed. Not the gradual fade after a game, but a deliberate blackout that stopped fans mid-stride. Conversations cut short. A collective intake of breath.

"What's happening?" I whispered, scanning the darkened rink where the players should have been celebrating.

Journey didn't answer. Just gripped my arm harder, her eyes fixed on something above us.

"Ari," Journey shouted, and I followed her line of sight to the jumbotron as it flickered to life, its massive screen illuminating the arena. I froze in place as words began to appear:

ARIELLA LEDGER, WILL YOU MARRY ME?
–ZAIDEN

The spotlight hit center ice where, somehow, all the players had cleared away except for Zaiden. He was down on one knee, his helmet removed, dark hair falling across his forehead. In his gloved hand was a small black velvet box.

The crowd erupted in cheers and applause. Someone nudged me. "Ari," Mila screamed over everyone. "That's you."

My throat closed completely. The lights blurred as tears welled up, turning the arena into a kaleidoscope of color and light. I managed only a trembling nod as an usher materialized at my elbow, his voice coming as if from underwater.

"Ms. Ledger? This way, please," he said with a smile, guiding me toward a gate at ice level.

My legs felt like jelly as I stepped onto the ice, careful

not to slip. The spotlight found me, and I squinted as the cheering grew louder. Zaiden's face broke into a relieved smile when he saw me.

"I thought you might not make it." His voice cracked, barely audible above the roar.

What if I hadn't? What if my taxi had hit one more red light? What if I'd given up at the airport?

"I'm so sorry I was late," I managed through tears, the weight of those almost-missed seconds crushing my chest.

Zaiden shook his head, a private grin forming at the corners of his mouth. "Your timing," he whispered, just for me, "is perfect."

His gloved hands trembled slightly as he opened the velvet box. The diamond caught the spotlight, fracturing it into a thousand glittering promises. Around us, the massive arena seemed to disappear until it held only two people.

"I know we still have a lot to figure out, like where we are going to live, but I know without a doubt that I want to spend the rest of my life with you." The corners of his mouth lifted into the smile I loved so much. "Ariella Ledger." His voice broke on my name. He swallowed, steadied himself. "Will you marry me?"

Eighteen thousand people held their breath, but I could hear only my heartbeat.

My lips parted, but no sound emerged. I nodded once, twice, tears streaming freely down my face.

Find your voice, Ari.

"Yes," I finally managed, the word barely audible at first, then stronger as I repeated it. "Yes! Yes, I will!"

The crowd erupted again as Zaiden slipped the ring onto my finger and rose to his feet, pulling me into his arms. His teammates burst back onto the ice, showering them with confetti and cheers.

The Jumbotron now read:

SHE SAID YES!

As Zaiden lifted me off my feet and spun me around on the ice, my laughter mingled with tears. Being late had never felt so perfectly timed.

I looked back at our friends in the stands as my shoes hit the ice, their excited faces confirming what I already suspected—they were all in on it. Sterling nodded, his smile widening. Journey covered her mouth with both hands, her shoulders shaking with emotion. Even Hawk, usually so stoic, wore a wide grin.

My heart swelled, but over the roar of the crowd and the confetti falling like snow, a familiar ache surfaced. That empty seat that would never be filled.

Kacie.

My fingers instinctively found the small silver bracelet on my wrist, the one she'd given me on my seventeenth birthday. I rarely wore it because I was terrified of losing it.

"She would have loved this," Zaiden whispered against my ear, his voice thick with emotion. He'd known exactly what, who I was thinking about.

I closed my eyes, feeling the weight of the new ring on my finger and the weight of the bracelet on my wrist. "She knew before either of us did," I whispered back.

A memory surfaced—Kacie, at sixteen, sprawled across my bedroom floor, pointing her highlighter at me. *"You're going to marry my brother someday, Ari."* At the time, it had been so ridiculous because we weren't even dating. *"I see the way he looks at you."* I'd brushed her off.

The arena lights seemed to brighten for just a moment,

or maybe it was my tears catching the glow. I looked up at the rafters, beyond the banners and beams, and smiled.

"You were right, Kacie," I whispered. "As always."

As Zaiden's teammates surrounded us in a jubilant circle, I felt complete—not because the missing piece had returned, but because I'd finally learned to carry her with me in a way that felt like celebration rather than loss.

Check out more by
Michaela Sawyer.